Partner Pursuit

KATHY STROBOS

Dear Nicole,
Thanks so much for
signing my book. I love
being in book club together.
Yay for Hunters moms!
Kathy

Published by Strawbundle Publishing
New York, New York

For Claus

Chapter One

*J*acket on the back of the chair. Check.

Desk light on. Check.

Now, Ms. Willems, your mission, should you choose to accept it: Get out of the office on the sly. Audrey snorted silently at her own badly-played movie line. She stuffed the Save the Children t-shirt she'd gotten from a Central Park Zoo benefit in her Tory Burch brown leather satchel, added as many legal pads as could fit, and plumped the bag to look like it held at least four case files. She casually leaned the bag against the side of her desk, in view of her open office door.

The excited chatter of the exiting assistants filled the hallway. She typed up the Popflicks engagement letter and then entered Popflicks as a new client into the law firm database. *Yes.* Her pulse quickened.

The office was now quiet. She put an uncapped red pen in the middle of a legal pad on her desk. It looked like she'd be right back. The scene called for something more. If only she had a permanently steaming cup of tea. She poured a bottle of water into a glass.

She should depart boldly, but leaving early was frowned upon by the partnership powers-that-be. They might even think she needed another assignment. She definitely did not. She had just landed Popflicks. She had stayed until 11 p.m. every night this week. *Okay, so I'm not always very good at saying no.* But now was not the time to say no to a partner—not when she'd been working so hard for seven years, her life on hold. Now that she was in the homestretch, she could practically see "Audrey Willems, Partner," embossed on her law firm's business card.

She'd promised Eve that she wouldn't stand her up—again—tonight. Best friends were supposed to be reliable. Especially when she'd promised said best friend and neighbor to be the guinea pig for her new catering business.

The towering stacks of papers on her desk made her hesitate. *But . . .* Promises to Eve. Promises to herself, her career. Promises to the senior partner. She could taste-test for Eve and then review the files . . . The mental image of her laughing with Eve morphed into her pale face lit by a fluorescent lamp reading a legal opinion. Her shoulders slumped.

She peeked out her doorway. No one was in the hallway. It was clear. With the *Mission Impossible* theme song running through her head, she snuck down the carpeted hallway and darted into the rarely used interior stairwell. Better odds to escape unseen than to chance the elevator. She jogged down several flights of stairs. So far, so good.

She was a few steps from the twenty-fifth-floor landing when the hard *snick-crack* of the crash bars sounded below on her left. The metal door swung open and the wiry figure of Lawrence

Malaburn appeared. He leaned against the emergency exit door as it softly clicked shut behind him. Audrey stopped short, gripping the cold railing with one hand.

"Audrey. I didn't realize you took the stairs." Malaburn raised his face, and his thin lips pursed slightly.

Malaburn. Her least favorite partner. Eight months of working for him had made her seriously consider ending her law career. Demanding and critical, he'd brought her to tears more than once—in the office, but not in front of him. It was every working woman's motto to never let them see you cry.

Note to self: Do not take the stairs.

Second note to self: Never let them see you sweat.

"It's my exercise for the week," Audrey said wryly. Maybe even for the month.

He waved for her to precede him down the cement stairway. Audrey stepped forward, her skin crawling. He was just about breathing on her neck. How about leaving the space of one step behind someone on the stairs? The jerk didn't even practice common courtesy. No way was she going to make small talk with him for twenty-five more floors. She quickened her pace.

He matched her steps.

"Yes, well, this is fortuitous. I was just thinking of you for an assignment. It follows up on that research you did a few years ago, so it shouldn't take too long. Could you fit it in?" Malaburn said, his nasal voice bringing back memories of his late-night calls with constant changes.

When hell freezes over. Or when I don't already have a full case-load. Same thing.

"Thank you for considering me. I'll check my schedule and let you know," Audrey said, forcing a polite, measured tone into her answer.

"Stop by my office tomorrow . . . or now?"

"I'm on my way to a meeting."

"Then tomorrow."

They'd reached the twenty-third-floor landing. Her chance to exit, get rid of him. Suddenly, she felt the heat of his body next to her. She tensed—way too close—but then he reached past her and slapped at the crash bar. Only after the metal door slammed behind him did she let out the breath she'd been holding. She shook her head. *Rules, girl, rules.* He needed to go through the assignment partner. That was the protocol to ensure work was assigned evenly. She would not be in his office tomorrow.

The cement block walls of the staircase mocked her. *Stop thinking about him.* She was about to defend the Popflicks litigation. Her Hen Bank case was busy, and its success crucial to the firm.

She jogged down the stairs and pushed open the exit door. This staircase exited separately from the lobby, on the other side of the building. Total bonus. She checked to confirm no law firm colleagues were in sight and stepped into the sauna that was Manhattan in the summer.

She merged into the throngs of suits heading for the subway station. Black sedans were double-parked, waiting to pick up the office building escapees. Her phone buzzed. Watching where she was going, so she kept pace with the fast-moving current of New Yorkers, she read the text from Winnie: *Need to talk ASAP. Just stopped by office.*

She side-stepped out of the herd and stood off by the curb. Winnie was wasted as a lawyer; she should've been in CIA intelligence.

She texted back: *Escaping. Promised Eve dinner. Why?*

The heat shimmered off the asphalt street. A messenger guy on a bike swooped in and out of the cars on Eighth Avenue, blowing his whistle.

Winnie: *This is my friend Audrey, right? Who lives at the office? Who wants to make partner in six months?*

Audrey: *Haha. Very funny.*

Winnie: *Call you later. Have fun!*

She darted across the street before the light changed. She jogged down the metal subway stairs, the familiar dank smell of ammonia mixed with sweat greeting her. The countdown clock showed her the 1 train was arriving. She slid her MetroCard through the turnstile and ran down the next set of stairs just in time to squeeze onto a train. She reached around the woman in front of her to hold onto a pole, trying not to touch her, to maintain an inch of physical distance. There were definite benefits to working late and taking a car home on the client. A couple smooshed in behind her. The man had his arm tightly around the woman, holding her balanced against the jerking of the train. Audrey averted her glance and focused on the subway posters. One had a picture of a couple on a beach. That was the opposite of her summer so far, working nights and weekends. But romance suddenly seemed possible—not this summer, not before she made partner, but maybe after. Tim had reached out to hug her at the end of their Popflicks pitch, out in the hallway, under the portraits of the founding partners. But he'd stepped back as if electrocuted by that professional work-colleague boundary. Still, it was something, and it made her smile as the train pulled into her stop.

She pushed through the subway turnstile at 72nd Street. She passed by the Gray's Papaya with its slogans in bright red letters on its yellow façade and turned the corner to walk down the brownstone-lined block. Birds chirped; a teenager walked their golden retriever up ahead. Trees grew within small, fenced-off, neighbor-planted flower beds, with different variations of "Don't let your dog pee on me" signs.

She reached the corner Korean grocery store and admired the sea of pink roses, sunflowers, and hyacinths for sale. The bright yellow sunflowers stood especially tall outside. Eve would like those. Audrey picked out a bunch and paid the man at the makeshift counter at the end of the row of flowers.

Walking away, she slid her wallet back into her purse just as her phone rang. *Winnie.* Fumbling to check it with her one free hand, she bumped into a hard body and dropped her phone.

The owner of said hard body was tall with wavy brown hair and chiseled cheekbones, and he was carrying a case of beer. His fitted, worn gray t-shirt showed off his lean muscular frame.

"Sorry, I was distracted." She blushed as she bent to pick up her phone, trying to do so gracefully in a pencil skirt and heels while holding the long-stemmed sunflowers.

"No worries," he said, turning away from her. "I was trying to make the light." The light glowed red.

She checked her phone so she looked busy as she stood next to him, waiting for the light to change. That hard contact had her flustered. Had she stared at him like a lovestruck teenager? She really needed to get out of the office more often. Fortunately, her mobile had survived the fall. The caller ID had identified the call she thought was from Winnie as a scam call. Now his phone rang.

He shook his head. "Being on call. It's so . . ."

"Essential, right?" She nodded. It allowed her the freedom to leave the office, but still be available wherever she was.

"I was going to say annoying." He answered the phone. "Jake here." He listened to the caller and then said, "Yes, come on by. You know my opinion: you've got to shake it off and get out there. Dating in New York for a guy is like shooting fish in a barrel." He slipped his phone back in his jean pocket.

"I've always preferred the metaphor that honey catches more flies than vinegar," Audrey said. "You might want to try sweet bait on your hook, rather than your shotgun approach." She raised an eyebrow, less than charmed by his remark.

He laughed. "You're right." Her gaze met his; his eyes were warm blue with hints of green and gray, like the Atlantic Ocean on a calm day, and her stomach did a little flip. "Can I help you carry anything?" He waved at her purse and the flowers.

"Thanks, but I'm good." She was tempted to hand him the flowers to carry, just to keep talking to him, but he was carrying a case of beer.

A little boy scootered past them, over the curb, into the street, towards the busy intersection. She stared in horror, her feet glued to the sidewalk as if stuck in cement. Jake bolted after him, scooping the child up with one arm as the scooter fell to the ground, just past the parked car. And then her feet moved and she sprinted over, picking up the dropped scooter from the street and following Jake back to the safety of the sidewalk.

A mother with a baby stroller laden with Trader Joe's shopping bags ran up, screaming. "I told you to stop at the curb, Eddy!"

"I tried, Mommy, I tried." The boy started crying. "I missed the brake."

Audrey and Jake exchanged a look of "that was close." Her heart was still hammering. And she felt shaky. Jake wiped his hand on his jeans.

The mother hugged her son tightly and turned to Jake. "Thank you so much."

"No problem." Jake bent to his knees so he could look Eddy in the eyes. "I've got a niece about your age who likes to scooter. And you know what I've told her? She can scooter ahead, but she has to stop where the buildings stop. Then if she misses the brake, that gives her time to find it. What do you think about trying that?"

Eddy nodded. Audrey found herself nodding as well; that was good advice.

"Thank you both again," the mom said. Audrey just waved it off. She felt guilty that she hadn't moved fast enough—that she'd been stuck in shock.

"No worries. I've had practice with scooter crises." Jake looked embarrassed at the mom's gratitude. The light changed, and he quickly crossed.

Audrey followed him, still quivering from the near-accident. Her phone rang again. This time, it was Winnie.

"Hey, what's the important news?"

"I heard a rumor that litigation isn't doing well. They might only make two partners instead of four. I was going to wait and tell you tomorrow because you deserve a night off, but then I thought I'd better call you."

Audrey stopped in the middle of the sidewalk. "That's not good." *Only two? All this effort and I'm not even going to make it?* She leaned against a stone wall of the steps of a brownstone, her leg muscles jittery. "But Tim and I got the Popflicks case."

"It's not going to be enough. Two cases suddenly settled, so that means Colette and several other attorneys are no longer billing those crazy amounts, except that Colette is sure to get on another case soon. She's not one to sit around," Winnie said. Colette had joined the firm two years ago. She'd rebuffed Audrey's friendly overtures; they were both in consideration for partner, but she was friendly with Tim.

"That's game-changing." She had to do more, but she was already working more cases than anyone else. And if she made partner, it would be even worse. She sank down onto the steps. Her hand gripped her phone tightly, as she stared down at the paper garbage littering the street.

Audrey shook her head. She had to think positively. It wouldn't be worse. She would make it—be judged and found to merit becoming a partner with the best and brightest legal minds of the country. It was the final rung on the ladder. She would prove herself as one of them. She took a deep breath, stood, and strode forward. *Eyes on the prize. Don't be deterred by doubts.* Her mom's favorite expression, other than "be nice." Kevin had often imitated her mom saying that, and not in a nice way.

Kevin, who she'd broken up with four years ago, who'd said she'd never make partner.

She glanced up to see Jake turn into the five-story brownstone next to the one where she and Eve lived. The one with the apartment for rent. But that would be too much to hope—that he was her new neighbor. He was only her type in looks anyway, given that he was comparing women to fish and strolling around the streets on a Thursday carrying a case of beer—that he had managed not to drop while rescuing the boy. Impressed, she bit her lip. Better to hope that he wasn't; she didn't need that type of distraction.

"I still just have to do my best," she said to Winnie.

"I tried to find out more, but that was all I got. So far." Winnie's voice promised that she was on it. "They should pick you over Tim or Colette or that guy in London."

"I feel like I don't fit the image," she said. Especially now, with her caramel blond highlighted hair frizzing from the heat and exercise. And her face probably matched her pink blouse. "Colette and Tim are always so polished."

"Yeah, *you've* got a personality," Winnie said.

"They might prefer polish over personality."

"You're the whole package. Remember that. When you're on, you take over the room." Winnie's voice was reassuring.

She nodded. She recognized that. She wasn't conventionally pretty; she had a strong nose—far from an all-American button nose. But if she was animated or laughing when walking down the street, men and sometimes women turned to give her a second glance. Her mom said she had presence, but she had to feel confident; otherwise, she'd fade into the background.

"Tim's like the firm's golden boy. If they're only making two, he'll definitely be one of them." Audrey stopped outside her brownstone door, hoping Winnie would contradict her.

"Unfortunately," Winnie said.

Indeed. That was the thing about Winnie—she could trust her for the truth. But that meant there was just one spot for three contenders. And she wouldn't bet on her being chosen over the other two. Her shoulders slumped.

Winnie continued, "Anyway, let's grab lunch tomorrow."

After saying yes, Audrey hung up. She should go back to the office after dinner. But she'd promised Eve they'd hang out tonight. And they barely saw each other because they both worked nights even though they lived across the hall from each other. Eve was only off tonight because the restaurant where she worked as a pastry chef was closed for a private function and the group was bringing their own birthday cake.

If Eve went to bed early, she could sneak back to work after dinner and dessert. Maybe she should've thought of joining the CIA. At least then she'd have the disguise skills to escape the office.

Chapter Two

udrey hurried up the stairs of her brownstone building to the second floor and pushed open the unlocked door to Eve's street-facing apartment. She had to put Winnie's news aside for now and enjoy her time with Eve.

She had met Eve at a party freshman year in college. She was dancing with a group from her dorm, watching these three women dance on top of the trestle table in the center of the banquet hall, admiring their confidence. All of a sudden, one of them reached down and helped her onto the table, saying, "You've got good moves. You need to strut your stuff up here with me." That was Eve, cajoling her to come out from the library when they were in college and graduate school, and now from the office. And it wasn't that Eve didn't work hard. She did.

Eve called out hello from the kitchen. A cozy curry smell beckoned. Audrey's stomach growled. She slipped off her shoes in the hallway and joined Eve in the kitchen.

"You made it," Eve said. "I was sure you'd have to cancel."

"I didn't want to disappoint you again," Audrey said.

Eve's curly black hair was pulled back from her forehead by a bright pink kerchief, which complemented her warm brown complexion. Eve was tall and thin, with toned arm muscles that Audrey envied—but not enough to do the required planks. Audrey smiled when she saw Eve was wearing a pink tank top that said "Bakers Gonna Bake."

Audrey handed her the sunflowers. "For you. Thanks for cooking me dinner."

"My favorite. Thanks." Eve reached up to take down a vase from a shelf. Eve's kitchen had open shelving stacked high with pans of all types, cookbooks, and glass containers filled with all varieties of sugars and flours.

"I think I just met our new neighbor." Audrey filled the large blue vase with water.

"And? I was hoping some hot guy would move in next door."

"I think you got your wish," Audrey said wryly.

"A hot guy?" Eve smoothed her hands on her apron and raised her eyebrows.

"But he thinks dating in NY for guys is like shooting fish in a barrel."

"He said that to you? What kind of conversation did you have?"

"No, he was on the phone with a friend who was just dumped," Audrey said, arranging the flowers in a vase.

"Oh, I see. He must be really good-looking then."

"Yes, but he knows it. So that makes him less attractive." Or it should have.

"I wouldn't hold that against him," Eve said. "My good-looking guy friends always say how easy dating in New York is for them. And remember when Max had that consulting gig down south for six months and complained about how much harder he had to work to get a date there compared to New York?" Max was part of their tight circle of friends from college.

"We were *so* not sympathetic," Audrey said with a smile. "And that's why dating in NY is such a nightmare. Men always seem to be searching for that better girlfriend option around the corner."

Eve shrugged. "New York is tough. Let's eat on your balcony. You can enjoy a summer night outside now that you've escaped."

Audrey carried the salad bowl across the hallway to her rear duplex apartment. The minute she'd walked into it, she'd wanted it: light and airy, huge sliding glass doors, hardwood floors, exposed brick walls, clever closet solutions, outdoor space. The kitchen and living room were upstairs, with a small balcony, and a spiral staircase led to her bedroom downstairs, where a sliding glass door opened out onto a little backyard garden. Perfect apartment: check.

And she had been able to afford the down payment. Ever since her dad had died when she was in high school, she and her mom had had to worry about money. Her social life had taken a definite hit, but living at home with her mom for law school and for her first three years at the law firm had paid off. And her mom had been so relieved and proud that Audrey could buy this apartment. *Yes, Mom, you don't have to worry about me.*

Several months after her father's death, she had tried to bring back their family game night, making tacos, putting out board games for two. Her mom had shaken her head, crying, and abandoned the table. Audrey had then remembered her all A's report card and run after her mom, whose expression completely changed when she looked at it. Her mom was so happy that Audrey was keeping up her grades. That she was going to get into a good college. No more game nights. Just discussions about schoolwork.

Eyes on the prize. And that prize was now the financial security and professional recognition of partnership.

Which was now at risk. A cold shivery feeling snaked through her. It had never been a sure thing, but now it seemed farther away. She was tired; she'd been working so hard this past year that she didn't have the reserves to pull up to mount this one last push. She shook her head. She could do it.

The salad had fresh strawberries and blueberries. The tart, fruity smell of the balsamic vinaigrette dressing drifted up. Definitely a keeper for Eve's menu. Audrey set the salad on the little square table on the small iron balcony that overlooked the gardens, going back inside to fetch wine and glasses.

Her phone beeped. She picked it up as Eve passed by with the cranberry curry chicken dish and a bowl of rice on a tray.

Eve stopped abruptly. "Are you taking the night off or what? Put that phone away."

She dropped the phone as if it were a hot pot. "Look who's talking. Are you or are you not about to cook a new recipe on your night off?" She followed Eve out onto the balcony.

"That's my love of cooking. And you. You need to eat a home-cooked meal every once in a while."

"You're the best," Audrey said as they sat down at the table. "I'll add someone who cooks to my list of boyfriend requirements. Make it impossible. It's hard enough finding someone intelligent and attractive." That was another reason she liked work. Law was logical. Case precedents gave guidance, and sometimes even black-and-white answers.

"Good luck with that. What boyfriend is going to put up with these hours?"

"Another lawyer?"

"Well, that's one point in Preppy Boy's favor."

Audrey smiled at the nickname Eve had given Tim. He was a preppy dresser, which wasn't exactly her style. But he was still a good guy, ironed khakis notwithstanding. "His name is Tim."

"I prefer Preppy Boy," Eve said.

"What happens if we start dating?"

"Preppy Boy doesn't have the guts to start dating you while you're both up for partner at the same firm. I've told you that. But if he does, he's got my respect and I'll call him Tim." Eve took a bite of her salad. "Or Preppy Man."

"Lovely." Audrey poured two glasses of wine. "Anyway, I'm not going to date him either while we're up for partner. I've learned that lesson."

An evening breeze lessened the heat of the day, carrying the smell of barbecued steak from a neighbor's grill. She filled Eve in with the exact details of her bumping into the good-looking guy and how he'd rescued the little boy. A glow of warmth made her cheeks blush as she recalled his glance meeting hers, but she didn't share that with Eve. It was nothing but two strangers smiling at each other on the street.

"Looks like they're setting up a party down there," Eve said, gesturing with her glass of wine to the garden next door. A bar with a bright yellow surfboard as the countertop dominated one corner of it, and citronella candles and strings of Chinese lanterns provided dim, atmospheric lighting. "Let's see if your hot guy shows up."

"A surfboard—impressive!" Audrey said.

"Do you think he surfs?"

"Maybe that's how he catches all his fish." Not that she was surprised that he caught a lot of fish. That intrigued glance when he'd laughed at her comment. Her stomach flipped again. She would've swallowed a hook if she hadn't overheard his remark to his friend.

Eve asked Audrey to point him out to her if she saw him. Audrey took a bite of the curried chicken and said, "Oh wow, Eve. So good."

"So, it's a yes as a menu option for my catering gig in three weeks?" Eve asked.

"Yes. The mix of spices—it's delicious."

Eve smiled. "Chef Burns seems to be feeling me out for the executive pastry chef position."

"That's amazing." Audrey savored another bite. "But you're still doing the catering? Shouldn't you just focus on getting that position?"

"I can't do these hours forever. I don't want to be working nights and weekends. I never see Pete. Especially because he works all the time too. But, we can't both continue like this." Eve lived with her boyfriend, Pete, who was in finance. Eve rested her head on her hand. "I thought being an executive pastry chef at a restaurant was the holy grail, but I'm thinking I need to check out some back-up options."

"But you shouldn't be the one giving up your dreams," Audrey said. That's what her mother had done. And she never failed to tell Audrey she deeply regretted it—having to start over when her husband's death meant she had to return to the workforce.

"My dream is a balanced life where I get to see my boyfriend, my friends and family, and be a chef." Eve sipped her wine. "I'll still work." The music volume from the party next door increased.

Audrey shifted uncomfortably in the iron chair. She wanted a balanced life too, but having it all was a myth. She was going to have to live at the office 24/7 if she wanted to be a partner. And Eve had been pursuing her dream of a pastry chef with the same single-minded determination. "But what if Chef Burns promotes you?"

"If he promotes me, I'll put my all into that. Then I'll be able to create my own menu. But until then, I'll try the catering or apply for jobs as a pastry chef for a chain where the hours are better, you know, explore other options. And you?" Eve gave her a look as if to suggest she should do the same.

Now was not the time to be exploring other options. The window to leave the firm had been one or two years ago when she was a fifth or sixth year—that's when her peer girlfriends had departed, but she'd decided to go for it. She leaned forward to be heard over the music. "Tim and I won the pitch today for a new case."

Eve clinked her wine glass against Audrey's. "Congratulations!"

"It's a really cool case. Cutting edge legal issues, an entertainment company, a female general counsel." She waved her hand expressively, smiling as she recalled the smart questions of the general counsel. Answering them correctly had been invigorating. "It's my dream case. And my other case is high-stakes too, with a great team. I spent the earlier part of the week at that client's New York office, pulling relevant documents for the document production."

"Are the employees there?"

"Oh yes, they get to watch me go through all their stuff. I had to go through one guy's gym clothes." That guy had not been happy.

"That's a clever hiding place—right next to the smelly socks!"

Audrey shuddered. "You have no idea. The clothes were still slicked wet with sweat and it smelled rancid. But a file was in there."

"How do you know what might be relevant? It's not like they're tagging it 'smoking hot bad document.'"

"If only they would . . ." Audrey looked out over the brownstone backyards. Kids were being called in for the night, their childish voices disappearing from sounds of the night. "No, we have to read through everything. The team has been there for days now. But people generally don't hide things well. Maybe they're too confident they won't get caught. When I kept a diary on my laptop, I named it 'calculus homework' so no one would ever be tempted to review it."

"Except a math geek."

"No plan is foolproof."

"Did you find any juicy admissions?" Eve asked.

Audrey shook her head. She'd finished her curry chicken, her plate completely empty.

"That's just scary that you read everything," Eve said.

"Well, don't mix personal and work. You should be safe."

"What do you mean? Every recipe I make is a little love letter." Eve gave a chef's kiss. "Besides, you're one to talk what with your little office crush on Preppy Boy."

"True. You'd think I'd learn not to have office crushes." Audrey sighed. It had been two years of late-night chats, and Tim still hadn't asked her out. Eve was right that she should stop mooning over him. Especially after her break-up with her last boyfriend, Kevin. They had dated when she was a fourth-year associate and he was up for partner at the firm. When he didn't make partner, he left. And they'd broken up soon after that.

"Kevin was a jerk," Eve said. "And he was the worst kind of jerk because he seemed like a good guy. Even I was taken in. But you can't let him define you.'"

"I'm not. I still think I can be promoted to partner." She shifted in her seat. Or so she had thought—before Winnie's news.

"Given how much you work, it makes sense you'd meet someone in the office." Eve ate her last bite.

"Someone online asked me for a date this Saturday."

"And you said yes, right?"

"No," Audrey said. She kept forgetting to take down her on-line dating profile. She really had to add it to her to-do list. No time for dating now. "I haven't replied."

"Say yes, now."

She should tell Eve about Winnie's news, but Eve always argued that she should be able to date while being a lawyer. "Does that mean I can get my phone?"

"Okay. You can have five minutes on your phone to say yes and check your work email. I'll get dessert."

Audrey carried their dishes into her apartment and deposited them in her sink. She'd do clean-up. She picked up her phone and typed yes to the date. He had seemed funny—he'd made a joke about being a workaholic, and she was taking Saturday off to re-charge.

Eve brought out a strawberry-rhubarb pie for dessert, and they sat back outside in the balmy evening air. Audrey took a bite, the tart flavors of the berries and rhubarb exploding on her tongue. As they threw around ideas to kickstart Eve's catering business, Audrey suggested she throw a party to show off Eve's appetizers and desserts. It would have the added benefit of being one last chance to see all her friends before she buckled down into a black hole to make partner. Eve agreed. The garden next door was now packed with people. "The Man" by Taylor Swift was playing, and some guests were swaying to the music. Glass clinked in a toast between several beer bottles. Audrey helped herself to a second sliver of pie. The rest was for Pete.

"Okay, I see him. He's in the light gray shirt by the bar talking to the girl in red." Audrey looked away so he wouldn't see both of them checking him out.

"Mmm, yes, he's hot." Eve nodded and smiled mischievously at Audrey. "And they say fairy godmothers don't exist. Definitely what I was wishing for you. He has the same type of looks as that guy you had a crush on in college but never asked out."

Suddenly a male voice broke through their conversation. "Juliet, Juliet, wherefore art thou? Fair maidens, come down and join the party." A guy beckoned to them from the party in the garden below.

A buzz of anticipation flickered through her veins. She looked at Eve to see if she wanted to go. If they went, there was no way she could return to the office.

"Yes, definitely." Eve gave her a "you'd be crazy not to go" look. "You have to get out there."

"But I have to be at work early tomorrow," she whispered, trying to resist the siren call of laughter, music and conversation.

"It's only eight. Don't tell me you go to bed earlier than midnight. I've heard your footsteps in the hallway coming home from the office. That gives you at least three hours. This will be fun. Like old times."

Best friends don't disappoint each other. She would work late on Friday night.

Audrey called down, "But it might be better to use 'Rapunzel, Rapunzel, let down your hair' if we want a happy ending to our meeting."

"Rapunzel it is! I'm all for happy endings, plus that hair. Who could resist?" the guy said. He was attractive, with long brown hair in a ponytail. She imagined he played guitar. "I'm Rafael."

"We'll be right over."

"Ring doorbell 1B."

Audrey loaded all the dishes onto the tray and carried it back inside.

"You should wear that little black dress you bought in Paris." Eve followed her inside, carrying the rest of the pie.

"Won't it be obvious that I changed?"

"You'd be crazy not to look your best with the hot male quotient there. I plan to dazzle in a dress myself, and I'm pretty much a happily married woman, but not quite." Eve fluttered her ringless finger.

"Has Pete given any signs that he might propose?" Audrey turned on the light in her white galley kitchen. A lone blue tea mug was upside down on the drying rack.

"He's crazy busy at work right now, trying to get this promotion. And that's okay with me. I'm trying to figure out my career stuff. It's not like I need to be married right now, although my mom would like it."

"My mom doesn't dare bring up dating or marriage because she doesn't want to add any more pressure to my life." Audrey scrubbed the dishes.

"Did she say that?" Eve dried a plate.

"Last Thanksgiving, my aunt asked if I was dating anyone, and my mom said, 'she has enough on her plate right now.' And I don't think she was referring to my turkey dinner."

Eve laughed. "Your mom seems to think that you can only do one or the other."

"She thinks I should make partner first, and then I can find a relationship. Which makes sense."

"I'm all for you finding a relationship now," Eve said. "And I mean, right now, after you put on a dress."

Chapter Three

As Audrey and Eve entered the apartment, Rafael crossed the room to meet them, making his way through bright-colored balloons floating around a bare room. Either the new tenant was an extraordinary minimalist or his stuff hadn't arrived yet. After they exchanged real names (although he joked that he might want to keep calling Audrey Rapunzel), he said that his friend had just moved in and offered to introduce them. He took them out the sliding back door and through the crowded garden, aiming straight for the guy Audrey had bumped into on the street. *Jackpot.* For a minute, she was tempted to invent an excuse to leave before he thought she was pursuing him, but he turned her way and their gazes collided. He raised one eyebrow. She flushed.

"Eve and Audrey, this is Jake," Rafael said. Jake smiled warmly at them, but there was definitely a teasing light in his eyes. As

Rafael explained how he'd invited them, he remarked that Eve looked familiar. They started comparing names of schools and jobs.

So, here was her chance to talk to Jake, but she couldn't think of a sparkling opening.

"We meet again," Jake said. "So, you're my neighbor—a woman who knows her fairy tales as well as Shakespeare."

"Doesn't everyone know their fairytales?"

"Valid point. Brainwashed at an early age to believe in happy endings."

"You don't?" she asked, surprised. He gave off a happy-go-lucky vibe.

"I do. But why is it called a happy ending rather than a happy beginning?"

"Sounds accurately titled to me, given that I end up as a slaughtered fish," she said, wryly. It was kind of an accurate description of dating in New York for women.

"No shooting needed. That's my whole point. I just have to stand here and a woman will approach."

She wished she had that self-confidence, but . . . She smiled innocently. "You are the host. I'm going to presume they're asking you where the bathroom is."

He laughed and nearly choked on the sip of beer he'd just swallowed. "Nobody has ever asked me that." He looked at her as if intrigued.

Well, at least he was a good sport when challenged.

He reached out to gently pull her out of the way of someone vigorously gesturing. "Anyone here look like he could be your Prince Charming? Or you're dating him already?"

"I'm not sure I've met him yet." He looked like her Prince Charming, but there's no way she'd tell him that. He was already very much aware that he was a catch.

"Aren't you supposed to 'just know'?" His eyebrow arched up again.

"Apparently, but I've never believed that." She tilted her head. Kevin had ticked all the boxes, but he had definitely not been the one.

He smiled and sipped his beer, his gaze meeting hers as his lips touched the rim of the bottle. Her pulse quickened. He asked, "So, you may have met him?"

"This feels like a cross-examination. Are you a lawyer?"

"God, no. Can't stand lawyers."

"Lovely." Just her luck to have an attractive, competent, self-confident neighbor—who hated lawyers.

"Don't tell me you like lawyers?" he asked in a tone of mock disbelief.

"I am a lawyer."

He looked surprised, but recovered quickly. "My dad's a lawyer, so I've some exceptions. Do you like being a lawyer?"

"I wouldn't do it if I didn't like it." She crossed her arms. She'd met so many people who hated lawyers on principle, and she'd made it a personal mission to prove them wrong.

"Not doing it just to pay the bills while you plan your escape to something more creative?"

"No." She tucked her hair behind her ear. "And being a lawyer is very creative. What type of lawyer is your dad?"

"He sees himself as the creative type as well," he said. "He's a partner at White & Gilman."

She nodded, acknowledging knowing the firm. She'd been offered a position there but had chosen its competitor, Howard, Parker & Smith, instead. The best of the best.

"Are you trying to make partner?" he asked.

"Yes. Six months until the decision."

Jake stepped back. "Law firm partner. That's quite a commitment." He looked over her shoulder, focusing on something happening in the party. More guests were arriving.

Not wanting to be the one left, she said, "I should continue circulating—with no phone, see!"

"It's not in your purse?"

"I left it at home."

"You took my advice?"

"No. Please, I just met you," she said dryly. After Eve's rebuke, it had seemed wise to leave her phone at home. And her dress didn't have pockets.

"Well done, anyway," he said. A man in a Nirvana t-shirt elbowed Jake gently and asked him the title of a song playing and if he had any details on the artist. Leaving her, Jake said, "Sorry, party duty calls."

Audrey joined the conversation between Rafael and Eve. They had met before—at a cooking course. Audrey teased Rafael that he must have lots of women after him if he was a good cook. As she talked with them, she couldn't stop her gaze from following Jake, who was chatting with one of the bartenders by the surfboard. When a striking blond woman in a purple mini dress and gray strappy platform heels came up to talk to him, he looked over at Audrey and winked. She blushed at being caught watching. She turned back to join the conversation with Eve and Rafael, determined to ignore him.

"So, how do you know Jake?" Eve asked Rafael. He explained that they played soccer together on weekends.

"Jake, when's your stuff coming?" Rafael asked as he passed them. "Do you need help with the move?"

"Saturday. That's why I had the party tonight—nothing can get trashed."

"As if you'd let anyone touch your record collection," Rafael said.

"True, no need to make enemies on the first day," Jake said, adding he'd welcome Rafael's help on Saturday.

Rafael introduced them around the party. They met several soccer players as well as high school and college friends of Jake's. People were friendly and easy to talk to. Audrey caught Rafael studying her at one point, and she smiled back at him. Rafael was greeted by a woman and turned to talk to her. A golden retriever slipped past Audrey, followed by Jake.

"Is that your dog?" Eve asked.

"Meet Biscuit," Jake said. Audrey petted Biscuit's furry head.

A girl with bright blue hair in a bob haircut and an orange dress suddenly appeared and gave Jake a big hug. Stepping back, but still holding him, she said, "It's been ages! I'm so happy to see you. And even more delighted you've seen the error of your ways and disentangled yourself from the clutches of that she-wolf."

"Penny! You're still the same, even with blue hair. Never one to mince words." Jake kissed her lightly on the cheek.

"Like it?" She tossed her hair.

"You'd look good in any hair color," Jake said and introduced Eve and Audrey. Audrey could feel Penny appraising them subtly.

"You know you should take a break from serious relationships and just enjoy single life," Penny said to Jake.

"That's exactly what I intend to do," Jake said.

If he waited six months, that would be perfect.

"Hmm, we'll see how long that lasts," Penny said. "I give it a week. If you would date someone for a while before jumping into a relationship, you might save yourself some agony." Then she turned to Audrey and Eve. "It's been ages since I've seen him and had a proper chat because"—her voice dropped to a low whisper—"he was dating this woman who watched him like a she-hawk, and anytime he as much as glanced at another woman—even a long-time friend like me, she'd swoop in and"—Penny's voice took on a Southern accent—"just desperately need him."

"I don't think Audrey needs to know all this," Jake said.

Yes, I do.

Switching subjects, Jake asked, "How's your acting career going?"

"Great, but that's what I want to talk to you about. Do you mind if I steal him to catch up?" Penny linked arms with Jake.

Eve and Audrey shook their heads. Audrey watched them go, then chided herself. She was here to enjoy a night out, not find a boyfriend, not if she wanted to make partner. A candle flared, punctuating the dusk, and the smell of citronella wafted over.

"I'm so glad we came," Audrey said to Eve. "I haven't been to a party in so long." The party conversations murmured and swelled as if keeping time to the music.

They dropped into two folding chairs placed in the corner at a good vantage point to check out the party. "Let me know if you see anyone of interest. Happy to play wing woman. I like Rafael."

"Yes, he seems really sweet."

"Sweet. That's the kiss of death for dating. He's tall and definitely handsome. And fit. And he cooks." Eve gave her that look that said "your list is not so impossible after all."

"I wasn't meaning sweet as the kiss of death."

Eve raised an eyebrow. "If you say so."

"I didn't feel that electricity. But it could be there . . . just grounded temporarily." Her chair was rocking. She shifted it to more even ground.

"Make the most of it, this is happening. You don't get out that often anymore."

Suddenly, a woman in high heels in front of Audrey lost her footing on the brick path and fell back, spilling her white wine on Audrey's black dress. The cold liquid hit her skin and she cried out.

"Oh, I'm so sorry." The woman pushed her wispy blond hair out of her eyes. "I'm really sorry, your dress is so wet."

"No worries. It will come out, I'm sure." Audrey looked across the backyard to where Jake was talking to someone, his back to her. "Can you do me a favor and ask the host where his bathroom is? I'll try to fix it there."

"It's the least I can do." The woman made a beeline for Jake. Smiling wickedly, Audrey hurried to the bathroom, which was in the same location as in her apartment.

She left the bathroom, and at the door to the garden, she ran into Jake. He put his arm around her. The warmth of the physical contact surprised her. He smelled like fresh cotton laundry with a slight whiff of beer. He leaned in, one hand on the door next to her, her back against the sliding glass door. She held his gaze, her body buzzing. Enveloped in their own little bubble, the party noise receded into the background. It was just him and her.

"So, surprise, surprise, a woman actually asked me where the bathroom was," he said in a low voice.

"And you wanted to share that with me?"

"I thought you might have had something to do with that."

"Did you?"

"Yes." He laughed. "You totally did. You're so not good at keeping secrets."

She laughed. "Maybe. I might've."

"Are you sure you're a corporate lawyer?"

"Positive. Why?"

"You seem too mischievous." He brushed a strand of hair away from her face. His touch left a warm tingle. Her brain blanked. She couldn't think of anything witty to say in response.

"It would have worked better if my apartment was bigger," he said.

"Got to work with what I've got. I'm thinking it succeeded." Raising her chin, she gazed directly into Jake's eyes. He leaned in closer. She held her breath. Did he feel that pull of attraction too? Penny passed by, singing the words "I'm Staying Single." Definitely no subtext for Jake there. Audrey caught the glance Penny gave him. He pulled away, smiling ruefully.

"Do you know the band The Jane Austen Argument?" he asked.

"No, but cool name."

"They actually titled their hit song 'Staying Single,' the one Penny is singing. I should not have introduced her to that song," he said, raking his fingers through his hair distractedly.

Two guys approached Jake. Both looked like they'd played sports in college. One was tall and lanky, with brown wavy hair; the other had blond curly hair and the build of a football player.

"Jake, nice place."

"Rory, Bill, great to see you guys!" Jake said. "This is Audrey, my neighbor."

"I never thought I'd see you on the Upper West Side," Rory said. "I miss having you nearby."

"I'm still a text away. Although I can't quite believe I moved uptown either," Jake said.

"Nobody moves uptown once they've lived downtown." Bill took a sip of his beer. A burst of laughter broke out in the corner of the garden, and the three tall men looked over. All three men were good-looking, but Jake had this joie de vivre magnetism. Audrey could feel her body swaying towards him.

"My sister needs help, so it seemed easier if I moved up here—at least for now. Especially since I didn't particularly want to be in Tribeca," Jake said.

"You missed some great waves at Long Beach," Rory said.

"Hopefully next weekend," Jake said.

Apparently, these guys had jobs that allowed them to go surfing on weekends. She had to take a moment to process that. No Malaburn demanding they spend every waking moment devoted to legal jurisprudence. Go away, thoughts-of-Malaburn, she was going to enjoy this party.

"Nice to meet you. Jake's a lucky guy. My neighbor is at least seventy-five and has three cats," Bill said. Audrey shook his hand.

"But she does accept your dry-cleaning deliveries." Rory smiled.

"What can I say? I'm like a grandson to her. But better. I get her flowers," Bill said. Jake winked at her, and she felt warm inside.

"You didn't tell me that. That's why she tried to set you up," Rory said.

"Yes, unfortunately, only seventy-five-year-olds see my appeal," Bill said.

"I'm sure that's not true," Audrey said, smiling.

"Really?" Bill put his arm around her. "C'mon, your drink needs replenishing. Let's go to the bar and leave these two Neanderthals behind." Bill led her to the bar. She tried to casually ask him what he did; she didn't want to seem like she was focused on jobs. He was in sports marketing. That hadn't even been an option on her career menu. Doctor or lawyer were the choices.

Eve popped up beside them at the bar. "I need another drink. It's hot." Eve fanned herself.

"This is Eve. She lives next door too," Audrey said.

"Another gorgeous neighbor! What am I doing wrong in life?" Bill asked.

Rory joined them, and the four ordered their drinks from the bartender and moved away from the bar. They all continued talking easily, with little ripostes ricocheting back and forth between them. The music volume suddenly increased.

"It's not a Jake party if there isn't dancing," Rory said.

Jake was swing-dancing with Penny, the two of them grinning as he spun her around, her orange dress flaring around her.

Bill asked if she wanted to dance, and with one last look at Jake and Penny, Audrey said yes. She danced with Rafael next, and he asked for her number. Eve gave Audrey a thumbs up. As Rafael left to get a drink, she thought about asking Jake to dance, but he was used to women chasing him. She didn't want to be another woman pursuing him. Especially when she had to focus on making partner—not hankering after guys who had to time to surf on weekends.

At midnight, Jake turned off the music and announced that the party was moving to a nearby bar to avoid pissing off his new neighbors. Eve asked Audrey if she wanted to go home or set off with the party.

Audrey glanced to where Jake was surrounded by friends. She hadn't spoken to him again. He'd spent the night as the host talking to lots of different people. But if he was "staying single," then there would be time to get to know each other as neighbors. And not when she was tired. Or when Penny was standing guard.

She said, "Go home and leave it on a high note."

"What happened to my college roommate—the girl who believed in closing down the party? Once I got her out of the library, that is," Eve said.

"She grew up and became a corporate lawyer." Audrey gave her a wry look. "Don't tell me you're not tired. I saw you yawn a few minutes ago."

"Caught in the act. I'm cool with going home."

They walked over to Jake to say goodbye and thank you.

"Are you sure you don't want to come out with us?" Jake asked. He tilted his head, encouraging, and she was tempted. All her senses came alive, as if they were ready to box in another bout of bantering.

"I have to be at work early tomorrow." It wasn't like college where she could sleep in. Tonight was a temporary respite, but tomorrow she had to make up for it.

The air stirred behind her, and the smell of Chanel perfume wafted over. Jake's open smile disappeared.

"Veronika," Jake said flatly.

"Jake, I took an early flight to make your party." Veronika swept between Audrey and Eve to envelop Jake in a hug. The night air suddenly felt chilly, and Audrey wrapped her arms around herself. She turned to Eve and tilted her head towards the door. Penny joined them as they were leaving.

Penny held open the front door for them. "She's like quicksand. She appears harmless, but she's not going to let him go that easily. And Jake's too nice. He shouldn't have told her about his party. He told me it was safe because she had a modeling commitment in Italy. He doesn't want to hurt her feelings, but there isn't a nice way to break up with someone."

"No," Audrey said, still filled with regret at the way she'd broken up with Kevin. Eve and Audrey waved goodbye to Penny as they turned into the entrance of their building next door.

As they jogged up the stairs, Audrey said, "That was fun. I miss college and those all-night parties." And that flickering of anticipation that something might happen. All-nighters filing briefs were not the same. Any flickers then were of fear that she had missed something.

"It doesn't have to be all-night or nothing. There is a middle ground. I told you that you just have to get out there," Eve said, behind her on the stairs.

Audrey nodded, but any middle ground was fast disappearing. She trudged up the dark stairway to their floor. A hallway light was out, and the walls felt like they were closing in. Winnie's news and Malaburn were lurking in the shadows. She shook herself and hugged Eve goodbye at her door.

Chapter Four

udrey's office looked occupied, just as she had left it. Not that the deception had worked. She should've taken the elevator. She had to call the assignment partner and head off Malaburn's attempt to work with her.

As she walked around her desk, her bag swung out and knocked over the glass of water. Agh! All over her papers. All her edits and notes. She blotted the papers with napkins from one drawer devoted to extra napkins and plastic utensils from her take-out dinners. Still wet. She draped a few papers over the backs and arms of her guest chairs. Finding a ribbon left over from a wine bottle gift at the close of a trial, she strung it from her floor lamp to her bookcase, and using binder clips, hung papers off it. She quickly closed her office door so nobody could see her paper laundry. She laid out some papers on the floor. She'd quickly input her edits on the first ten pages while the others dried. Winnie was going to find this hysterical.

A knock sounded at the door, and she opened it to find Malaburn. Her back tensed. He took in the scene in her office and raised an eyebrow.

"I knocked over a glass of water." She removed the papers from her guest chair, felt the cushion to confirm it was dry, then carefully stepped over the papers on the floor to return to her own seat.

Sitting down, he peered at her through his tortoise-shell rimmed glasses, like she was a bug he wanted to squash. "Glad you could make time for my little assignment. You're on such high-profile cases nowadays. I see the Rothman case frequently in the news. That was a nasty article in the *Wall Street Journal* the other day."

Really nasty. It had quoted the plaintiff in the case, this French multi-millionaire, Pierre, and his public complaint alleging that Mr. Rothman had made a $200,000 trade in Pierre's account without his approval. Only one sentence noted that Rothman and Hen Bank disputed those allegations vigorously.

"We're working with our communications team to get more favorable press this weekend."

"Bit behind the ball." Malaburn sniffed.

She wasn't even responsible for press. "Not necessarily. We know more about their approach now, and now we get to counter it and leave a positive impression."

He steepled his fingers. "And I hear you won the Popflicks pitch."

"I'm excited. Hopefully this client will bring in a lot of work for the firm." *Hint, hint.* A new client demanded utter availability and commitment, not an overloaded, stressed-out associate. And the firm recognized that. It was like a legal "get out of jail free" card.

"My assignment shouldn't take much time," he said. "It's updating your past memo for a pitch."

Preparing for a pitch could be just a short-term assignment, but he'd probably get the business. Her stomach knotted. She was too busy for this, but she needed his vote for partner. She couldn't see how she could just say no. "I'll talk to the assignment partner."

Her assistant Gertrude appeared at the door. "Anderson is on the phone. He says it's urgent."

A reprieve.

Audrey said, "I have to take this call." She should ask Gertrude to say she had a call whenever Malaburn was in her office. Not that Gertrude would ever agree—she was too deferential to the partners.

He stood. "I'll call you later." As he closed the door, he said, "I'd suggest you take down the papers and give them to your assistant to input quickly."

She picked up the call from Anderson, the partner in charge of the Popflicks case. The Popflicks general counsel had requested her—not Tim—as the senior associate to run the case. Anderson looked forward to working with her on it.

"I'm thrilled. It's my dream case," she said to Anderson over the phone, and she meant it. Tim must be disappointed.

She called the assignment partner. He was out on vacation, so she left a message. Of all the times for him to be away. She shouldn't worry yet; he was sure to check messages and call her back. She finished the engagement letter, sent it off to Anderson, input all her changes from the wet papers, and then reviewed two associate memos, giving comments.

Now to write a memo about their recent document pull at the Hen Bank offices where John Rothman worked. Minus the details about the gym bag she'd shared with Eve. They had been hoping to find a written authorization signed by Pierre allowing Rothman to trade in the account. They had not.

She stared out her window, up at the blue sky with just a few patches of clouds, biting a nail. She had a hunch, but she needed to speak to the Hen Bank compliance officer to confirm it. She called Genevieve, Hen Bank's in-house counsel, explained her theory, and Genevieve patched in the compliance officer.

Audrey asked, "If a written authorization allows a broker like Rothman to trade in an account, what procedures are followed? Is there any follow-up by the compliance office to make sure the trading is within the approved boundaries and not fraudulent?"

"Yes," said the compliance officer, explaining how those accounts had a higher level of supervision that involved certain sign-offs on the order tickets.

That made sense. They were not just going to let those "masters of the universe" trade willy-nilly without anyone looking over their shoulders.

Audrey hung up and clicked on the folder storing the images of the order tickets for Pierre's account, recently scanned from the document pull. The order tickets had those signoffs. So, Pierre's account was being treated as a discretionary trading account. She sat up straighter, feeling lighter already. It was something, but they still needed that written authorization signed by Pierre. She rubbed her neck and shoulder muscles. She needed to win this case. She wasn't going to be promoted if they lost this case—and possibly then the client.

Was there another reason why Pierre, a reputed multi-millionaire, would sue her client, Rothman, destroying their twenty-year friendship for a $200,000 trade? Especially when the stock was volatile and might recover? John Rothman had been upset about the loss of their friendship. Not overtly, but a few heartfelt remarks here and there when he'd explained how they had been family friends; their wives, best friends. A personal reason made more sense, given the ramifications. That wasn't something she usually considered as a lawyer, but an emotional rationale could appeal to a jury.

Winnie called to see if she was still free to pick up lunch. "I need to vent," she said.

"Oh no. What happened?"

"They told me I'm going to Texas to manage our document discovery. Just one week, but still." Winnie sounded frustrated.

"Oh no." Audrey saved her document. "Meet you downstairs."

She caught the elevator right before the doors closed. Swooping in, she nearly bumped into senior partner Gene Whitaker.

"Wherever you're going, it's not worth losing your hand over," Gene said, his bushy eyebrows rising up as he leaned back against the wall, his blue eyes crinkling at the corners.

"Lunch. I heard you were retiring. I'm really sorry to hear that. You'll be missed," she said. Gene was one of her idol partners. Tough, but fair. Willing to mentor young lawyers.

He harrumphed. "More like, don't let the door hit you on the way out."

Her brow furrowed. "When is your retirement party?"

"I'm not having one. The firm's got enough to worry about right now, without planning my party."

"I hardly think that planning your departure party is a hardship that the firm can't handle," she said, shocked.

"So you'd think."

The doors opened onto the lobby. Winnie was texting by the window. Audrey admired her white military-style dress with little brass buttons in a vertical row. It was cutting-edge chic, almost too hip for the law firm. Winnie visited her grandmother in Hong Kong every summer and inevitably returned with a few stunning tailored pieces.

She joined Winnie, whispering, "The firm isn't even throwing a departure party for Whitaker."

Winnie nodded knowingly.

They pushed through the revolving doors to the street. It was muggy, the air heavy. The sulfur smell of the steam rising from a New York City manhole cover hit them.

"No need to do the sauna too, in this heat," Audrey said. "They should add lavender or citrus to that steam to de-stress New Yorkers."

"Yeah, the perfect way for New Yorkers to get sauna health benefits while still rushing to their next destination," Winnie said. "And we could create an app that alerts people to the next steam stack to blow and make enough money to quit law." Winnie was quite certain that she didn't want to make partner.

"I can't believe you have to go to Texas. Should I write a note to the senior associate about how essential you've been to the Hen case?"

"Then he'll just want more of my time."

"True." Audrey sighed. "Malaburn just asked me to update a memo."

"How'd you get assigned more work? You have a full plate," Winnie said.

"He caught me in the stairway yesterday."

"I'm not surprised he haunts the stairway. But he's supposed to go through the assignment partner. Did you tell him that? That's the whole point of the assignment partner. He can parcel out assignments fairly and make sure that no one associate is over-burdened. It's just like Malaburn to bypass that."

"I did tell him. And called the assignment partner." Assignment partners should assign someone else to cover this when on vacation.

"Malaburn. The problem is he's really influential. He's one of the highest-billing partners because all he does is work," Winnie said. "What's he on? Like divorce number three?"

"I don't see how I can say no," Audrey said. Winnie didn't contradict her. This was definitely a job for the assignment partner. "Anyway, Whitaker seemed depressed about it. I'm going to talk to HR and see if it's true. Maybe it's a surprise party."

"I don't think they throw surprise parties for seventy-year-old partners. Too much liability," Winnie said.

They ran to catch the light and cross the street. The sidewalk seemed less crowded than usual; probably most preferred to stay indoors in the air conditioning. A wise choice. Her shirt was sticking to her armpits. The sun burned her arms. The heat was radiating off the buildings. So, this was how it felt to be a piece of toast. She was getting cooked walking down the street between the two buildings.

"But he's a legend. I can't believe they're not throwing him a party. It's not that much effort." Audrey shaded her eyes to see the figures down the block. "Is that Colette and Tim?"

"Yeah, I forgot to tell you that I ran into him as he was on the way to lunch in the cafeteria. You could've met him for lunch there."

"Because lunch in the cafeteria is so romantic."

"Your crush, not mine," Winnie said. "Maybe they found each other in the cafeteria and decided to go out for lunch."

Colette's shiny brown hair was pulled back in a tight ballerina bun. Tim bent his head slightly as if to catch what Colette was saying. Even though she wasn't close enough to see Tim's eyes, Audrey could visualize his chocolate eyes giving that cozy "we're in this together" feeling.

"They look rather together," Winnie said.

Audrey bit her lip, considering this. Colette would definitely appeal to someone like Tim; Colette was so polished and sure of herself. Her breath hitched and she felt a slight ache of disappointment. Colette wouldn't wait around for two years, content with casual stop-bys. Audrey waved as they neared. Tim said hello with an intimate smile at Audrey.

"Congratulations on getting the Popflicks case," he said. "I could tell the GC liked you."

"I'm sorry it's just me."

"It's okay. Gives me more time to focus on my current case," Tim said.

Exactly. He had only one case and she, three very busy ones. She wiped a trickle of perspiration away from her brow. She seemed to be the only person sweating. Tim was wearing a highly starched, still-crisp white shirt, and Colette's sleeveless silk shift looked cool in the heat.

"I'm taking Tim to lunch." Colette placed her hand on his arm. "I found this charming French bistro that opened last week. I met the French owner, so it might be authentically good."

"Your father's French, right?" Winnie asked.

Colette stilled. "Yes."

"I didn't realize your father was still alive. But you're visiting only your mom this weekend?" Tim asked. Audrey glanced at Tim sharply. He seemed interested, if he was asking about her parents.

"I am visiting only my mom this weekend. My father's still alive, physically speaking, but we don't talk." Colette smoothed into place a stray shiny brown tendril escaping her sleek bun.

"That's terrible," Audrey said. She would give a lot to have one more chance to speak with her father.

"It's not a loss. He slept with his assistant, divorced my mom, didn't always pay child support, but appears demonstratively physically happy with his new wife." Colette shuddered.

"That would do it," Winnie said.

"Yeah," Audrey said.

"I don't need him." Colette shrugged. "But I do need to find a new partner to work for. My case just settled. Maybe I can get your thoughts on which one over lunch, Tim." She gazed up at him. "It has to be someone whom I haven't worked with before. But someone influential who will advocate for me for partner."

"I'd be glad to help." Tim patted her hand on his arm. "Will you be in the office tomorrow, Audrey?"

"Yes, after lunch," Audrey said. Their body language was certainly giving an impression of being more than office colleagues.

"I thought you were taking Saturday off?" Winnie asked.

"Not if I'm going to work on that pitch with Malaburn," Audrey said wryly.

"Another pitch?" Colette asked sharply. "You're really racking them up."

Audrey glanced at Colette warily. She didn't want to compete against her. A passing pedestrian bumped shoulders with Audrey, and rubbing her shoulder, Audrey moved closer to Winnie.

"Audrey gave our whole team the weekend off," Winnie said.

"Is that the Rothman case? I thought that was busy," Colette said, narrowing her eyes.

"It is," Audrey said firmly. The last thing she needed was a rumor that the case wasn't busy. "But the team needs a break."

"Junior associates shouldn't be tired yet." Colette gave a short laugh. "I hear Hunter is a sweetheart to work for." Hunter was the partner in charge of the Rothman case.

"It wasn't Hunter who gave us the weekend off. It was Audrey," Winnie said.

"But Hunter agreed to it," Colette said.

"I said I'd cover any issues," Audrey said.

Colette shrugged and pulled Tim away. "Come, Tim, we should get lunch."

They walked away, and Winnie said, "Well, if he's interested in both of you, at least, it's a clear choice."

"I think so," Audrey said dryly, but she wasn't sure that the choice was in her favor for a preppy guy like Tim. They waited for the light to change to green.

"Anyway, it sounds like they'll be discussing work," Winnie said.

"Partnership plotting—but which type of partnership?" Audrey asked, making light of it. She didn't want Winnie to see that she was shaken. She hadn't realized that Tim was so friendly with Colette.

"I wouldn't put anything past Colette."

"I discuss work all the time with Tim."

"And that should tell you something right there."

Audrey nodded, her shoulders slumping. Hence the reason Eve called him Preppy Boy—Eve had said, "You want a man who likes you so much, he has to ask you out—not someone who can wait around for two years."

Eve was right. And her mom had also always said that at least she'd had a great love with her father. She should be looking for the same, not trying to read tea leaves to decipher Tim.

They passed the Juice Java, and the smell of citrus and lime lured them inside. As they waited in line to order and pay for their strawberry smoothies, Audrey said, "I'm certainly not competing with Colette for Tim. Two professional women fighting over a man—no way." She shuddered.

"On the positive side, if they fall madly in love, maybe they won't be able to concentrate on work, and you'll have a clear path to partner."

Audrey laughed. "I don't see either as that type." She held the door for Winnie as they left Juice Java to walk the final block to the salad place. "It's bad enough if it's four of us competing for two spots." Her stomach churned. She couldn't lose hope. "I hope she's not thinking of asking Hunter for work. I guess it'd be okay. We could #leanintogether."

"Colette's definitely leaning in."

"But I don't think she got the memo on leaning in together."

"No, not with you anyway. Maybe Tim."

"Great," Audrey said sarcastically. They entered the salad restaurant and picked up their salads from the pre-ordered take-out shelf. "At least Colette seems upfront. So that's good. I respect that." Sipping the Juice Java ice-cold smoothie definitely made the heat more bearable. "Also, the dad thing means we have somewhat similar backgrounds."

"How?" Winnie asked as they ambled back to the office. "Your dad died. He didn't cheat on your mom."

"No. He adored my mom. But still, she lost her dad, in a sense, and her whole unit of family changed. And it sounds like they were far worse off financially."

"Interesting. But I still wouldn't trust her. I mean, you shouldn't be intimidated by her, but you shouldn't trust her." Winnie glanced at her. "You should ask Hunter for advice about Malaburn."

"I don't want him to think I can't handle it." Hunter was the main partner supporting her. She couldn't create any doubt in his mind.

"You're not superwoman. He could help you," Winnie said. "Colette's looking for work; she should've been assigned to work with Malaburn. She was envious that you were doing another pitch."

Audrey nodded. "And yet I don't think she'll ask Malaburn for work."

The sky darkened. One of those sudden New York monsoon thunderstorms was about to erupt. They sprinted the last block back to the office. Winnie pushed open the doors to the lobby, and the cold air-conditioning hit them like an ice blast.

"No," Winnie agreed. "Malaburn is too much of a nightmare. Are you really going to say yes?"

Audrey shivered. *Frozen hell.* "If it's just updating one memo, I can do a good job and leave him with a favorable impression." They entered the elevator, and Audrey pushed the buttons for their floors.

Audrey checked her messages when she got back to the office, but no return calls saved her. She quickly ate lunch at her desk and then called Malaburn to agree solely to update the memo. She could do it. He wouldn't make her cry this time.

Chapter Five

Her online date had suggested a bike ride, so on Saturday morning, Audrey rolled her blue bike out the front door of her brownstone onto the street. She probably should've cleaned the dust off of it. At least there was a breeze and not too much humidity.

"Hey, Audrey, going for a bike ride?" Jake asked.

She jumped. She hadn't been expecting to bump into Jake. He had a coffee in one hand and Biscuit on the leash. Biscuit was intently sniffing the tree in front of a neighbor's townhouse.

"Yes, perfect day for one." Audrey grinned at him.

He stepped closer to her. Her heart was fizzing like she'd just swallowed a highly-caffeinated drink.

"I could join you if you wait a bit," he said.

That would've been perfect. But no, she had to reply, "Umm, actually I'm meeting a blind date for a bike ride."

"Really?" He looked surprised.

"Yes, really." *Unfortunately, really.*

"I've never done a blind date. That takes guts."

"Or desperation," Audrey muttered.

"No need for desperation. You just need to leave your office every once in a while, and you'd do fine."

Audrey felt herself glowing at the compliment, and she looked away briefly before he could notice her mooning over him.

Biscuit finished inspecting the tree and was now pulling to go down the block. Jake waved goodbye.

This date had better be worth it. She bicycled to their established meeting spot: the John Lennon memorial circle. Quite a crowd of people was gathered there. A young man with long hair was playing his guitar, singing "Yellow Submarine." Another guy had a sign that said, "$1 for a joke; dollar back if you don't laugh." She didn't see her date, who was supposed to be on a green ten speed. She scanned the crowd again and then looked back at the entering pathway.

A guy was bicycling towards her on a green ten speed—in a full-body black speedo outfit.

He stopped in front of her. "Hi, I'm Dan. Are you Audrey?"

"Yes." Wasn't he sweating in that Lycra suit? Not much was left to the imagination.

"Are you ready to go? Your bike doesn't look like it goes very fast," he said.

"No, but it's dependable."

"Perhaps we should meet up? I want to get in a good workout. I like to be efficient with these things. Want to meet up by the boathouse and we can get a drink there?"

Flustered and surprised, she said, "Um, I guess so."

"Okay, see you there."

Dan quickly bicycled out of sight.

She texted Eve: *Date in full-body black Speedo!?*

Eve: *Does he look good? How are you biking and texting me? While on date?*

Audrey snorted. She started to text a reply and then decided it would be easier to explain by calling Eve.

"Not that good. He's bicycled off so he gets his workout. We're meeting at the boathouse," she said as she wheeled her bike down to the bike path with one hand on the handlebars.

"Are you serious? What kind of a date is that? Why didn't he just work out beforehand?"

"He likes to be efficient."

"Efficient? I'm not even going to go into how nuts that sounds. Well, at least you're getting drinks at the boathouse—that should give you time to talk, if you still have any interest. Oh, man, gotta go. Stop by later and give me all the gory details."

Audrey bicycled up to the boathouse. No Dan at the boathouse entrance. Out of the corner of her eye, someone was vigorously waving. Dan. He was sitting on a bench on the other side of the road.

"Over here," he said. She biked over to him.

"There's a vendor over there who sells water if you're thirsty." He pointed to the vendor. "I already got mine." She should continue biking, but she had a morbid curiosity to see what he was going to say. She bought herself a water bottle and sat next to Dan on the bench.

"So, what are your interests other than spin class? Do you do any other sports?" he asked.

"Not anymore," she said. "Do you?"

"Fly fishing."

Was fly fishing a sport?

"I am hugely into fly fishing, and biking, of course." He leaned back against the bench. "I'm kind of into those solitary sports— you know—man on his own. I'm kind of like a monk."

"Interesting." He hadn't mentioned that he aspired to be a monk in his profile. And she had definitely written she was seeking someone outgoing. Any online chemistry had disappeared. She searched for something to say as she sipped her water. "So, where do you go fly fishing?"

"Up in the Catskills. Have you ever been fly fishing?"

"No."

"It takes enormous skill and strategy. And patience. I've got this amazing collection of fishing lures."

"How does that work?"

"Different lures attract different fish. It's really an art form." He took a gulp of his water. "Finished your water? I want to do another turn round the park. It was great meeting you. Maybe we can get together again sometime. I'm going to a fly-fishing lecture next week on Wednesday, if you'd like to join me."

"I've got to work late that night." She was not wasting any more of her free time on this guy. Not when she could have been biking with Jake. What a disaster.

"Okay, well, maybe I'll see you on the loop around." Dan bicycled off, and she bicycled home.

Back home, she knocked on Eve's door to tell her the date was over. "Fastest date yet, pun intended. He must have found me ugly."

"You're not, so I doubt it." Eve hugged her.

"He did invite me to go to a fly-fishing lecture on Wednesday," Audrey said in a voice that made it sound like it was an invite to something special.

"And you didn't take him up on that?"

"Clearly, I wasn't thinking straight."

"You could've thought of it as advice on dating men—any time they reference fish, just think of men."

Audrey laughed. "Maybe I should email him back and say I'll go."

"No, no, that one needs to be put back in the water and left to swim free."

"My profile says outgoing and looking for same." Audrey sighed. "I need to give up on this dating thing until after the partnership decision."

"No, you shouldn't," Eve said. "You have to be able to have a life and do your job."

She had argued about this with Eve before, but Eve just didn't understand. Theoretically, she agreed with Eve. Just practically, it seemed impossible.

Eve gave her a knowing look. "Pete and I are both workaholics, and we manage it."

Audrey nodded and said goodbye, retreating to her own apartment. She'd like a relationship like Eve's. Pete and Eve both worked really hard, but still made time for each other—still supported each other. And the way Pete looked at Eve—like he couldn't believe he'd gotten so lucky as to be with her. She sighed romantically.

She should call back her mother, who'd left two messages during the week, but Audrey knew she would ask about work. And her mother would worry if she told her about Malaburn and about Winnie's news. She didn't want to distress her mom. She could still see her mom biting her nails as she balanced the checkbook while Audrey did her homework at the dining room table.

She looked out the window at her backyard. The surfboard bar had disappeared and in its place was a wooden picnic table. That was quick. She had felt so alive Thursday night. She'd really had to keep on her toes with all the bantering. Her exchange with Jake had been so sparky—the opposite of this date. It wasn't that she had time for a serious relationship, but she didn't want to lose the connection. What had Jake said: he expected a neighborly welcome? She'd bake him chocolate chip cookies. She had time and it was only a small overture to keep a dialogue going. Either that or she needed to wheel her bicycle around, hoping he'd ask her to go biking again.

She mixed together a batch of cookies. While the cookies were baking, she found a round red tin leftover from Christmas, and taped her hand-written note to the lid:

Saturday, NYC

Dear Jake:

Welcome to the neighborhood and thank you for the party on Thursday.
Etiquette suggests I give you a welcoming gift. Here are some homemade cookies and take-out menus for seafood restaurants.

Best,
Audrey

She chuckled. Now . . . how to deliver it?

She could leave it by the front door of his building, but lately, packages were being stolen. And it would be devastating to think he'd declined to reply, if he had in fact never even received it. She'd leave it in his backyard. She could throw it over the fence, but crushed cookies would not look appetizing. She could slip through the hole in the fence, but what if he saw her in his backyard? *Meet your new deranged stalker neighbor.* Maybe leaving the cookies in the foyer was the best bet. No, she didn't want that uncertainty. With some sort of hook, she could lower them down from her balcony into his garden.

She found a large paperclip and fashioned it into a hook shape. Then she tied a string around it. She put the tin into a Trader Joe's paper bag and taped on it a handwritten sign saying "Welcome to the neighborhood."

Her balcony was close to the property line. She attached the hook to the paper bag handles and gently lowered the bag over the side. The bag swung out, but landed on the pavement outside his door. But she couldn't maneuver the hook out. She pulled this way and that way; the hook did not want to leave the bag. She dropped the string. Not quite as smooth as she'd hoped—he'd know how the bag arrived—but at least the bag was well-positioned right in front of his sliding glass door, with its welcoming sign. Mission accomplished. Now off to work.

Chapter Six

udrey packed up her briefcase Sunday morning. Biscuit was barking in the backyard. She glanced out the upstairs glass sliding door. The blue summer sky beckoned. A thin woman with straight silky brown hair, luminescent pale skin, and large brown eyes was sitting at the rustic wooden picnic table in Jake's garden, drinking from a coffee mug and flipping through a magazine that looked like *Vogue*. The table was set for two, with placemats and even flowers. Jake walked out with muffins and a pitcher of liquid resembling strawberry smoothies.

He was dating someone! What if she'd slept over and they'd opened the curtains this morning and both saw the bag with its huge "Welcome to the neighborhood" sign?

> She texted Eve: *Are you up? SO SO embarrassed! Need to talk!*

> Eve: *Coming.*

She opened her door, waiting for Eve. Eve emerged from her apartment, putting her fingers to her lips, and closed her door softly. "Pete's still sleeping. What's the crisis?"

Audrey pulled her inside and wailed, "I'm so embarrassed! I sent Jake homemade cookies yesterday as a funny welcoming gift, and it looks like he's already dating someone else." She tiptoed over near the window and flattened against the wall, hiding behind the curtain, motioning Eve over. "Look, he's out there with this absolutely gorgeous woman having breakfast."

Eve snuck over to the wall and discreetly peeked from behind the curtain into Jake's garden. "Well, they could be just friends. I don't recognize her from the party."

"That's true," Audrey said. If only she had been able to say yes when Jake had asked her for a bike ride.

"He said that he was going to stay single for a while."

"But Penny doubted he'd even last a week."

"They're not eating your cookies." Eve stepped away from the window.

"No, not for breakfast anyway."

"It could just be interpreted as a neighborly thing to do."

"From the single woman next door? It looks like I'm pursuing him, when he just told me women pursue him all the time."

"And weren't you?"

"Yes." She gave Eve a "Do you really have to call my bluff?" look. "That's why it's embarrassing. But it was under the guise of a neighborly welcome."

"Do you want me to send over some food as well? From me and Pete?" Eve laughed.

"That would make me feel much better," Audrey said. "But no need for him to think we're all nuts."

"How did you get it to his front door?"

"I didn't. I left it at his garden sliding door. I lowered it over from my balcony. It wasn't easy."

"Girl, you are crazy."

"I know."

"But that's why I love you." Eve hugged her. "Cheer up. It's not that embarrassing, even if he is dating her." The two friends peered out from behind the curtain again.

"From the body language, it doesn't appear they're romantically involved," Eve said. "Your chocolate chip cookies may yet work their magic."

"Maybe. But he did say he didn't like lawyers, so I shouldn't be interested in him either."

"He dislikes all lawyers?" Eve walked away from the window and sat on Audrey's couch.

"He has exceptions," Audrey said as she joined Eve on the couch.

"You should steer clear of someone with a hang-up about lawyers," Eve said. "Although he seemed fun and I liked his friends. I probably prefer him to Preppy Boy."

"Tim would be more supportive of my legal career."

"Unless it conflicts with his own," Eve said dryly.

Like Kevin. Audrey looked down. She'd been swept up by Kevin's attention when she was a fourth-year associate. And impressed by his experience as a senior lawyer. But then he hadn't made it. She shivered. That could easily be her in six months.

Kevin had moved down to DC. He'd wanted her to leave the firm too, to go with him. She didn't understand how he could even ask that of her, given her mother's regrets. And he'd been angry when she'd said no, that she wanted to stay in New York working for a Wall Street law firm and make it as a partner. But then he seemed to recover, to be willing to date long distance. And she had believed him. Until they'd attempted a romantic weekend together at this charming bed and breakfast in Virginia. The setting was from a Jane Austen movie, but Kevin moping about how he hadn't made partner and looking like he'd been stabbed if she mentioned anyone's name from the firm had not been conducive to fulfilling its romantic promise.

The next morning, with the sun streaming through the frilly-curtained window, she'd woken up to find him tenderly staring at her. He'd gently pushed the hair away from her face and said, "You know you'll never make partner. You're too nice." She'd stared at him, hurt, her stomach sinking, vowing she would make partner.

Feeling betrayed, she hadn't been nice then. She'd told him that she was sick of his whining about not making partner. His shocked, hurt face still haunted her. It hadn't made her feel better to tell him that. Just guilty that she'd hurt him. Even if he had just hurt her. And then they'd broken up and that was the note it had ended on. So, her mother was right that it was better to be nice.

"Tim's never shown that he would be like that," Audrey said. But then, Kevin hadn't shown that initially either. She needed a boyfriend who fully supported her career.

Eve suddenly noticed Audrey's packed bag. "You're not off to work, are you?"

"Yes."

"I prefer your cookie craziness to your work craziness."

As if on cue, Audrey's work phone buzzed. Eve waved good-bye. "See you tonight."

Chapter Seven

*A*udrey had already emailed the updated memo to Malaburn around noon after spending the morning writing it. She was making good progress. She'd be on time to meet her friends at eight for a movie. On the whiteboard on her office wall, she drew a green line in a flow chart detailing her proposed strategy for the Rothman case. Green for yes. The alcohol smell of dry-erase markers charged the air. Figuring out how to win cases was like a thought-provoking puzzle with real-life consequences. She studied the pros and cons of starting with Rothman as the first witness. Lists were always her first tool to figure things out. The final picture was emerging. She nodded crisply. Once she was finished brainstorming, she'd write a memo for Hunter proposing her case strategy. Her phone beeped.

Eve: *Saw Jake. Alone.*

Audrey: *That could mean she slept over, he made scrumptious breakfast, and she left because she had other plans.*

Eve: *If you've just slept with Jake, you cancel those plans.*

Audrey: *I'll keep that advice in mind. Doubt I'll need it.*

Eve: *Conservative lawyers = dating slump. Still on for movie tonight?*

Audrey: *Think so.*

She almost typed yes, she was so sure she'd make it, but she had learned not to make that promise.

Audrey continued working. She ate a sandwich she'd brought from home for dinner. She hadn't wanted to go out and waste that time.

When it was almost seven and time to leave, her phone rang. As she picked it up, Malaburn's raspy voice said, "Thanks for the updated memo. I have some separate ideas to research for the pitch slide deck. I'll send that to you to work on." She quickly wrote down his thoughts as he rattled them off.

She slumped deep into her chair after he hung up. That would take her a few more hours. She would have to cancel on her friends, again. It was so like Malaburn to call on a Sunday night too. She could feel her blood boiling. She focused on a poster of a Rothko blue painting she had hung on her wall, trying to let its deep hues relax her. It was just a movie. She could catch up with her friends another time. She called Eve to tell her she couldn't go. Luckily, Eve was going with Pete and Max, so she wasn't stranded, but she sounded disappointed. Disappointed with her, her unreliable best friend. Audrey sighed and turned to research the new points.

Her phone beeped. The car service was waiting downstairs. Law firms paid for a car service on weekends after a certain number of hours worked and on weekdays if you worked past 8 p.m. She'd forgotten she'd arranged for it. She'd finish this at home. Her footsteps were hushed on the plush carpet as she passed by the closed doors of the other offices and waved good night to the cleaning lady. Leaving the building, she entered a waiting black sedan that smelled of peppermint air freshener. She opened the window. This was her chance to feel the warm night breeze on her skin.

As the black sedan sped up Madison Avenue, she looked up from her iPhone out the car window. The shops were closed, but their brightly-lit windows beckoned. The restaurants were packed, the tables spilling out onto the sidewalk, with couples sitting and chatting over candlelit dinners, enjoying the balmy night. She wondered what they did for a living. Most of her friends worked similar hours to hers.

The car stopped at a red light, and her attention was caught by one couple. The woman, her hair in a sleek, dark bob, was talking animatedly, while the man was listening intently, staring straight in the woman's eyes. They seemed very in love. She stared out the window at them, craning her head to see them even as the car turned the corner.

Her phone flashed red in the dark interior. She tensed before clicking on the email, but it wasn't from Malaburn. The car turned left to go across Central Park towards the Upper West Side. She and Eve joked that the Upper West Side must be filled with single women based on the types of stores: cupcakes, cookies, and clothing. It seemed contradictory: who could fit into the clothes after eating the cupcakes and cookies?

The car dropped her off in front of her building. As she entered the foyer, she saw a long rectangular moving box on the table with AUDREY handwritten on it in black capital letters. That was weird. It was tightly taped. Maybe she should put on her cleaning gloves and open it outside in her yard. She picked it up gingerly. It was light for its size. She left the package outside her apartment door as she went inside to get gloves from under the kitchen sink—if she had any. Her cleaner came every two weeks with her own supplies, but Audrey had bought some when she'd first moved in. She'd had visions of domesticity, dinner parties galore—before she'd started her job as a lawyer and realized her apartment was mostly a place to sleep. Luckily, Eve periodically threw impromptu gatherings anchored by delicious food, all of which she made look effortless. But one day, she would have dinner parties too, with witty conversation. Maybe when she was an established partner.

She found the gloves, still in their package, and put them on. Grabbing scissors, she carried the box to her yard, and sitting on her chaise lounge, she opened the package. Red, yellow and pink tulips greeted her (*flowers!*), and a pile of papers tied up with string. A folded-over note was taped to the flowers. She carefully un-taped the note and read it:

Sunday, NYC

Dear Audrey,

Thanks for your warm welcome to the neighborhood—those cookies definitely helped fuel me through the unpacking process! They were amazing—you should give up being a lawyer and make your fortune selling cookies.
I can never have enough take-out menus.

So here you go: legal disclosures for your lei-surely reading and this small bouquet of flowers as a thank you.

Cheers,
Jake

Surveying the pile of legal disclosures, she laughed. It didn't seem like he was dating the woman from breakfast if he was sending her flowers. Putting on pop music, she shimmied over to her desk and opened up her laptop to finish the research for Malaburn.

.

Chapter Eight

To: Winnie Chu
From: Audrey Willems
Date: Tuesday, August 24
Re: Whitaker retirement party

I called HR and they're not planning a party for Whitaker(!), so I volunteered to organize it. They gave me a budget and the names of the various vendors. I just need to fill out a sheet for the cafeteria to cater it and order flowers. How's Texas?

To: Audrey Willems
From: Winnie Chu
Date: Tuesday, August 24
Re: Texas

Isn't that too much to add to your plate? Texas is hot. But all I do is go from the hotel to the office, review documents, and go back. Hotel food is good. Only four more days until I'm back home Friday.

To: Winnie Chu
From: Audrey Willems
Date: Tuesday, August 24
Re: Texas

I couldn't NOT do it. He's often grumpy and very demanding, but he takes the time to mentor young associates. I vividly remember his welcoming speech about how we're all thoroughbreds and they want to train us to be the best possible lawyers. I need to do the invite list too. It will be fine. (I know, I know, I keep telling myself that.) That's all there is to it. And finding some people to give nice speeches about him (in addition to me). Do you have any good stories?

As she clicked send, Malaburn knocked on her door. It was like being haunted by a ghost. The ghost of her past failures.

He marched in and said, "We won the pitch. The client just called me. Let's meet this afternoon in my office."

Her stomach sank. He knew the rules about going through the assignment partner, and he wasn't following them. She had to be more forceful.

"That's great news that you won, but I can't meet this afternoon. I have meetings already on my other cases. As I mentioned before, I don't have the time to give this case the attention it deserves. I have to talk to the assignment partner first. My other two cases are really busy right now."

"I extolled your research abilities to the client," he said. "We need you specifically. I'll talk to the assignment partner. How about tomorrow? Does 11 a.m. work for you?"

So, he presumed the assignment partner would support him. On the plus side, she seemed to be back in his good graces. But she'd like to stay there, which was why she didn't want to work on this case when she couldn't do her best because of her current workload. But she was loath to tell the assignment partner she couldn't handle more. She was damned either way. He was standing there, waiting, staring at her, his eyes narrowed.

She said yes to 11 a.m. Malaburn whipped around and left.

She sighed, rubbing her forehead to ease the tension headache gathering there.

To: Audrey Willems
From: Winnie Chu
Date: Tuesday, August 24
Re: Horror Stories, yes

No, not of the type you're looking for. But if the theme becomes general law firm horror stories, let me know.

To: Winnie Chu
From: Audrey Willems
Date: Tuesday, August 24
Re: horror stories, yes

I'm about to star in my own horror story. Malaburn won the pitch. I can't believe I have to work with him in this final run-up to partner. Now I wish Stacy hadn't found me crying in my office and gotten me pulled off his case three years ago.

She slumped in her chair. She had known then that Malaburn would not forgive her for leaving his case. The senior associate Stacy had said not to worry about it—that they had easily found another associate to replace her, that the partners recognized that she had had an unfair workload, that Malaburn would forget—when Audrey had worried out loud that Malaburn would hold this against her when she was up for partner. Which she had felt silly saying as a fourth-year associate. But even then, she had been aiming to make partner.

To: Audrey Willems
From: Winnie Chu
Date: Tuesday, August 24
Re: Horror Story Take Two

Stacy was right to insist that you get pulled off his case. You had been working for him for eight months straight AND the last two months with no days off. Of course, Stacy found you crying in the office.

And it was THREE YEARS ago.

What is with him that he's bringing that up? He's mean. He has no life outside the office, so he doesn't want anyone else to have a life either.

He might be better now. He knows he can't pull that again—now that partners are supposed to watch associates' time sheets and make sure they get a smidgen of time off. They don't want an associate dying in the office.

It was time to talk to Hunter about Malaburn. After seven years of working together, she had to believe that Hunter's insider knowledge of her work ethic and ability would withstand any aspersions cast by Malaburn. She knocked on Hunter's door that afternoon. He gestured that she should come in. Hunter looked a bit like Clark Kent, but she would never tell him that. His office was decorated in a soothing, warm, mid-century modern style. They'd find a solution. She quickly explained her predicament and asked again if he advised working for Malaburn.

"Yes, I talked to Malaburn." He looked down and straightened the pile of papers in front of him. "Malaburn thinks you don't have what it takes."

She clenched her jaw. She hated Malaburn. A white-hot anger filled her like a tea kettle about to boil. But she couldn't let it show.

"What am I missing? He just extolled my research abilities to the client. I've been working here day and night for seven years." Her voice cracked. Hunter still hadn't looked up. *He couldn't believe Malaburn.*

Hunter met her gaze and said softly, "He thinks you're too emotional. He does think you're a great researcher, but he thinks that's a good senior counsel trait."

She was emotional, but she was not "too emotional." She would like to show Malaburn her being emotional. Emotionally angry.

"Is that code for I'm a woman?" Leaning forward, she gripped the seat.

"I don't think so. He's supporting Colette. He's concerned about the time you were pulled off his cases because it was too much." His voice lifted on the last part of the sentence, almost making it into a question.

Heat flushed her body. "It was too much. And I was pulled off only one case. But adding him to my caseload now is too much. I'm being set up for failure." She was proud that her voice was firm. She had to counter Malaburn. She had not given up her life to be a senior counsel. No way was she letting Malaburn derail her bid.

"He says you can't handle a lot of work—that you'll crack under pressure and that you won't pull your weight as a partner."

Hunter grimaced. "I told him you had more than pulled your weight as an associate. But I can't see a way out. He'll oppose your bid otherwise. You need to show him you can handle it. Because you can, Audrey." He said it as if he was stating a closing argument.

She nodded. She had to show confidence. But she hadn't been able to handle him earlier. She had to believe she could do it. It was just one case. But it wasn't the case, it was Malaburn.

"But to free you up, I'll also staff Colette on this Rothman case," Hunter said.

"What? Why? But you just said I could handle all three cases. Do you doubt my ability?" she asked, her voice rising in frustration.

"Not at all, but I want to help," Hunter said. "This is a good solution. You and I have worked together for years, and I already know you would make a good partner. I'm one of the few partners who hasn't worked with Colette. She asked me the other day for an assignment. I need to work with her so I can make an informed recommendation on her as a partner. Unfortunately, I don't have any other cases that are really suitable for her." Hunter explained that she would retain overall case strategy under his direction and offensive discovery, and Colette would manage defensive discovery. "This gives you more time to work on your trial case with Anderson and your case with Malaburn."

"It's a bit complicated when both Colette and I are the same level," she said hesitantly. *Wrong move, don't express doubts to Hunter.* Hunter was hard to get to know personally, although he had opened up after he had kids—but just in that area of his life. As a lawyer, he presented a confident, impenetrable strength.

"Well, yes, but you're a great team leader. I'm sure you two will work well together." He looked at his watch. "I have to run. I'll ask my assistant to schedule a meeting with the three of us so we can all start from the same page." He stood abruptly.

Dismissed.

"Great," she said, schooling her voice to be positive and firm, and she trailed him out of his office. She walked quickly to her office. She could use more time for Malaburn and her Popflicks case. How dare Malaburn say that she didn't have what it took? Especially after seven years of working here around the clock. She'd prove him wrong. Her stomach clenched.

She needed to prepare for her meetings that afternoon.

Tim knocked on the doorframe. "Hey, can I come in?"

"Sure." Normally, she loved chatting with Tim, feeling a little thrill when his brown eyes met hers or he nodded in acknowledgement of a point she made, but now she was on edge and upset. And she didn't want to show him that side of her. Especially after Malaburn's remark that she was too emotional.

Tim closed the door with a click. "I hear Colette was just staffed on your case."

"Word travels fast."

"Colette told me." He pulled out the chair in front of her desk and sat. He was frowning. His hair was gelled into place—not like Jake's tousled hair.

"Did you suggest Hunter as a partner for her to work with? You could've warned me." Her throat tightened. She had thought he was on her side—even if not interested romantically.

"No, I mean we did discuss him as a possibility, but I told her that he's so keenly in your corner, that it would be better for her to go with Stromen," he said. "She hasn't worked with him either, and he's certainly influential."

"But he's difficult." Although not as difficult as Malaburn. It wasn't a fair trade. She got Malaburn; Colette got Hunter. She shook her head. She needed to look at this positively. Wallowing in self-pity was not going to get her anywhere.

"Probably why she didn't ask Stromen," Tim said dryly.

"I guess it should help me. This will give me more time to focus on my Popflicks case, and now I'm not responsible for defensive discovery on Rothman."

"Still, it's a bit awkward. You're really being put head-to-head there."

"But we have different areas, and surely our being able to work together helps our partnership chances," she said. "I've never worked with her before, though."

"She definitely views you as the competition. She thinks they'll only make one woman partner, if any. But, hey, I'm friends with both of you, so I don't want to get in the middle," Tim said. "But her having defensive discovery—that's not good for you. If she's responsible for preparing all the client's witnesses and pulling all their documents, she could establish a relationship with the client such that they prefer her."

"Are you trying to cheer me up or scare me?" Her stomach was tensing.

"I'm trying to weigh the pros and cons with you."

"I have to work with her. I'm sure we can work together." Audrey didn't want to share her doubts, if Tim didn't want to "get in the middle." So, he wasn't on her side, he was staying neutral. She looked down, her throat feeling tight, and swallowed. The competition for partner was feeling more direct, more personal. She looked back at Tim. Was that a pitying look from him?

He leaned forward. He ran his hand through his hair, staring at the floor, seeming to consider what to say. "Audrey, Colette is determined to make partner. She's not going to play nice in the sandbox. You've got to be prepared."

"What do you mean?"

"Just be on your guard. Don't assume you're both on the same side."

She made a face. "We're on the same side: representing the client. This is a big case for our firm."

"You're on opposite sides competing for partner."

"Is that how you view us too?" The office felt small, tight.

He paused. "She may be right that they'll only make one woman partner."

"But what am I supposed to guard against?"

"I don't know."

"Hunter likes teamwork. It's not going to win her any points with him to screw me over."

"If he realizes . . ." He raised an eyebrow.

"I feel like I've stepped into an episode of *Survivor*." She bit her nail. And Winnie had told her not to be intimidated by Colette. Tim was making her out to be formidable, as the French would say. She doubted he could be dating her if he really thought this way about her.

"I may be wrong. You're such a hard worker, but you also need to promote yourself. You can't assume your hard effort will be recognized." He leaned forward.

"I don't have time to get all this work done and promote myself." She hadn't had the time with two cases, let alone three. Tim had only one. And Colette was volunteering for more work. No wonder they had time to wander around politicking.

"You need to make that time. You need to consider it part of the job." He straightened in his chair.

"And how do you go about doing that?"

"I stop in partners' offices and I let them know what I'm doing—maybe even in the guise of asking their advice on what I'm thinking about in terms of a legal argument."

She sighed. "I feel like that conversation is not going to go in my favor. Remember the time in the elevator that Stromen regarded me like I was an alien from another planet because I tried to make conversation by noting that the merger of those two airlines would not be good for people."

"That airline was one of our biggest clients."

"I resolved never to make conversation in the elevator again."

"As I remember, Stromen couldn't stop asking you about it."

"Yes," she said. "Apparently I represented the view of the 'common people.'"

"But as I recall, the opposition made some of your arguments, and Stromen was grateful for your input."

"Yes, but I don't think his image of me ever improved." What if Stromen didn't support her for partner? The knot in her stomach was tightening.

He covered her hand with his. It was comforting, but there was no zip of energy. He said, "You're a rockstar lawyer. You just need to get out there and do some politicking."

"Aren't rockstar and lawyer contradictory?"

"That's what I mean—no self-deprecating remarks." Tim's phone beeped, and he stood. "I've got to go. Think about what I've said."

He closed the door behind him. *Click.* How could she *not* think about what he said? She wasn't good at promoting herself. She knew she should, but she felt pushy and exposed when she tried it. And then Tim's warning about Colette—what was she supposed to do about that? And saying yes to others was so much easier than saying yes to herself. She'd been brought up to "be nice." Before she'd found her current cleaning service, she'd hired a one-time cleaning service from the internet, and as she was working on her laptop in her bedroom to supervise, the cleaning guy had said, "I don't have to clean in here, right?" And she'd agreed, even though she'd paid for the whole apartment to be cleaned, including her bedroom. Then she'd berated herself for being taken advantage of.

Kevin was right. She was too nice. She was going to get steam-rolled by Colette. *Roadkill.* Like that coyote in the *Road Runner* cartoons. But coyotes were pretty resourceful animals. They were even moving into Manhattan. People underestimated them. And now she'd been warned, so she should be more prepared to be— what? Less obliging? Less nice? Aggressive back? She sighed. On guard? She pictured herself in a fencing outfit. Stick-thin Colette would rock a fencing outfit, whereas she'd resemble the Pillsbury Doughboy. A flattened Pillsbury Doughboy. *Great.* Better to think of herself as a wily coyote. But not Wile E. Coyote. He was often flattened too.

She had to see what Colette was going to do, if anything, and be prepared to strut her stuff when they met.

Chapter Nine

*T*hat evening, at home, Audrey turned to Amazon for gift suggestions for Jake. She clicked on various links and giggled. She drafted a note:

Dear Jake,

Thank you so much for the beautiful flowers—and those riveting legal disclosures.

Knowing of your interest in surfing, I thought you might like this Surf's Up Dude. It's THE adult coloring book featuring surfing and meditation designs. Coloring can relax you like surfing waves.

And this book: Travel, Surf, Cook. It seems to have it all.

Enjoy!

Best,
Audrey

She was still elated she'd received a response to her cookies. Jake's eyes had crinkled at the corners when he had leaned in to tease her. He even had a dimple when he smiled. *Swoon.*

Cookies could be taken as a neighborly gesture, but if she continued sending gifts, then it could no longer fall under the pretense of a "neighborly welcome." She was upping the ante, and the gifts had to reflect that. Plus, she knew she'd be attracted to someone who challenged and intrigued her, and so her gifts back, she gauged, should be a little mischievous.

Game on, she thought happily.

Chapter Ten

A udrey changed from her flats to heels. Tim had called
that Thursday morning to suggest meeting for a coffee
and to ask if she still had her files from that antitrust
case she had done years ago. She pulled out the files for Tim. She
hoped he hadn't called her just for her research. It wasn't the first
time he'd asked. To be fair to him, though, others also asked. She
had a reputation for thorough research ever since, as a third-year
associate, she had found some obscure case for Malaburn that was
straight on point that local counsel hadn't even found. Malaburn
had then staffed her on all his cases—and proceeded to make her
life hell for eight months. He'd been in the middle of divorce number two. Approaching his door, she'd overheard one conversation
when he'd said, "You should be glad law is my mistress. It's not
like I'm cheating on you with a person." She'd quickly retreated
from his door.

Although she'd worried that Tim was staying "out of it," he had warned her about Colette; he was being there for her. So, she should ask his advice on Malaburn; Tim had never mentioned any issues with him.

The firm's spacious reception area was on the top floor of the skyscraper so that the floor-to-ceiling windows could impress visitors with the views of the New York City skyline. Tim was on his phone, leaning against one of the marble columns, looking out the windows, one hand in his pocket. Her heart felt a little pang. She still found him attractive, even if she wasn't sure where she stood with him anymore. And even if he was off-limits for the next six months.

She nodded to the guard at the mahogany reception desk with Howard, Parker & Smith emblazoned across it in brass letters. As her heels clicked on the white marble floor, Tim smiled at her and ended his call. Straightening, their glances meeting, he said, "Glad you could make it. Is that your research file?"

"Yes, but it's from a few years ago."

"I'm sure it will help." He took the file and tucked it under his arm. As the elevator doors closed, he said, "I'm happy you could come. I need the break." He shook his head as if to clear it. "I worked all weekend and stayed late every night this week. I can't believe the hours I'm putting in." That didn't sound like he and Colette were dating.

Once they were out on the street, with no colleagues around, she asked, "Do you have any advice on working for Malaburn?"

"Malaburn?" He looked at her. "You should be able to knock it out of the park if it's just research."

"I hope. But you and he had no issues, right?"

"No, I mean I was a second year. I don't think I wowed him as much as you did, and he was quite fine to see me go onto another case. He yelled at me for my formatting. I think I underlined something that was capitalized and that ticked him off."

"Yeah, he's got a thing for formatting. When he explained his formatting peeves, I couldn't believe he was serious."

Starbucks was around the corner, so it was a quick trip. She wished that they were walking slower so she could enjoy the warmth of the sun on her face and arms before they had to return to the air-conditioned offices.

Tim held the door for her as they entered the crowded shop. She offered to grab a table while he put in the orders. The free table was wedged between a man working intently on his laptop and an older woman, wearing three colorful scarves and a bright yellow muumuu, reading a newspaper. A shopping cart filled with newspapers was parked next to her. Audrey slid into a seat against the wall facing the counter. A mothball odor drifted over from the older woman. Tim was giving their orders to a barista, who seemed to be flirting with him.

"I always take this seat," the woman said, unsolicited. "Gives a great view of all the action."

"It does," Audrey said.

"Waiting for someone?" the woman asked.

As she said yes, Tim strode up and put the folder and his phone on the table. "Do you need sugar or anything?"

"No thanks."

The older woman spoke up as he left: "Ooo, he's a keeper, honey."

"He's not mine," Audrey said.

"Don't let that stop you," she said. "He's yours at the moment."

Audrey looked at her, bemused.

Tim returned with the drinks. "One chai tea for you and one big bolt of caffeine for me." He sat down and pushed back his chair so he had room to stretch out his legs. "I've got friends coming into town this weekend. I wanted to get ahead so I'd have time to hang out with them. But working for Dan is pretty intense." He pulled the cases out of the folder. He flipped through the stapled documents and asked her which ones he should start with. She examined the cases, reviewing her notes at the top of each case, and suggested various avenues to pursue.

"Did Malaburn call you all the time when you worked for him?" she asked.

"No, but I was junior. Stacy was the senior associate on the case. She definitely complained about him. Is Hunter taking you as his guest to the business development conference at the Marriott?" Tim asked. "Alastair just invited me." Alastair was Tim's partner mentor—a similar relationship to hers with Hunter.

"No, at least he hasn't invited me yet."

"Maybe he's not going. He does like to get home to his family."

"Yes." She pressed her lips tight, disappointed that she would miss out on this event.

"But you should ask him."

"Ask him directly?"

"Yes, why not?"

She shrugged; Hunter must have a good reason, and she didn't want to be too pushy.

Tim said, "The focus is on high tech and finance. I'm hoping I can make connections that can lead to new business."

"Yes, I'm worried about that—the business development part of being a partner. Our firm has such established clients. I mean, I have good relationships with my peers at the banks . . ." she said.

"Exactly, and as they move up the ranks, they'll want you. I've seen you with clients at our firm's events. They love you. And not just as their lawyer. You're calm and organized and have a good sense of humor—it's the same reason so many associates want to work with you."

"That's so sweet of you to say." That was the warmest thing Tim had ever said to her. A glow of pride suffused her.

Loud coughing from her talkative neighbor interrupted their conversation. Tim looked over, concerned.

"Do you need some water?" he asked.

"That would be lovely," their neighbor said.

Tim looked surprised she'd accepted his offer, but he strode to the counter.

Leaning close, her watery eyes peering into Audrey's, words fast and clipped, the older woman whispered, "All right, I think he likes you."

So, she hadn't been imagining that their relationship was more than just a friendship.

The older woman continued, "But you need to dress up more for him. What is it with young women today? You're wearing black pants and a white blouse, like a waiter. You need to wear a dress. And flirt! In my day . . ." Tim returned and handed her a glass of water.

Audrey's lips curled into a wry smile. The dismal state of her love life was so obvious that strangers in coffee shops were giving her advice.

Batting her eyelashes, the woman offered a wide smile. "Thank you. I didn't think that they made gentlemen like you anymore."

"At your service." Tim looked embarrassed as he slid into his seat.

The woman winked at Audrey and shifted slightly away. Audrey wasn't sure how to flirt with Tim, especially with an audience. But she wasn't about to be bested by her muumuu-wearing neighbor. She tried a wide smile.

Looking down as he flipped through the documents, Tim frowned. "I'm thinking of having a party with some college friends who became investment bankers so I can get back in touch, but my schedule has to free up first. And they work the same crazy hours as me, so it's hard to schedule with them."

"That's such a coincidence. I'm planning to have a party in the fall so Eve can showcase her catering. I hope you can come." She felt awkward emphasizing the "you," even though it was a totally normal sentence to say. Since the smile hadn't worked, she casually stretched out her heeled foot and touched his shoe with hers.

He moved his foot away, but at least he looked up. "Well, you go first then. Maybe your friend can cater my party as well—although I was thinking more along the lines of a well-stocked bar."

"Good food makes it classier." She leaned forward and twirled a strand of hair.

"True." Tim nodded, not seeming to react at all to her flirtatious gestures.

"Although it's the company that makes the moment." She held Tim's gaze, but doubted that qualified as flirtatious enough for her eavesdropper.

"It's an unbeatable combination." He smiled at her and put down the cases.

Hmm, maybe her neighbor was right and she did need to flirt more. She took a sip of her tea, unsure of where to go next in the conversation. Flirting with a work colleague was hard. And she wasn't sure what more to do. There was the hair flip, the leaning forward, the standing closer, the meeting glances, the teasing . . . but that's not the kind of relationship they had.

She tucked her hair behind her ear. "Did you decide to join your college friends on the hiking trip in August?"

"I decided not to. I'll go home briefly to see my family, but other than that, I'm going to power through all this work. If I scheduled something, I'd be afraid that I'd have to cancel it. Or work through it, which wouldn't be worth it."

"That's always so frustrating."

"Yeah, you can never find adequate Wi-Fi, you're seen as 'no fun' because you're working, you're grumpy because you're working, and it's not worth the stress. But I'm planning a hiking trip with them in Canada, in the spring. I'm looking forward to that." He stirred his coffee and looked pensive. "And if I don't make partner, who knows, maybe I can reassess my priorities up there." He looked intently at her.

"You're not thinking of giving up being a lawyer, are you? You're good at it." She couldn't imagine Tim *not* being a lawyer. And she couldn't imagine not being a lawyer either.

"Probably not, but I don't really want to stay around as a senior counsel if that's the consolation prize. I haven't done all this work for that."

She had to agree. She also didn't want to watch others make partner, especially after seeing how bitter that had made Kevin. Tim's phone buzzed, and he picked it up immediately.

"Dan's called a team meeting in an hour. I'd better go back. Do you want to walk with me?" He stood, picking up his coffee cup, his phone, and the file.

"Of course." She grabbed her half-finished cup of tea.

"Have a good day," she said to the woman as she left.

"You too dearie," she called out after her, "Remember what I said!"

But she couldn't think of how to flirt with Tim. As they walked back, Tim called his assistant and told her to print out various documents for his meeting. Her phone beeped. It was her best male friend, Max.

She texted back: *Having coffee with Tim.*

Max: *Don't let me interrupt. Go back to flirting!*

She wasn't flirting with Tim—not like with Jake; this couldn't qualify as the same energy.

Tim was still talking to his assistant. Audrey whispered that she was going to stay outside and take a walk around the block. Tim nodded. She waved goodbye and called Max. She needed to talk about this with someone, and he was always good for the male perspective.

"That's just the thing. I realized I can't flirt with Tim," she said.

"I never flirt at work. Too risky nowadays," Max said.

"Maybe that's it." She frowned. The fact that he was a work colleague was definitely making it difficult, but it could also just be an excuse. Or maybe it was that any thoughts of romance between them were quickly dwindling with the cold reality that the partners were going to possibly choose only one of them for partner. And she wouldn't take it well if he made it and she didn't. She had worked as hard as him for the past seven years—if not even more.

Chapter Eleven

udrey heard her name being called as she closed the door of the black sedan dropping her off at the curb of her street on Thursday night.

"Hey," Jake said. He was walking Biscuit.

"Hey yourself." She walked over. "Thanks for the beautiful flowers. Tulips are my favorite. I'm sorry my thank you is delayed . . ."

"Too busy with work?"

She petted Biscuit. "No, thinking of a worthy reply."

Jake stepped closer. "You can always send over more home-baked cookies. Those were good."

"I'll keep that in mind, but I did think of something." She grinned. "You'll see it soon."

Jake's phone beeped. He read the text. "A bunch of friends and I are going to see a band play at Irving Plaza. Do you want to come? The show starts at ten. I came home to walk Biscuit and then head down."

She hesitated. Oh, she wanted to say yes. She wanted to hang out with Jake. So much for getting a good night of sleep to plow through work in the morning. But she could reward herself. She had emailed Malaburn a finished assignment before she'd left the office.

"I'd love to." Renewed energy filled her. "I'll change while you're walking Biscuit. Is there a dress code?"

"Anything goes. You could wear what you're wearing now. I'll be wearing jeans. Shall I ring your doorbell in about 30 minutes?"

"Yes."

Jake held open the door to the Uber car as Audrey slid in, trying not to let her dress slide up too much. She didn't have supermodel thin thighs. She had put on a yellow dress, deciding that she should put some effort into this and that jeans might be too hot. Jake was wearing a white button-up, open at the neck, and jeans. He looked amazing.

The taxi felt intimate in the dark. She could feel the heat of him next to her in the cab seat.

"I'm glad you could come," Jake said. "I'm sorry, I have to reply to a few texts. I invited a bunch of people. My friend in A&R, Devon, is trying to sign this band, and he wants to get a crowd together to hear them."

"No problem. What's A&R?

"Artists and repertoire—he finds talent."

"Is that what you do too?" she asked. Another career she'd never considered.

"No. I started in A&R, but marketing was more my thing. If he signs them, I'll be doing the marketing." His phone beeped. He typed a reply.

"So, is this work for you?"

Jake grinned. "In a sense. But you can't beat it for work, can you?"

"It definitely beats my late nights of running around like a drill sergeant trying to file a brief."

"I can't see you as a drill sergeant." As the headlights of a turning car illuminated the interior of the cab, Jake's glance met hers.

"No, that's true. I'm more of a 'we're all in this together—let's get it done' team leader."

"That's the best kind."

"Let's hope the law firm partners agree."

"Even if they don't, it still is," he said. "Look at Central Park lit up. I never get tired of that sight." They were speeding down Fifth Avenue, past the streetlights illuminating trees against the milky black night sky.

"You grew up here, right?"

"Yeah, Upper East Side. Where did you grow up?"

"Upper West Side," she said.

"Oh, a west side New Yorker. That explains it."

"Explains what?"

"Explains why I like you." His phone rang, and he picked it up.

Her stomach fluttered. Did he mean *like* you or just like you?

His head was turned, but she could see his profile, the street-lights playing off his angular cheekbones, his tousled brown hair, his kissable lips. She had to get ahold of herself. She didn't have time for full-blown crushes.

Their glances met, and his mouth tipped up, then he looked back out his window. "Yeah, the vocalist is amazing. Like shivers down your spine when she sings. You need to rally and come out," he said into the phone. He hung up and turned to her. "She really is incredible."

The Uber stopped in front of Irving Plaza. Jake held the car door open for her. She took out her wallet as they approached the entrance, but he stopped her and said, "You're comped as my guest."

The concert space at Irving Hall was already packed. Disco balls and crystal chandeliers hung from the metal ceiling as if mixing remnants from its ballroom heritage with its 1970s concert hall inception. Jake held her hand and steered her towards a group at the bar. His hand felt solid and warm. He introduced her around, and she recognized several people from the party, including Rafael and Penny.

"What do you want to drink?" he asked. He had to talk into her ear to be heard above the crowd, and his breath on her neck tickled. She smelled his familiar fresh-laundry scent.

"A Diet Coke," she said.

"Don't go too wild here."

"Don't worry. I'll keep up."

"No pressure."

Devon came over, and Jake introduced her. While Devon and Jake discussed final strategy notes for signing the artist, Lolly, Audrey said hello to Rafael.

"Good to see you again," Rafael said. "Are you and Jake dating?"

"Dating?"

"I thought from the way you came in together. . ."

A glow filled her. She hoped that she was reading the signs correctly and Jake was interested romantically, but she was afraid to misinterpret his just being friendly. And she didn't want to say that it was more than it was.

"Jake just invited me when we ran into each other on our block. We took a car down here together," she said.

Rafael nodded. "Jake does like to collect people."

She hoped she wasn't just part of a collection.

Penny joined them, and Rafael offered to get her a drink. The crowd milled around as upcoming show announcements displayed against the stage curtain.

"So how do you know Jake?" Penny asked.

"We're neighbors," Audrey said.

"Oh, neighbors. What do you do?"

"I'm a lawyer."

"Legal Aid?"

"No, corporate. I work for a law firm," Audrey said.

"Like a Wall Street law firm? Like his father?" Penny asked.

She nodded.

"Oh." Penny put her arm around her. "Well, some sisterly advice—it's probably not welcome, but here goes: it's hard not to have a crush on Jake. I had one for ages until I finally realized it was never going to happen. And that was a good thing for me. Jake's got some serious issues with his workaholic lawyer dad. He refused to talk to him once for weeks in high school after he canceled Christmas vacation. I don't see him ever dating a lawyer. I'm just telling you to save you some heartache."

Too late. She already felt a pang of hurt. Was it so obvious that she had a little crush on Jake? But it was nice of Penny to warn her. She was hoping Jake didn't like lawyers because they were boring or arrogant—not because they were workaholics. Like her. That would be tough to prove wrong. Although she was out tonight.

"Thanks, I guess. Jake obviously likes you," Audrey said, hoping she came across as only interested in Jake as a friend.

"He likes me as a friend."

"That can develop into something more."

"Sometimes, but I don't see it happening here." Penny glanced at Jake. He was laughing full-heartedly, his head thrown back, at something Devon said.

"Veronika was also really bad news," Penny said. "She was incredibly needy and demanding and cut Jake off from all his friends. You may have noticed by the way she entered the party and ignored everyone, as if she hadn't met us all."

"What are you all discussing so seriously?" Jake asked as he suddenly came up behind them. He handed Audrey a drink.

"Girl things, Jake, things you wouldn't know about," Penny said. "No drink for me?"

"I have an older sister. So, I know more than you think. What are you drinking? I'll top you up next time."

"White wine," Penny said. "I don't think she discusses these things with you."

"You'd be surprised. There's not much my sister finds off-limits, unfortunately."

Rafael brought Penny her drink. Jake grinned at them as they launched into a heated discussion about a recent play they'd seen.

"Let's get closer to the stage," Jake said to Audrey. "The love-birds won't even notice we've left. The set is about to start." He took her hand and pulled her through the crowd. His hand felt sure about hers, and she was buzzing with hope and excitement, despite Penny's warning. The lights dimmed, and pink-flamed strobe lights sparked around the venue. It had been years since she had been to a show. "Lolly's pop but a little subversive."

The stage lit up, and out came Lolly, dressed in a white fluffy fake fur coat. With cat ears. She belted out a ballad about longing, and it was as if that yearning reverberated through Audrey's whole body. She wanted so much more. She didn't want to miss out on living her life.

Jake glanced over to see her reaction, and he nodded. "You feel it, she's brilliant."

"Wow. I feel like her voice filled me up and then left me wanting when she stopped," she whispered back into his ear.

"I hope she signs with us. The competition is here." He nodded at a guy dressed in a black suit over in the corner. Lolly sang an upbeat pop song next, and they both swayed to the music. Jake was singing the words. The crowd was moving back and forth as they followed Lolly prancing across the stage.

Her work phone buzzed. It was most likely Malaburn. She took a photo of Lolly on stage and surreptitiously checked her email. When Jake glanced at her, she clicked her phone off before she could read the message.

Devon squeezed through the crowd to join them, and Audrey saw him gesture towards their competition.

"Can I refill your drink?" Audrey asked.

"Now?" Jake asked.

"While you talk," she said.

"We're done. I told him I saw him already," Jake said. "Stay for the next song." It was a slow love ballad. Couples around them started slow-dancing. Jake asked her for a dance, and it was so easy to say yes. As he pulled her into his arms, she wanted to pinch herself that this was happening. He was so solid and smelled so good. Her pulse quickened.

Her phone buzzed, right next to his hand at her waist.

"Is that work?" he asked, pulling back to look at her.

"It could be." She bit her lip. It was always work. Her shoulders tightened and she forced them to relax before he could sense that she was frustrated.

"That's the problem with lawyers. No boundaries. People shouldn't email you at 11 p.m. at night unless it's a work crisis."

"There's no work crisis. He's probably emailing because he's thought of something and doesn't want to forget it in the morning." She leaned against his chest.

"That's why they have the scheduled delivery function."

She nodded against his hard chest, but the earlier mood had changed. She wasn't as relaxed, worried instead that her phone would buzz again. And Penny's warning sounded in her head.

The slow ballad ended, and Lolly sang another pop song. They danced, their glances meeting in the sparkle of the disco ball. The fizzing feeling returned, and his light touches—at her waist, her elbow—teased and made her think he felt that spark too.

At the break in the set, she excused herself to go to the bathroom so she could check her email in the bathroom stall. It was a lengthy email from Malaburn with more suggested angles to research along with darts of criticism. She shook her head. He couldn't bring her down now. She was having too much fun. She sent him a reply that she'd be on it first thing in the morning. She shouldn't stay out too much later.

The next set went quickly. Rafael and Penny were dancing close. Like dancing with a cute guy was something Penny did regularly. Dating seemed so easy for everyone else.

"Do you want to come to the afterparty?" Jake asked. "I'll introduce you to Lolly. We hope to sign her tonight."

An afterparty with a pop star. That was another life. And she'd just been invited to peek inside. She darted a glance at Jake. He looked expectant, waiting for her answer.

She sighed. She wished she could stay out longer, but as Eve had said, it didn't have to be all-nighters. She just had to take a balanced approach. "I better go home. I have a lot of work tomorrow."

"Understood." He didn't look surprised that she said no. He kissed her goodbye on the cheek. "It's going to be a late night for me."

Empty city streets with darkened store windows passed by the Uber driving her home. She was buzzing; it seemed like Jake *liked* her. Their heated glances, his touch, that warm buttery feeling when he'd held her in his arms. She hugged herself happily. If only she could have stayed out longer, but after all, Jake was working too, and it seemed like he understood. She was going to have a hard time falling asleep. But if she couldn't sleep, she could always start addressing Malaburn's latest email. Not likely.

Chapter Twelve

Her phone was ringing. Half asleep, as it was Saturday morning, she fumbled for the phone, only finding it after it ceased. It was her mom with a message to call her back before dinnertime in Paris.

If only she was having dinner in Paris. She had visited her mom in Paris for a week in June in her exchange apartment there. Suddenly, being a romance literature professor able to take a sabbatical in France seemed like a very good career option. With French doors opening onto a balcony, croissants and fresh bread every morning, she'd been tempted to stay herself. Her question of the year was: would the French lifestyle mellow her workaholic mother?

She called her back. "Hi Mom."

"How are you doing?"

"Good." Her mom's voice warmed Audrey.

"How's work? Are you at work now?"

"No, I'm working from home today." She stared at the pile of cases on the table in front of her. Highlighters, Post-it notes, pens, all ready to go.

"And how is work?"

"I won a pitch for a new case on Thursday."

"That's wonderful. Marjorie's daughter was promoted to managing director. I was just telling Marjorie about your case last year when I got to watch you argue in court and win. That was so thrilling."

"That's impressive that her daughter is a MD."

"A partner at a law firm is just as impressive."

Butterflies churned in the pit of her stomach. Her mom didn't mean to add to the pressure, but she did. "How's your work going?"

"It's great." Her mom waxed on enthusiastically about the people she was meeting and the research she was doing. She couldn't wait to introduce Audrey to her new friends. "But I think Benedict is trying to sideline me while I'm here." Benedict was her department rival.

"How?"

"My teaching schedule for next year is a nightmare. He volunteered to do scheduling, and I think he planned it so I would have less time to write and publish."

"Did you confront him?"

"Not directly. I asked him nicely to reschedule some of my classes."

"What about alerting the department head? He wants you to publish, for the benefit of the department's reputation." Audrey leaned forward, her elbow on her dining room table, her head propped in her hand.

"He hates to be bothered with these details. I'll try to get as much published this year as I can. As you know, you can only depend on yourself to get it done. So, how's Eve?"

"Good. We have a new neighbor in the brownstone next to us."

"I hope he's a quiet one, not someone who's going to throw a lot of parties and play music at all hours."

Audrey swallowed her laugh. "He had a party his first night, but it was really fun."

"You went to a party at his house already?" her mom asked.

"Eve and I were eating dinner at the balcony, and we were invited over."

Her mom said, "I was worried you'd be working too hard. But it is only six months until the decision, so you need to focus on that. You'll have the rest of your life to go to parties and travel."

That's what Audrey kept telling herself. That once she was partner, it would be better. She would have more control of her schedule; she had to believe that. Tiny slivers of doubt made her shiver. She wasn't going to regret going to Jake's party or the concert. But she wasn't going to tell her mother about the concert either. Instead, she reassured her mom that she was focused on work. They talked for a bit longer, and then Audrey's doorbell rang. The postman announced she had a package over the intercom. She said goodbye to her mom and ran downstairs to get it. She quickly opened the package and read the note.

Dear Audrey,

I might start planning my next vacation based on Travel, Surf, Cook—I'll just need to bring the soundtrack.
     The coloring book was certainly a thoughtful gift. And different. I can't say I've received a coloring book as a gift before. I could never stay in the lines.

I found you this fairytale coloring book—guaranteed to reduce stress!

Cheers,
Jake

She laughed. He didn't seem to be ruling her out based on her career. And the close dancing and the glances last night had intimated that she was more than just a friend—more than a person added to his collection. She'd love to be traveling with Jake in Central and South America. Hanging out on the beach, listening to the music, swimming in the waves, eating dinner over a little table near a grass-roofed cabana by the moonlight, the lapping of waves in the background as she gazed into Jake's blue eyes with the soft sea air caressing their skin. Okay, she was getting ahead of herself. He'd sent her a coloring book. If anything, the romance factor was going down. And right now, she had to concentrate on work. And then there was her mother's voice telling her to stay focused on making partner. It was the final stretch.

She texted briefly with Winnie. Winnie had been asked to spend another week in Texas and was *not* happy. She was planning a surprise party for her boyfriend's birthday in two weeks, so as long as she came back Friday, she was resigned.

Invited by the birds chirping in the garden and the beautiful summer weather, Audrey decided to spend the day reading cases in her garden. Nothing like the smell of suntan lotion to remind you of summer. She lay out on the lounger in a t-shirt and shorts, a homemade strawberry smoothie on the little wooden side table, iPhone music on, highlighter in hand, and read cases. The heat of the sun warmed her face and legs. The smell of fresh-cut grass filled the air. She finished reading late in the afternoon and leaned back, took off her headphones, closed her eyes and breathed in.

A rough tongue licked her foot and she jumped. She opened her eyes to find Biscuit wagging his tail.

"Oh my god! You completely scared me. How'd you get in here?" She looked over at the fence and saw a hole where two slats of the fence had broken off. Biscuit must have squeezed through.

"Oh, I see. Very innovative . . . I'm glad you didn't hurt yourself. Did you want company?" She patted the lounge chair, and he jumped up and settled in on her legs. When he rolled over, exposing his belly, she gave him a belly rub until Biscuit rested his head on her legs. She closed her eyes. Even better.

Twenty minutes later, she heard Jake's voice in his yard. "Biscuit! Here boy!"

She opened her eyes. Jake was peering over the fence.

"Biscuit! And Sleeping Beauty! Or is it Snow White?" Biscuit thumped his tail but didn't move.

"I don't think either had a dog."

"Should have—always a good defense against witches."

"And murderous huntsmen," she said. "Should I go check my fairytale coloring book?"

"Glad to see it's of use already."

"I'm feeling much more relaxed."

"I installed one of those dog doors so he could go out whenever he wanted. I didn't realize he could get through the fence."

"Biscuit is always welcome. The hole has never bothered me, so I've never fixed it. I bought this apartment from a couple, and they said they used it to visit your predecessor."

Jake bent down and squeezed through the gap in the fence, smiling at her. "Sounds like a good idea to me." He surveyed her garden. "But I can fix it if you want. I'm positive there's something in Emily Post about good fences make good neighbors."

She glanced at the six-foot-two hot guy standing in her yard. She wasn't an idiot. Even if Emily Post recommended a fence, she wasn't going to follow it. "Might as well leave it for now." She added, "Robert Frost wrote a poem about fences—he's often quoted for the line 'good fences make good neighbors,' but in the poem, he's actually questioning that."

He looked impressed. "Well, there you go. I'll have to read that poem." He pulled the wooden chair next to her lounge chair and sat down. "Biscuit doesn't bother you? He's made himself comfortable."

"He's lovely. I wish I could have a pet, but I work too many hours. I thought about getting a cat, but then . . ." She stopped right before she said she'd be a single woman with a cat looking desperate. Phew. She'd caught herself just in time.

"Still too much work?"

"Cats aren't, but I travel."

"Well, I'd be happy to come feed it. Or my sister could when I'm traveling."

"That's quite a commitment on your part to volunteer to feed it." She raised her eyebrow. Maybe she should get a cat just so Jake would keep stopping by. And a dog so they could walk their dogs together. Every night.

"I like to find homes for strays. My first kitten followed me home as a boy one fall out in Fire Island."

"I hadn't taken you to be such a softie." She tilted her head, smiling.

"Why not?" he smiled engagingly and held her gaze. "I'm not the killer litigator."

"I'm quite friendly unless you happen to be opposing me in a lawsuit. Then you might be in trouble."

"Only then?" He leaned forward, elbows on his knees, resting his chin in his steepled hands and focused on her. As opposed to Tim, pushing out his legs, leaning away.

She raised her eyebrow, questioning, determined *not* to get flustered.

"So . . ." he drawled, maintaining eye contact.

"Yes?" she asked.

"A coloring book?"

She giggled. "It was billed as the perfect gift for surfers!"

"Don't believe the hype, and I speak as a marketing guru." She couldn't believe he was in her garden and they were chatting casually.

"So modest."

"No room for modesty in marketing."

"I'm a sucker for marketing," she said.

"I was hoping you'd say marketing men," he quipped.

"Too easy." She smiled. "I don't think I've met many marketing men."

"We can remedy that," he said.

Yes, please, but really, she just wanted to get to know one particular marketing man. And not just as a friend. But she shouldn't be distracted from her goal of making partner.

"Have you had dinner? I was thinking of ordering something in. Like fish," he teased.

"I wonder why." She peeked up innocently. "I've got a chicken cranberry curry dish that Eve made and froze for me. There's enough for two if you'd like that. It's scrumptious, and I'm not biased because she's my best friend."

"Sounds great. Does she cook for you often?"

"I'm her number one guinea pig. She's pulling together her menu for a catering business. And her cooking is so much healthier for me than take-out."

"Can Biscuit come in too?"

"Of course." She petted his head. "We're not going to leave you alone outside."

She slid open the sliding door to her bedroom, relieved that she'd made her bed that morning.

He commented that he liked the painting on the wall above her bed. It was a bright blue and green abstract painting she'd bought at a New York art fair. Jake and Biscuit followed her up the stairs into her kitchen. Jake stopped short at the cans of beer stacked up against her brick wall at the far end of the kitchen. "Why do you have a wall of beer? Or is that some kind of artistic Warhol statement?"

"I don't drink that much beer. And every time I throw a party to reconnect with my friends, the beer stack grows. I buy beer and then people bring more beer than they drink." She gave Biscuit a bowl of water and put rice in a pot of water to boil.

"I can throw a party that will take care of all that beer."

She laughed. "I don't know if that's good or bad, but you're welcome to it." The comforting smell of boiling rice filled the room.

"Can I help with anything?" he asked.

"No, it's really easy." His presence was making her nervous. She couldn't believe they were about to eat dinner together. In her apartment. Maybe they should've ordered takeout. Then he could have chosen what he wanted to eat. She tightened her grip on the curry dish as she poured it into a pan to heat, worried that she might be clumsy.

"We need music," he said.

She unlocked her iPhone and handed it to him so he could choose some songs.

He studied it and her bookshelves. "I see you still have CDs."

"This spoken by the man who still has records?" Although she'd inherited some of those CDs from her mother.

"I can't part with them. And records have a superior sound," he said. Her CD collection was mostly pop and dance, with just a few jazz and alternative pop CDs. Not deep or angsty. "There's a lot you can tell from a person's music and book collection. Very revealing—especially the *one* opera CD."

"As you may have guessed, that was a gift." It felt like she had passed muster.

"Well, I'm expecting you to throw good dancing parties." He hooked up his phone to her speaker and light pop music filled the apartment. Jake moved along to study her DVD and book collections. "We like a lot of the same books—unless these were all gifts or part of a college reading course: *The Sun Also Rises, The Great Gatsby, Catch 22 . . .*"

"*Pride and Prejudice?*"

"Well, I can't say it is in my top ten. But it has its wisdom, and my sister Fiona loves it, which is why I read it, so I can be wise to her tricks." He'd read *Pride and Prejudice*? Did she know any other guy who'd read it?

"'It is a truth universally acknowledged, that a single man in possession of a fortune must be in want of a wife,'" she quoted.

"Yes, which is the equivalent of my view that dating for men is like shooting fish in a barrel," he said.

"Touché. I hadn't thought of that." As he studied her bookshelves, she said, "Now you've moved to the college reading course shelf: all the World War II history books. But I'm not supposed to point that out. Just think how brilliant my reading taste is."

"Ah, I found the chick lit shelf—double stacked and hidden behind the literature?" he asked.

She smiled. "Caught red-handed." He seemed to be checking out all her stuff, as if trying to figure out who she was. That had to be a good sign—unless she was found boring. She didn't have any deep dark secrets—except her chick lit shelf.

"My sister likes romantic comedies too." A warm curry scent began to emanate from the kitchen. "Smells good. I'll set the table." He entered the kitchen and opened a cabinet.

"Not there, that's the pantry!" she yelped, pointing to another cabinet. "That's the dish cabinet."

"Too late. Interesting pantry items." He pulled out sneakers from the bottom shelf.

"I make a fabulous sneaker souffle, you should try it sometime," she said. The kitchen felt too small and too hot with Jake in it. It was impossible not to bump into him while passing. They both smelled of suntan lotion and warm summer days.

"I'll hold you to that." He winked. "But seriously?"

"To remind myself to work out instead of snacking. And I don't cook all that often, so it seemed like a good space to use."

"Does it work?"

"Not particularly," she said. "Do you want to open a bottle of white wine? There's one in the fridge. Or there's some beer in the fridge."

Jake opened the white wine and poured two glasses.

"All right, dinner's ready. Let's sit," she said.

He pulled out a chair at the white round table. She took the chair with her back to the couch. His presence seemed to fill up the entire room. Jake had this magnetism. He seemed so confident and yet friendly and easy-going, radiating a zest for life. She needed to pinch herself to make sure that this was happening. Biscuit circled round and round and then curled up at Jake's feet.

"Oh, that's so sweet," she said and indicated he should serve himself first.

"Biscuit's my girl. She's ever hopeful I'll drop some crumbs." Biscuit's tail thumped when she heard her name.

He took a bite of the chicken curry. "Wow, this is good. I was worried when you suggested reheating a frozen meal."

"Was that the reason for your look of panic?"

"I'm a guy. I've some basic requirements, like good food. And I eat a lot, so when you said there'd be enough, I had my doubts."

"Then I should be flattered that you were willing to risk it?"

"Yes." He smiled. "But it's still a pretty low risk calculus, given that I could order more food later—especially since I've yet to try all the takeout menus that you gave me."

"You know how to flatter a girl."

"Do you think I don't?" He quirked an eyebrow and held her gaze. Her face flushed. His gaze lingered on her face. He broke the tension first by serving himself more chicken. "So, did you always want to be a lawyer? Are your parents lawyers?"

"No, my mom is a professor, as was my dad, but he died when I was in high school." She continued quickly to move the conversation past that revelation. "But, no, I didn't always want to be a lawyer. I took several women's rights college courses studying the victories won via court cases, so that first piqued my interest. And then I did some volunteer work with families, which showed me how lawyers were crucial to getting needed services. But after law school, I started working as a corporate lawyer, and here I am." She took a sip of her wine. "Did you consider being a lawyer since your dad is one?"

"No, it had completely the opposite effect," he said in a flat tone. "He works all the time and is always at the beck and call of clients."

"Aren't you at the beck and call of your music clients?"

"It's not the same thing. I have to work hard, yes, and there are a lot of late nights for video shoots, TV appearances, tour dates— but I still have more control over my schedule. For one thing, most events are arranged well in advance because they have to booked on the artist's schedule, so I can easily plan my life around them."

"Video shoots, TV appearances . . . that sounds cool."

"It is. But it's helping someone achieve their dream, that's the really cool part." He radiated joy as if reliving those moments. He finished his last bite. "What do you like about being a lawyer?"

She leaned forward. "I like researching and writing, building a case, and defending clients. I feel like a detective as I try to find evidence and cases that will support my client. And there's a huge thrill when you get an admission from a hostile witness." She wanted to persuade him that being a lawyer was not all bad. "Not that that happens often. But I didn't expect to have to work as much as I do. I'm hoping it will improve once I become partner." She glanced at the pile of stuffed brown manila folders on her desk in the corner.

"My dad works constantly. Still."

Her stomach sank. She sighed at the prospect. "Did he work a lot when you were young?"

"Yes. He couldn't make it to games, school performances, and sometimes he even missed vacations." His chair scraped the floor as he pushed it back.

"Really? He had to miss vacations?"

"Several times—once during Christmas. A deal would suddenly flare up, and that'd be that." He looked away.

A chill went through her. "Wow. I thought the hours were worse now."

"I don't know. Back then, dads were expected to work. My mom would come, but I would've liked my dad there." He frowned. "And now it's still the same. He missed Thanksgiving last year for a merger deal. He's got grandkids. And Ned, their dad, is away serving as a combat medic. My dad needs to put his family above his work. Especially now. He's got enough money."

"It's probably too much a part of his identity."

He nodded slowly. "Yes. And he loves it. He loves the intellectual thrill and editing documents, all of it. The briefcase, the suit. He's disappointed I'm not a lawyer." Jake stopped as if he'd admitted too much. "For me, it was absolutely clear that the personal cost is too high. You don't think so?" His gaze challenged her.

Sometimes. She flushed, taken aback, and gazed at him, her brow furrowed. Remembering Kevin asking her to leave and come down to Washington, D.C. to work for the government, saying the partnership would just use her labor for seven years and then spit her out. She shook her head. "I work very hard and for long hours, but I also enjoy the work, and I have good friends at the law firm." She didn't admit that she liked the suit too. As soon as she put on her crisp black suit with her white blouse, she felt stronger, like she'd donned a suit of armor.

"But you can have both," he said. "You can have a good career where you make enough money and have a life. It's not easy. You have to make it a priority and make certain choices."

She frowned. "Do you really think it's your choice? My mom works hard all the time."

"Certain choices that may mean you don't get promoted. Veronika got mad at me when I decided not to put my name in the hat for an executive VP promotion this year. Her attitude was get to the top and then you can coast. But I don't see much coasting at the top. And if I look at my dad, it seems he can't give it up."

"I see that with my mom." She nodded.

"Did your mom want you to be a professor?"

"No, definitely not. And I didn't want to be a professor. Getting tenure just seems to involve so much being nice and collegial to everyone, at least as a woman. My mom wanted me to be a lawyer, a career with a really good income. She also thought there'd be less politics and less subjectivity in law."

"Is there?"

She snorted. "Probably less hand-shaking than getting tenure as a professor, but it seems political now that I'm trying to make partner."

"I hate the politics." He leaned forward. "Is being a lawyer part of your identity?"

Yes. Now she felt like he'd moved from studying her bookcases to her. What did he see? She lowered her eyelashes to consider the question. She bit her lip. "Yes and no. I don't like being defined as a lawyer, so there's still hope for me yet. But I like to say I'm a lawyer if I'm trying to impress someone professionally. Not that it worked with you." She looked at him as if to say *give me a chance.*

Biscuit shifted positions in the silence, lying full out on the floor. Jake reached down to pet him. He smiled at her, and some of her tension eased away.

He asked, "So, did you bake the cookies you gave me?"

Grateful for the change in topic, she said, "Yes, but don't get your hopes up. That's about all I can make."

"I can live for a while on good chocolate chip cookies."

She laughed. "That's what I've always thought. They're kind of an essential food group."

"But only if they're superior . . ."

"You've got to have standards." Their gazes met. She wasn't sure they were still talking about cookies. She flushed and asked, "So, were you able to sign Lolly?"

"Yes."

"Congratulations!" She clinked his glass.

"I'm excited." He looked happy about it. He fiddled with his iPhone, changing the playlist, the light glinting off his dark wavy hair as he concentrated on finding the next songs.

"So, did you always know you wanted to work in music?" she asked.

"I didn't know you could work in music! I fell into it, luckily. I was a DJ in college radio, so I got connected to some of the music labels. Then they asked me to go check out college bands and recommend them. Eventually, I realized it could be a career and I could be doing something I loved."

"Sounds perfect."

"There's nothing like promoting a new band—until you watch them succeed. It's just cool."

"Is that what you do?"

"I'm a marketing senior vice president. I prepare the marketing campaigns for the records released by my label."

"It sounds like you love it." When he spoke about his job, his whole face glowed, as if lit from within. This close to him at her table, she could feel all of that passion and heat, and she leaned forward, eager for more. "Why?"

"I love music, I like the creative challenge, I like being a part of the music scene, I like the people," he said, waving his hands as he expressed his feelings. "I like figuring out the essence of the band and their music and then crafting the message." He played some songs on his iPhone from the bands he covered.

"They sound amazing. Do you miss living downtown? That's where the action is, right?"

"Not as much as I thought I might. I miss the sizzle—I mean, the streets can be electric at night down there, and that's not the case here. But I like being near the park and my sister and her kids. And I met you." He said this part in a low voice she wasn't used to hearing from him, one corner of his mouth kicking upward. His usual confidence seemed to fall away for a moment, and the shyness that replaced it made her blush. "Plus, as was pretty clear at the party, I just broke up with my girlfriend, and it seemed like a good move."

"Why'd you break up?" She was curious, but she wouldn't have dared ask if he hadn't brought it up.

"I wasn't in love with her, and I'm not sure she was in love with me. She was in love with the image of me—the up-and-coming marketing executive and the cool parties and the scene. Plus, she was pushing me to work more, and I don't want to." He looked hard at her, as if daring her to question that.

She held his gaze as if to reassure him that she wouldn't do that. "Why'd she want you to work more?"

"She thought I had a slacker attitude and I'd get farther ahead if I worked more."

"But you're a senior VP!"

"Ah, yes, but I could be an executive VP. There's always another rung on the ladder to climb."

"So, there is—if that's what you want." Although for her, making partner was the final rung. The rest was icing on the cake. "It seems you've found a good balance." She only wished she could find the same.

"I try." The silence lengthened. "Do you believe in a balance?"

"I believe in it, but achieving it is another thing. There's so much to learn, and the only way I'm going to be good is if I get enough experience. Plus, now I've got five months until the partnership decision." She piled up the plates. "Do you want any dessert? I don't have any chocolate chip cookies, although I assure you that that's rare. Ice cream?"

"We could go for a walk and pick up dessert," he said. "I have to walk Biscuit anyway." Biscuit thumped his tail and got up.

"That'd be great." A walk outside in the balmy summer night air sounded ideal. When they both stood, he was close. Only inches away. To break the tension, she asked where he went to high school. High school was so defining in New York.

"Collegiate. Where did you go?"

"Stuyvesant. All boys school, huh?" she teased.

"No distractions."

"Are you easily distracted?"

He smiled warmly. "Not easily." Her gaze met his and held. Her stomach fluttered.

"She Works Hard for the Money!" sang her phone's ringtone. She picked up the phone. He turned off the music.

"Hi Lawrence, yes, excuse me, okay, not in front of me, no, yes . . ." She grabbed a pad and started writing.

Malaburn was speaking fast. She scribbled down notes. Jake took the dishes to the kitchen. Out of sight. She hung up the phone. She stared at the legal pad, tears welling. She hated Malaburn with a visceral intensity right now. She took a deep breath, blinking back the tears and wiping them away before Jake could see.

She joined him in the kitchen and wrung her hands. "I'm sorry—that was this partner, Malaburn. He has changes to this client memo, and he also asked for more research. I have to go into the office to put the changes through now."

"You're serious? Now? On a Saturday night?"

"Yes, well, unfortunately, Malaburn has criticized me for not having what it takes to make partner. This memo is due Monday to the client. I can edit it and give the changes to the overnight secretarial staff, but I also have to research some additional points now, and I'm not sure how long it will take me. I'm sorry. I was really having fun. So maybe a raincheck on the ice cream?" She looked beseechingly at Jake. *I'm not your dad. I have to prove Malaburn wrong.*

"Raincheck it is. Come on, Biscuit, let's head home and go for your walk." He didn't look at her, and he said it in a tone as if he'd expected this to happen. He zipped down the spiral staircase, Biscuit behind him.

She locked the door behind him and watched him cross the garden, stoop to go through the hole in the fence with Biscuit, and disappear. He didn't look back. Her stomach sank.

Picking up her bag, she left to hail a taxi to take her to the office. She didn't have a choice. *Eyes on the prize. Don't let doubts deter you.*

But what if this was the wrong prize?

Chapter Thirteen

*A*udrey finished the client memo late on Sunday and emailed it to Malaburn for final approval. The whirring of a vacuum cleaner interrupted the evening office silence as the cleaning staff neatened the vacant offices, emptying out bins of paper and small wastebaskets of Diet Coke cans, coffee cups, food wrappers—the discards of small bursts of energy used to power the lawyers through the day. She slumped down in her chair and looked out her office window at the bright twinkling lights of a New York City night.

She bit her lip. She'd probably ruined it with Jake. He'd said "And I met you." She'd caught her breath when he'd said that. *Why did I leave so abruptly?* She should've gone for the ice cream and then left for the office. She chastised herself for her almost Pavlovian response to report to work. It had been going so well too. This could have been her chance for a romance with Jake.

She needed to be able to balance both her job as a lawyer and a life outside her job. She shouldn't check her phone all the time. If she was in the middle of a date, she shouldn't pick up a work call. If she had not answered the phone, they couldn't blame her. She could have been at a movie or asleep. Then again, she had needed all that time to make the changes to the brief. From a work perspective, it had been the right call. She sighed.

All right, she vowed, she was going to be better at creating boundaries between her life and work and balancing both. She wasn't going to put work first automatically. Then again, maybe she should start this resolution after the partnership decision. But she sensed that Jake would be long gone by then.

No, she could do it. She had to be able to have a life and a career. Partners had families. They managed to do it all. Then again, how often did they see their families—definitely on weekends. Hunter sometimes went home for dinner and then worked after dinner from home. It was doable. She just had to be more flexible in her approach and mindful—taking time to consider how to do both—like going for the ice cream and then leaving for the office.

Now, she had to salvage her sudden departure on Saturday. Maybe she could re-start their flirtation with a different gift—with a play on "brief."

Dear Jake,

Thank you for the fairytale coloring book. Here's my effort at coloring in Sleeping Beauty. You can see why I became a lawyer and not an artist.

I really enjoyed dinner. I'm sorry I left early to work on a brief.

It was unfortunately not a "brief" assignment. I'd "brief" you on the assignment, but that would be boring. However, this pair of "briefs" might be a *more "masculine" gift for you. I hope you like surf-board design. They're made by a company called "Brief Insanity." Which, unfortunately, is my life as a lawyer.*

Best,
Audrey

She couldn't decide if she should send it. Maybe it looked like she wasn't taking her sudden departure seriously enough—for a son disappointed by a workaholic father. But a sense of humor about it was good. And if any relationship was to emerge of this, they would need to be able to laugh about it. And what could she promise? She was a workaholic, but she definitely would try to do better.

Chapter Fourteen

Audrey smoothed down her skirt, took a sip of water, and then rolled her neck to ease the tension building there. As she picked up her notes, she chided herself for being nervous. It was just a meeting with Hunter—and Colette. She and Hunter had worked together comfortably for many years, starting from her first year at the firm. Usually, she considered this Monday morning meeting a pleasant start to her week—Hunter and she discussed the status of the case, what work she was giving to which associates, what they expected to get done during the week, any issues—and caught up on each other's lives and any firm gossip.

She smiled perfunctorily at some assistants she passed. She had to think positively. It was helpful to have Colette on the team. She shifted her binders and notepad to her other arm. Her goal for this meeting was to explain the case and her proposed strategy to Colette. And show Colette that she was firmly in control and not to be messed with.

Hunter's assistant was not at her desk, so she walked to the doorway. Colette was already there—in a cream-colored silk suit that radiated sophistication. Audrey had dressed up for the meeting, but she wasn't feeling the power of her pearls and black suit. Both heads turned as she knocked gently on the open door, and Hunter waved her in. She took her usual seat. They exchanged preliminaries about the weekend, with Colette saying she'd worked, volunteering nothing personal. Today, Colette was wearing glasses, as if she was channeling Lois Lane.

Hunter told a funny story about his kids playing on the beach. Normally, Audrey would have joked about her last bad date, giving a brief funny synopsis, but she didn't feel comfortable after her last meeting with Hunter, so she just said, "Oh you know, hung out with friends and worked." Hunter looked quizzical.

"Well, Audrey, do you want to bring Colette up to speed on the case? I've sent her the complaints and some preliminary documents," Hunter said. His assistant entered and set down some glasses of water.

"Of course. Colette, first of all, I'm glad you've joined our team, and I look forward to working with you," she said. There, she was starting this on a positive note. She handed Colette the binder she'd put together for her.

Colette gave her a tight, polite smile in response.

"We represent Hen Bank and its three brokers who are being sued for unauthorized trading."

Colette flipped the binder open to that tab.

"We're still in the midst of discovery," Audrey said. "John Rothman's case is the most critical for success from the bank's perspective because he's one of their long-time stars and heads its wealth management group." And he was a good guy.

"Have they said that?" Colette asked sharply.

"Yes," Hunter said. "Our firm has also worked with John for years, and he's solid—a straight arrow. These allegations are quite distressing and a real shock to his family and the firm. You may have seen some of the press."

"Especially at this time—his wife is undergoing chemotherapy, and so they just want the stress of the case to be mitigated," Audrey said.

"They want to settle?" Colette asked.

"No, they want to clear his name, but as soon as possible and with the least amount of disruption. But the case is—let me give you background first." Audrey relaxed. She knew this case cold. "John has a French client, Pierre, from a very wealthy family. He brought him in as a client to Hen Bank years ago when he started. They are family friends. So, it's a twenty-year relationship with no prior issues—as far as we know. About six months ago, Pierre calls John on his personal cellphone while John is at the hospital picking up his wife from her first round of chemo. Pierre wants to invest in this Brazilian company. John said he hasn't researched it, hasn't heard of it, wouldn't advise it. Pierre is insistent that he wants to buy it. John tells Pierre to call Mike, the analyst, and ask him to place the trade because he's at the hospital. Pierre is adamant that John has to make the trade—he only trusts John." Audrey paused to let Colette catch up as she was writing notes.

"This is from a recording?" Colette asked.

"No, unfortunately. John's memory. Because Pierre called John on his personal cellphone, no recording. John's wife overheard part of the conversation, but he doesn't want her in the case. And she's the wife—so a jury will probably consider her biased." Audrey took a sip of water; her throat felt dry. "But the telephone records show that John received a call from Pierre that day, and the hospital records show that John was at the hospital at that time."

Colette nodded and made some more notes.

Audrey leaned forward. "Pierre says that he wants John to make the trade or he'll use his other broker. What kind of client service is this? Blah, blah, blah. John agrees to make the trade."

Colette shook her head. "Shouldn't have done that."

"But he does. He gets on his laptop and manages to buy the amount in a brief dip in the stock. John then calls Mike immediately after and explains Pierre's request to him. So, we have Mike's testimony supporting John, but again, John's his boss. That conversation should be recorded, so we're looking for that recording. Then, John asks Mike to do some research on the company. That research comes back mixed. Rumors are swirling that the company found some huge mining spot, but it can't be confirmed. John sends the brief research analysis to Pierre. Pierre is using that document now to say that John suggested the stock to him."

Colette raised her eyebrows.

"John gets back to the office and sends an email asking Pierre to confirm the trade in writing," Audrey said. "No response. He calls. Voicemail. We do have that message recording. And that's in our favor because the stock is still up at that point. Pierre has ten days to send the written confirmation. But the stock goes south eight days later—and then Pierre writes that he didn't authorize the trade and wants the firm to reimburse him."

Audrey explained their first argument that Pierre instigated and verbally authorized the trade, per John's recounting of the facts. Alternatively, they would argue that this trade was authorized because Pierre signed a written authorization allowing John the discretion to trade on Pierre's behalf. "But we haven't found that written approval yet. I did find documents indicating that a higher level of review is being applied because it is marked as a discretionary trading account. That leads us to hope a written authorization exists." Audrey finished describing their additional arguments.

Colette was looking pensive.

Not the best case for making partner, is it?

"Hmmm." Colette put down her pen. "Did you see that recent verbal authorization case? It was in New Jersey."

"No, what did it hold?" Audrey asked.

"It torpedoes your first argument. The court held that there is no discretionary authority without prior written approval," Colette said.

Audrey was shocked. Her automatic searches should have alerted her of any decisions on unauthorized trading.

"I'm surprised you didn't see it." Colette looked slyly at Audrey.

"We aren't aware of that one," Hunter said, and Audrey appreciated that Hunter said "we." "How recent is it?"

"In the past two weeks." Colette handed a document to Hunter. Audrey noted that she'd only brought one copy.

I missed a case within the last two weeks. She rubbed her suddenly sweaty hands on her skirt under the table.

Hunter read the case. "Not good," he said, frowning.

She hoped he wasn't saying "not good" about her research. She was known for her research skills—for finding that winning case. Colette was looking very self-satisfied.

Hunter handed the copy to Audrey, and she skimmed it. She said, "It's in a different circuit, so it might not serve as precedent."

"The court will look to it as the most recent discussion of the issue," Colette said.

Audrey checked the date. It had been decided Friday. It wasn't as bad as two weeks. She hadn't checked for any case decisions over the weekend. The Malaburn and the Popflicks cases had kept her busy, and she'd had dinner with Jake. It was critical to know about the case, but now their legal argument was weaker. And she should've known about the case. She was falling behind. She couldn't fall behind. So, she should be grateful for Colette's help.

"We'll have to see if we can distinguish the facts of that case from John's situation," Audrey said. "That's the basic summary of the John Rothman case. We are confident we can defeat their class action motion because the facts for each broker's case differ."

"The courts have been pretty liberal in granting class actions lately. An article in the *New York Law Journal* highlighted the changing trend," Colette said. More bad news. Well, she's a Debbie Downer. Colette was really on top of this.

Audrey had not been aware of that trend, but she said, "Overall, we're fairly confident that we'll be able to show different facts. We definitely want to distinguish these cases because the plaintiff may be right in the James case."

"Really?" Colette asked.

"In that case, plaintiffs allege that the broker was making unauthorized trades to increase his commissions. The Hen compliance department is investigating, but initial reports are not good."

Colette raised an eyebrow and wrote more notes. Hunter's assistant popped her head in to let him know that a client was on the line with an urgent matter. Hunter wrapped up the meeting.

The two women stepped out into the hushed hallway. Audrey hugged her binder to herself and looked up at Colette. Colette met her gaze as if appraising her.

"That was a quick run-through," Audrey said. "Do you have any questions?"

"No," Colette said. She said it quickly as if she didn't allow herself questions.

"Well, then," Audrey said, "the team meeting is every Tuesday, although we get together all the time. We just did the first document pull from the three brokers' offices, so we're all review-ing it now. I was about to review archives and electronic storage records, but I'll leave that to you now."

"Yes, I'll handle that." Colette turned to walk towards her office, but looked back over her shoulder. "Was there anything else you wanted to discuss?"

"No, glad it's all clear," Audrey said. Clearly, they were not going to be "buddy buddy" on this case. And not only were they not going to be buddies, Colette seemed to want to score points against her. Some help this was. She'd rather run defensive discov-ery herself than deal with this. No, she had to be positive. Colette had found an important case. She should have checked before the meeting. She had to be more on top of her game. She walked down the hushed corridors to her office, passing the portraits of various male partners on the wall.

Chapter Fifteen

*A*udrey couldn't believe she was on her way to work at seven-thirty on a Wednesday morning. She was really stressed if she wasn't able to sleep in the morning. When she'd woken up early, she'd decided to go to a yoga class to see if that would help. Winnie swore by yoga and her dermatologist had recommended yoga (but not hot yoga) to reduce stress. She'd complained that her skin flushed when giving client presentations. That wasn't the image she wanted to project as a candidate for partner at her law firm, especially competing against Tim and flawless Colette. And what with working for Malaburn again, she needed a new mechanism to counter getting stressed. And she did feel more relaxed, although very sore. Apparently, it countered stress by making her too sore to be stressed.

As she let herself out of the door, she looked up to see Jake. *My note with the briefs is supposed to arrive later today. He'll probably just wave and walk by quickly.*

"Do you go to work at this hour?" Jake asked. *Making conversation, good.*

"Not usually. I just woke up early. Do you?" Audrey asked. He looked dressed for work.

"No. But I'm not off to the office immediately. My sister has some early team meeting at the hospital, so I'm picking up my niece and nephew to bring them to daycare."

"That sounds like fun."

"Want to come? You can meet my sister and her kids. She thinks that two adults for two kids is optimal."

"Sure," Audrey said. *Yes! Here's a chance to hang out, and I'm not even expected at the office until nine-thirty.* "I'm sorry again I had to work on Saturday."

"Life of a lawyer. I get it," Jake said.

That wasn't what she wanted him to get, but she wasn't sure what more to say.

They walked down an empty Columbus Avenue, past the bags of early morning bread deliveries tucked into the corners of restaurant doorways, and turned down a block leading to Central Park West. The early morning sun lit up the golden stonework of the buildings on the north side of the street.

"So, you moved here to help your sister?"

"Yes, my sister has two kids, and her husband is a medic in the military reserve and gets called away periodically. He's serving right now."

"That's impressive," Audrey said.

"Yes, I was the go-to fix-it guy in the family. Then she married Ned, and now I'm just the music guy." *So, he could be self-deprecating.*

She followed him into the art deco entranceway of a small apartment building. Jake greeted the doorman and then turned towards a staircase, saying it was just one floor up. Jake let himself in with his key and yelled out, "Reporting for uncle duty!"

The small foyer of his sister's pre-war apartment was neat but crowded, with a little bench for removing shoes, coats on a hook, bookbags, and a folded-up stroller. He hung his black leather messenger bag and Audrey's satchel on the one empty hook.

"I've brought a friend," he added.

His sister met them as they entered the living room, her nine-month-old son on her hip. She looked like Jake's sister. She even had the same dimple in her cheek.

The living room gave off a casual, friendly vibe. A comfortable gray L-shaped couch faced the windows next to a wall of bookcases filled with children's books, games, and bright bins of toys. A maple dining room table was off to the corner in front of an open kitchen.

"Hi, I'm Audrey," Audrey said, extending her hand.

"Fiona, so nice to meet you," his sister said, shaking her hand. "And this is Thomas."

"Audrey's my neighbor, so I invited her along when I ran into her," Jake said. "You're always saying one-on-one is better than zone defense."

"I knew my basketball example would hammer home the point. We both played basketball in school," Fiona said. She explained that it had been a disaster of a morning, and she had planned to have everything ready for Jake to just go, but she didn't. Despite all that, Audrey was impressed by how together yet casual Fiona seemed.

"Don't worry, we've got this," Jake said. Audrey nodded.

"Famous last words," Fiona said.

"Do you want us to help or not?" Jake asked.

"I desperately do. I'm deeply grateful. Really—moving up here was beyond the call of duty. You're the best brother ever." Fiona reached up to ruffle his hair.

Jake rolled his eyes at Audrey. "Don't push it."

"Do you have a brother?" Fiona asked.

"No, I'm an only child."

"So, you're neighbors?" Fiona asked as she walked back to her kitchen and put the bottles of breastmilk for Thomas into a little insulated pack. The kitchen was all white except for sprinkles of color here and there: a yellow pitcher holding wooden spoons, a blue dish towel, a red KitchenAid mixer. She yelled to the back of the house, "Luna, Uncle Jake is here!"

"We met when Jake moved in," Audrey said.

"How friendly," Fiona said, but it was in the tone of "there must be more to this." Which was a valid tone as Audrey wasn't in the habit of accompanying next-door neighbors in New York to babysit.

"I'm a friendly guy. You did tell me that the Upper West Side was a neighborly place," Jake said. He took the thermal pack from Fiona and added it to the Trader Joe's bag.

"So, I did. Are you happy you moved?" Fiona asked.

Jake nodded. "Very. It's easier to keep on good terms with Veronika if we're not running into each other all the time."

"I imagine it's a little harder for her to show up suddenly on the West Side."

"I thought you liked her," Jake said.

Fiona shrugged. "It was hard to get a read on her. She was good with kids, but so nervous around Biscuit. She seemed high maintenance—with all those outfits, although she did inspire me to think that I should vary my wardrobe from yoga pants and scrubs." Fiona paused. "And she was so physical with you—always clinging to you and petting you."

Note to self: Do not pet Jake—not that she would.

"Petting?" Jake asked.

"Petting," Fiona said. "And she didn't seem to have much of a sense of humor."

"Don't hold back now," Jake said, looking embarrassed. Audrey felt bad for him.

"Luna said she liked your friend the other day," Fiona said.

"Penny?" Jake asked.

"Oh, Penny. She has bright blue hair now?" Fiona asked.

"At the moment." Jake smiled. "I didn't know you were training Luna to be a spy."

"I'm not. She came home wanting blue hair," Fiona said.

"You and Penny both seem to think I can't be happily single," Jake said.

Happily single. She felt a pang. She was hoping he wanted to date her, but she couldn't date anyway, so this was better. *Just keep telling yourself that.* She'd probably lost her chance after she'd left their dinner abruptly.

"It's not your usual modus operandi," Fiona remarked as she loaded the breakfast dishes into the dishwasher.

"Work's really busy for me right now," Jake said.

"Of course." Fiona patted his arm. "Too close a call with Veronika?"

Jake winced. "Are you a doctor or a psychologist?"

"I took a psychology course."

"Apparently it wasn't Freudian."

Audrey swallowed a chuckle.

Fiona zipped the bag shut. "Finally, ready. I just need the diapers. Oh no, it smells like he made another poop. It's hard to talk when you've got to hustle kids out the door in the morning—you start talking and lose all track of time."

"I'll change Thomas. You finish getting ready. Don't worry." Jake picked Thomas up from Fiona, holding him under the arms, and baby-talked to him, rubbing noses. Audrey's heart melted. "Are you giving your mommy a hard time? Let's go get you changed and say hello to your sister while mommy gets a moment to herself." He carried Thomas to the back of the apartment, holding him slightly away to protect his crisply ironed shirt. He smiled at Audrey. "Audrey, come meet Luna."

"You're lucky your work is a bit more flexible with hours," Fiona called after him.

"One of the reasons I love my job. Just have to be on time for my label meeting this morning. And remember I'm in Las Vegas on September 23-25 for the IHeartRadio Music Festival, so you have to take care of Biscuit."

Fiona replied that it was on the calendar.

Jake led the way to the changing table in Fiona's bedroom. Jake looked at her and raised his eyebrow as he changed Thomas, and a poop smell filled the room.

"I'm impressed," Audrey said.

"Don't worry. I wouldn't ask you to change him on first meeting. Second meeting?"

His crisp blue shirt brought out his eyes. His shirt sleeves were rolled up, and his hands and forearms were tanned. He had beautiful, capable hands.

Audrey punched his arm playfully. "And I thought you said you know how to flatter a girl."

"I'm sure you'd be great at changing diapers," Jake said. He picked Thomas up and held him close.

"I don't think I can compete with you," Audrey said, smiling.

They found Luna in her room playing with her Playmobil castle. Luna grabbed Jake around the leg. "Uncle Jake!"

"Luna, meet my friend Audrey."

"That's a great castle," Audrey said. "I love playing with Playmobil."

"Can you hold Thomas?" Jake asked. Audrey took Thomas from Jake, reveling in his sweet baby smell.

Jake squatted so he was at Luna's height. "Luna, I get to bring you to school today. I'll meet your friends. But you need to get dressed so we can go. Look, Mommy put out your clothes." Luna glanced at her clothes on the bed but didn't seem interested.

Jake suggested they get their final instructions from Fiona while Luna got dressed. Carrying Thomas, Audrey followed Jake back to the living room, where Fiona was packing her purse, the various bags filled with children's stuff at her feet. Fiona told them what still needed to be done and explained that she couldn't be late again to the morning staff meeting.

"You and Mom." Jake rolled his eyes. "It's as if I've never babysat before."

"Trying to get them out the door on a deadline is entirely different," Fiona said. She kissed Thomas goodbye.

"I gather. Mom called me last night with all this advice— saying I should sing if I get frustrated and tempted to yell. As if I would yell. Anyway, she said it would lighten the mood and get them to listen."

"Oh my god, yes, she really liked that course that the preschool offered. She thought it was brilliant." Fiona yelled out, "Luna, Luna, Mommy is leaving now."

"Bye Mommy." Luna came into the living room, wearing just a pajama t-shirt and underwear, her guitar slung on, overwhelming her small frame. She was singing a song and strumming off-tune.

"Go," Jake said to his sister.

"Yes, don't worry," Audrey said, bouncing Thomas on her hip.

"You can strap Thomas in the stroller, and then both of you can get Luna ready. You can give Thomas a book. His books are over there." Fiona kissed both children goodbye, checked she had her keys and phone, and left.

As the door closed behind her, Jake said, "Sisters, no faith. She doesn't understand that getting everybody on board for a marketing strategy can be like herding cats. I can definitely handle getting two kids out the door."

Audrey put Thomas down on the floor with a fire truck and started zooming it around him. Jake unfolded the stroller.

"Uncle Jake, teach me guitar!" Luna said.

"I can't right now," Jake said.

Luna pouted.

"We have to get ready for school. I see you started getting dressed," he said.

"I hate school. I want to play with you. You told me you'd teach me guitar."

"You love school. You see all your friends there." He pulled out her chair. "Here, come finish your breakfast, and I'll go get the rest of your clothes."

Luna climbed into the wooden slanted highchair, and Jake pushed the chair in.

Jake looked at the clock. "I'm sorry, I thought I'd just be picking them up. I don't want you to be late for work."

"I have time." Some time anyway. "Do you have a work meeting?"

"I was hoping to do a final prep before my meeting presenting to the entire label." He looked chagrined.

Luna asked for more milk. Jake poured some and then left to get Luna's clothes. Audrey sat down at the table with Luna, holding Thomas on her lap. Luna eyed her warily and didn't eat her bagel.

Audrey picked up a little bunny in a pretty flowery yellow dress that was lying discarded on the table and said in a high-pitched voice as the bunny, "Hello Luna."

"Bunnies don't talk," Luna said.

"I talk," Audrey said in a funny squeaky voice, while moving the bunny forward, with her one free hand. "I like to talk. I also eat. That bagel looks yummy. Can I have some?"

"No," Luna said smiling. "It's my bagel." She took a bite.

"Is it good?"

Luna nodded yes, chewing.

"It's a very big bagel. Can you eat it all?" Audrey asked as the bunny in a high-pitched voice as Jake returned to the room with Luna's clothes. He raised his eyebrows at Audrey.

"Yes." Luna took another bite.

"Don't you think Uncle Jake looks hungry?" The bunny came closer to Luna and Audrey loudly whispered in a squeaky voice as the bunny, "You better eat it quickly before Uncle Jake tries to eat it."

Luna looked up at Uncle Jake and took her final bite.

Audrey moved the bunny to the cup of milk and made the bunny peer into it. "Do bunnies like milk?"

"No. Cats like milk." Luna drank her milk.

"Good job," Audrey said in the bunny voice. "Now let's get Thomas in the stroller."

While Audrey strapped Thomas into the stroller, Jake said, "Great job, Luna and bunny."

"That's Bella."

"Great job, Luna and Bella. Now let's get you dressed." He sat down and turned her chair to face him and helped her put on her sweatpants and a pink sparkly unicorn shirt.

Audrey loaded the various bags onto the back of the stroller. She handed Thomas a small truck to play with in the stroller.

"I like the unicorn," Jake said.

"No unicorns," Luna stamped her foot. "No pink."

"Pink unicorns give you special powers," Jake said.

"Like what?"

"They can make you fly." He picked up Luna and flew her around the room. Luna giggled excitedly. He was so natural with his niece and nephew.

"More."

"We'll have to fly to school if you don't hurry up," he said.

"No unicorn." Luna crossed her arms. "My best friend Lucy doesn't like pink."

"Pink is a great color," Audrey said.

"You're not wearing pink," Luna said.

"That's true," Audrey said. "But I do wear pink."

"Audrey was wearing a pink top when we met," Jake said. Their gazes met. *He remembered that?*

"No pink." Luna shook her head.

"Maybe you should get another shirt. C'mon Luna, let's brush your teeth," Audrey said. Luna took her hand trustingly, and Audrey felt flattered.

"Yes, I don't want her to end up in therapy from the time I made her wear a pink shirt. But personally, I think she should ditch this Lucy," Jake said.

Audrey finished brushing Luna's teeth as Jake returned with a smorgasbord of non-pink shirts, hoping there was one she would like. Luna looked skeptically at the shirts.

His eyes, frustrated, met Audrey's. She smiled wryly and said, "We're about to be defeated by two kids."

"No, let's use my mom's advice," he said. "Luna, my love," he sang to the beat of "Fight Song," "Let's get this shirt on, sock and shoes. Socks and shoes. Can you get your shirt on? Shirt on, Let's get this shirt on! Socks and shoes, we can do it." Luna sang "socks and shoes" too and cooperated.

"Let's get jackets on! Jackets on!" He roared as if it was rock and roll, and strummed an imaginary guitar. Audrey could see Jake as a rock star; he just needed to unbutton a few more buttons, not that she didn't appreciate the view of the two already unbuttoned.

Audrey handed Thomas a drum that was in the toy bin by the dining room table, and he banged on it. Audrey grabbed a toy broom from that basket and, using it as a microphone, crooned, as best she could, "Jackets on!"

"Jackets on!" Luna yelled back, also strumming a pretend guitar and putting on her jacket.

"Knapsack on!" he sang.

"Knapsack on!" Luna yelled back.

"Stroller ready!" Audrey sang.

"Way to go!" Jake chorused as he shut the door behind them.

"I've got to remember to call my mom to tell her that the advice is brilliant," Jake said as he wheeled the stroller out the door down the block back towards Columbus Avenue, Luna skipping alongside him.

"Super brilliant. Who knew?" Audrey said.

"Thanks for all your help."

"It was fun."

Their glances met. They'd been a good team. And he looked even hotter wheeling a stroller loaded with bags and holding Luna's hand. The streets were crowded now, with parents rushing their children to school and single adults walking with purpose towards the subway. Luna started telling Jake about her school project.

As they reached the green subway entrance in the traffic island in the middle of 72nd Street, Jake asked, "This is your subway, right? The daycare is over on West End Avenue a few blocks down, so we'll make it in time."

She nodded reluctantly.

"Say goodbye to Audrey," he said to Luna.

Luna hugged her. Audrey loved those little arms holding onto her.

Then Luna said, "You should marry this one. Mommy says that if you marry, I might get cousins I can play with."

Audrey blushed bright red.

"Fiona is determined to marry me off," Jake said. "Sometimes I feel like I'm in *Pride and Prejudice*, with Fiona playing the role of Mrs. Bennett."

"Your sister is not remotely like Mrs. Bennett."

"You have no idea. She invites me over to dinner, and half the time, she's also invited a single girlfriend. It's fu…n and awkward."

Audrey laughed. "At least she thinks you're a good catch."

"I'd hope. But still, I think I can find someone on my own." He smiled warmly at her. "Thanks again for coming out on the spur of the moment and helping me. Your talking bunny was super helpful."

"Your singing was key."

"You can see why I'm in marketing and not out in front."

They stood there, staring at each other, while crowds jostled around them, streaming towards the subway. Luna tugged at Jake's hand.

"We have to go," Luna said. "Daddy usually kisses mommy goodbye here, and then we go."

"All right." Jake kissed Audrey lightly on the cheek. She closed her eyes and breathed in his clean smell.

"Good luck with your meeting."

"I'll start singing if it gets tense." He pushed the stroller towards West End Avenue and the daycare. Audrey watched him go. And then he turned his head and saw her, standing there, transfixed by a kiss on the cheek. He smiled and waved. She waved back. Caught again. Subtlety was not her forte.

Chapter Sixteen

"They want to keep me here another week," Winnie wailed on the phone on Friday.

"Did you tell them about your boyfriend's surprise birthday party next Friday?" Audrey asked.

"I tried, but Alex had to go. Some partner was at the door," Winnie said. Alex was the associate in charge of the case.

"I'll go talk to him," Audrey said.

"What do you mean?"

"I'll tell him that they can't keep you down there for three weeks in a row. That's insane," Audrey said. "And if that doesn't work, I'll tell him we need you back for the Hen case. He's not allowed to monopolize you."

"No, you don't have to. Maybe I can finish up by Thursday next week."

"I'm doing it. I'll call you back." Audrey hung up the phone and marched down the hallway to Alex's office. Alex was a year

134

younger than her, and, similar to Tim, seemed a shoo-in for partner. He looked the part and radiated that assurance. She pushed open his door without knocking. "Alex, Winnie has been down in Texas for twelve days straight, working without a break and without returning home. You can't ask her to stay another week."

Startled, Alex looked up.

"That would be three weeks in a row. Without coming home. You told her a week," Audrey said.

"I didn't realize."

She shook her head. Caring about junior associates should be higher on the partner criteria list.

"You're supposed to rotate associates, if it's going to be a long document review. Not do a bait and switch, telling them one week and then leave them there for as long as it takes," Audrey said.

"I didn't mean to, I thought she didn't mind. I'll send down Martin and let her come back. She just needs to brief Martin. I'll ask him to go on Monday and they can talk today. She wrote me she was enjoying the food," Alex said.

"When did she write that?"

"Now that I think about it, when she first got down there," Alex said. "Thanks for telling me, Audrey. I wasn't paying attention. I've been so busy on this other case."

Audrey nodded. She walked back to her office. Alex was a nice guy, just really dedicated—so much so that he wouldn't mind being away on a document production for three weeks. When she was a younger associate, she'd liked long business trips—all meals accounted for, and usually just the one case to worry about. Often there'd even been time to work out at night because client's offices closed at 5 p.m. But unlike Winnie, she didn't have a boyfriend back home.

Winnie: *Alex called. Going home tomorrow.*
THANK YOU!

Audrey spent the next few hours trying to find a case contradicting the case Colette cited. She'd read one, and if it referred to a former case, hinting at similar facts to the Rothman case, she'd pull it up and consider if the law or the facts helped—and keep searching for the perfect case. *Just one more,* she'd tell herself. Then she'd read yet another, lured by its potential and the thrill of finding the one that could win the case for her client. Finally, she found exactly what she was looking for. Still, it may not be enough. But it gave them something to argue. She shut down her laptop and called the car service to go home.

She wrote an email to her mom on the way home, asking her what was happening with next year's schedule. She used to call her mom during these taxi rides home late at night to catch up, but she couldn't now with the time difference. She wrote her that she was on a case with Malaburn, but it was okay. She was drafting a motion to dismiss, and if they won the motion, she'd be done working with him.

Arriving at her apartment, she picked up an Amazon package addressed to her left on the landing outside her door. *Please, let it be from Jake.*

She shut the door of her apartment, dropped her bag, and sliced open the box with a pair scissors. It was from him! She smiled as she pulled out a pink and yellow book, *Love in the Cookie Bakery. Ooh, love in the title.* With a note:

Dear Audrey,

Thanks again for helping me with Luna and Thomas. The label meeting seemed pretty smooth compared to persuading Luna to wear a pink unicorn shirt.

I found you an even better coloring book: Outside the Lines: An Artists' Coloring Book for Giant Imaginations *for relaxing when you finish writing briefs. I'm never going to see legal briefs in the same way. I hope nobody brings up a brief at my father's next cocktail party.*

I should probably buy this coloring book for Luna too.

And you might like this book for your collection.

Cheers,
Jake

She smiled. *Yes! The flirtation is on!* She hadn't completely messed up. She was so relieved.

She looked at the coloring book. *I'm not an "outside the lines" person. I've always stayed in the lines. Probably too much so—at least in my personal life.* But she was flying counter to her usual approach now, pursuing this flirtation with Jake, and it was giving her more energy for work.

She read the book summary—she couldn't wait to read it. *Love in the Cookie Bakery* even had cookie recipes. She'd bake Jake some cookies using the recipes in the book. That's what she'd send back.

Chapter Seventeen

*A*udrey moved around, trying to get comfortable in her office chair. The cushion seemed to have lost some supportive oomph with her non-stop sitting on it. *Could you ask for seat cushions to be replaced?*

She opened up the yellow inter-office folder. A note on vellum paper with flowery handwriting from Mrs. Whitaker greeted her. Mrs. Whitaker wanted to help plan the party. She had also written that the Whitakers were now gluten-free (and salt-free to lower Gene's high blood pressure). Okay, hopefully Mrs. Whitaker could recommend a gluten-free, salt-free caterer, but she was concerned that Mrs. Whitaker seeking to help was going to add to the amount of work.

> Winnie: *You didn't tell me about bus-dev conference event at Marriott tonight. Colette and Tim outside my door—excited about it.*

Audrey: *I wasn't invited. Otherwise, I'd have told u.*

Winne: *Odd.* ☹

Sad face indeed. If both Colette and Tim came back with potential clients, that'd be a real plus in their partnership bid and a real negative in hers. She didn't understand why Hunter had not invited her—he could have just sent her alone as his guest if he had another commitment.

Winnie: *Colette's going as Hunter's guest!?! What's up with that? They just passed together.*

That answered her question as to why he hadn't invited her. But not in a good way.

It was time for some office gossip due diligence, so she decided to pop by Mary's desk. Mary was Hunter's assistant.

As she approached, Mary said, "Audrey, what are you doing here? You're supposed to be at the Marriott event." Then Mary's eyes widened as she realized she'd said something wrong, and her face flushed.

Audrey decided to take the upfront approach. "What happened with that? Why did he take Colette instead of me?"

"Oh, honey, he intended to invite you. I kept sending him emails reminding him to ask you and get it on your calendar. But then he said that Colette asked him straight out to take her, saying it would be a good opportunity for them to get to know each other, and he couldn't argue with that."

"Thanks, Mary. I feel better knowing that." She did. She should've followed Tim's advice to be aggressive and ask Hunter. But, had Tim told Colette that Hunter hadn't invited her? She shook her head. *I need to be more assertive, especially if I'm being put head-to-head with Colette.*

Chapter Eighteen

alaburn's office was devoid of any hint of personality, aside from the legal tomes that lined the bookshelves. As Malaburn skimmed her letter to opposing counsel and her brief to dismiss the case, she looked to see if he had any personal pictures or even keepsakes. None.

"You're too nice in this letter," Malaburn said.

Audrey stared at him, swallowing, her brain fixated on *You're too nice.* She heard Kevin saying that again, as if he was in the room. And Malaburn had known Kevin, obviously, when Kevin had been up for partner. She shook her head. Malaburn couldn't know that Kevin had said that to her.

She had missed whatever Malaburn had just said. But he was still talking. "You need to add a sentence here, right at the top of the second page: 'If not, we'll see you in court.' That's the kicker."

She had to focus on rebutting his assertion. "Isn't that obvious? I wrote, 'Here are the reasons you should settle.'"

"You need to be aggressive and say it." He laughed. But it wasn't a joyful laugh. "Litigation is not about being nice."

That's what Kevin had said. Her mom's "Be Nice" mantra whispered in her head. But she could be aggressive. She could.

Malaburn looked back down at the brief. "Interesting first point here. Potentially risky. I'll think about it."

"That argument will win the motion to dismiss," Audrey said.

"You're surer of yourself than when we last worked together."

"I have three more years of experience."

"But do you have what it takes to be a partner? I mean, we can't very well have a partner who has to get pulled off a case because it's too much work." His voice was mocking, and he stared at her. His green eyes almost looked yellowish in the light, like a lion's. "How's that going to look to the client? Unprofessional. And that's what it looked like to me."

He stood and walked around his desk, stopping behind her chair.

She didn't turn around. She sat up straighter. "I was on four busy cases that year, three of them yours. More than any other litigation associate. And I hadn't had a day off in months."

"That can happen as a partner." He was still behind her. *Like a voice of doom.*

"I'm prepared for that," Audrey said. She still didn't turn around.

He walked back to his desk. Apparently, he didn't like looking at the back of her head. Point for her.

Malaburn shrugged. "It's a matter of emotional stability." He smiled thinly.

Audrey gasped. He was deliberately trying to provoke her. He was the one who seemed unstable. She could feel her skin flushing on her face and neck. She counted to three in her head and thought of the yoga teacher's chant. *Let it wash over you.* "I can handle a demanding workload, as I've done during my career here. Even that fall, I was still on three cases." Her voice wavered. She stood. "Let me know what you decide about my proposed argument. I've got to run to another meeting."

"We need more research on your two last points. They're not compelling. I'll expect a revised brief Wednesday," Malaburn said.

"You'll have it."

"And take out that risky argument," he said.

And he was criticizing her for not being aggressive.

She escaped from his office to the bathroom, where she washed her face with cold water to lessen the redness. She'd change the ending of the letter. That was easy enough. And not let his digs get to her. That was harder. He was just striking out at her—trying to throw her. He wanted a reason to say no to her bid for partner. She wasn't going to give him one. She straightened her shoulders in the mirror and took a deep breath. It was time to be "on" again.

She rushed to her first meeting with Colette and the rest of the team. Hunter had asked Audrey to run this first meeting to give Colette time to catch up, although Colette should feel free to interject her own thoughts. Audrey feared that "interjection."

Winnie and three other junior associates were gathered around the long cherry wood conference table. Colette was leaning back in her chair, arms crossed. In-house counsel from Hen Bank, Genevieve, had also joined them. Genevieve looked all-business as she leaned forward, notepad on the table, pen in hand, her curly black hair pulled back by a barrette, but her stylish violet glasses made Audrey think that she'd be fun to befriend. Audrey wished that Genevieve wasn't there to witness her first joint meeting with Colette; she had no idea how Colette was going to act.

Audrey launched into a discussion of the case.

"For our first argument—that Pierre called John to make the trade—we have the phone records as evidence. Mohan, were you able to get the recording of John's call to his analyst Mike relaying that Pierre had just called him to make the trade?"

"Yes, yesterday," Mohan said, a fifth-year associate on the case.

"What does it say?"

"It matches exactly what John told us in his interview."

"Excellent. That's huge," Audrey said.

"For the second argument, everyone please look for a written authorization by Pierre. And continue to tag any documents showing that a higher level of supervision is being exercised over the account to ensure the trader makes appropriate trades on behalf of the client. Also, let's do a thorough review of prior trades to find out Pierre's trading history. Is he himself a risky trader? We want to argue that this trade was not excessive, consistent with past trades, and appropriate for Pierre. Mohan and Marcia, can you work with our expert witness on that?"

They nodded yes.

"Any emails or other documents in any way related to Pierre should be tagged. I still question why Pierre destroyed a twenty-year family friendship for a $200,000 trade, especially since I believe John that Pierre was the one who wanted to make the trade."

"Two hundred thousand dollars is a lot of money," Colette said.

"For me, yes, but Pierre's a multi-millionaire. Hasn't he had trades go bad before? Maybe we should look for that," Audrey said.

"Would that actually help?" Colette asked. "Wouldn't that hurt us because it would show that he has lost money on trades before and not sued?"

"That's true," Audrey said. "But we should be prepared for that argument in case the plaintiff raises it." She looked at her notes.

"Marcia, you were running some French news searches to see if there's any talk of Pierre being in financial difficulties. Anything?"

"No," Marcia said. "It seems to be the opposite. His company's about to invest in some huge deal."

"Are you seriously spending time trying to find another motive for his suit?" Colette asked. Audrey flushed. Mohan looked at Marcia with raised eyebrows. Audrey could only imagine what Genevieve was thinking.

"Yes," Audrey said evenly. "If it is Pierre's word against John's, then it helps if we can find another motive, because that might impact Pierre's credibility to our benefit. A jury might be less likely to believe him over John." Winnie looked like she wanted to add something, but Audrey gave a tiny shake of her head, indicating not to get involved.

Colette raised her eyebrows. "You shouldn't be using Marcia for that. She's more valuable doing *legal* work, not following some hope that this is a soap opera drama."

Audrey could feel her face heating up. "Marcia is the only one who reads French. It's a twenty-year friendship. John made very clear in our meeting that he's shocked by Pierre's accusation."

"If the friendship is so valuable, maybe John should repay the money himself. He's pretty wealthy as well."

"That would set a strange precedent. John's not the one who wanted to make the trade. He's not the one at fault," Audrey said.

"Still, that shows how valuable the friendship is. Money trumps friendship. There is no other motive. It's not like it's all 'pure friendship' on John's side either. He benefitted from being able to pull Pierre in as a significant client when he was starting out. That certainly helped propel his career."

Audrey was silent. It was likely that money was the sole reason, but a different motive could change the whole paradigm of the case. Looking at the case solely through a "legal" lens was too limiting. And she felt sorry for Colette if she believed money trumped friendship. But arguing that point further with Colette didn't seem productive, particularly not in front of Genevieve.

"Is Marcia assigned to the defensive discovery team?" Colette asked. Audrey nodded reluctantly. Colette inclined her head and wrote more notes.

Audrey took a deep breath, discussed their third topic, and then said that each of the associates would take a deposition. Audrey and Colette shared tips on preparing for depositions and promised they'd practice with each person to make sure they were ready. Audrey wrapped up the meeting, and the junior associates left the room. She was left alone with Colette and Genevieve. Genevieve said goodbye and walked towards the door.

Colette said to Audrey, "We shouldn't waste Marcia's time reading the French news, so I'm asking you to stop requesting that of her. I'm in charge of defensive discovery, she's assigned to the defensive discovery team, and I need her full-time on defensive discovery."

"Are you sure? I really think it could help with motive."

Colette rolled her eyes. "Yes, I'm positive."

Audrey left the meeting deflated. Maybe she was not "serious enough" for pursuing this non-legal argument. She jumped when Genevieve popped up around the corner.

"I overheard your conversation with Colette," she said.

"I'm sorry. It probably sounded unprofessional."

Genevieve shrugged. "Politics can be brutal in-house too. I can speak French. And both Mr. and Mrs. Rothman raised that same question. They don't understand any of this. Why would Pierre do this? John is checking with his contacts in the French financial community to see if there are any rumors about Pierre's financial straits."

"I think it has to do with Pierre's wife. Isn't she the connection between the two couples?"

"Yes. Really? Why?"

"You're going to think I'm ridiculous. Do you have some time to come to my office?"

"Sure."

The women walked down the hall. "I went to the library at the French Institute on Madison Avenue," Audrey said. "I searched on Pierre through their digital French magazine collection, and it looks like he and his wife stopped attending events socially together in the past six months. Before that, they were always together. I'll show you the articles I copied."

When they reached her office, Audrey pulled out her copies and showed them to Genevieve on her desk. Pierre and his wife were pictured together in photographs. "And then starting about six months ago, right before this trade, it's just him." She showed the pictures of Pierre alone at various French art galas. She said, "Oh, and I should mention that I didn't bill you for this. I went there on my free time—because I was curious. It's not legal research."

"Wow. When you see all the pictures of them together, and then this absence, it is striking. Unless his wife Laila is sick too."

"Yes, I thought that too. That would be bad, both for Laila and the case. It would make Pierre more sympathetic—maybe he needs the money for some treatment for her. But we still don't want to find that out as a surprise during the trial."

"It seems unlikely that both wives could be sick at the same time. Mrs. Rothman will be interested in this. She may have some insight. Can I have a copy?" Genevieve asked.

"Of course. As you know, Colette thinks I'm completely crazy to be thinking about this. I'm glad if anyone is interested. I don't know how to get any further, though. If Mrs. Rothman has any suggestions or thoughts, please let me know."

"I will. It's good you thought about why. It shows a willingness to think outside the box."

Chapter Nineteen

She sipped her steaming tea, breathing in its fruity smell, hoping it would revive her. She hadn't slept well last night. Even after the encouraging meeting with Genevieve, she'd been upset about Colette challenging her. Still, there had been moments when they'd worked well together at that team meeting. She had to foster that. She also didn't understand why Malaburn was reluctant to proceed with her suggested argument. And she needed to persuade Malaburn that she was not "too nice" but still *be* nice. She definitely didn't want to end up like him.

She opened up Colette's reply to her team email.

To: Audrey Willems
From: Colette Caron
Date: Tuesday, September 14
Subject: Please Circulate Deposition Outline

Dear Audrey,

Thanks so much for drafting and circulating your summary of our team meeting.

Also, per Hunter, please circulate a draft of your deposition outline when done.

Regards, Colette

Audrey narrowed her eyes as she read the email. She was probably being too sensitive, but Colette seemed to be asserting herself as the dominant senior associate.

Gertrude knocked at the door and said that Mrs. Whitaker had called with a list of gluten-free, salt-free caterers to meet and taste-test. Audrey looked at the list in shock. Twenty names were on the list. She didn't have time to attend taste-tests. This wasn't a wedding. It was a departure party—all right, a departure party after a long and distinguished career, but still. She'd tell Mrs. Whitaker to hire whatever caterer she liked; Audrey didn't have to attend the tastings. She called Mrs. Whitaker and suggested that, but Mrs. Whitaker insisted that Audrey come along because she'd been eating without salt or gluten for so long that she wasn't sure what others would find delicious. Audrey asked her assistant to coordinate some dates with Mrs. Whitaker. It would be just her luck if Malaburn came looking for her when she was out of the office eating cake with Mrs. Whitaker.

She re-read Colette's email. *Should I ask Winnie what she thinks? Or just let it go?* She decided it was too subtle to address without looking thin-skinned. She would let it pass.

Chapter Twenty

Returning home after a late-night dinner with Winnie, Audrey popped in on Eve to ask her advice on how to handle Colette. Eve was curled up on her couch reading a cookbook, with index cards spread out all around her, brainstorming recipes. Pete was traveling again this week.

She plopped down on Eve's couch. "How was your week? Did Chef Burns approve your new dessert for the menu?"

"He did. He actually mmm'd when eating it." Eve grinned. "So satisfying. And your week?"

"I'm so happy for you. Not that good. I need your advice on Colette. And Winnie started meeting with headhunters to look for another job."

"Why?"

"She doesn't want to work these hours. The Texas trip was the last straw. But I'll be so sad if Winnie leaves. She's my last close girlfriend at the firm."

"You'll still see Winnie. And if she's the client, you can take her out for dinner. How about some dessert to cheer you up? I just finished making concord grape sorbet and pumpkin spice cookies, and I need a guinea pig." Eve jumped up and disappeared into her kitchen.

"Sounds delicious." Audrey smiled.

Eve reappeared and handed her a bowl of sorbet with two cookies. Sitting cross-legged, Audrey happily savored the sorbet. "Mmm. This is so good." She finished and put the empty bowl down on the coffee table. "These cookies too. Just the right hint of spiciness. They're much better than anything I would've eaten out with Winnie."

Eve smiled. "They're good, aren't they?" The kettle whistled, and Eve went into the kitchen.

Audrey followed her. "What's happening at the restaurant?"

"Ugh, this new management, it's a mess. Chef Burns said he's looking at other options—with a position for me as executive pastry chef." A huge smile spread across Eve's face.

"Yes!" Audrey high-fived Eve. "I'm so happy for you." She reached over and gave her friend a big hug. Eve had worked hard for this and put up with a lot. It wasn't easy working as a woman in a professional kitchen, which were mostly male-dominated. Eve had chosen pastry in part because pastry had its own space.

"It'll be good. I'm working on my menu. I can't believe I can actually say that." Eve did a little shimmy. "Pete bought me this mug to celebrate." She held it out, displaying the slogan emblazoned in pink script across Eve's white mug: *Chef. Because Badass isn't an official title.*

"Aww. I can't wait to make a reservation," Audrey said.

Returning to the living room with their mugs, they discussed Eve's menu choices. And then Eve asked what had happened with

Colette. Audrey hugged one of Eve's dark-red tasseled throw pillows. "I had such a disturbing conversation with Tim. He warned me against Colette. He said she thinks it's a competition between me and her as the two women vying for partner."

Eve shifted to face her. "Maybe Tim is trying to pit you against each other."

"I considered that as well, except that Colette isn't very friendly and does seem to be challenging my actions."

"That's annoying."

"It really is." Audrey shook her head. "But maybe I'm just being sensitive."

Eve sat up. "I'm sure you're right. You shouldn't doubt yourself. And don't let her make you question yourself."

Audrey sighed. "I just don't need this."

"What's your game plan?" Eve asked. "When I was first hired and that guy was hassling me all the time, I had to show him not to mess with me. Remember, he was always calling me offensive names, and then he switched my sugar and salt. And I made these horrible cookies, although luckily, I tasted one before I sent them out, but still, I was so behind. And then I made a regular batch for the kitchen staff for our communal dinner dessert, but gave him one from the bad batch." Eve laughed. "Oh, the expression on his face."

Audrey laughed. "That was brilliant."

"He never messed with me again." Eve chuckled.

"The thing is, I don't see the benefit to scoring points off Colette. That won't help either of us to make partner. Even if I make her look incompetent, which she isn't, I'll look bad. And that's not the way I want to make partner. But I also don't want to be a total wimp and pushover for her. I get so annoyed with my mom when I think she is being too accommodating so as to not ruffle any male feathers in her department. I need to convince Colette that we should work together."

"Good luck with that." Eve poured more tea. "What's happening with Jake?"

"Jake told his sister that he wants to stay single when I was with him at his sister's. I thought he was romantically interested before, but I think now it's just friends. He hasn't called to set up a date, and he seems like he's the type who would if he was interested."

"He definitely seems like the go-getter type."

"And frankly, how can I date him now when I'm up for partner? Work is crazy right now," Audrey said.

"If he was interested, I'd say you still need to go for it, even with work."

"And lose out on making partner?"

"You're not going to lose out on making partner by dating someone. He'll support your goals."

Audrey nodded. Even if Jake did not support the goal of making law firm partner, she still couldn't help liking him. "Hey, I was planning to throw that party in October to showcase your catering. Do you still want to do it if you're about to become an executive pastry chef?"

"Yes, definitely. I'm closer to my dream, but I'm not there yet. And I like keeping my options open."

"Except for Pete."

"Well, Pete stole my heart on our third date when he convinced the bread chef at our favorite bakery to give us a lesson. Sometimes it's pretty clear when they're keepers." Eve yawned.

"Pete's definitely a keeper." Audrey stood. "I'll let you get to bed. But thanks for listening to me."

Eve rose too and gave Audrey a hug. "Any time. I'm here for you. And you're in the home stretch—only three more months until the announcement, and then you won't have to worry about that."

"Unless I don't make it."

"Don't even go there."

"I know. As Mom would say, eyes on the prize, don't let doubts deter you." Audrey washed her bowl in the sink.

"Well, your mom's right that you have to think positively, but your mom also knew exactly what she wanted, I mean, in terms of her career. She wanted to be a professor of French literature."

"What are you trying to say?"

"I love cooking, but I don't know what the right prize is. For now, it's to be an executive pastry chef. But later on, I don't know. I just think you have to be open to possibilities."

"I am trying to be open to the possibility of dating Jake," Audrey said.

"And I'm proud of you." Eve hugged her. "It's hard when jobs require so much sacrifice of your outside life."

Audrey sighed. "I'm going to need some of those cookies to go. And don't you dare send any to Jake. Right now, he thinks I make very good cookies."

Chapter Twenty-One

Friday, New York City

Dear Jake,

I baked these cookies from the recipe in Love in a Cookie Bakery. *These cookies are VERY GOOD. They taste best with milk, so feel free to pop by again if you're out.*

I'm looking forward to reading the book too. I gather you weren't able to find a book called Love in a Law Firm?

Best,
Audrey

Audrey slipped through the fence between their backyards and left the cookies with the note outside his sliding glass door. Then she rushed off to her morning meeting with Mrs. Whitaker to sample salt-free, gluten-free food. Please, let the first caterer be great so they could hire her and be done.

Chapter Twenty-Two

*A*udrey settled into her lounge chair to spend her Saturday morning escaping into *Love in the Cookie Bakery* and go into the office around 2 p.m. She hid her romantic comedy behind a law treatise in case her psychiatrist neighbors looked over the fence. She didn't want them psycho-analyzing her taste in literature.

She was so engaged in the book that she almost didn't hear Jake ask, from over the fence, "Want to go for a bike ride?"

A bike ride was not in the plans. She had piles of work waiting at the office. But she'd definitely forgo reading for an hour bike ride with Jake.

"Sure. What are you going to wear?" she asked.

"Is there usually a dress code?"

"The last person I met for a bike ride was dressed head to toe in a black bike-racing speedo outfit."

"No way."

She just nodded as Jake eased through the hole in the fence.

"A law treatise made you giggle?" he asked. She looked up in guilty surprise as he grabbed the treatise. "Caught you red-handed. So much for Shakespeare. Hope that book is as good as your cookies."

"You seem to have very good taste in romance novels. Is that based on experience?" she asked.

"Just good at reading the Amazon summaries." He smiled.

"So, are you going to be dressed in a speedo?"

"Red speedo, but it has a cape as well. Aren't you holding out for a superhero?"

Recognizing the title of the Bonnie Tyler song, she continued the riff: "Only if you're faster than the speed of light."

As did Jake: "That's definitely asking for a heartache."

"That's on my heartache playlist!"

"You have a heartache playlist?"

"You don't?"

"I do." He looked intently at her. "It's one of the reasons I love music. If I want to motivate myself or cheer myself up, I just play certain music."

"Me too." She reverted to their initial topic. "I would love to go, but my Wonder Woman costume was damaged in my last rescue mission—can I go incognito as a normal human?"

"Much preferred. See you outside in fifteen?"

She nodded.

Fifteen minutes later, she wheeled her bike out front. She snapped on her helmet.

"What's in the backpack?" Jake asked.

"Suntan lotion, picnic blanket, water and a bare minimum of food supplies in case we get hungry." *And no work phone.* There was no way her job was going to interfere this time, and she didn't trust herself not to check her phone if she brought it.

"And there's no vendor within sight?"

"What can I say? I get grumpy when hungry. I like to be prepared."

"Spoken like a true scout." He asked, "Any chance you've got some of your homemade chocolate chip cookies in there?"

"I gave all the homemade ones to you except for those I sampled to make sure they were edible. But I have some apples and some power bars."

"Wine?"

"I thought we were going for a bike trip."

"I'm not the one who brought an emergency food supply." He biked towards Columbus Avenue. "Let's pick up cookies at Levain Bakery."

"Now you're thinking."

They biked over to Levain Bakery, and she held the bikes and his helmet while he went inside.

"This completely defeats the purpose of the bike ride," she said as he handed her the bag of heavy cookies and she added them to her knapsack.

"Depends on the purpose. I'm thinking of a fun afternoon enjoying the view of the Hudson River and the park." He biked ahead. Audrey kicked herself mentally, thinking that maybe the online dating algorithm understood her better than she did herself, and Dan really was her right match—why, oh, why had she said that the purpose of a bike ride was exercise? She was doomed to a life of fly-fishing lectures. She raced to catch up to Jake and pulled next to him at the red light.

"Okay, up or down along the river?" she asked.

"We're heading up. I have the afternoon planned, including dinner."

The whole day. Including dinner. Audrey buzzed with excitement, but she couldn't. She should go into work. She really should. And she had left her work phone at home. She couldn't even check it in the bathroom. He bicycled ahead towards the river. But she'd regretted it the last time she had ditched their date to write a brief. She might not get another chance. She could work really late on Sunday and Monday.

She caught up. "I'm impressed. I love going for bike rides. I did a semester abroad in Amsterdam and I loved that I could bike everywhere."

"One of my best summer jobs was working as a travel editor for my college's travel guide. I covered Holland one year, so I spent the summer there. I loved it," Jake said. They passed the bronze statue of Eleanor Roosevelt and entered Riverside Park.

"My semester abroad at the University of Amsterdam ranks as one of the best times of my life," she said. She'd been "off." The classes had been stimulating yet doable.

As they entered the biking lane by the Hudson River, Audrey glanced over at the rippled blue water. A few sailboats floated out and about; a tugboat chugged up the Hudson. Across the river, New Jersey's coasts were green forest with tall beige buildings poking out like sentinels.

"I did a year abroad in Australia. Great fun. If music hadn't taken off, I might've moved back there after college."

They swapped stories about their adventures abroad, laughing out loud as each sought to impress the other. Jake won. They moved to bike single file to allow another person to pass and then returned to biking next to each other. She breathed in the salty air.

"Okay," Jake said. "Top five favorite countries that you'd return to in a heartbeat."

"Holland, United Kingdom, Kenya, Costa Rica, Spain. You?" she asked.

"Australia, Kenya, Vietnam, Italy, Scandinavia."

"Scandinavia is not a country," she said.

"Technicality. It's a way of living. I covered Denmark the year after Holland."

"Not Sweden?"

"Lost out to the guy who spoke Swedish," he said. They bicycled comfortably up the Hudson River.

"What'd you like about their philosophy of living?" she asked.

Jake stopped his bike and looked out over the river: "That you should take the time to enjoy life and it's not all about making more money. It's about making time for friends and your relationships. Something *hygge* can be a good meal, candles, and friends over." He turned to look at her as if to gauge her reaction.

Audrey, stopping her bike next to his, returned his gaze. "Yes," she said. "I wish I knew how to be better at that." She did. But today was a step in that direction.

He nodded. Their eyes met as if some bond had just formed. They cycled up the path.

Audrey's bike suddenly swerved. The back tire was deflating.

"I have a flat," she said, dismayed, and stopped her bike. A flat back tire was about to torpedo this outing that was going so well. So much for her backpack of supplies.

Jake got off his bike to take a look.

She said, "I'm so sorry. I can google bike shops nearby."

"No need. I have a tire repair kit."

"Now who's the scout? Do you think you can fix it? That's cool."

"We could also stop here and eat some of your snacks. This looks like a good spot. Why don't you set up a picnic while I try to fix your tire?" They wheeled the bikes over to a grassy spot in the lawn beside some trees. Salsa music was playing in the distance, punctuated by the happy shouts and cries of kids playing soccer nearby. He turned her bike upside down and pumped up the tube to find the air hole.

"Where'd you learn how to fix a flat tire—Holland?" she asked.

"Boy Scout training,"

"I didn't know they had Boy Scout troops in NYC." She spread out the picnic blanket and unpacked the water bottles and the cookies.

"Haven't you met any other NYC Boy Scouts?"

"Not that I know. But then I'm not an elderly lady trying to cross the street. Although you did save that little boy from scootering into the street. You might have to show me some of your other Boy Scout skills, like building a fire, before I believe you," she teased.

He paused in his fixing of the tire to meet her gaze. "I'm pretty good at building a fire. And you?"

She felt herself heat up under his gaze.

"I probably need a little practice," she said, flustered.

He turned the bike right-side up, cleaned the grease off his hands with wipes from his bike repair kit, and lay down on the blanket next to her. *He was so close.* Her pulse beat faster. The silence between them lengthened. The background salsa music was a drumming beat matching her heartbeat. The salty air from the Hudson mixed with the smell of dirt from the ground. She was afraid to move. If she touched him, she felt like she'd ignite an electric shock. A seagull soared in the sky above them.

He rolled back up to sit on the blanket and made some joke about the best cookies in New York. She laughed, but she was on edge, her pulse hammering, not sure if she should say something to indicate she liked him as more than a friend. When he handed her a cookie on a napkin, his fingers lingered while touching hers.

Whoosh. A soccer ball from the game nearby rolled right next to them. Jake stood and kicked the ball back. And when he sat, talking about his soccer league, the mood was lighter.

The rest of the afternoon flew by. They biked at a comfortable pace, chatting companionably and laughing—with hints of flirtation. They ate dinner at a café in Inwood, at the top of Manhattan, overlooking the river. Jake texted his dog walker to ask him to walk Biscuit.

"What are you doing in the city on a summer weekend? I thought you'd be in the Hamptons or somewhere else." Audrey finished her dinner and sat back.

"I covered a concert last night, so it was a late night. And I promised my sister I'd babysit tomorrow so she could go out on a brunch date with her friends. And you—how are you out on a Saturday?"

That was a good question, and she bit her lip as she contemplated how honest to be. "I was planning to go into the office, but this seemed like a better option." She smiled ruefully at Jake.

He grinned. "Then let's make your playing hooky count. Let's check out a jazz show in Harlem after dinner. We could go to Bob's Place or the Smoke Jazz Club. Have you been to either?"

"No, but I'm up for anything. I'm not exactly dressed for it."

"Well, neither am I, but it's a casual place. We'll be fine. Let's go to Bob's—it's a classic. Bob's started as a speakeasy in 1920. That whole area was known as swing street because of the number of speakeasys there."

"That's so cool. I've always wanted to go to a speakeasy. Do you cover jazz artists?"

"No, I prefer not to work on my weekends, if I can help it, especially since I worked last night. I just like jazz. I'll call to make sure we can get in."

"What music do you cover?"

"Alternative pop." He called Bob's as Audrey unlocked her bike.

Their headlights shone straight ahead as they cycled down the bike path in silence in the deepening dark. Pools of luminescence from the street lamps punctuated the murkiness. Across the Hudson River, they could see the lights of New Jersey. The air was cooler, but not cold.

At 145th Street, they headed east and left the park, riding single file down the brownstone-lined streets until they reached Bob's Place.

They locked up their bikes. A man wearing a jaunty fedora was sitting on the stoop in front of the lamppost.

Jake said, "Lenny here is like the neighborhood watchman. Can you look after our bikes, Lenny?" He handed a five-dollar bill to the man on the stoop.

Lenny nodded. "You got it."

"I've left my bike here before, so it'll be okay."

"I'm not too worried someone's going to want my bike," she said.

Swinging their bike helmets, they walked towards the door of Bob's Place, which had only a small sign announcing its presence, befitting its history as a former speakeasy. In the entry hall, Jake chatted briefly with the woman who was taking the money, introducing Audrey and asking after a friend in common. Bob's Place seemed to be a ground floor railroad apartment, and the jazz set was performed in an elongated living room. The "stage" was a slightly elevated platform taking up most of the living room, with space for only one row of chairs in front of it. Those were already filled, but Jake guided her to the back, his hand lightly touching the small of her back. They passed through an open archway into the adjoining room where he grabbed two seats with a view of the band.

"Or we can sit out in the garden, but this is better for seeing the band," he said.

"This is perfect." And she meant it. She couldn't believe that she was out with Jake in a former speakeasy.

She held the seats while he made his way to the bar, saying hello to several people. He started talking with one person, gesturing towards her. Glasses clinked, and the general buzz of conversation and rustling as guests settled in heightened the vibe of expectation. The crowd seemed to be a mix of locals and out-of-towners, and the atmosphere was friendly, as if she were at a party at a friend's house. Three Scandinavians sat in front of her, speaking Swedish. Several musicians came out and started warming up, chatting comfortably with the people sitting right in front of them. She inadvertently made eye contact with the drummer, and he winked at her and she smiled back. Then the lights dimmed, and Jake slipped back into his seat. As he handed her a soda, the music filled the room without even an introduction. The band began with one of her favorites, "Begin the Beguine," and the clear clarinet notes seemed to pierce the hushed crowd.

When the song finished, the band leader, Bill, introduced the players and shared some history. The pianist then played the opening notes of "Just One of Those Things" while Bill sang, the trumpet joining in. The venue was so intimate that she could see the musicians communicate with each other as each played off the other. She could not stop herself from moving to the rhythm. She looked at Jake, who was also nodding his head to the music and tapping his foot, and their glances caught and he smiled. He moved to hold her hand. She squeezed his hand back. The last line of "Just One of Those Things" was apt for the day—today had been like "a trip to the moon."

She had entered another New York world—completely different from the one that she lived in. It wasn't as if she had not been to jazz clubs in New York City—she had been to some downtown clubs—but this was different. It was like being a part of the whole jazz scene rather than just watching a show.

"And we've got our very own emerging star in our midst. Where's Emmeline?" Bill asked. "I know I saw her. Emmeline, come up and sing a set with us."

From the back of the room emerged a young Black woman in a flowing green dress. She walked up and took the mic from Bill. After some whispered conferring, Bill snapped his fingers, the drummer picked up the tempo, and Emmeline's clear soprano rang out over the room: "It don't mean a thing . . ."

She then sang scat, her voice flipping up and down the scales. The abilities of scat singers to improvise vocally and imitate a physical instrument always amazed Audrey. The whole club roared its approval when Emmeline finished and gave her a standing ovation.

Bill asked for any requests, and someone yelled out "Stardust" from the back of the room. Bill took a few more requests, and then the band continued with some songs that Audrey had never heard before with lots of improvisation and solos, leading up to a crescendo finish. The audience gave another standing ovation, and then the band retreated from the stage, taking their time to talk to some of the audience members. A warm glow seemed to pervade both Audrey and the club atmosphere.

"That was magical," she said, and Jake nodded. Their gazes caught. He understood, and she didn't need to say more.

Chapter Twenty-Three

*A*s Audrey and Jake waited to pick up their bike helmets from the coat check in the narrow hallway, she moved closer to Jake to make room for passersby. It was like stepping closer to a fire. He was studying her. She returned his gaze. His look was intense.

She swallowed. *Don't say anything.* She could inadvertently say something to ruin the mood, or even worse, put them in the friend zone. A crowded hallway waiting in line for coats was even worse for making conversation than being alone in an elevator with a partner.

His phone beeped. Then it rang. Checking the number, he answered it.

"Fiona," he said.

"Are you serious?" he asked. "No, I'm not home. I'm at Bob's Place in Harlem—the jazz club." He listened to his sister. "No, I'm not alone. I'm with Audrey." He ruffled his hair distractedly.

"We're on bikes. I guess I can be there in about thirty minutes. What do you want me to do?" After a brief pause, he said, "Sure." He hung up. "Great." He looked ruefully at Audrey. "My sister and Luna have some stomach bug. They're both throwing up, so she asked me to come help. Luna woke up and threw up in her bed. Fiona took her to her bed, and then Luna threw up in that, although mostly on the towel. Fiona then puked too—and not just from cleaning up the vomit. So now both of them are hugging the toilet in the bathroom. Thomas luckily is still sleeping and seems okay. She wants me to come over and sleep on the couch in case Thomas wakes up, because if she's still sick, she doesn't want to infect him. And I should put the sheets in the wash."

"That's terrible." In more ways than one. *So close.* Jake handed in the ticket for their helmets, and they went out the door. The warm evening air hit Audrey like an embrace. It would have been such a perfect night to bike home and invite Jake over. Audrey clipped on her helmet. They thanked Lenny for watching their bikes.

"Should I come with you?" she asked. "I can help with the laundry."

"Ha! That'd serve Fiona right—if she met you again in her current state," he said. "But I don't think she'd ever forgive me. And this might be contagious. Now that'd be a ploy from *Pride and Prejudice.* Doesn't Mrs. Bennett send Elizabeth over in the rain so she gets sick and has to stay at Bingley's house?"

"Ha, but not a stomach bug. That's a little hard to work with if you're trying to seduce someone."

Jake stilled, but then smiled at her. "Especially in front of your sister."

They unlocked their bikes. Jake looked over at her and shook his head.

"Here, let me check your helmet, since we're biking home at night." He adjusted the helmet on her head and then tightened the straps, his fingers lightly touching her face. It looked as if he might lean down and kiss her. Suddenly the door opened from Bob's Place, light spilling out onto the sidewalk, and a chatty crowd descended the brownstone steps.

Jake smiled wryly, and his hands left her.

"Let's go down the St. Nicholas bike path. That's probably the safest route."

She nodded yes.

As he turned on his bike light, he glanced at her and said, "You didn't check your work phone once today."

"No," Audrey said. "I'm trying."

Jake looked like he wanted to say something, but then he nodded and started pedaling.

Chapter Twenty-Four

*I*t was back to work on Sunday—back to reality after Saturday night's enchantment. Audrey felt like she'd dreamt it—until the end. The end was in line with her usual luck in dating. Something seemed about to happen, but then disaster.

An email from Genevieve reported that Mrs. Rothman was obsessed with the articles showing Pierre and his wife no longer attending social events together. Mrs. Rothman had reached out to another friend in common. That friend had just been in Paris on vacation and inadvertently bumped into Pierre's wife, Laila. Laila looked healthy and was just about to leave for the south of France with the grandchildren. Laila had asked after Mrs. Rothman, seeming to indicate she was sorry for her husband suing John.

It seemed as if there was no issue other than money. Colette was right. She should stop chasing false premises and focus solely on the legal arguments.

Winnie knocked on her door and entered, shutting the door behind her.

"Did you hear about our firm's failed pitch to Peters Securities to defend their money laundering litigation?" Winnie asked. "White & Gilman won it—and Tim worked on it."

"I heard. I can't believe White & Gilman beat us," Audrey said, her tone serious. "I'm sure the partnership was counting on that business. Peters Securities was one of our main clients. We've been their outside litigation firm for years. And now we're not. It's bad." The atmosphere on the litigation floors of the firm had felt tense as the news had filtered down.

"Is Tim upset?" Winnie asked.

"Hard to tell with Tim. Stiff upper lip and all that."

"You should be careful what you tell Tim. I don't trust those two. I see him and Colette together a lot now."

Audrey nodded. She had noticed that too, but her concern was more their allying against her for partnership than the loss of Tim as a romantic prospect—especially given her zingy flirtation with Jake.

Audrey mused, "Maybe they get the best of Tim and me if they make Colette a partner."

"Colette's not the best of both of you. They just get a smart woman. And she doesn't care about mentoring young associates. Nor does Tim. They should've pushed Colette to next year for partnership. I understand that she was a star during her clerkship, but still, next year, she would've been a shoo-in."

"She wouldn't have come here if they hadn't agreed that she was still on the same partner track timeline. She's good at negotiating, you've got to give her that."

"They get the best of Tim and Colette if they make you a partner. They get a smart woman who's also collegial like Tim. You should think of it like that," Winnie said.

Audrey smiled wryly, warmed by Winnie's support. "I'll try. Thanks."

"Anyway, I'm heading home now. Jae and I have a cooking class tonight," Winnie said.

"That'll be fun."

"If we manage not to burn the food, ourselves, or the teacher."

The door of the neighboring office was locked shut. It was already past seven. As she scribbled some notes in the margin of a document, Tim popped his head into her office.

"What are you working on?" he asked.

"I'm writing my outline for direct questions and the cross for my trial witnesses—and I am finishing up a strategy memo for Hunter. I'll be here late." Audrey sighed and rested her head on her hand.

"Feel like talking your strategy out? Sometimes that helps me." He leaned against her doorway.

"Thanks for the offer, but right now, I just want to finish up my direct and cross. Talking about it will just add to my stress that I haven't finished it yet."

"Okay, but I'm here if you want. I can read it over when you're done and give you my thoughts."

"I have a feeling I'll be working on it until I hand it in," Audrey said.

"Well, could you look over one of my briefs? I'd really appreciate your insights. Whenever you look over my stuff, you add so much. I feel like you're my good luck charm."

She frowned. That's what Kevin had called her. He'd always wanted her to look over his briefs. She had been doing a lot of his work, too, as she had researched additional angles and improved his arguments. She had forgotten that. In the end, she hadn't been much of a good luck charm for him.

Tim's gaze lingered. She hadn't been hanging out with Tim much lately. She felt differently towards him and was wary given Winnie's observations about him and Colette. But she and Tim had spent a lot of late nights these past two years bouncing ideas and strategies off each other. She didn't want to cut that off, although she didn't need the additional work of looking over his brief. But politically, she wanted to keep him on her side.

He said, "Frankly, I'm worried about my partnership chances because of the failed pitch."

"I think you'll still make it." She wanted to console him, but she didn't know what else to say. She was the one who might not make it because she didn't fit the mold. She couldn't express how she didn't fit—other than not being particularly preppy—she just felt it. "Sure, I'll look over your brief, but not tonight."

"Great. What's happening with the Rothman case? Are you getting along with Colette?" Tim asked.

That was a weird question to ask, given that he was friends with both of them. "As well as can be expected," Audrey said.

Tim held her gaze, then he nodded and left. *Hmm, those intense looks.* Like he was attracted to her. But he was also getting closer to Colette. Keeping all options open. Which made her sad if he thought that either one of them would do. Or if it was just for making partner purposes. *I'll drive myself crazy trying to figure it out instead of getting my work done.* Audrey turned back to work.

Chapter Twenty-Five

*A*udrey closed her apartment door and dropped her bag on the floor. Ten p.m. She shouldn't have worked so late on a Sunday—now she'd be tired the rest of the week. But she'd wanted to accomplish as much as she could so she had more flexibility to be available if Jake called.

She should try that face mask cream—before it expired—and watch some TV to unwind before going to bed. She walked down the stairs to her bathroom. She splashed her face and opened the mirrored cabinet to find that cream. She hated that she felt compelled to buy products she would never use after listening to the facialist sales pitch. *Shit!* Out of the corner of her eye, she saw a black scurrying movement. *Ugh!* A huge water bug in the tub. And Pete and Eve were away this week for vacation. Okay, she could handle this. She just had to get the vacuum cleaner. She hurriedly backed out of the bathroom and closed the door, stuffing a towel under the door so that the sucker couldn't crawl out into her bedroom.

Water bugs were at the top of the short list of things she hated about summer in New York. She grabbed the vacuum cleaner and rubber gloves from the closet. She pulled her socks up over her work pants so the bug couldn't crawl up her legs. She pulled her hair into a ponytail and wrapped a scarf around her hair. She didn't want it flying into her hair. She pulled on the rubber gloves. *Ugh.* Okay, she was going back in. She removed the towel. Holding the vacuum cleaner hose like a weapon, she gently opened the door and scanned the bathroom. It was still in the bathtub, its antennas moving back and forth.

She turned on the vacuum cleaner and lunged for it. And missed. *AAAGH.* She inadvertently closed her eyes as it zoomed at her and she waved the vacuum hose in front of her face. *Perfect.* It was one of the flying ones. It now taunted her from the corner of the ceiling. Great. She needed to call in reinforcements. And this was a good excuse to see Jake—although not the most romantic occasion. There are times in life when you have to acknowledge your weak points. She backed out again, closed the bathroom door, and re-positioned the towel under the door.

She carried the vacuum cleaner across the bedroom to the sliding door and put it down. She wanted her weapon at hand should the bug escape into the bedroom. She went outside into her garden and peeked over the fence. The light was on. Jake was up. She slipped through the hole in the fence and, with the dim light peeking through the curtained windows, carefully followed the path to his sliding door. She banged loudly on the glass. Biscuit barked.

Jake, pulling back the curtain and opening the sliding door, looked shocked. Jake was bare-chested. All hard muscle. She flushed.

"Wow, is this like a 1960s cleaning visit fantasy?" he asked. "Not that I ever had that dream, but you know, I do like the James Bonds from that period—especially the headscarves. I'm not sure about the socks over the pants though."

"Very funny. A giant water bug has invaded my bathroom, and I need you to kill it."

"You look pretty equipped to do the job yourself."

"Yes, well it's up in a corner I can't reach."

"Okay. But I'm not particularly fond of them myself."

"It's tough being a boy," she said.

"I thought you were one of those women who could do it all."

"No one can do it all. And I especially can't do water bugs."

He grabbed his t-shirt from the couch and pulled it on. He started to put on his sandals and stopped. "Do I need to add the socks?"

"I'd recommend it unless you don't mind if it crawls on your foot. You might want to put on long pants as well."

"Too hot. But I'll add the socks in case I try to step on it. I'd better get a heavy shoe as well. C'mon, Biscuit, we're going to battle a bug."

They walked back through the two gardens in the warm night air. Audrey opened the sliding door and picked up the vacuum cleaner, slinging the hose over her shoulder.

He said, "You know, it's the vacuum cleaner slung over your shoulder that really adds that flair."

"You're just jealous because you've only got a shoe."

"I hope you're going to share. Otherwise, I'm going back to get mine."

"It's all yours." She handed the vacuum cleaner over to him.

"Are you ready?" she asked as she prepared to remove the towel from the crack between the bathroom door and the floor.

"You really aren't taking any chances."

"I definitely don't want it in my bedroom." She slowly opened the door, and she and Jake quickly slipped into the bathroom, shutting the bathroom door behind them. The bathroom was small, with not much room for the two of them and the vacuum cleaner. Biscuit whined at the door.

"Sorry, Biscuit, I don't think you can fit in here too. Where is it?" he asked.

"It was up in the corner over there, above the cabinet. Let me see if it's still there." She stood on the inset tub wall again. "Yup, still there."

"I can't see it from here either. All right, you direct me and I'll try to get it with the hose."

"It's straight back in the corner."

"Going in!" He turned on the vacuum and pushed it quickly against the wall over the cabinet. He missed and it flew towards him, making him jump back and nearly hit her. "Fuck, it flies!"

"Sorry, forgot to mention it could fly."

"I should've guessed, but you didn't have a beekeeper hat on."

"No, but I do have the headscarf."

"At least I can see it now." He lunged again with the nozzle. "Got it."

"Let's leave the vacuum cleaner running so it definitely dies. I'll get some tinfoil to put over the nozzle."

"Sounds like you've done this before."

"There's at least one every summer," she said.

"Who usually kills them?"

"Pete. But he and Eve are on vacation. Unless they're the slow-moving, crawling type—in which case, I can kill it myself."

She went up the stairs to the kitchen, yelling down, "Would you also like a drink of water or something?"

"You really know how to treat a guy. Water would be great."

"It is a school night. Do you want beer instead?"

"Yes. You're telling me. I'm still shattered from being up last night dealing with the throw-up crisis. I was just about to go to bed."

"How is everybody?"

"All good by the morning. Just up all night. We all slept in."

She grabbed two beers from her refrigerator and the tinfoil. She came back down and put the tinfoil over the nozzle, reinforcing it with a rubber band.

He suggested they drink the beers in the garden. A frisson of anticipation zipped through her. They walked outside and settled into the two lounge chairs. Biscuit followed and climbed onto the bottom of Jake's chair to rest at his feet.

"It's a pity we can't see any stars," he said. The night sky was cloudy.

"Just the lights of other lives in the windows—far more interesting than stars."

"Spoken like a true New Yorker," he said. "Looking up at stars with the right person is good too, though."

"How do you know you've met the right person?"

"I don't know. I'm still figuring it out. I do have my top five questions."

"Really? What are those?" she asked, turning her head to look at him. He was shadowed in the dusk.

"Do you want to know all my secrets?"

"Only the good ones," she said. The lights of the next-door apartment came on, casting a warm glow over their chairs, illuminating their faces.

"Well, what if you wanted to get to know someone and you only had five questions—what would you ask?"

She bit her lip. "Difficult. Top five favorite books?"

"Yes. Here's another: five favorite countries to travel to or what five countries would you like to travel to?"

"You asked me that one." A zip of hope buoyed her. *Was Jake vetting her?*

"So I did. I also have to ask about musical taste and pets, because those could be deal-breakers for me. And then the fifth question is, what is your perfect day?"

"If they're from New York, I always ask what high school they went to, but I don't want that to be one of my top five."

"All right, you've three more questions—what would you ask?" he asked.

"Children—but I'd never straight up ask." An apartment light went out.

"Yes, it's easier for me to ask if she likes dogs, because I can sleuth it out when I bring up Biscuit. And I can sleuth out kids when she meets my sister's kids." He petted Biscuit.

Her pulse quickened. Had there been an ulterior motive behind the drop-off date? "Does your sister know you're using her kids as bait?"

"She suggested it. She'd be pissed at me if I didn't have kids and dogs as deal breakers. You have two more."

"I'm stealing yours: perfect day." The night air was invigorating, heightening her senses. Off in the distance, the slight hum of nighttime traffic buzzed. "And then my fifth is tell me about your friends."

"Good one. I'm still keeping musical taste. I'll probably meet her friends."

"I thought you'd borrow their iPhone to check out their music, as you did at my apartment."

"As I did indeed." He smiled. Their glances met.

"And did I pass?"

"You passed, but we can expand your repertoire from dance parties. But the main thing is not to fail."

"What would fail?"

"No music whatsoever."

She laughed. "All right, let's go to next top five—less pressure: beach or mountain person?"

"Both."

"Okay, that works." She asked, "Morning or night person?"

"Night." He raked his hand through his hair. "Or usually night. But since I was up all night with my sister and Luna, this beer might put me to sleep." He stretched out in the deck chair, looking relaxed. The clouds shifted above, forming frothy patterns in the sky, with hints of discernible shapes. The wind whispered, as if to promise more. And she hoped something would happen. "Next?"

"Bicycle or motorcycle?" she asked.

"Bicycle," he said.

"Really? I could see you on a motorcycle."

"I can't see you on a motorcycle."

"No, I'm too cautious for that." A pleasantly warm night breeze caressed her skin.

"And being a lawyer tends to strengthen that tendency, I've noticed. But I would say too smart," he said. "My turn: hamburger or foie gras."

"Hamburger." A cat meowed several backyards over, followed by the sound of a door opening and closing.

"My type of girl." He asked, "Comedy or drama?"

"Comedy. You?"

"Comedy clearly. I get enough drama in my job."

"Do you? Like what?" she asked.

"Like the talent deciding that they suddenly don't feel up to doing some radio promo I've set up for them," he said. "And you—any day-to-day drama in the law firm?"

"More than I'd like, lately."

"Like what?" he asked.

"The litigation department just lost a key bid to defend this big lawsuit. The client picked another firm, even though we've been their outside counsel for years. It's a huge loss. If the litigation department isn't doing well, they may not make us all partners."

Another apartment light went out. It was getting late.

"How many of you are up?" he asked.

"Four. One guy in London who seems to be a sure thing as he just closed a large corporate deal, a guy here, another woman, and me," she said. "The other woman thinks that the partnership will make only one woman, so I feel like she's trying to undermine me in the case we're working on together. I'm probably just being sensitive."

"Do you think they'll only make one woman?"

"No, but they may make only two partners if litigation isn't doing well," she said.

"I thought the process was getting smoothed out: that you'll be told if you're not going to make it."

"You're definitely told if there's no way they'll consider you. But it's still not a sure thing that you'll make it," she said. Not with the firm's current fraught financial situation. "Your dad's firm won that bid."

The lights went out from the windows in the adjoining garden, bathing them in darkness.

"I guess that's our cue to call it a night."

"Yes," she said. Now was the chance for something to happen. She glanced at him, then looked away.

The silence lengthened. Some crickets chirped. The cold aluminum of the lounge chair pressed into her back.

He stood and stretched. "I'm beat. C'mon Biscuit."

She stood as well. "Thanks again for killing the water bug."

"Anytime." He smiled. Their gazes held for a pulse too long. It was a perfect night for a kiss. She could feel his gaze lingering on her face. She stepped closer.

"That reminds me. I don't have your number or email," he said. "I'm leaving for Las Vegas tomorrow for the iHeartRadio music festival. And then we're going to London. I'll be gone for about two weeks. Can you take Biscuit next weekend? My sister is going to take him this week and next week, but she's going away that weekend to visit friends in the Hamptons. My mom can do it, but . . ."

"I'd love to," she interrupted his flow of words.

"I'll get my keys and give my sister your email." He disappeared through the hole in the fence, and the cold night air swooped into where he'd been standing.

She shivered and went back to her apartment to get her spare set of keys and her phone to store his number and email.

She met him back outside. He was on the other side of the fence. The leaves of the trees rustled as a small breeze passed through. They exchanged numbers and email addresses.

As he handed her his keys over the fence, looking into her eyes, he mused, "Sharing keys."

She waited to see if he would say more.

He just smiled and shook his head.

He's driving me crazy. Should I go for it and kiss him? He might be really tired. And he's about to go on a business trip. Also, there is a fence between us. Logistically, it seems challenging—at least for me. I'm not super smooth at this.

To fill the silence, she said, "You're also welcome to help yourself to my beer supply. I can't seem to get rid of it."

"I'll keep that in mind." He leaned over the fence and kissed her on the cheek. "I'm shattered from last night. I'll see you when I get back. Thanks for taking care of Biscuit."

"It's my pleasure. Have a safe trip." She walked through the dark yard to her door. The vetting had seemed like a sign of interest, but then nothing happened. She had been so sure that something would have happened yesterday had his sister not called. But tonight had been a second chance, sitting outside in the dark, sharing secrets.

As much as the kiss on her cheek moved her, a kiss on the cheek might mean that they were just friends. Maybe she wasn't flirting enough or giving signals that she was interested in more? That was what the Starbucks lady had said to her: you need to flirt more. But their conversation had been flirtatious. The hushed air in the garden gave her no clues. She was sometimes surprised by how quiet it could be in New York, the silence only periodically broken by the wail of an ambulance siren in the distance. She was so frustrated. She should have kissed him. At least then she'd have an answer. No, the current status quo was still filled with possibility. She would value these nights of slowly learning more about each other. She had to have faith in herself.

Chapter Twenty-Six

As Audrey exited Malaburn's office, she ran into Whitaker. "Are you working for Lawrence?" Whitaker asked.

"Yes," she said after a pause; she was so used to referring to him by his last name that she'd forgotten Malaburn's first name was Lawrence. They walked down the hallway together.

"That's unfortunate. He's a wet drip."

She looked at him, surprised at his openness. "Yes, we mutually dislike each other."

"But he chose to work with you?" he asked.

"Apparently he needs to confirm I have what it takes to make partner."

Whitaker harrumphed as they reached his office. He motioned for her to join him inside. The office was filled with packing boxes. Framed pictures in bubble wrap leaned against the walls. "I didn't think he had what it took to be a partner. He's not a thoroughbred. We shared a secretary, and he was borderline verbally abusive to her, so I reported his behavior. If he's not behaving with you, let me know. I'd be happy to hoist him up again." He rubbed his hands together, looking like he relished the thought of the conflict.

I'm a litigator who doesn't relish conflict.

"What's your case about?" he asked, pulling out a chair for her to sit at his conference table.

She described the case and outlined her legal arguments, including the one argument that she thought was pivotal but that Malaburn had dismissed as too risky. Whitaker nodded as she spoke.

"That's clever. It reminds me of an argument I once made and won. Let me find my files and see if you can buttress it," he said. The two of them flipped through the cases in his file and discussed various ideas.

"I'll miss this," he said. "The brainstorming and satisfying, chills-down-your-spine moment when you realize you've got the winning argument."

She nodded. She loved this part too, and it was even more satisfying working as a team.

"You should propose it to the client and let them decide," he said.

"Malaburn doesn't invite me to the client meetings."

Whitaker shook his head. "Just show up. He can't cut you out of meetings."

She hadn't minded when Malaburn hadn't included her in the pitch meeting because she was hoping not to join the team. But when he'd insisted she work on this case but still didn't invite her to client meetings, she'd been upset. She'd tried to rationalize the exclusion: at least she could use that time to work on other cases. But now he refused to make a winning argument, and if they lost the motion to dismiss, she would have to continue working with him. And she definitely did not want to do that.

"He's meeting them today at four," she said.

"It's almost four. In the office?"

"Yes."

"Excellent. I'll ask my assistant to find out where. We'll run into them." He chuckled. *Who knew that retiring partners were so feisty?*

His assistant called back with the meeting location, and they walked to the conference room. It was empty.

"I can stand here and text you when they come, and then you can appear," he said.

"Or we can pretend we're meeting in the conference room, and they'll walk in on us," she said.

"That's even better," he said, his blue eyes gleaming.

They entered the room and sat down at the conference table.

"You need to look more relaxed so it doesn't look like we're expecting them. You keep looking at the door, and you're sitting on the edge of your seat. Try sitting back," he said.

She leaned back in her chair. "Now you're checking out the door."

Whitaker chuckled. "We used to play pranks when I was an associate, before it became serious business to be a law firm partner." He pulled a legal pad from the center of the table towards him. "Back in the days when you left the office to eat dinner at home. Before the practice of law changed."

The door opened. Malaburn, accompanied by two men, entered and stopped short. "Audrey. Gene."

"Lawrence, good to see you. We're just finishing up here," Whitaker said. "Audrey was just telling me all about your case.

Fascinating. Particularly that new argument she's come up with that could win the case for you."

Malaburn opened and closed his mouth.

"I don't think we've met yet," Audrey said, standing up to shake the clients' hands. "I'm Audrey Willems. I've been working on your case."

"Great to meet you. We've seen your name on the memos and wondered when we'd meet you in person. You have a new argument?"

As they sat down, Audrey explained her latest argument. Whitaker didn't leave, even though Malaburn looked pointedly at him. Whitaker was like a craggy eagle presiding over the meeting. The clients loved her argument and wanted to use it. Malaburn sank lower into his chair.

"Did you just come up with this?" the client asked. Malaburn's head whipped around to face her.

"I just refined it with Gene," Audrey said.

Malaburn looked down.

The meeting ended, and Audrey slipped off to her office to revise the brief, excited to add the argument. When she finally finished writing the revised brief, she emailed it off to Malaburn and called the car service. Another late night, but worth it.

As the black sedan sped up Madison Avenue, Audrey looked up from her iPhone out the window. The shops were closed, but their windows were brightly lit. Some stores still displayed bright summer fashions, but others were showcasing clothes with the more muted tones of green, gray, black, red and orange as they shifted to the upcoming fall season. Summer was coming to an end, and she had spent most of it in the office.

To distract her from her morose thoughts, she checked her email.

To: Audrey Willems
From: Jake Miller
Date: September 22
Subject: Go Women!

I asked my dad about that case. An all-women team pitched for that engagement and won it. You might want to mention *that* to the powers-that-be.

Cheers,
Jake

She smiled. That was sweet of Jake. It wasn't exactly a romantic email, but it was even more touching and significant because it was supportive. The car cut across the Central Park 66th Street transverse, and she looked out the window at the entwined trees reaching towards the sky behind the stone walls.

Chapter Twenty-Seven

*A*udrey, Eve, and Max sat in a booth in their favorite brunch place in Tribeca, where they'd been meeting since they'd all first moved to New York after college. The white-washed wooden shipboard siding and a worn wooden sign with a picture of a black and white cow swinging above the counter gave it a homey-farmhouse-in-Vermont vibe. With scents of pancakes cooking, butter sizzling, eggs frying, warm bread baking, and hazelnut coffee brewing, the restaurant was like a warm hug. Max had found it only a few blocks away from his apartment.

Audrey stirred her tea. "So that's it. I feel like there are hints that something is going to happen, but then it doesn't." The waiter set down their brunch plates.

"It sounds to me like something would've happened after the jazz club if his sister hadn't needed him. And then it was just bad timing that he was traveling for work for two weeks." Eve signaled the waiter for a coffee refill. "Clearly he likes you, or he wouldn't keep coming by."

"He likes you, but you're in the friend zone," Max said, his brown eyes sympathetic.

"But how did I get in the friend zone? I don't want to be in the friend zone."

"You missed a pass," Max said.

"I don't know. Do you think men and women can just be friends?" Eve asked. The smell of waffles wafted over to their table as a waitress passed with a tray full of plates of freshly-baked waffles and strawberries.

"Of course, they can. We're all friends," Max said, leaning back.

"Well, yes, but he already has lots of female friends based on the number at his party," Eve said.

"I hope he holds another party soon so I can meet all the female friends," Max said. "Audrey's cooking him dinner—so Jake gets food and companionship."

"I thought women wanted companionship and men wanted sex." Eve nodded thanks to the waiter as he poured her coffee.

"Men like companionship—especially if it comes with food. Data shows men live longer if they're married," Max said.

"Hello! Hello!! I am still here!" Audrey waved her hands, sitting up straighter in the plush booth.

"And so you are . . ." Max sipped his coffee.

"I seem to be in the friend zone with both Tim and Jake. With Tim, I can understand—we work together, but why Jake too?" Audrey asked. "Let's get back to the crucial question: how do I get out of the friend zone?"

"Answer the door in a negligee." Max raised an eyebrow suggestively.

"Are you serious?" Audrey asked.

"Right now, you're like Mother Theresa/Julia Child—you've got to get his mind in the gutter."

"But he knows I wear sweats to bed."

"Good God, why are you doing that? And how does he know?" Max asked.

"He popped by once in the morning to borrow some milk."

"Late at night, and I would say there's where you missed the pass . . ." Max said. "Well, start wearing lingerie in case he comes by again. Or at least dress up."

Eve stirred her coffee thoughtfully. "Or you could try to make him jealous with Preppy Boy."

"Do we like him more than Preppy Boy?" Max asked.

"Definitely. Preppy Boy is a bit boring—and I don't trust him because they're both up for partner," Eve said.

"And you, Audrey, who do you like more?" Max asked.

"Jake," Audrey said without hesitation. "But I've had a crush on Tim for so long. And maybe Jake's not even interested. Maybe I'm just not in his league."

"Please, just stop that," Eve said. "If he doesn't make a move soon, he's not in your league. Because he's an idiot not to realize how good you are."

"Maybe he thinks I'm a workaholic and he doesn't want to date someone like that, so that's why he hesitates," Audrey said.

Max and Eve looked at each other. "You are a workaholic."

"It'll get better once you're a partner. You'll have more control over your schedule . . ." Max said.

"Unless I'm even more at the beck and call of clients," Audrey said.

"Or on trial. You always disappear completely when you're involved in a trial." Eve frowned.

"I'm about to go on trial," Audrey said.

Eve rubbed her back. "Maybe he'll have to travel again, and he won't notice."

"Before you disappear, let's plan your party." Max rubbed his hands together. "I can check out if either is interested." As the waiter cleared their brunch plates, they asked for the check.

"I want to see you with them too, but I'll probably be too busy with the food. Maybe at the end, I can get a sense," Eve said.

"Well, don't make it obvious, you two."

Both of them protested that they were very subtle. Audrey raised her eyebrows in disbelief.

"I'm excited to see your subtlety at work—especially you, Max." Audrey turned to Eve. "And you still want to cook for it, right?"

"Yes, definitely."

"And you said that you have off the second Saturday in October?" Audrey asked.

"Yes, that'd be perfect timing for me," Eve said, adding that she was excited to plan the menu.

"Two weeks works for me," Max pulled on his coat.

"All right, let's do it. Let's invite everybody."

Chapter Twenty-Eight

As Audrey tried to squeeze by two guys to check on Eve in the kitchen and re-stock the ice, the tall dark-haired one, a little plump, clearly tipsy, wrapped his arm around her shoulders and told her to pass his compliments to the chef. She inhaled the smell of beer mixed with cologne.

"Is that big fellow in the kitchen the chef's boyfriend? I don't want to propose if he is, but otherwise I'm really thinking about it," he said, his speech just slightly slurred.

"He is indeed." As she conveyed that sad news, he sagged against her, and she staggered slightly.

"Roland, you're going to squash her," the friend said, who was quite cute, winking at her. "Buck up. You can always ask the chef if she has any friends who cook."

"Do you cook?" Roland asked her.

"Not well."

"Lost art, I tell you. Lost art." Roland shook his head forlornly. "I like to cook myself, but want to share the art."

"Okay, let's release the nice lady—she looks like she's trying to get more ice—and go console ourselves with more canapes." The friend tried to pull Roland away.

"A lot of cooks are here because Eve—that's the name of the chef—invited friends in the business," she said.

"See there, canapes and cooks, let's go back to the dining table and see who we can meet. By the way, I'm Oliver. Great party."

"Audrey. Thanks. Nice to meet you."

As Roland removed his arm from around Audrey, Oliver said, "Maybe we'll see you on your way back."

Her apartment was starting to feel like a bulging suitcase where every time you tried to close it, a sock (or in this case, a person) popped out in the way of the zipper. But when three different friends—Eve, Max and herself—invited everyone they knew, that guaranteed a good crowd.

But Tim had not come, and Jake seemed to be fully occupied serving as the party DJ. At this point, it looked like neither of them was interested in her. Her friends must think she was completely delusional.

It was only an hour into the party, so Tim could still show up and Jake could start hanging out with her. She reminded herself that the purpose of the party was to kick off Eve's catering business and introduce her cooking to as many of their workaholic friends as possible. Secondary to that was her opportunity to interact with Jake again in a party setting and Tim in a non-work setting—and let her friends judge if either was romantically interested.

She'd had her caramel-blond hair highlighted and blow-dried so it fell in waves around her face. She was wearing a sophisticated midnight-blue dress that brought out the blue of her eyes, or so the salesgirl had told her. And she was even wearing heels—sparkly sapphire heels that had been an impulse buy. Jake's eyes had widened when he'd seen her as if he was impressed, but then he'd just made a "buddy" comment that she cleaned up nicely. The comment wasn't totally unwarranted. That morning, he'd popped over, having arrived home from London earlier in the week, and helped her move most of her furniture against her whitewashed exposed brick wall to prepare for the party. Not having expected him, she'd had her hair in a ponytail and been wearing sweats. So much for following Max's advice to be wearing lingerie! And then he'd rushed off to meet his mom. But now she'd heeded Max's advice to dress up.

With several "excuse me's" and holding the ice bucket aloft, Audrey skirted around a group of Max's friends and entered the kitchen. Pete was carefully chopping basil in one corner, wearing one of Eve's aprons. The flowery apron was quite a contrast to Pete's muscular frame, but he looked at home. Eve and Pete were chatting comfortably as Eve placed another tray into the oven. She was managing to keep the food flowing using Audrey's kitchen as her base. This also gave her a chance to meet guests.

"The food is a huge hit. People keep telling me how delicious it is," Audrey said.

"It's going well so far," Eve said, looking pleased. "Several have come into the kitchen to tell me. One asked me to cater a Hamptons party."

"We might have to make a weekend of it," Pete said, rubbing Eve's shoulders.

Audrey left the kitchen, maneuvering around two unknown guests discussing a *New Yorker* article (resisting the temptation to butt into their engaging conversation). The smell of fresh bread and melted cheese wafted from the kitchen. The dining table was in the center of the room, piled high with food. Spinning tiered trays showed off all the appetizers. Eve's new business cards figured prominently on the table. Elegant tea lights sparkled on the table and the fireplace mantel. Guests were congregated around the dining table, eating, crunching on the avocado-topped crackers and other appetizers prepared by Eve, talking, having a good time.

Bursts of loud conversations acted like a crescendo periodically over the music in the background. Jake remained in the corner, working the music playlist. He had not only helped in the morning; he'd also arrived early to help set up the food and had brought extra alcohol and friends. Jake had made fun of her party "To Do" list until Eve had produced her catering list and Max had staunchly defended the use of lists. Jake had laughingly conceded then. Overall, he and Max seemed to get on, although they'd briefly tussled over DJ'ing the party.

She delivered the ice to the bar. She was asking the bartender for a white wine when Max slid his arm around her and said, "Hopefully he won't be too distracted by DJ'ing. I offered to DJ to free him up to hang out."

"Oh, was that the reason? I wondered why you all of a sudden wanted to DJ. But his playlist was much better."

"Always looking out for you."

"You're so sweet . . . sometimes," Audrey said. "Do you think he seems interested?"

Max shrugged.

The front door opened. It was Tim—and Colette. That was not a good sign. Not quite the answer she'd been expecting, but if they were together, that eliminated Tim. She told Max, who had his back to the door.

"I'm finally going to meet Tim?" Max whispered. "After two years of hearing about him?"

"Behave!" Audrey said.

"Is he someone I need to behave with?"

"I mean, don't tell any embarrassing stories about me."

"What am I going to talk about, then?"

"Ugh. Thanks."

"Don't worry. I shall extol your abilities to hire help, to throw dinner parties . . ."

Audrey punched him lightly.

Max said, "Ouch! I just want to meet him and see this paragon you've had a crush on. Jake is some tough competition, though. I want to see who's right for you." Max turned around. "Well, hello, is that Colette?"

"Yes. And what if he isn't right?"

"Then there's still time for sabotage," Max said. "I can see her appeal."

So could Audrey. Colette was dressed in a little black sheath mini-dress with a mauve silk scarf, spiky heels, and tortoise-shell glasses. It made her look like a leggy 70's pop star crossed with a strict librarian. How did she do it? As small consolation, Audrey realized that she would never look good in that dress; she was just too curvy.

"Thanks. You're supposed to be on my side," Audrey said.

"I am, I am. I'm offering myself as a sacrificial lamb. And I'd love to be the stay-at-home house husband. I'm perfect for her. Anyway, you should be talking to him, not Colette. Let's go over, and I'll distract her."

"Thanks, I think." Max was good-looking, but he wasn't preppy, and Audrey suspected that was Colette's type. It was a shame that she and Max were not attracted to each other. They got along so well as friends.

Audrey and Max joined Colette and Tim by the center table, and Audrey introduced everybody.

"The food is delicious," Colette said, gesturing to the platters. "I took your friend's card. I'm hosting a baby shower in April, so maybe Eve could cater it. I've been worried about what to do for food. I don't want to rely on my cooking skills."

"You're a good cook," Tim said.

"You're being kind. I have one dish, and that's an omelet."

Max and Audrey looked at each other, and Audrey suspected that they both had the same thought: an omelet—Tim had stayed over and had breakfast with Colette? Tim and Colette were dating, then. But Colette continued, "I think you were just really hungry that evening." She smiled up at Tim and then explained to Audrey and Max, "It was the Unicorn project team dinner, and the portions were tiny. Even I was hungry afterward. Since my apartment was around the corner from the restaurant, I invited Tim over for an omelet."

"It was a very good omelet," Tim said staunchly. His buttoned-up dress shirt and khaki pants made him seem stiff in this party environment.

"I do make good omelets, but that's it. I am not sure that's going to work at this baby shower, although it is a brunch. But then I'd rather not be cooking and hosting—especially with all the various baby shower games I have to pull off. I had no idea it was so complicated."

Max said he would introduce her to Eve and led Colette away, leaving Audrey alone with Tim. Max was a good wingman.

Tim mentioned an issue he was having with a junior associate assigned to his case and then asked her a legal question he was wrestling with. She concentrated on giving her best answer. She hoped he wasn't going to talk about work the whole time. They moved away from the appetizers to the balcony doors, where the air seemed cooler. He looked out the glass doors to the murky darkness beyond, the black night tempered by the twinkling Christmas lights around the balcony railing.

"This is fun. It's been a while since you had a party," he said.

"Too long, probably."

"I still remember vividly your garden party our first year at the law firm. We barely knew each other, but you invited all the litigators. You were wearing this very summery yellow dress."

"Wow, you remember that?"

"Distinctly. And you started dancing with some of your college girlfriends on top of the picnic table in your backyard." His warm brown eyes looked into hers. She could smell his woodsy cologne. Maybe the party setting was going to work.

"A bit wilder then."

"Law firm life does tend to tame one." He gestured out the window. "What happened to the picnic table?"

"It broke. Either the winter weather or the dancing destroyed it. I've been meaning to replace it . . ." She paused. Like so much of her life, it was on hold while vying for partner. And if a partner, she doubted she would be dancing on picnic tables—except for the day she made it. "Lately we've just been dining at the little table out here." She gestured to the balcony table.

"A table for two—much more intimate."

Audrey was not sure whether to leave him with the impression that she might be dating someone (per Eve's advice: don't let him think you're completely available) or clarify that she was usually eating with Eve on the balcony (also per Eve's advice: let him know that you're interested). Flirting was so complicated.

At that moment, Jake walked up and put his arm around her. Her body warmed. She had no reaction when Max put his arm around her, except for a comfortable big brother feel, but when Jake touched her, she could feel the contact through her dress.

Jake said, "I'm so sorry, I have to steal our hostess away for a second. Party demands."

Jake still had his arm about her, and she wanted to stay within his embrace.

Tim, surprised, said, "I understand." He pulled out his phone.

"What's the party emergency?" she asked as Jake tugged her back to the table.

"I need your opinion on which dip is better," Jake said. "And I thought I'd rescue you from that guy who looks like a very serious work colleague. You're off duty now, you know." Grabbing her hand and pulling her through the crowd to arrive at the center table, he surveyed the dishes, took a cracker and spread dip on it.

"Now, which dip do you think is better? Try this spinach dip, or maybe this one." He handed her a cracker topped with a black bean and sweet potato dip. "Also, Eve is about to clear the food and put out the desserts, and I'm not sure you've even eaten."

She hadn't. "Mmm, yes, this one is good." She tasted it. "But hostess duties mean I shouldn't leave him with no one to talk to."

"Shhh, he can fend for himself. Now try this bruschetta with tomato and avocado—really special." He put the cracker up to her mouth, and she ate it; their glances met as his fingers touched her lips. She wasn't sure what she'd just swallowed. She took another bruschetta to taste it this time.

"There you go, he's already been scooped up—by that woman with the very strict haircut—no nonsense there. They seem well-matched. Another lawyer?" Jake asked.

"Yes, that's Colette."

Tim was smiling at Colette. Colette handed him a drink, set hers down, and used both hands to pull her hair away from her face.

Max was talking to Winnie. Audrey was relieved that Jake did not seem to find Colette attractive. What if Max, Tim, and Jake had all pursued Colette? It wasn't beyond the realm of possibility in her life.

She turned back to Jake. "Did I look bored?"

He handed her an empanada.

"You looked very serious. Not smiling," he said. "And I could have sworn you were discussing a case because you have this little crease in your forehead when you are thinking hard." He gently touched her forehead and smoothed it down, and she shivered.

"We were. I'm amazed you figured that out."

"I'm afraid it's genetically ingrained. At my parents' parties with work colleagues, we were all under strict instructions to pull my father away from any conversations that looked boring."

"Really?" she asked. She had been worried that Tim was just going to talk about work, but the conversation had just shifted to be more personal.

"Absolutely. To his credit, my father said that parties were for getting to know each other better—not for discussing work. But some people just can't help themselves. So which appetizer?" Jake asked.

"I can never pick. I love the chicken skewers with satay sauce, the pizzettes and the banana black bean empanadas. And the bruschetta with the basil and the surprise twist of mint. That seems to be the most popular. Wait until you see the desserts—they're coming out next." Pete and Max cleared the appetizer plates.

"I'm going to play 'Sweets for my Sweet' when Eve brings out the dessert, so I have to get back to the music, but I have a serious party hostess question: do you want this to be a dance party? After the desserts, we can turn this into a dance party if I switch the playlist and you dim the lights."

"Definitely a dance party," she said. So much for returning to talk to Tim. Anyway, she didn't feel like battling Colette for him. He chose to come with Colette.

"Save the first dance for me. I see Eve now with the desserts."

Audrey helped Eve carry out the desserts as Jake played "Sweets for my Sweet" and some other similarly themed songs. The guests oohed and aahed as the pastries came out. Audrey was glad people were so appreciative. As everyone tucked into devouring the desserts, there was that moment of silence when the enjoyment of the baked delights and the sorbet precluded talking.

Upon finishing her dessert, Audrey caught Jake's nod from across the room, and she went to dim the lights. "Holding out for a Hero" burst out and Jake's eyes met hers across the room and he smiled.

He crossed back and clasped her hand, pulling her to him and dancing swing with her, spinning her round. The party crowd moved back to clear space. Her hair spun out, and she felt a bit like a princess—like a teenage dream when you're the center of attention at a party with a cute boy—she just needed a billowing skirt. He pulled her close, and she closed her eyes briefly, enjoying resting against his hard chest, breathing in his familiar fresh laundry scent. She looked up, and their eyes met. He smiled, his dimple appearing in his cheek. He spun her out again. They separated hands, but kept dancing close, mimicking each other's moves, totally in sync. Others were now dancing around them (although not Tim or Colette). Winnie and Eve came out and joined them, dancing as all the women sang "I need a hero."

"Are you trying to set impossible standards?" Max asked Jake as he joined the group.

"Just raising them," Jake said. "Don't worry. We've got a mix of musical messages coming up."

The song switched, but Jake didn't leave her. They separated from her group of friends to dance together.

A spark of electricity passed as their hands touched. She couldn't tell if he felt it too. She turned away and shimmied back, and Jake did the same, their moves in perfect rhythm, their glances heated, his hand lingering at her hip as he spun her around. *Is it just for the fun of the dance, or does it mean more?*

A friend of Jake's came to say goodbye, and Jake stopped to talk to him. She couldn't hear what he said, but Jake leaned in to listen to him. They stepped away from the dance floor. As they did, Jake looked over briefly as if to excuse himself, and she nodded.

Winnie and Eve ventured over, and she danced with them. Max joined them.

Eve said, "Pete's going to clean up."

"Definitely a keeper," Audrey said.

"No doubt."

Colette came up to say that she was leaving, but she'd enjoyed the party and the food. A tall preppy guy was standing behind her. She introduced him to Audrey, saying that he was an old friend from college; neither had known the other was now living in the city. He put his arm around Colette as she talked and she glowed. Audrey watched them leave together. So, Colette was not dating Tim.

As Jake rejoined them, Pete appeared and scooped up Eve for some swing-dancing.

At midnight, Audrey shut down the music and most guests left. Max and Jake pulled the couches out along with the coffee table, and Eve and Winnie piled the remaining food on the coffee table. Jake briefly opened the door to let in the fresh cold night air and let out any smell of alcohol. Audrey sank gratefully into the soft cushions of the couch, Jake sitting next to her. The heat of his thigh against hers warmed her. As the crowd thinned, Tim appeared and perched on the edge of the couch. But seeming to note that Audrey was flanked by Max and Jake on the couch, he said his goodbyes.

The remaining close group of friends—with Jake and Winnie joining in easily—hung out, doing a party post-mortem analysis until the food was finished. Most of Eve's business cards had been taken, so that seemed positive. Eve had landed three engagements, one with Colette. As the conversation wound down, Max and Winnie both said they had to leave, and Eve and Pete also stood up, saying they'd help with any remaining clean-up in the morning.

That left Jake.

Chapter Twenty-Nine

*H*aving said goodbye to her friends, Audrey bounced back to the living room where Jake remained on the couch. *Finally!* Max's parting comment had been auspicious: "I want a full update in the morning."

The lighting remained dim; candles still flickered, giving it a romantic atmosphere. Jake, his dark, tousled hair hiding his face, was bent over, looking at his phone. She shivered. She couldn't quite believe that it might happen, that it might work out with this funny, warm, up-for-anything guy.

The floor creaked as she approached the couch, and Jake looked up. It was as if a shadow had passed over him. His eyes looked dark, and his face had paled so much that she could see his midnight shadow beard.

"Is everything all right?" she asked, shocked at the change.

He ran his hand through his hair and looked down at his phone.

"Sometimes I don't know how she knows," he said. "My ex-girlfriend texted me—she's got some crisis . . ."

"At one in the morning?"

"That's when her emergencies happen," he said sadly. "I probably should head over there and just make sure it's nothing serious. It's not that we're together anymore, but I still feel responsible. I'm her closest friend here. We started dating shortly after she moved to the States, so she hasn't made many other friends." His eyes were looking intently into hers, as if to will her to understand. "And she's a model, so it seems that the other women . . . are super-competitive. She can't let them see her weak or distraught."

It was a lot to take in.

"When did you break up?"

"A few months before I moved here." His phone beeped again. He read the text.

"What's the emergency? Is she okay?" she asked.

He looked up and shook his head, "She's just young and she gets anxious, and she doesn't take criticism or pressure well. And she needs a lot of attention. I'm being too harsh here . . . because of the circumstances." He hesitated. "She seems happy when you first meet her. But there is a darker side underneath the gaiety."

He typed a message. "I have to go." He stood. She walked him to the door. He looked torn. He moved to kiss her cheek and she tilted her head so he ended up kissing near her ear. She didn't want to be kissed if he was leaving to see his ex-girlfriend.

"Did you have a jacket?" she asked.

He said no and pulled her into a tight hug. It felt like he was drawing support from her. They parted, and he disappeared down the stairs.

She leaned, drained, against the door, flattened by the toll of hosting the party and the disappointment that nothing had happened with Jake. Whereas before she'd been floating, she now crashed to the ground. She shook her head. *Jake is a nice guy doing the right thing.* She'd thought it was over with his ex-girlfriend. *Clearly not.* But he'd moved uptown. *That is pretty drastic. Is he still emotionally involved? He is involved enough that he cares when she texts him and leaves in the middle of night to go to her. And leaves me.* Maybe he hadn't made a move because he still had feelings for Veronika. She wasn't sure if that made her feel better or worse.

Chapter Thirty

An emergency meeting convened at their Tribeca brunch place once Audrey texted Max that nothing had happened. She slumped against the turquoise diner seat as she finished recounting how Jake had left. After a brief pause, both Max and Eve jumped in.

"He has a dark side. That makes him much more interesting than just a party boy," Max said thoughtfully.

"OMG, it's the plot of *Rebecca*—get out now!" Eve said, talking over Max.

"Okay, okay, hold on here. He doesn't have a dark side—his ex-girlfriend does; and his ex-girlfriend is alive, there's no scary housekeeper, and he seemed to be trying to make clear that he isn't still in love with her," Audrey said. The clatter of plates from the kitchen punctuated Audrey's defense as a waiter with a tray full of food emerged from the swinging kitchen door.

"My advice is to steer clear of men with crazy ex-girlfriends—especially those who call in the middle of the night and require the guy to come over," Eve said.

"And interrupt potential fooling around. I'm seeing Eve's point here. Potential sex vs. consoling ex-girlfriend. No contest," Max said.

"Man, you guys are so right. But I really like him."

The three friends considered options.

"Well, on the bright side, he's interested," Max consoled. "Aside from the possessive ex, he's a good catch."

"Personally, I wonder if she was just so attractive that he didn't probe deeper," Eve said.

Max conceded that men may *initially* prioritize looks without a deeper analysis. "But to give Jake the benefit of the doubt, he probably didn't know she was possessive when they first dated," Max said, defending his gender. "And what about women who are attracted to bad boys? Case in point here."

"Jake is not a 'bad boy,'" Audrey said.

"Putting aside his ex, I still prefer Jake to Tim. Although I did talk to Tim at the party, and maybe he's not as boring as I thought," Eve said.

"Compared to Tim, Jake is definitely 'the bad boy.'" Max snorted.

"Really, you liked Tim?" Audrey asked Eve.

"He was kind of sweet, and apparently he likes to cook. I talked to him for a while in the kitchen. He was even helpful. He said he'd heard a lot about me from you."

"Points for Tim!" Max said. "I couldn't tell if he liked you. You didn't talk to him much, although you did look intimate together by the glass door."

"No, Jake pulled me away from Tim, and we started dancing. And I really felt like there was chemistry and it was going to happen."

"I thought so too," Max said, rubbing her shoulders.

"And Tim came with Colette, so I thought that they might be dating. But then she left with some friend from college. Tim probably thinks I'm dating Jake."

"After last night . . . yes."

Audrey's work phone beeped. She rummaged around in her bag looking for it and said that it was probably Malaburn. "We're filing our brief, and he keeps texting me changes. He dribbles them out like a sort of torture."

"It's good you can joke about it." Max exchanged a concerned look with Eve.

Audrey intercepted that glance. "I'm better at handling him than I was the first time. But I'll be glad when this is filed and he doesn't have an excuse to text me every day." She read the text. "It's Tim. And he's asking me if I want to see a movie tonight!"

"Way to go!" Max said.

"Men. Competition works. And he's asking you for tonight to see if anything happened last night." Eve shook her head.

"Well, be coy about Jake. Don't admit that nothing happened," Max said.

"Great, so I'm going to look like a slut," Audrey said.

"No, she should say nothing happened, and act surprised that he thought something did, but that they're VERY close friends. It implies something could happen at any moment, and he better wrap this deal up!" Eve said.

"Damn, Eve, you're devious," Max said, shaking his head.

"I can't believe I'm going on a date with Tim after the party last night. But I wish it was Jake asking me. Maybe I should say no."

"You might as well go out to a movie with Tim and see what's going on. You've had a crush on him for two years. And I don't know what's up with Jake. This ex seems to have made him really hesitant to get involved again," Eve said.

Audrey nodded. She had had a crush on Tim for two years, before she met Jake. And he did support her career, warning her about Colette. She texted back yes to Tim.

Chapter Thirty-One

*A*udrey came out of her bathroom, smoothing down a wrinkle in her little black dress, her hair blow-dried straight. Hearing a knock on her backyard glass door, she looked up and saw Jake. She slid open the door to be greeted by a rush of cold air.

"Jake." Surprised, she felt she had to be a little distant after the disappointment of last night. Normally she would've opened the door wide and invited him in, but now she stood partially in the door entrance and just looked at him.

He looked down for a minute and then looked up, sheepishly. "I want to apologize for last night. It won't happen again. It's over with Veronika. I mean, it's been over for some time, but I also told her that her 'I'm depressed' texts at night have to go to another friend—unless she is depressed. But she can't write me that text and then meet me at the door in lingerie." He took a breath. "I thought maybe we could hang out tonight, but you're dressed up. You look great. Are you going somewhere?"

She stepped back and let Jake in the apartment, closing the door behind him, playing for time. How to respond? *I shouldn't have said yes to Tim.*

"I'm meeting Tim for a movie," she said reluctantly, embarrassed given their last charged encounter and this new overture.

His eyes flashed. "Tim? Isn't he the lawyer from your firm?"

"Yes, that's the one."

"You're dating him?"

"We're meeting for a movie. I don't know if it's a date." It probably wasn't even a date.

"He seems like a player to me."

She snorted. "Tim is not a player. He's such a . . . straight arrow."

"Is that your type?"

"I'm a lawyer. I'm not exactly wild—I obviously chose a conservative career path."

Jake came up close to her and gently pushed her hair away from her face. "But you've a bit more spark. Like me."

Flustered by his touch, she said, "Like you." Then she worried that he would think she said that she liked him. She blushed.

He stared into her eyes for a moment. "What are the plans for tonight?"

"Dinner and a movie at Lincoln Center." Which definitely sounded like a date.

"Where's his apartment?"

"He lives in Murray Hill. I've never been. And I've known him for years."

He seemed reassured by that and followed her up the spiral staircase. "Can I check out your movie collection again? I was hoping to watch a movie tonight, but nothing on Netflix is grabbing me."

"Sure, feel free." She waved to the DVD shelf as she checked her watch. "I have to leave." They both stood there. She was reluctant to leave. He didn't say anything. She was tempted to ask Jake, *Is anything going on between us?* But now was not the time, not when Tim was waiting. Her phone beeped. Her Uber was at the door. "Goodbye."

"Bye," Jake said. "I'll go back out the back door. I left my keys at home."

She walked out. She felt like she'd see him standing where she left him if she turned back around.

The night air was chilly as she and Tim walked back to her apartment. Although they had put their work phones away, agreeing no emergency was likely to happen, they had only discussed work during dinner. She'd much rather have spent the evening with Jake. After the movie, Tim had suggested that they pick up Magnolia cupcakes and enjoy them at her house, since the movie theatre was so close to her apartment.

As they entered her apartment, Audrey saw light from under the living room door.

"That's weird. I don't recall leaving the light on," she whispered. Jake could have left the light on, but what if he'd left the sliding door unlocked? She shivered.

"I don't think an intruder would leave the light on."

"Should I get an umbrella, just in case?"

"An umbrella? For what?" Tim asked.

"For bopping the guy on the head."

"I took martial arts self-defense. I can defend us. Stay behind me." He put out his arm and moved her behind him. They inched up the hallway. She was right behind him. It was odd, but this was the closest physically they had ever been. She could smell his aftershave.

"I think there's someone in there," she whispered.

"I don't hear anything," he said. They reached the door. Tim slowly turned the handle and pushed the door open.

The sight of the back of Jake's tousled head with headphones watching a movie sprawled out on her couch greeted them. Biscuit barked. Jake looked up from the movie and pulled off his headphones. His beer was on the coffee table.

"Jake, what are you doing here?" she asked.

"My Blu-ray player is broken, so I didn't think you'd mind if I used yours. And I thought I'd make a dent in your beer stockpile," Jake said. He stood and walked over to Tim, introducing himself, holding out his hand. Shaking hands, Jake said, "I think we met briefly before."

"Did we? Sorry, I don't recall." Tim shrugged.

Jake walked over to the kitchen, asking, "What's your drink? Would you like a beer? Corona? Stella Artois? There's quite a selection left over from the last party."

"Umm, a Stella Artois," Tim said, appearing flummoxed.

"Anything to eat? Chips? There's even some amazing quiche in the freezer," Jake said.

"We bought Magnolia cupcakes," she said, trying to take control back from Jake.

Tim asked, "I'm sorry I don't recall—are you roommates?"

"I practically live here, but my apartment is next door. The food is much better over here, though. And the company, of course," Jake said, smiling at Audrey.

Jake disappeared into the kitchen, but before Audrey could say anything to Tim privately, he quickly reappeared with three Stella Artois and some plates, handing them out and reclaiming his seat on the couch. His legs seemed to spread out on the couch, taking up space. Tim sat in the armchair across from the couch.

"So, how was dinner?" Jake asked.

"Jake, don't you have to go?" Audrey asked as she pulled over a chair from the table. She didn't dare join Jake on the couch.

"No." Jake leaned back.

Audrey put the cupcake on a plate on the coffee table and cut it with the plastic knife from Magnolia. "Would you like a piece?"

"No, thanks," Jake said.

Audrey handed Tim a light-blue frosted cupcake on a plate with a fork. Tim cut a piece with his fork, but then put the cake down on the table.

"So, what do you do again?" Tim asked.

"I work in the music business."

"That's tough. Make any money in that nowadays?" Tim asked.

"It's up and down." Jake shrugged and didn't sound that concerned.

"But he's doing what he loves," Audrey said.

"I love law. There's nothing better than a good dispute: the strategy, trying to find a solution for your client." Tim's phone beeped, and he looked at it.

"Are you getting emails from work at this hour on a Sunday night?" Jake asked. Audrey shot him a warning look.

"Yes, this partner, Gerald, usually starts working again around 11 p.m. after his family has gone to sleep."

"Even on a Sunday?" Jake asked.

"Definitely. That's why they pay me the big bucks," Tim said.

They were both acting like cavemen, and it was ridiculous.

Jake said to Tim, "So nice to see love in the workplace. I never had the guts—I mean what if you had a break-up?"

"We're all civilized adults."

Jake said, "Somehow, I don't often think of civilization and love in the same sentence."

Touché for Jake.

Tim's phone beeped again, and he picked it up.

Tim said, "Oh, man, another round of changes. He talked to the client and the client really liked my new angle, but he wants to go on the offensive even more."

"Well, it's good that the client really likes it. You were worried that he'd find it too aggressive."

"And now we might be going over the top." Tim looked thoughtful, as if he was analyzing how to re-write the brief. "I'd better go and get to bed. It's going to be a long day tomorrow."

"Thanks for the dinner and movie. Let me walk you out."

Jake looked like he was about to get up and accompany them, but Audrey shot him a look: *Don't you dare!*

As they entered the hallway, Tim said, "So I gather that guy doesn't live here, or we wouldn't have been preparing for a robber in this hallway, but he certainly seemed comfortable here. Is there something up between you?"

That was direct. I should be so direct with Jake.

"We're very close friends and neighbors, so we have keys to each other's apartments. But I mean, we've just been friends."

Tim kissed her lightly on the cheek and said he'd see her tomorrow at the office.

As she re-entered the living room, she confronted Jake. "What are you doing?"

"What do you mean? I offered him a beer and even quiche, following the old maxim that the way to a man's heart is through his stomach."

"Does that work?"

"Competition works. Wasn't that your first date after he saw us dancing at your party?"

"Yes," she said reluctantly.

"I just provided a little competition. If he's really interested, he'll be back."

"And is that what you want? What about us? Is there any us?" Audrey asked.

"Is there? You just went out on a date with another guy."

"You left last night to comfort your ex-girlfriend."

"Just because I care that you don't date that corporate robot . . ." he said. He grabbed his coat and strode to the spiral staircase. "Maybe I'll leave you to it, then." He disappeared down the stairs. She followed him down, reaching the bottom step as he slid open the glass door and, without looking back, walked out into the dark. A cold blast of air hit her as the door slid closed.

She stood in shock. That answered the question about whether he liked her romantically. But it was not the response she'd wanted. Her shoulders slumped. She didn't understand why she could never move from the "fun friend" to the girlfriend. She turned around to get ready for bed. At this point, she just wanted to collapse in the soft sheets and give up on dating entirely—again. And retreat to the sanctuary of work. But that felt empty too now.

She heard the door slide back open, and she whirled around. It was Jake. He strode across the floor and stood in front of her, his eyes searching intently into hers. He bit his lip. "Except I think there is an us. Don't you?"

"Yes."

"Don't date that android. Date me. Please. Yes?"

"Yes," she said, almost at the same time as he asked. She gazed into his eyes, depths of blue that she could get lost in. The radiator sputtered in the background as the heat came on.

He took a step closer; her senses zinged in response. As he gazed into her eyes, she tilted her head up. He smelled of chocolate and beer.

He hesitated. The moment stretched out. Was he nervous? She was. She could see him swallow. He smiled slightly, and she moved towards him. *That should make it easier.*

He kissed her firmly on the lips as his hand moved back to cup her head and tangle in her hair, and he pulled her closer, his other hand curving around her waist. He tasted like chocolate and smelled like Jake. As his fingers teased patterns in her hair, she shivered with longing from his touch. She melted into the kiss and hugged him tightly. He gentled the kiss, but every part of her felt on fire. All sensibility was lost except for the consciousness of Jake and this kiss and his fingers. Her fingers caressed his cheek and pushed back his errant hair. The stubble on his cheek grounded her back in her room.

They parted for a breath.

In a low voice that set her body humming, he said, "I messed up last night, but going out with that guy was a low blow in return."

She pulled back to look at him. "I wasn't going out with him to get back at you. How would I know you were interested? It seemed last night you made a pretty decisive choice that nothing was happening here."

"I was going to ask you if something could happen, but then Veronika foiled that." He feathered kisses across her cheek. "Does this feel like nothing?"

"No, there's definitely something; we may need more research to determine what, exactly," she murmured teasingly.

Jake kissed her neck, and tingly feelings cascaded through her. As he trailed kisses up her neck, her eyes closed and she tilted her neck to give him more access.

"I'm up for more research," he said. "But it's definitely something good?" He put both hands in her hair, smoothing it away from her face and looking deep into her eyes. She soaked him in, his warm blue eyes, his face that was so familiar and dear to her. Her hand cupped his firm butt, delighting in the knowledge that she now had permission to touch him so intimately.

"Better than good," she said.

He kissed her again, lightly at first, then more urgently. She ran her fingers through his hair. They couldn't stop kissing each other. The air was sparking around them. Moving backward while still kissing, he hit the bed, and they tumbled onto it. She lay there for a moment in his arms.

"Well, that's convenient," he joked.

"Yes," she said, rolling him around and pinning him under her. "I've got you right where I want you."

He relaxed on the bed. "I'm all yours." She pulled off his gray t-shirt, the worn shirt that he'd been wearing when they'd first bumped into each other, and she tenderly ran her hands across his chest.

He took a quick indrawn breath and moved slightly. "I'm ticklish."

"You are?"

"I'm embarrassed to admit that I am." He was tightening his muscles as if preparing for her ticklish touch.

She lay down next to him and kissed him. "You shouldn't be. That just makes you all the more endearing."

"Are you?" He tickled her, and she giggled.

"Stop, yes, some places." She laughed and moved away.

He kissed her again, and his hand moved down to hold her tightly against him. They fit together perfectly. Their glances met, and the air shimmered around them.

"We need to pull the curtains shut," she said.

"On it," he said, leaping up to close the curtains.

They spent the rest of the night researching just how good it was between them.

They fell asleep holding hands, and she only woke up when Jake tickled her in the morning. She opened her eyes to see his blue eyes smiling at her, his muscular chest leaning over her in the bed, the sheet only up to his waist.

"Hi." He kissed her quickly, his lips firm.

"Hi," she said shyly.

"Do you have to work, or can we spend the day together?" he asked, almost hesitantly.

It was Indigenous Peoples/Columbus Day. Technically, it was a holiday, but she had planned to work. She remembered Eve's words: if you sleep with Jake and you've got plans, you cancel those plans. She hadn't imagined that those words would ever apply to her. She'd had so many unrequited crushes, but here he was—with her. And last night—her face flushed.

He kissed her. "You're so cute when you blush."

"I hate that I blush."

"No, you shouldn't." He tenderly ran his fingers through her hair.

"I don't have to work today," she said. "What do you want to do?"

"I have a really fun idea. Let's go mountain biking."

"Mountain biking?" she asked, surprised.

"Have you ever been?"

"No."

"You'll love it. Perfect for today's fall weather. I know a really good beginner's path. We can either go to a trail in Queens or Staten Island. If you're up for it, I'm pretty sure I can rent a bike for you."

It was not what she'd expected him to suggest, but it would be fun to be out biking on a crisp October day, especially with the leaves turning a kaleidoscope of colors: yellow, green, orange, burnt umber.

"I'm up for it," she said enthusiastically.

He smiled. "That's my girl."

And she felt like she was definitely his girl.

Chapter Thirty-Two

On Tuesday, Audrey floated into work, although her body was sore from biking over rough terrain. Jake was so easy and comfortable to be with. He didn't seem to mind that she clearly wasn't the best mountain biker around, especially when he showed her the mountain biking position (stay loose, butt slightly over saddle and torso low on the handlebars, elbows bent) and she'd stayed too loose, falling promptly over with the bike. But she'd gotten up quickly, although she had a hard time both staying loose and maintaining the athletic body crouch. He'd been a good teacher—so sweet and protective. He'd tried her bike first to make sure that everything worked.

What am I doing working in the office every weekend when I could be out in the crisp fall air biking through trees, joking around with Jake?

Her mother's voice sounded in her head: "Building your career takes dedication and time to accumulate the deep reservoir of knowledge and expertise." But the day of biking reminded her of hiking Bear Mountain with her dad and mom on weekends when she was a kid. Her mom had become so work-intense after her father died—as the sole breadwinner. Yesterday's trip reminded Audrey that her mom hadn't always been that way. That was one of the shocks of losing her father—she hadn't just lost her dad, but part of her mom. Her whole family life had changed.

Working all the time at the law firm had also changed her. But she still wanted that validation of making partner. *And I'd be a good one.*

Tim emailed, asking why she hadn't been at work yesterday and if she wanted to meet for coffee, but she said that she couldn't meet and she didn't answer the question. She would have to tell him she was dating Jake, but not today. Not when it was all so new.

At two in the afternoon, Jake sent a text: *Change of plans.*

Her heart dropped.

> Jake: *I've found the perfect place for our first official date. It's a restaurant called . . .* Her heart resumed beating.

> Jake: *Wait for it.*

> Audrey: *Waiting with bated breath*

> Jake: *Bated or baited? The restaurant is called Live Bait. Have you been? It's fun. Very lively.*

> Audrey: *Because the bait is still alive?*

> Jake: *Lol. Made a reservation for 7:30. See you there.*

She arrived early to the restaurant. She told herself she'd come in early and stay late tomorrow. The large hand-painted Live Bait sign on the front of the restaurant façade looked like it had been written by a child in a mix of upper- and lower-case letters, and underneath it, large neon letters flashed "Bar Restaurant" in red. More neon signs ("Dixie, BBQ, Raw Bar, Beer") adorned the two aluminum-framed windows on either side of the door. A hand-written sign in the window said, "If you want home cooking, stay home" next to a medal for cooking. Buoys filled the bottom of the window.

Jake was waiting at the bar, which was against one wall, taking up the front third of the restaurant. She could barely see the mirrored back behind all the bottles of alcohol and the sparkly lights. He came over and kissed her firmly on the lips. He put his arm around her and notified the hostess they were ready.

"Trust you to find a restaurant named Live Bait," she said.

"Yes, it's not the most romantic place, but it's fun," he said. "And the food is good."

"It's classic you." The relaxed vibe, a group of friends standing in a circle, beers in hand, laughing at some joke—it was a place designed to foster informality and high spirits.

"I hope I don't smell of stale beer," he joked.

"No." She hugged him close. "You smell of you."

"Eloquent."

"I didn't get a lot of sleep last night." She winked at him. Pop music was playing, and some people were swaying by the bar. They walked to the back of the restaurant where white aluminum-sided tables with colorful plastic chairs were surrounded by turquoise booths on the side. Fishing nets, Mardi Gras beads, and a large mounted swordfish decorated the walls. The waitress seated them at a turquoise booth and handed them menus.

"Work was a bit tough today. I was distracted," she said.

"Distracted, huh?" He smiled and took her hand across the table.

She leaned forward and gazed into his eyes. "Most definitely." Maybe they shouldn't have gone out for dinner. She didn't have much appetite for food. The waitress interrupted the moment, and she quickly echoed his order for fish tacos.

"My friend Rory is having a Halloween costume party. Do you want to go with me?" he asked.

"Yes, definitely," she said, happy that he was asking her out for something in the future.

"When do they make the partnership decision again?" he asked.

"December."

"No hints?"

"Not as far as I can tell. But then I may not be that good at reading tea leaves." Audrey sipped her water. "You, for example. I had a really hard time figuring out if you were interested. Why did you take so long?"

"What? It was almost impossible for me to tell if you were keen."

"What do you mean?"

"You sent me all those gifts—I was sure you were, and then we have dinner and you get a call from that partner and totally revert to work mode and leave immediately."

"I so regretted that," she wailed. "I'm such a dork."

"You're definitely not a dork," he said with a warm glance. "But I was worried you were a workaholic—like my father—and so I was determined not to be interested, especially since it seemed like work could trample any interest you had in me."

"You doubted I liked you?"

"I knew you liked me as a friend. I thought you liked me more than that, but still, you are a lawyer trying to make partner," Jake said.

"What changed your mind?"

"It seemed like you could leave your work phone at home. You didn't take it out when we were biking—unless . . . did you check it in the bathroom?"

"I've been known to check it in the bathroom, but I left it at home that day because I didn't want to be interrupted."

"So that seemed like a good sign," he said. "And I was gun-shy. Veronika was such a total disaster. And I couldn't seem to get out of it—as you know." He glanced sideways at her. "But responding to her call Saturday was a mistake. And I was so frustrated and mad that she finally got the message. Then she told me she'd met someone new, and I told her that I was thrilled for her and she should be calling him, not me. I think she thought that would make me want her back." He ruffled his hair. "But I don't."

The waitress set down two plates of fish tacos and two beers. Jake started eating.

"Was there something also with Penny?" Audrey asked.

"Penny dared me to try old-fashioned dating. And I kind of liked it—the flirtation and getting to know you slowly. But not if you were going to date Tim. What a life you'd have—what with both of you working all the time." He shook his head. "And then my dad said not to get involved with you when you were in your last few months up for partner—you needed to concentrate on that and I should wait until you made it and then ask you out."

"You discussed me with your dad?"

"No, my sister did, after you helped take the kids to daycare. She totally grilled me. She should've been a lawyer. She laughed so hard when she heard you were a lawyer—and trying for partner.

And then she told my dad that he might yet get a lawyer as part of the family." He ruffled his hair. "She likes you. She's sorry she interrupted our jazz date. Throw up dates are not usually my offer."

"Really? I would've thought your rock star life would involve throw up periodically."

"Not in many years." Jake grimaced. "And then the next night, I was wiped out and about to go on a business trip. I considered kissing you—you looked adorable in your outfit—but then I thought, I've waited this long, I should wait for when I return from my trip."

"I thought about kissing you that night, but I didn't have the nerve." Her work phone in her bag vibrated next to her thigh. *Ignore it.*

"Am I that intimidating?"

Not at the moment. His disheveled hair and warm gaze made him look enticingly kissable.

"To kiss? When I'm not sure you like me? Yes." She nodded.

He whispered, leaning across the table, "I like you. You can kiss me whenever you want."

She kissed him. "Time to go home, don't you think?" She finished her dinner. The phone buzzed again against her thigh.

"My apartment so I can walk Biscuit?"

"Perfect."

"Okay, let's get a car." He checked his phone. "Looks like there are a bunch nearby."

"Let me just run to the bathroom before we leave." Finding the bathroom in the back, she locked the bathroom stall. She couldn't decide if she should check her work phone. She had told him she could not check it. If she checked it, it could be nothing and then she didn't have to think about it again. *Until it buzzes again. Or it could be something. But I can't respond. So then maybe*

I'll get stressed. Better to not check it. I'll read my emails tomorrow at the office.

Jake was waiting by a car when she walked out of the restaurant. They entered the car, and she snuggled up against him. He held her close. As they chatted softly, she remarkably and wonderfully and unbelievably stopped thinking about work.

Chapter Thirty-Three

The next week passed in a blur of racing home from the office to Jake, tumbling into bed for can't-get-enough-of-you sex, sleeping little, waking up in tangled sheets, bodies entwined, feeling warm and loved, breakfasts together in the morning, and coasting through work as much as possible.

Audrey had told Tim she was dating Jake. Tim looked shocked for a moment, his body tensing, although he recovered quickly and wished her well. He made one remark: "Is that wise in these last few months?" He sounded like her mom. She ignored that, just as she had ignored her mom who'd asked the same question. She was still working as much as possible, but also delegating more so that she'd have more time at home—an important partner skill. She could combine both.

Knock, knock. Hunter stood in her office doorway.

Striding in, he said, "I have some questions on your memo outlining your proposed strategy for the case. And you'll be interested in this." He put an email on Audrey's desk.

To: Hunter Evans
From: Colette Caron
Date: October 19
Subject: Rothman Case: My Strategy Analysis—Privileged and Confidential

Dear Hunter,

I know that Audrey is responsible for strategy, but we should share it as we are both the same level. Also, since I am in the trenches and responsible for defensive discovery, I've written my own strategy memo.

In summary: We should lead with Rothman, our stronger case, so that we dominate. The Rothmans also want this case resolved quickly.

We should not offer to settle the James case even though the facts are bad and may indicate fraud. We should hold out and see how the case develops. We can always offer that as the first bargaining chip if necessary when settlement negotiations are raised.

We look weak if we offer settlement immediately.

Very truly yours,
Colette

Audrey huffed out a breath; she should've guessed that Colette was not content with just defensive discovery.

Hunter said, "She raises some good points. She should share strategy. And maybe we should hold out longer and not offer up James. It will make us look weak if we lead with a request to settle that."

A cold distance widened between them. It was as if she was facing litigator Hunter and not colleague-and-friend Hunter. How had Colette changed him so quickly?

"We are not offering up settlement immediately," she said. "I proposed deposing the James case plaintiff first to get intelligence about him, a sense of opposing counsel, and to smoke out any arguments counsel may use in other cases. If that plaintiff is a highly sophisticated investor, then James has a legal defense. If not, only after that deposition, did I suggest settlement. And what other option do we have if the internal investigation finds that James was fraudulently trading? What does Colette say about that?"

Hunter sat in the chair facing her desk, leaning back, one leg crossed over the other. "She said the internal investigation can't find intent as required for a finding of fraud, so we can still argue that James didn't *intend* to make the trades to increase his commissions. She suggested we put the investigation on hold while the litigation is pending." His look was assessing.

"That doesn't set a positive precedent at Hen. Hen's anti-fraud policy doesn't look at intent. It looks at the number of trades and any justifications. Hen won't agree to that. And ultimately, Hen is our client." She was sounding defensive. *Easy, you've still got this.* "I'll read her memo in detail, but I've already thought about the points in her email. They are good points, but when I plot out various possible outcomes, ultimately I still think my approach will be more successful."

"You plotted out various outcomes?" He leaned forward.

"Yes, of course. Like flow charts." Her dating experience was proving to be of some benefit for litigation strategizing. But she wasn't going to share that thought with Hunter—especially at this moment. He'd hand the whole case to Colette.

She pulled out her huge charts and tacked them to her bulletin board on the side wall. She had thought this through, and she could prove it. Hunter swung around his chair to view them.

She took a sip of water and then faced Hunter. "Here, this red line shows our starting with Rothman first. First, let's ask the million-dollar question: how strong is that case? My answer: not a slam-dunk, although the recordings are really helpful."

Hunter pulled back, surprised. "John didn't do it. And you found that case with the facts directly on point supporting our legal argument, countering Colette's New Jersey opinion."

"Hopefully we can rely on that case and get it dismissed on legal grounds. This arrow shows that winning outcome. But we have to consider all the options. Let's say we lose the motion to dismiss." She traced the alternate arrow. "We continue with discovery of the facts. If Pierre didn't authorize John to trade on his behalf, it's John's word against Pierre's. We know John, so we think he'd be a good witness, but Pierre sounds pretty charming too."

"What?"

She opened up her file drawer and pulled some magazine clippings out of a folder. "Look at him. He's frequently in French society magazine pages: he's good looking, charming—the jury could go for him in a 'he said, she said' case."

"I can't believe you researched French society magazines," he said.

She couldn't tell if he was being derisive or thinking she'd been very thorough. She suspected the former.

"It's important to know about Pierre, especially if it comes down to personality and jury appeal. I hope we can get the case dismissed on the law. But it seems pretty factual at this point, unless Pierre executed a letter authorizing discretionary trading. We didn't find that in the first document pull. Colette's now in charge of finding the rest of the documents in the archives," Audrey said. "Given that we need to complete discovery, it makes sense to delay the Rothman case. If we follow Colette's suggestion to litigate the Rothman case first, and Hen Bank's internal investigation of James concludes that James violated Hen anti-fraud policy, that's going to create a negative inference for John that his report committed fraud."

"Won't that inference remain even if we proceed with the Rothman case after settling James? Plaintiffs can still say your employee committed fraud on your watch."

"Not if James is fired. Then John can say: 'I don't tolerate fraud. We investigated, he violated policy, and I fired him.'" She traced the red lines on the chart. "But if we start with the Rothman case and the James case is promptly settled once the internal investigation concludes, then we lose any intelligence we would've learned from proceeding with James first."

"I see. Getting information from the James case is helpful," Hunter said. He studied the flow chart. "But if we start with the Rothman case, John can say that he fired James here and that would mitigate the damage." He pointed to the red flow chart red arrow showing the James case intersecting the Rothman case.

Audrey looked at the intersection on the chart. "Unless you follow Colette's proposal and the investigation is put on hold and he isn't fired." *Yes, good point. Quick thinking.* She could see Hunter register that as a good point. "Then John gets all these questions because he's James's boss about why he hasn't dismissed James. That will be a nightmare." She needed to add that point to these charts. She hadn't ever considered the possibility of putting the company's investigation on hold. *I know Hen wouldn't agree to that.*

Hunter acknowledged that she had thought this over and asked for copies of the charts. He looked at Colette's memo again.

Her muscles tensed as she debated whether to say more. Then he said, "I agree with Colette that she should direct strategy too, because she is the same level as you. This doesn't diminish your position."

She worried that it did—that it would look to the other partners like she needed help.

He said, "You'll be co-leaders. It's always good to have more perspectives, although she should have raised her points with you directly. I don't think she realizes that we've worked together for years and how much I value teamwork."

Cold dismay coursed through her. *I just lost strategy.* He was bending over backward to be fair to Colette. She didn't want to share strategy with Colette. She might've, if Colette seemed inclined to work with her, but she doubted that was going to be Colette's approach. Hunter's speech implicitly recognized that, but still rewarded Colette when she hadn't worked as part of a team. *It would be too confrontational to call him on this. And my ultimate goal is for both of us to make it.*

"I need to ask you a question. Am I competing head-to-head against Colette for a partner position? There are rumors to that effect. As long as we are being frank, is that true?" she asked.

"That's ridiculous. We need more women partners, not less."

"Can you share with Colette that you think the firm needs more women partners?"

"I will." Hunter stood.

"I'd appreciate that."

He nodded and said, "I'll review both your memos again and come to a decision as to approach. Remember that it's crucial to the firm that we win this case. We can't afford to lose this client. I'll tell Colette that she'll share strategy."

Chapter Thirty-Four

After Hunter left, Audrey closed her office door and locked it—to digest this in private. She slumped down into her chair and looked out the window at the New York City skyline, buildings crowding against each other, each trying to be taller than the next one. She should've been less conciliatory when she'd suspected Colette was challenging her.

She read Colette's memo and thought about the points raised. She had to address Colette's memo with Colette directly. They needed to work together as a team. But she didn't relish confronting Colette. She rubbed her eyes. She liked fighting for a client or a friend. She had to think of herself as the client. She stood.

She slowly descended the internal staircase and walked down the hallway to Colette's office. Colette's door was open, and she was typing. Audrey straightened her shoulders, took a deep breath, and walked into Colette's office.

"Colette, do you have a moment?"

"Sure, just let me save this," Colette said. Colette wore a white silk blouse that had no wrinkles despite the lateness of the day. Audrey had already been through the wringer and looked it—after that tense meeting with Hunter. She probably should've waited until tomorrow, but no, she wouldn't have slept for worrying about this confrontation.

Audrey looked around Colette's office. It was neat, with no piles of paper. Fresh iris flowers in a white vase added a touch of elegance. A framed photograph of Colette and an older woman who looked like her mother stood prominently on her credenza by the window. A blooming orchid filled the office with a sweet flowery smell.

"Maybe I should close the door," Audrey said.

Colette raised her eyebrows. "If it is going to be that kind of discussion." She leaned back in her chair and crossed her arms. She stared at Audrey impassively.

"Well, yes," Audrey said, closing the door and turning to face Colette. "Hunter gave me a copy of your strategy memo. And I have to say that I was a bit shocked given that that area was assigned to me. I feel like you are trying to undermine me." There, she'd said it. Her face flushed.

"I'm your level. We're both up for partner. Why do you get to determine our entire approach to the case and I just do defensive discovery? That puts me in a junior position. I should be able to give my opinion," Colette shot back. It seemed as if she had prepared for this meeting. Her eyes and voice were hard, and her body seemed coiled and alert in her chair. "Maybe I should've approached it differently, but it seemed to me that my best tactic was to show my ideas as to how to win this case."

Audrey stepped forward. "You have another case that you direct as the senior associate."

"I'm asking to share strategy, not to take it over," she said. "That's an important distinction. You have to be able to see these nuances." She straightened the paper clips on a stainless steel bird-shaped Alessi magnetic paper clip holder. "I doubt anything could hurt your standing with Hunter. It's awkward for me—Hunter favors you, and the team loves you. It would've been much better for me if I had my own case with Hunter rather than joining your case as a second to you."

"Yes, it's not ideal." Audrey nodded, but made direct eye contact with Colette. "But I don't think the solution is to try to backstab me."

Colette flushed then. "It's not as if you are my best friend. I barely know you."

"We're supposed to be a team," Audrey said, walking towards Colette to stand by her desk. Colette stood up, towering over Audrey.

"Hunter gave me a similar lecture about being a team player. But unfortunately, in this circumstance, it is not as if the whole team is going to the championship and will win a trophy ring. There's a good chance only one of us will get picked for partnership, and it won't be me if I'm the junior player and you're the star. I have to do what's best for me and show Hunter that he's not treating me fairly by relegating me to some junior position."

"You should do what's best for the client," Audrey said.

"That's what I did," Colette snapped. "We should lead with Rothman. It's ridiculous to lead with your worst case."

"It's not. Prosecutors in white collar cases start at the bottom and work their way up so that they have the best case against the main target. In this case, we are building up our defenses."

"Unless this approach works better for opposing counsel because they're the plaintiff. That's more akin to a prosecutor."

"We don't have a strong case for Rothman right now, so I don't see the advantage of starting with him. Even the points that you cite in your memo—I don't find them compelling," Audrey said.

"Well, Hunter did, and that's what counts, isn't it?" Colette said.

Audrey was silent. She was still shaken that Hunter had been so persuaded by Colette's memo. She'd read it, and there'd been some good points, but nothing earth-shattering.

Maybe she should try a more conciliatory approach. She perched on the chair in front of Colette's desk. "I agree with Hunter that you should be sharing strategy because you now know everything about our defensive case. I can see that. But I don't think it helps either of us if we're discrediting each other. There's a better chance both of us will make it if we support each other."

"That seems naively idealistic to me," Colette said. "It's highly unlikely that they'll make two women partners given the current financial situation."

"They need more women partners. I asked Hunter, and he said that."

"He has to say that. He can't say that they have a quota." Colette sneered.

"They've more junior female associates than male associates."

"That doesn't seem to have persuaded our male bosses in the past. They presume most of those women will leave to raise families." Colette leaned forward and bit out each word. "They have never appointed two women partners in the same year. And you can't say that the candidates haven't been worthy."

"No, I can't," Audrey said quietly, remembering the talented women senior associates who had not made it.

A tense silence filled the room as both women stared at each other. Audrey felt her flush flooding her neck and shoulders.

"They may have worked against each other—maybe that's what defeated the other women," Audrey said. "And you want us to repeat that."

"Oh, please."

"I just don't think we should accept that they'll make only one. We should change that construct and act as if both of us will make it."

"Are you trying to appeal to some sense of decency?" Colette asked. "This isn't some kindergarten contest where everyone wins a prize."

"No, I'm well aware of that," Audrey said. "I don't expect that they'll feel compelled to make us both partners because they don't want to hurt our feelings. It's a business. But you acting as if they'll only promote one woman just legitimizes that premise. If we work against each other, there's a good chance that neither of us will make it. We'll both end up tarnished. Advocating for each other is the way to go."

"I'm not going to support you, Audrey." Colette crossed her arms.

Audrey stood up. She turned as if to leave, but then turned back to beseech Colette: "At least, let's communicate—including any disagreements."

"I just did that." Colette smiled. It was not a warm smile. "But I can cc you in the future."

Chapter Thirty-Five

*L*eaving Colette's office, Audrey ran into Tim. Sometimes she wondered if he spent the entire day walking around, chatting with partners, working that good old boy network. She internally chastised herself for that unkind thought.

"Hey, you look flushed. Are you okay?" Tim asked.

Audrey honestly didn't know if she could trust Tim. It felt awkward between them now that she was dating Jake. "I just had it out with Colette."

"What do you mean?" Tim followed her into her office.

"Close the door," Audrey said. "I know you warned me, but I just didn't think it would be this bad. She wrote a memo contradicting my strategy."

A pained *I don't want to hear this* look crossed his face. "She's just trying to show her stuff to Hunter. I'm sure she didn't add anything you hadn't already thought of."

Seeing that expression, Audrey stopped talking about Colette. *Had Tim known that Colette was writing a counter-strategy memo?* "You know, I just need to blow off some steam. I'm going to go work out." She circled back around Tim to open the drawers in the credenza and pulled out a bag of gym clothes. Then she turned around, looked at Tim, and made a shooing motion with her hand.

"Oh, uh." Tim looked surprised at being thrown out so quickly. He'd just settled into the chair. "Right now?"

"Yes." She was about to elaborate, but decided she didn't have to explain.

Tim stood up. Audrey held the door open for him and followed him, pulling on her coat and slinging her gym bag over her shoulder.

"Wish I could go with you."

"Probably better if you don't. I've some thinking to do."

Tim walked with her towards the elevator. As they entered the elevator, Tim turned to Audrey and said: "Remember *The Godfather*: this is business, it's not personal."

"I prefer: 'Leave the gun. Take the cannolis.'"

"Really? I wouldn't think you'd like that scene," Tim said.

"I like cannolis." Perplexed that he had come with her into the elevator instead of walking down one flight of stairs to his office, she asked, "Are you going downstairs with me?"

"I'll just walk you out and grab a coffee; I haven't seen you in a while, and it's not every day I get to analyze *The Godfather* with you. I thought you didn't see violent movies," Tim said. This was classic Tim—he'd realized she was upset with him, and he was going to rectify that. "But isn't the cannoli/gun scene the same approach: that it's just business and not personal?"

"What do you mean? Isn't that scene saying 'don't use force: leave the gun' and let's use persuasion and sweets or, in other words, the cannoli?" she asked as they exited into the marble lobby.

Tim stopped cold, and she bumped into him. He raised his eyebrow. "Have you seen *The Godfather*?"

"No," she said. "I've seen *You've Got Mail*." She folded her arms and faced him.

He chuckled and shook his head. "In that *Godfather* scene, one guy murders their long-time chauffeur by shooting him in the back of the head, and the other guy returns to the car and tells that guy to leave the gun and take the cannoli—that cannoli is next to the dead chauffeur's body and he needs that because his wife told him to buy some this morning. It shows how murder is just their job. It shows how inured they are to violence. It's the opposite of sweet persuasion." He started walking again, out the door to the street.

"Oh," she said. "Hmmm. I prefer my interpretation as an approach for dealing with Colette. Use sweets, rather than force."

He laughed, but shook his head. "In any event, Colette wouldn't be interested in cannoli."

"No." She waved goodbye as they reached the coffee place and she walked on to the gym. She suspected Tim had known that Colette was writing an alternate strategy memo. *And didn't warn me. And discussing* The Godfather *is not going to smooth that over.* Rationally, it made sense for Tim to stay out of it and not tell her, but as her friend, he should have told her. She would have warned him if she had known that one of his team members was writing a memo criticizing his strategic approach. *Was his last remark now saying that her approach to Colette wouldn't work?*

At the gym, Audrey bicycled furiously, with her headphones blaring pop music. Round and round, her thoughts circled about what to do about Colette. She believed firmly that mutually attacking each other was ultimately not going to help either become partners. And it was against her whole sisterhood philosophy. She was going to go with her own version of the "cannoli" approach.

Audrey felt better after her workout. She stopped in Barnes & Noble on the way back to the office and was relieved to find a copy of the remake of *Miracle on 34th Street*. She would've preferred the original, but this would do. She also bought a copy of *Feminist Fight Club* for Colette.

Upon returning to her office, she closed the door and wrote on a post-it:

Colette,

Macy's and Gimbels send customers to each other, and business booms. It's a movie, but I think it also would work in real life. Think about it.
    I also thought we could form our own Feminist Fight Club. Have you read this book? Here's a copy.

Audrey

She hesitated before she slipped the DVD and the book with its note into the inter-office envelope. Maybe she shouldn't send the movie because it was just make-believe. She wasn't sure Colette had a sense of humor. She still believed in its message, though.

Her phone beeped. Jake was texting to ask if she wanted to have dinner together later. He was meeting someone for a quick drink first. Business, he added. She immediately said yes. She put the inter-office envelope in the pick-up tray, pulled on her coat, and left.

Jake texted that he'd stop by Fairway to pick up some food for dinner. She texted back that she'd meet him by the subway station as she was already on the way home.

She waited by Gray's Papaya, looking for him. It was dark already at 7 p.m., but the street lamps lit the sidewalk. She pulled on her hat. She spotted him first. He was wearing this blue scarf that brought out his eyes. She suspected an ex-girlfriend had bought it for him, but he did have an innate sense of style, so he could've bought it.

Their glances suddenly met and he waved. A huge smile lit his face. He put away his earbuds and quickened his pace. He lightly jogged to make the light, and he kept jogging right on up to her, crushing her in a big hug.

"Got you!" He laughed and he kissed her hard. As soon as his arms hugged her, she cared less about Colette. That contact was better than a workout.

"But have you a shopping list?"

"Definitely. I've my priorities. You and food. I need to stock up for a few days, at least."

They walked hand-in-hand over to Fairway. Jake chose some apples from the carefully stacked rows of colorful fruit on the wooden green display stands outside while Audrey commandeered a cart. As she wheeled the cart inside and turned into the fresh vegetable aisle, she suggested a salad.

As they passed one of the freezer sections, he put his arm around her. "Let's grab frozen cookie dough. It's a chocolate chip cookie night, given your voicemail message about Colette."

She sighed. "It was also Hunter's reaction. I was just so surprised that he was so easily persuaded by her arguments. And he seemed so distant and almost hostile when he first came into my office."

"Inwardly defensive and outwardly offensive."

"I think I persuaded him that this is still the right strategy."

He rubbed her back. "I'd like to have been a fly on the wall when you pulled out your flow charts."

"Are you mocking my flow charts?" she asked, half-joking.

"No, honestly, they sound brilliant. I do project management charts all the time as I plan marketing campaigns. I'm a huge believer. But I got some resistance persuading the lawyers to adopt them."

"But you did?"

"Eventually." Jake smiled. He pulled her around and put both hands on her shoulders and looked deep into her eyes. "And you'll persuade Colette. It makes more sense to work together."

"I hope so." Audrey shook her head. She didn't want to dwell on Colette when she was with Jake. "It didn't sound like you had a bad day."

He looked down and smiled at her. "That's the beautiful thing about chocolate chip cookie dough. It works for both bad and good days. But it was challenging trying to get everyone on the same page with this marketing campaign."

"Did you succeed in the end?"

"Yes, but legal was giving me a hard time." He steered the cart nimbly around some others that were nearly blocking the narrow aisle.

"Don't they always?" she asked.

"Some lawyers are feistier than others." He held her hand. "They insisted on certain cuts made to the video. The artistic director said they were killing his creative vision. It was brutal. Legal was being too conservative."

"What'd you do?"

"I showed a cat video—the one you showed me that you used once to raise morale in a meeting with associates who were depressed after working the weekend."

"You did not!"

"I had to. It was tense, and both sides were yelling."

"And?"

"It worked. Both sides laughed. Ultimately, I said we'd compromise: we'd cut some scenes and take the business risk on others." He shrugged. "I also showed some music videos I'd found where the content seemed equally close to the line—with no repercussions. Legal seemed more comfortable then." He added chicken to the cart. He wheeled the cart into the narrow breakfast food aisle. They squeezed past another shopper. "I had drinks with the lawyer just now—to show no hard feelings. What happened with Colette?"

She explained the day's events. She picked up some chicken soup for Eve, who had said she was getting a cold, while Jake added penne to the cart. They joined a check-out line behind other customers.

After she relayed Colette's parting remark, Jake said, "Ouch." They checked out.

Each took a bag, and holding hands, they walked out. Passing a newsstand, the Halloween-themed front cover of *Time Out* reminded Audrey that they needed to shop for Halloween costumes for Rory's costume party. Jake suggested they shop for them tomorrow night.

They stopped at a red light and waited for the cars to pass.

Jake said, "Colette might be able to do a lot of damage." A taxi cut off another car, provoking honking and a screeching of brakes.

She shrugged. "I'm still sticking with my approach." She wanted to make partner by being nice and working together and using humor. She didn't want to have regrets about the way she made partner.

"I find humor more persuasive."

"So do I, but I'm not sure Colette does."

Jake's phone buzzed. He looked at the message. "Change of plans. I got you on the list for the concert tonight at the Bowery Ballroom. I'll make some quick omelets and then let's go there. It's one of my developing artists, but I think the group is going to be big. I saw them perform last night. The music is this funky popsicle pop dance—very upbeat. You'll feel a lot better after a night of music and dancing."

She looked at him, unsure what to say.

His eyes held hers. "It's better than sitting at home with today's events going on repeat through your head."

She nodded and astonished herself by agreeing. She suspected that she even surprised Jake. He smiled and kissed her.

Chapter Thirty-Six

The next morning, she felt energized and ready to take on Colette.

The night of dancing at the concert had been the perfect antidote to her stressful meeting with Colette. Dancing to the music, feeling the positive energy flowing around her, flirting with Jake, whispering into each other's ears to be heard over the music, teasing little touches had made her forget all about Colette and work. And afterwards they had hung out in the basement of the Bowery Ballroom. Jake was so passionate about his work—she loved watching him rave about a song or a set. Even though he'd been working, he'd made sure to include her and introduce her around. She'd met so many people—and seen so many tattoos. It was another world from a law firm.

She could also now see what Jake meant about being a A&R executive versus the marketing person. The A&R executive in charge of finding this group was friendly, but he had one eye on the crowd, trying to see who else he needed to talk to. His attention had centered on Jake, though, when Jake was brainstorming marketing ideas with another executive. The two of them were inspiring each other like musicians riffing off each other. That's the relationship she would like to have with Colette.

She hadn't received any response from Colette to the note. Not that she'd expected one. But she wasn't done yet. She'd found some articles about a Columbia Business School case study. That study showed that students reacted more positively to the man's successful career compared to the woman's, even though the career case study was exactly the *same*, only the genders had been changed. The woman was considered "too aggressive," "not a team player," "a bit political," "can't be trusted" or "difficult" for the exact same behavior as the man's.

Winnie knocked and entered. "What are you doing? Working on the Rothman strategy again?"

"Working on a strategy . . ." Audrey said.

Winnie saw a tabbed copy of *Feminist Fight Club* on Audrey's desk. "Are you reading that to inspire yourself?" she asked.

"No, I sent a copy to Colette, but now I'm copying specific pages for her to show her that ultimately, her approach isn't going to help her. Studies show it's better for women to work together— like that lecture Jae attended," she said. Winnie's boyfriend Jae had attended a lecture at his bank by two women executives who had explained how they had made a pact to support each other, and how their strategy was one method women could use to advance themselves. They had met for lunch, sharing their accomplishments, their concerns, and then touting each other's achievements. "So, I'm writing that we should follow their strategy. Women don't look good if they brag about themselves, but they do look good when they do it for their colleagues. It's what you and I do, not on purpose, but because we're friends. It's also recommended in *Feminist Fight Club*: 'Find a Boast Bitch.'"

"Jae was really impressed by that talk. But I can't see Colette as anyone's boast bitch. I don't think Colette has any problem touting her own accomplishments."

"No, she doesn't. But that's why I am sending this study. The research shows that women come off as arrogant and self-serving when they do."

"She's going to take her chances with that."

"And it's a depressing statistic. She should advocate for herself," Audrey said. "Just not at a cost to me."

"Maybe we should ask those women to stage an intervention with Colette," Winnie said.

"We should," Audrey said.

"I was joking," Winnie said.

"No, it's a brilliant idea. If we could find them, it's worth asking if they'd be willing to have lunch to tell us what they did. Colette would totally want to meet with them—potential clients and all that."

"All right, I'll ask Jae their names," Winnie said as she left.

Audrey stuck the case study articles in an inter-office folder along with a copy of the page in *Feminist Fight Club* about touting other women's accomplishments and addressed it to Colette. "Here goes missive number two." *It's a pretty slim chance to persuade her, but this is legitimate research supporting that we should work together.* She was enjoying this strategy.

She turned off her laptop, closed her door, and bumped into Malaburn.

"Leaving already?" Malaburn asked.

Her stomach dropped. "Yes." She had dinner plans with Jake.

"I hate to interrupt your busy social schedule. I stopped by last night, but you weren't here."

"No, but I've been here since 8 a.m. this morning."

"I thought you were trying to make partner."

"I am," Audrey said, her shoulders tensing.

"I noticed Tim and Colette were in their offices last night."

"Isn't it the quality of work over the hours spent?" She wasn't sure she even believed that.

"That's what I want to talk to you about."

Audrey stilled.

"This reply brief is not persuasive. The research is sloppy. It's the writing product of a first year, not a potential partner. You need to rewrite it, unless you want to leave me with this unfortunate impression of your work."

Audrey frowned. She had spent last week writing the brief. It was good. Whitaker had reviewed the section on their argument and had had only a few revisions, but other than that, he'd said he liked it.

"Did you find a case contradicting my research?"

"No," Malaburn said. "I'll expect a re-draft in the morning." He handed her the brief, marked with red slashes. He turned and walked away.

Audrey stared after him, her arms slack, her hand tightly holding the papers. She unlocked her office door. It was a good brief. Her experience taught her that. She slammed them down on her desk. She hated him so much. She was tempted to just ignore him and give the same brief back to him. That's probably what he wanted her to do so he could give a reason for not supporting her for partner.

She sank into her chair. Deep breaths. She'd have to cancel dinner with Jake.

Any writing could be improved.

She'd read his comments and see if there was a way to improve it, but give herself a time limit. If she got home by 10 p.m., she'd still have some time to talk to Jake.

Chapter Thirty-Seven

To: Audrey Willems
From: Colette Caron
Date: October
Subject: Deposition of Plaintiff in James case

Audrey,

I just read your deposition transcript of the plaintiff from the James case. You let plaintiff's counsel walk all over you. Counsel talked more than the plaintiff. How will that help us in your strategy? We were supposed to impress them, not be a doormat.

Yours truly,
Colette

"*L*ovely," Audrey said. At least Colette was sharing her thoughts and hadn't cc'ed the team.

Winnie entered her office, her mug of coffee in hand. "What's lovely?" she asked.

"I'll let you read Colette's latest friendly missive yourself."

Winnie crossed the office to stand behind Audrey's computer screen.

Winnie finished reading the email and shook her head. "Did she read what the plaintiff's lawyer said? We totally made the right decision to let him talk. What he was saying was helpful for us. He came off as a total idiot," Winnie said, walking back around the desk and sitting in one of the office chairs.

"I'm surprised she doesn't see that," Audrey said. "I mean, we did discuss it at the break: that he kept cutting me off and whether I should stop that."

"He was telling us his entire strategy. I wondered if it was because we were women and he thought we were completely clueless." Winnie stretched out the word "clueless."

"We should have told him we didn't appreciate his 'man-terrupting,'" Audrey said.

Winnie laughed. "I would've loved to see the expression on his face."

"But I'm surprised she doesn't see how much he told us."

"She's just pissed because Hunter decided to go with your recommended strategy. What are you going to write back?" Winnie asked, leaning across Audrey's desk. "You should reply with some of his better admissions from the deposition." Winnie stood and puffed out her chest, sticking her nose in the air, and imitated the counsel's patronizing deep voice when he'd said: "Are you asking about his sophistication? You don't need that. I'm not pursuing a federal securities claim."

"And we worried that he might. I still don't understand why he wouldn't. That was shocking." Audrey leaned back in her chair.

"You should also tell her that this is part of the strategy. You didn't give up your game. He mistakenly thinks you're a pussycat. Wait until he meets a tiger in court."

"Her approach is we scare them off before we get to court."

"I'm surprised she's not more sympathetic to the feminine wiles approach," Winnie said.

"There's no way we're going to scare them off. He has a good case with James. That plaintiff was a sweetheart grandfather who's lost some of his life savings by entrusting them to James. And who's in the jury pool? Other retirees." Audrey stared at the blue painting. "I don't think I should respond."

"What?"

"Why should I waste my time defending my actions and explaining how it's good for us?" She wanted to get home to Jake. She hadn't seen him at all this week. She'd been working so late. He hadn't said anything, but he didn't need to.

"Because otherwise she is going to walk around and tell Hunter and others that you were a total wimp in the deposition," Winnie said.

"The record speaks for itself. I'm not, and those 'others' should know that based on my past successes."

"You need to control what she says about you. I don't think you can rely on the past. You need to be talking yourself up."

"I don't have time." Audrey sighed. "I need to have good reasons for what I am doing and make sure I win this case too. I don't want to get distracted by her. And this deposition transcript also speaks for itself. If I tell her why I think it's good for us, maybe she'll twist that."

Winnie shook her head. "I'm going to tell Hunter we elicited some great admissions in the deposition so he has a counter-narrative in case she says we were doormats. Remember, you need to stand up to Colette. That's the only way to handle her."

Audrey glanced out the window at the slick, shiny skyscrapers crowding out the sun and then looked back at Winnie. She breathed in the hazelnut coffee smell from Winnie's mug. She associated the smell of coffee with Kevin. He was always drinking coffee. But never hazelnut. *I do have to stand up to her.* "You're right. In fact, we should write a short summary outlining all the good things we learned of plaintiff's strategy from the deposition and send it to the team and our client."

"Yes." Winnie high-fived her. "Exactly."

"I've worked too hard to establish my reputation to let a few well-placed comments by Colette besmirch it."

"She's not going to succeed." Winnie put her hands on her hips.

Audrey was glad Winnie was on her side. Winnie looked sweet, but she was tough.

"Let's write the first draft together now. I'll get my notes from my office." Winnie walked out.

Women working together is a great thing—a force for good. Then she texted Jake that she wouldn't be home for dinner. Again.

Chapter Thirty-Eight

*A*s Jake fiddled with his iPhone playlist, Audrey came up her stairs, newly changed into jeans and a t-shirt. She was looking forward to a night at home with Jake. The reply brief with Malaburn was filed, so his texts had stopped.

"Should we order in?" Audrey asked. "Or I could make hamburgers."

"I can pull together a ground beef vegetable dish."

Biscuit's ears perked up.

"Is this how you seduce all the girls?" Audrey asked, teasing.

Jake smiled ruefully. "Somehow, I was never cooking home-cooked meals with the other girls. They were more interested in going out and being a part of the music scene. I like cooking with you."

She hugged him. "I like cooking with you too."

Jake rolled up his sleeves. Audrey didn't think she could ever get enough of looking at Jake's forearms and slender hands. She hugged him.

"And you, have you been seducing men with your hamburgers?"

She laughed. "I haven't dated anyone in a few years." Three years.

"That's a long time. And before that?"

"I dated a law firm colleague, but it didn't work out. And before that, I dated someone in law school."

"Why'd you guys break up?"

"He fell in love with someone else."

"Tough."

"Yeah, he did a Supreme Court clerkship and fell in love with his co-clerk. We'd been drifting apart for a while. My father died when I was in high school and his father had died recently, so we bonded over that. But in a way we were both still recovering, so we didn't want to fully let go into our relationship and risk any type of loss. Still, I think we're both grateful to each other for creating a space to express our grief. I think our relationship enabled him to succeed in his current one." *He had been braver than me.* But she didn't think she had been using work to avoid attachment. She had dated Kevin. *And even thought Kevin was the One.* Kevin had seemed so established and secure.

"I'm sorry about your dad. I'm happy to listen if you ever want to talk about it." Jake's eyes held hers, and he rubbed her back.

"Thanks. It was a long time ago, but sometimes something will set it off, and then the pain of his death will feel raw. Like, you definitely don't want me for your date at a funeral. It's so bad I bring my own tissue box." She shook her head as if to clear it. "Anyway, I do have one seduction dish—at least when I cooked it for Eve, she said it was that good. It's my fallen chocolate cake and vanilla ice cream."

"I'm already intrigued." He kissed her. She felt safe and secure in his embrace.

She said, "I'll start making it while you get the stuff for dinner. It can sit in the fridge until we're ready to bake it." As she cracked eggs into a bowl, he ran over to his house to pick up the ingredients he needed.

She was just putting the chocolate batter into the refrigerator when he returned. He placed all the ingredients on the counter.

"Welcome, audience, you have now joined the Audrey and Jake kitchen show, where absolute marvels will be produced," Audrey announced in a fake French accent. She pointed a spatula at Jake like a microphone. "We turn to Chef Jake and ask: what's your secret?"

He gamely spoke into the spatula. "Butter, sugar and salt. Every chef should have those ingredients, and he will be masterful. My sous-chef here will put all the spices into little bowls, and I will demonstrate how to cut up this onion with what I call the Jake technique. Don't be fooled by the techniques of other chefs: this is *the* technique." Jake expertly cut the onion.

"Wow. Did you go to chef school or take cooking courses?"

"I may have taken a cooking course here or there."

"Wait until I tell Eve," she said. She'd found someone who cooked. "What inspired you to learn to cook?"

"Hunger." Jake let that sink in. "I was always hungry first in my family. If I wanted to eat something, I had to cook."

"And what are you planning to make for us tonight?"

"Jake's beef vegetable mish-mash."

"A mish-mash, not many people know how to make that," she said in a serious tone.

"It's all in the wrist. Now let me put you to work; you need to cut the carrots, beans, sweet potatoes, and red peppers so that we have the vegetable part. And I'll start cooking." Soon, the smell of sautéing onions filled the kitchen.

As he was washing up the dishes after dinner, she removed the bowl of chocolate cake batter from the refrigerator and mixed it again before pouring it into ramekins. He splashed her with water.

"Hey, no water in the cake!" she said.

"You're right. I'd better taste it to make sure it hasn't been contaminated." He reached for a clean spoon from the drying rack.

She grabbed his hand as he put the spoon into the bowl. "No previews!" She pushed his hand back, and chocolate sprayed inadvertently on his face.

"You know, this means war." He wiped some chocolate off his face and smeared it on her.

She laughed and sprayed him with chocolate from her mixing spoon. They eyed each other warily, waiting for who was going to strike first with more chocolate. She jumped into his arms and kissed him, then licked the chocolate on his face. He laughed and his tongue licked the chocolate off her face.

"That tickles." She shivered.

He hugged her tighter, and he held her gaze as he kissed her again.

The chocolate cake was eaten much, much later.

Chapter Thirty-Nine

*G*ood point, Audrey thought, as she read Colette's legal analysis on a churning/fraud defense. The articles didn't seem to be working, so the next step was praising each other. She typed out the following email.

To: Hunter Evans
From: Audrey Willems
CC: Colette Caron
Date: November 3
Subject: Colette's Legal Analysis

Dear Hunter,

Colette found an insightful legal solution that will be critical to our defense of the fraud case. I wanted to make sure you saw it.

Best,
Audrey

An email popped up. The motion to dismiss in her case with Malaburn had been granted. She jumped out of her chair and did a happy dance.

"Yes!" She raised both arms in the air and shook them. She'd survived Malaburn, and this time, she hadn't cried. Much.

Chapter Forty

To: Audrey Willems
From: Winnie Chu
Date: November 5
Subject: Mentors Found

Jae talked to those two executives at Global Capital who were on the panel, and they would be interested in meeting for lunch and talking about how they work together. (Yes, he's a keeper!) He gave me their contact info.

Winnie

Chapter Forty-One

The murmurs of people in dark suits filled the conference room, creating a hushed air of expectancy. John Rothman was in the corner talking to his lawyers, with his wife standing next to him. His wife's cancer was thankfully in remission. Hunter was seated across from Genevieve, next to Colette. Genevieve looked up and nodded hello. At the credenza in the corner, two associates were double-checking that the documents were in the proper order. Audrey took her seat next to Colette. Colette ignored her. Mohan brought over a document and held a rushed conversation with Colette.

Hunter asked if everybody was ready to begin. Mrs. Rothman asked if there was a room where she could make a private phone call.

Genevieve asked, "Perhaps Audrey could help us find a room?"

Colette said, "Of course. Audrey would be delighted to escort you."

No, not really. Audrey stiffened. A junior associate could have taken Mrs. Rothman; now she was missing the beginning of Rothman's deposition preparation. But she said, "Of course. I'm sure we can find a conference room nearby."

Genevieve was nodding. The three women left the room as Colette began.

"I'm so sorry to take you from the beginning of the preparation," Mrs. Rothman said.

Audrey felt guilty that Mrs. Rothman had seen her reaction. She smiled warmly at her and said, "It's really no problem. It's just the preliminaries, and I'll get the notes later. Now let's see if I can find you a private room. And I was so glad to hear your cancer is in remission."

Audrey walked down the corridor to the small room at the end. It was booked.

Audrey said, "There's another room around the corner. We can check there. If not, let's go to the main reception and see what's available."

"You know, John and Pierre go back years. I introduced them," Mrs. Rothman said.

"I know," Audrey said. "That's why I find it so surprising that Pierre is making these allegations."

"Exactly. I find it odd too," Mrs. Rothman said. A shared glance of understanding passed between them. "Laila, his wife, was my college roommate. That's how I introduced them."

"Oh, I didn't realize she was your college roommate. But you know, I'm the company's counsel."

"Oh." They'd reached the room at the end of the hall. It was free. The three women stepped inside and sat around the small round conference table.

Mrs. Rothman said, "Thing is, this was not the first time Pierre called John on his cellphone to make a trade. There was at least one other time. About twelve years ago. John said he doesn't remember it. But I do."

"Why do you remember it?" Audrey asked, the room quiet.

"I was annoyed he was working while we were on vacation. He'd promised me he wouldn't work. And then Pierre called him and they were arguing. John didn't want to make the investment. He didn't think it was a good one. Pierre was insistent."

"But we've looked through all the records. Do you remember the month?" Audrey wished she'd brought a pad or something to write notes. She looked around and saw the firm pads on the credenza by the wall, along with pens. She scooted her chair back slightly and reached for it.

"Yes, it was March of that year. We were in Bermuda. I remember because I went out to sit on the balcony to wait for John to finish and to calm down by looking at the water because I was so annoyed. Is this useful?"

"Extremely." Audrey sat at the edge of her chair. This could be the break they needed. "John said he'd never done oral trades before. But why doesn't John remember this? I don't understand."

"He doesn't remember. He said there'd be records that the law firm would have found if it had happened. I don't know why this trade isn't in the records. But I told Genevieve, and she suggested we tell you, even though John doesn't remember."

"What happened? Did he make the trade?" Audrey asked.

"Yes, after a lot of discussion, John made the trade on his laptop. I'd come back into the room, and I was sitting there tapping my foot loudly. And I remember John making the trade and saying 'I hope he sends me the written authorization.' You know, as we discuss this, I think I told him to send him an email confirming the trade," Mrs. Rothman said.

"Did he?"

"I think he did."

"We can ask him to check for that." Audrey wrote a note. "And did Pierre send the written authorization after?"

"I don't know that for certain, but I presume he must have because I didn't hear more about it."

"But why didn't John tell us that you remembered this?"

"John doesn't want me involved. But I am. I'm the reason he wasn't at the office that day, because he was taking me to chemotherapy." Her voice rose in frustration. "I couldn't believe it when Pierre denied that he had requested this trade. I mean, I know the stock tanked, but I just don't understand. He's the one who wanted to buy that stock! And John's not some random financial advisor—we were family friends for years, before they entered into a business relationship. To ruin John's reputation for money."

"Well, quite a lot of money," Audrey said. As Colette had pointed out.

"This is not a lot of money to them. I tried to reach out to Laila initially—when Pierre didn't acknowledge that he'd sought the trade. I mean, we've had a regular correspondence for years. We usually visit each other every other summer, although I'd been lax in writing back earlier this year, what with the cancer diagnosis and chemotherapy. No energy."

"Did Laila respond?"

"No."

"A regular correspondence." Audrey read from her notes, thinking aloud. "Do you think you wrote her after this March call—saying you were annoyed?"

"I might have. I can check my email. We often complained to each other about our workaholic husbands."

"Thank you very much Mrs. Rothman. This could be a significant breakthrough." Audrey's tone was measured, but inside, hope was billowing. "I will pull the records from that month and see if we missed something. Are you sure it was March, twelve years ago?"

"Positive."

"But can we ask your husband now if he remembers this?"

"I'd prefer you to see if you can find any records. John doesn't want me involved. I wanted to talk to you specifically, but we didn't tell him I was going to talk to you. If you find the records and then ask him, as if you discovered them unprompted, then he need never know that I mentioned this to you. So please let me know first if you find anything. Without the records, I'm not sure it does much, does it?"

"I asked Pierre in his deposition if he'd ever before called John on his cellphone to make a trade, and he said no."

Mrs. Rothman harrumphed and shook her head. "We can't trust anything he says now."

"Do you mind if I leave you now to call my Hen contact to check that month? You can make your call."

"I didn't have to make a call," Mrs. Rothman said. "I just wanted to talk to you in private. Genevieve agreed with me. It was a bit of a covert operation. Sometimes you have to work around men's egos." The three women smiled at each other. *This is the feeling of camaraderie that I want with Colette.*

"Okay, then you don't mind if I make the call here?"

"I'd be delighted."

Audrey called her Hen contact and asked her for the records related to March twelve years ago and to double-check that all the records had been provided. It turned out that some paper records were in offsite storage and had never been scanned. Audrey asked for them all to be sent to her.

"Can you let Genevieve know what you find?" Mrs. Rothman asked.

"Yes, I'll call Genevieve as soon as I review the documents."

"And thank you for the society articles," Mrs. Rothman said. "Something is up. Laila accompanies Pierre everywhere, and she loves those events."

Chapter Forty-Two

The boxes full of paper documents arrived at 5 p.m. in Audrey's office. She had chills as she opened the first box. An earlier phone trade could be a huge break for the case. Audrey called Jake and told him she wouldn't be home. He was working late too, busy coordinating a marketing campaign for this album. They agreed to meet for a quick dinner around 9 p.m. near Audrey's office.

She finished an initial review of the contents of the boxes late that evening and arrived at the restaurant first, a small Italian place in the neighborhood that was nearly empty at 9 p.m. The waiter greeted her by name—she'd been coming there for seven years now—and led her to one of the best corner tables.

"Just one, right?" he asked.

"No." Audrey smiled. "I'm meeting someone."

"Ah, Winnie coming too?"

"No, my boyfriend," she said, the claim still feeling awkward on her tongue. And it didn't seem to adequately describe Jake's role in her life.

"Boyfriend!" the waiter said. "That's marvelous! We'll dim the lights some more." He lit the candle on the table with a flourish.

She laughed and looked up to see Jake arriving, pulling his hat off his wavy brown hair. Their glances met across the room, and Audrey felt as if he had physically caressed her. The waiter turned to see who had entered the restaurant.

"Yes, I see he is here," he said.

And then Jake was hugging her and giving her a hard kiss on the lips. She leaned into him, breathing in the comforting smell of him, and looked into his blue eyes. He smoothed back her hair, and she kissed him.

"It's good, then." Jake looked at her as he took his seat. "I can see you're bouncing to tell me something."

"Better than good. I found that trade, and even better," she whispered, "I found the written authorization allowing discretionary trading." Just saying it out loud gave her chills again.

"You've got it."

"I do," she said. "Finally, a big break in this nightmare of a case. But now how do I tell them?"

"Tell whom?"

"Well, first, I have to tell Genevieve. I promised I'd tell her if I found anything, and she'll let Mrs. Rothman know. But this will make Colette look terrible—because she should've seen this gap in the records and followed up."

"She should've. That's not your problem. She certainly hasn't had any problem pointing out your mistakes."

"But my mistakes were not this big. This could've made us lose the case. I don't want to be responsible for her not making partner."

"She's the one who made the mistake. It's her responsibility," Jake said. "Don't you dare feel that it's yours."

"I don't. I'm pretty upset that this wasn't found earlier." She shook her head. "But I still don't want to throw her under the bus."

"And I respect you for that," he said. "But you may also want to be prepared for her trying to pin it on you."

"What?"

"She sounds like that type," he said. "At least in these circumstances."

"Ugh, she is. And especially if she thinks this might ruin her partnership chances."

"Could she make it look like it's your mistake?"

Audrey bit her lip. Colette might try to blame her. The waiter, seeing the pause in conversation, came to take their order. After he left, she said, "Only if she argues that she thought I'd finished pulling documents when I handed it over. But I'm pretty sure I sent an email outlining what still needed to be done, and that included the rest of discovery. I'll check when I get back. But do I send an email to both Hunter and Colette—or just Hunter first?"

"What's your gut?"

"Send it to both. Otherwise, I'll look like I'm screwing her over."

"I agree. Nothing to be gained by not telling both at the same time. How will you explain why you didn't alert them immediately to the possibility of these missing boxes—especially when Colette is responsible for discovery? You could've let her make the find."

"Except Mrs. Rothman asked me not to tell anyone unless I found something."

"And you can tell Colette separately you didn't want to point out the hole in the production unless there was good news."

"Good angle, but I don't want to write her that there was a 'discovery hole.' She'll feel attacked and go on the offense." She took a sip of water. "I'll write that I acted per Mrs. Rothman's instructions—which is what I did."

"Yes, I'd keep the note positive—all good news, etc.," he said. "But then call Hunter afterward to give it more of a personal touch and show how excited you are. You should write it and call him tonight."

"Bonus points for the late-night work."

"Unfortunately, yes. And I want you to get extra credit if you're not coming home with me now."

She held his hand. His beautiful hands were warm and solid around hers. "I wish I were. Just a few more weeks, and then I'll have a whole week off. You may get bored of me," she said flirtatiously.

"I don't think I'll ever get bored of you," Jake said, his eyes becoming blue pools, his hand tightening around hers. "And my sister said she still learns things about Ned all the time." He looked at the calendar on his phone. "We should plan a vacation together."

She asked, "What about that second week in December?"

"Maybe, but it's not ideal. What about between Christmas and New Year's? Our offices are completely closed that week."

"I already booked a ticket to visit my mom in France that week. You could come?"

"That's not quite the romantic getaway for two that I had in mind. Let's do the second week in December." Jake looked at the calendar on his phone. "The Christmas rush is mostly before Black Friday. I don't have anyone releasing any albums on Christmas Day, but I have to start preparing for the top-of-the-year music releases. I can do that week. I may miss some networking opportunities if there are holiday parties, but that's okay. And the Jingle Balls are the following week. You'll love those."

They spent the rest of the dinner deciding where to go on vacation until Audrey said she better get back to work to call Genevieve and Mrs. Rothman, write Hunter and Colette about the find, and call Hunter.

Chapter Forty-Three

Hunter swung around in his chair to face Audrey and Colette.

"I asked you both to come to my office to brainstorm our approach given this latest development in the case." He turned to Audrey. "Thank you, Audrey, for pursuing this lead and finding this documentation. Now that we have Pierre's consent for discretionary trading, we might even be able to settle without a trial. It eviscerates their case."

"They may still argue that the trade was inappropriate," Colette said.

"They'll have a harder time with that argument. Pierre signed this consent while asking John to buy into a speculative venture in Brazil," Audrey said. "Not to mention this chart of other risky trades made by Pierre." She pulled out a chart of Pierre's trades created by Marcia and Mohan with their outside expert. The expert had rated many of the trades highly risky.

"That's true. That chart is great work by Marcia and Mohan," Hunter said. "We needed these documents to win this case."

"It's too bad you didn't find these documents at the beginning," Colette said.

Audrey's mouth dropped open. She closed it quickly. *She is trying to blame this on me. Jake had called it.*

Hunter turned to Colette and said firmly, "Colette, it was your responsibility to find these documents. You were in charge of defensive discovery. Audrey handed that over to you after she did the physical document pull from their offices. We're incredibly lucky that Mrs. Rothman remembered this trade and that Audrey looked back through the document production log and found this gap. We're also fortunate that our client is ecstatic right now and not asking *why* these were not found earlier." Staring straight at her, he said, "You should have identified that gap in the production and followed up."

Colette flushed. In the strained silence that followed, Colette stared down at the table.

Finally, Colette lifted her chin and looked him in the eyes. "You're right. I should have found those missing months and been relentless in getting those documents pulled. I won't make that mistake again."

"I appreciate your acceptance of your mistake, but I am perturbed that your first response was to blame Audrey. Especially when Audrey avoided placing any censure on you and bent over backwards to note that this stuff happens in discovery." Hunter was now being relentless. Colette was sitting up straighter, but two spots of pink dotted her cheeks. Audrey shifted in her chair, almost wishing she had not been invited to this meeting. Hunter then gentled his tone. "Mistakes like this, however, do tend to be better learning experiences than constant success. They sear themselves into memory and so I'm sure that you will be a better lawyer as a result of this." That was Hunter's generosity, thought Audrey—accepting Colette's apology and giving her a way out.

But Colette interpreted it as an opening for a rebuttal and said, "My only defense is that I've been incredibly busy on this Stromen case, and I did think that the production was complete."

Hunter's reaction was swift. "Audrey has a trial in three weeks and she worked until midnight on this, so that's no excuse. If you can't balance both, maybe I need to talk to Stromen."

"I can handle both," Colette said quickly. "There's no need for you to talk to Stromen. As I said before, it won't happen again— ever. I immediately reviewed the entire document production log to make sure that there were no other gaps. There were not. And I reviewed my Stromen case production too."

"Also, Colette, being a member of the partnership is being a part of a team." Hunter leaned forward. "I've said this to you before, but I expect to see you working together with Audrey. This is not a zero-sum game."

"Audrey and I do work together, don't we Audrey?" Colette turned to Audrey.

"We could work together better," Audrey said. She was not going to let Colette pretend a strong working relationship.

Colette shot her a dagger look. "But we do work well."

That look wasn't encouraging. Her head throbbed.

"Enough said. Let's discuss our strategic approach now productively so we can present it to the client tomorrow," Hunter said. He pulled a legal pad towards him.

Chapter Forty-Four

As Colette and Audrey walked out of the office, Colette said, "So all that stuff about being nice and let's support each other as women was just a ruse?"

"No. Definitely not. Mrs. Rothman asked me to confirm before I told anyone. I just did my best not to throw you under the bus," Audrey said. "You should have found this document. As you've told me before, defensive discovery is your jurisdiction,"

Looking annoyed, Colette turned away.

"But I absolutely believe we should try working together," Audrey said to Colette's back.

Colette faced Audrey. "Please. I'm not falling for that again."

"Did you fall for it? Because I haven't seen you acting like you're supporting me. Didn't you notice last week that Hunter praised your analysis to the client saying it was 'insightful'—exactly what I'd written him? It was practically like a magic trick."

"You probably told him to do that."

"I didn't. And it's not like I'm making this stuff up. I've sent you the research."

"You don't need my support now. You have Hunter wrapped around your little pinkie."

"Please. As you know from the fact that we're sharing strategy, Hunter is his own man." *Hmm, but it would be good if Colette thinks I have Hunter wrapped around my finger. I shouldn't refute that.* "Hunter and I have worked together for years. He's not giving me special treatment. If he's in my corner, it's because I've earned his support as a team player. He'll support you as well, but not if your approach is to one-up me. You're the one who asked to be on this case. Hunter told me last night. Why?"

"You're my competition. I wanted to know what I was up against," Colette said. They reached Colette's office door, and Colette leaned against it. "And I thought you were a bit wimpy."

Audrey stepped back and turned away from Colette. *I don't have to deal with this.*

"But not anymore," Colette said. "You've more of the killer instinct than I thought. I misjudged you. And I've learned from you—you totally subsumed your ego for that deposition, for example, letting that guy walk all over you, but you got some great admissions."

Audrey faced Colette. "I tried my best not to damage you with that email."

"Yes, my mother thought your email was quite fair, all things considered. Of course, she works in Washington, D.C. She thinks I should befriend you."

"I don't see the downside. If you think about it, our strengths are complementary," Audrey said. "If it doesn't work, we can revert to being colleagues who don't quite trust each other—or know not to trust each other."

"I'll think about it," Colette said, entering her office and closing her door.

That was so Colette. She has to get the last word in, and she won't actually promise anything.

Chapter Forty-Five

*H*unched over her office desk, Audrey was revising her cross-examination questions for her trial.

> Jake: *While you're stuck at work, think about this: I thought you might want to do a yoga session while I'm surfing in Santa Teresa. Should I book?*

She googled the link.

> Audrey: *Looks fabulous! YES! Thanks! Wish I could do that yoga session right now.*

> Jake: *What about snorkeling with sea turtles?* He texted a picture of sea turtles. *Excited for river rafting. But dry season in December. We may have to go back in September—also prime whale watching then.*

Audrey: *Yes to sea turtles. So excited for river rafting! I can't wait.*

She felt guilty. They should be planning this together, and instead, Jake was doing all the Costa Rica vacation research. She'd have to find some fabulous activity once she finished preparing for her meeting with Popflicks tomorrow.

Jake: *Going to bed now.*

Audrey: *Sleep well. I'm sorry I couldn't make it home tonight in time.*

She sighed. She wanted to be going to bed now with Jake, joking around, Biscuit taking up the bottom of the bed.

Chapter Forty-Six

*A*udrey took a seat on the comfortable purple couch in the Popflicks reception area to wait for her client, the Popflicks general counsel. Two large flat screens playing Popflicks movies enlivened the reception area. Pop music played in the background. And next to the receptionist, a red 1950s-style popcorn machine churned merrily, periodically making popping noises. Bright bags of popcorn jumbled joyously in a bowl on the coffee table. And it sounded like ping-pong was being played in the room behind her.

Betty emerged from a side door and greeted her enthusiastically. What always struck Audrey most about Betty was her confidence. She'd seen Betty give a presentation at a New York bar association meeting, and she'd dominated the room upon entering, even surrounded by men in dark suits. She'd made a quick-witted joke to start her talk, and the audience had been enthralled, leaning forward.

Audrey followed Betty down a hallway lined with framed pictures of movie stars. Laughter emanated from one office that they passed.

"I should have told you that it's completely casual here. We all wear jeans," Betty said.

Audrey said. "I'm going back to the office afterwards anyway."

"Ah yes," Betty said. "I don't miss that life at a law firm where leaving at 5 p.m. is frowned upon. The work-life balance is better here. As long as you get your projects done, you can leave when you want to, which is great when you have kids and need to see some school performance or soccer game." Betty had previously told Audrey that she had two teenagers, a boy and a girl.

"I sometimes wonder how I will balance family life with being a partner," she said hesitantly. Discussing the desire for work-life balance may not be appropriate with a client.

"Many women do it, so they make it work," Betty said, "but it's not easy. Hopefully it will change. It helps if your male colleagues also have kids and obligations. Our CEO, Sebastian, has four kids, and he's very open about taking time off for them, so he sets the tone."

They entered a light-filled conference room in the corner of the building. Audrey placed her laptop on the white laminate table and pulled up a chart that showed a summary of the plaintiff's allegations—that Sebastian was only allowed to provide such news via corporate press releases and filings, not via Facebook. The plaintiff hadn't seen Sebastian's Facebook update and thus didn't sell his stock when others did, so he was harmed.

Audrey clicked on the next slide and said, "But his discovery production is helpful. I think he heard about the update that day. If he decided not to sell, that's his own fault, and we win the case." She moved to the next slide. "His discovery production is filled with folders of stock research. He does extensive analysis before he invests in a stock. At a minimum, we should be able to prove he's an experienced investor who should be held to a higher standard." She switched to another document on her laptop. "More importantly for the case, I think he gets automated news alerts on his stocks, as suggested by this chart I created. This column shows the time the news alert was issued and this column shows the time of the news alert printout in his discovery production. Here's a news alert on United getting the Turkey route at 3:06 p.m. His printout of that news article is stamped 3:10 p.m. So he printed out the news alert four minutes after the announcement. And this repeats across the majority of his stock holdings. So, either he's glued to the news or he has automated news alerts. If he's set up automated news alerts for United and his other stocks, I'd imagine that he also has automated news alerts for Popflicks because he holds significantly more Popflicks stock than United. If he received an automated news alert on the Popflicks news, he can't make the case that he didn't know about the announcement."

"That's amazing that you figured that out," Betty said. "Sebastian will love it. He loves charts and graphs."

"I will email you a copy to show him."

"Oh, he's coming by. He wants to meet you."

Audrey was surprised. Anderson, the senior partner on the case, was not going to be happy to learn he'd missed a meeting with Sebastian.

"But no printouts of the Popflicks news in his discovery production?" Betty asked.

"No."

"That would have been too much to hope for. Still, this is good sleuthing."

Audrey explained the rest of her proposed strategy for the case.

After about a half hour, the door opened and Sebastian walked in. Mid-forties, he seemed to radiate energy. He shook her hand firmly and asked her a few questions about herself. He then took a seat across from Audrey, leaning back. He listened carefully to her succinct presentation of the current case status and the planned approach to the trial. It felt surprisingly informal for a meeting with a CEO. As Betty had foretold, he loved the chart. He asked several thoughtful questions, and she had to think fast to answer them in an invigorating give-and-take discussion.

His assistant poked his head through the door and called him to his next meeting. Joking about how his assistant kept him on a tight leash so he could make his daughter's soccer games, he left the room. Audrey could see how he'd managed to persuade people to invest in his start-up. He came across as really smart but also charismatic and congenial.

"Well, that went well," Betty said, smiling, after checking an email on her phone. "I'm going to a professional development event in January at the Marriott in Times Square about developing the next generation of women leaders. Perhaps you'd like to join me as my guest?"

"I'd love to."

"Excellent. I'll have my assistant send you the details." Betty typed on her phone. "Why don't I give you a tour of the offices before you head back? But whatever you do, don't agree to a ping-pong match with the account executive Chris."

"Ping-pong?" Audrey asked, doubting she'd be playing ping-pong in front of a client.

"He'll decimate you. Do you play?"

"I haven't played ping-pong in years—not since before law school," Audrey said, packing up her stuff.

"Better wait until you've brushed up your skills before taking him on."

Audrey wasn't sure when she was going to brush up on her ping pong skills or be at a Popflicks office event, but she nodded obligingly. She loved the atmosphere of Popflicks, so welcoming and lively compared to the formality of Howard, Parker & Smith. This must be what Jake's workplace felt like.

And she had to admit, she had a little work crush on Betty.

Chapter Forty-Seven

A udrey sat next to Winnie at the firm-wide meeting. The faces of the various partners attending were somber and reserved, the atmosphere in the room subdued.

The managing partner of the firm, Michael, gave a brief overview of the state of affairs. Litigation was not doing well. Michael didn't say it, but he implied that making litigation partner was going to be difficult this year because the firm had fewer litigation clients. Michael said that that the firm wanted to start an associate mentoring committee and was looking for associates to head it under partner supervision. Hunter entered the room.

Colette raised her hand and said, "I'd like to recommend Audrey Willems to head that. She's a great mentor to younger associates." Colette took a deep breath. "I've had the"—she searched for a word and then she bit it out—"privilege to work with her on the Hen litigation. She takes the time to develop their skills and to provide targeted, practical advice."

Audrey was stunned, although Colette sounded like she was talking through a mouthful of nails. Winnie seconded the nomination. Mohan jumped in to say that Audrey had helped him with taking depositions, and he had learned much from her.

Michael turned to her. "Well, Audrey, we hope you'll accept this nomination. Those are quite some testimonials."

"Yes, of course, thank you," Audrey said.

"I'd be happy to support Audrey in that endeavor," Tim said. Audrey flashed him a grateful smile.

"And me as well," Colette said.

"Great," Michael said. "Lawrence Malaburn has offered to be the lead partner on this initiative." Audrey made a choking sound. *Malaburn again? How was that possible?* The associates around her seemed to recoil in shock. What had she gotten herself into—or been volunteered for? She looked over at Colette. *Is that why Colette recommended me?*

But Colette looked horrified. She mouthed: *Are they kidding?*

"I presume there are other partners on the committee as well. We'd propose a confidential associate nominating process if those partners have not already been decided," Audrey said, trying to save this.

"Good idea," Michael said. "I'll leave you and the others to work that out." He moved onto the final business of the meeting.

As she left the meeting with Winnie, Audrey asked, "Do you think Colette set me up?"

"I couldn't tell. She looked appropriately horrified. She also volunteered to help."

"I thought that was because she didn't want to be left out if both Tim and I were on this."

Winnie laughed. "Yes, I thought the same thing."

"I don't think she did, but this is a nightmare assignment, especially now," Audrey said. "So not only are they making fewer partners, but I have to work with Malaburn again. I just finished with him."

And critically, it shows that the firm is not taking this mentoring initiative seriously. She loved mentoring; it was one of her favorite aspects of working at the firm. But putting Malaburn in charge was not a good sign.

Chapter Forty-Eight

*A*udrey rang the doorbell and then used her copy of Jake's key to enter his apartment. Biscuit bounded over, licking and jumping on top of her. Nothing beat a dog greeting to cheer one up after a long hard day. Jake came out and kissed her. She clung to him for a moment. She could feel the soft fleece under her cheek and hear his heart beating.

"You look down. What happened?" he asked.

"I met with Malaburn today about heading up the associate mentoring committee with him. He's such an asshole, but still he said—out of the blue—that I was too effervescent to make partner. And this after I just came up with this novel legal argument on our last case. I was hoping now he would support me for partner."

"You do realize that's total bullshit. First of all, they should be happy to have someone who is happy and bubbly, if that's what he meant—good for the clients and good for the firm culture. I thought that's one of the reasons you were recommended for this committee."

"I've no idea. Maybe he was warning me that I come across as air-headed."

"That's ridiculous. You never come across as air-headed."

"Hmm," she said. "Maybe I need to wear my hair in a bun." Like Colette. Maybe that was the secret signal of seriousness.

"Don't let them change you," he said earnestly, holding her tightly. "It's not worth it. You don't need to change."

She grinned. "Can I quote you on that?"

"Seriously, don't listen to him. You need to be true to yourself in your job. You need to be who you are and not live up to some image."

"Funny, when you first told me you were in marketing, I thought you'd be concerned about appearances."

"No. I like music marketing because I really believe in the bands and their albums. I want them to succeed." He ran his hand through his hair. "Sometimes it's about creating an image, but to work, it has to be true to them."

"My ex-boyfriend said that I'd never make partner because I was too nice."

"Your law school boyfriend?"

"No, my boyfriend three years ago. He didn't make partner, and then he said I would never make partner because I was too nice." Her voice wavered.

"That's a damning indictment of law firm culture, not you. Being nice should be an asset. It should help you make partner."

Her brain froze. *I am right to be nice. It should help. And if not, it is their mistake.* Biscuit rolled over, exposing his belly. Audrey stretched out next to Biscuit, breathing in his doggy smell and rubbing his belly, feeling the soft fur underneath her hands.

Jake sat down on the couch, next to where she was lying on the floor. "My dad always says that you have to watch out for the soul-suckers in corporate life."

"Who are those?" She sat.

"The people who don't have a life and don't want you to have one, either."

"But I thought you felt that your dad works too much."

"He does. But I guess still not as much as he could have, now that I think about it. I guess he did try to be there for us—when it was really important." He slid down to sit next to Audrey on the floor and rubbed Biscuit's belly. "You're helping me see something I never thought about before."

"It's a tricky balance."

"You have to establish boundaries. Especially nowadays when everybody is expected to be available 24/7. It's the only way to succeed in life." He stopped rubbing Biscuit. Biscuit shook himself and meandered over to his water bowl.

"I thought having no boundaries was the way to make partner and succeed."

"In work, maybe—but not at life." He moved back up on the living room couch, clearing away some clothes to make room for Audrey.

She joined him. "And how did you get so wise?"

He put his arm around her. "Easier said than done. We have some assholes in the music business too—though probably not as many now that there's less money in it. But there's still the glory. Seriously, don't listen to him."

She leaned into him. "I won't, but I needed to talk it over with someone. I still don't understand why the partnership put Malaburn on this committee."

"That's not a promising sign." He rubbed her back. "Maybe you need to hold full committee meetings rather than meeting alone with him."

"That's a good idea." Not that she wanted Malaburn to insinuate she didn't have what it took in front of Colette and Tim.

"I've some difficult clients too in the music business, and I've learned it's better with back-up." He stood and stretched. "On to more cheerful things." He disappeared into his kitchen and reappeared with a small white bakery box. "What do you think of this new cookie? How's it doing in the ranking scale?" They had established a mission to rank the best chocolate chip cookies in Manhattan.

She tasted it. Very buttery. "Good, but too old-fashioned. It reminds me of a bakery butter cookie with chips."

"That's what I thought too." He sat back down on the couch and ate his cookie.

"I talked to Mrs. Rothman. She's going to Paris to confront Laila."

"No way."

"Yes." She smiled. "She offered to take me along. She might've been joking—but I've got too much work."

"You're working too hard as it is." He pulled her over to snuggle against him.

"I know."

"How about coming on a ski trip this weekend?"

Her shoulders slumped and she sighed. "I can't. It's not just the boys?"

"Those with girlfriends are bringing them along."

She still loved when Jake said she was his "girlfriend." The thought of going and being "Jake's girlfriend" with his friends was so tempting. It was almost worth ditching work, but as she thought of everything still to be done, she felt her chest tightening. *Think, think, how to do it?*

Jake looked at her. "I can also stay here if you need support."

"No, you should definitely go. You should spend time with your friends and get out there skiing."

"Why don't you believe that for yourself?" he asked, looking into her eyes.

She stilled.

"Are you sure you can't join us for two days?" he asked. "We'll leave from the slopes around four. You could even go into work Sunday night if you need to. I've found that sometimes I'm even more productive at work if I have some time off to recharge."

She was tempted. She'd resolved to be better at balancing life with work, and she ought to be able to make this work, but when she thought of all that she had to do . . .

"I just can't," she snapped. "I've got two weeks until the Popflicks trial, five weeks until the partnership decision. Colette and Tim live at the office, and I have to write the opening statement for the trial," she said, her voice rising, "and review everybody else's cross-examination questions again. I probably shouldn't even be here!" She closed her mouth and looked horrified that she'd just yelled at Jake. Like she'd yelled at Kevin to stop moping around—right before they'd broken up.

He nodded, his face unreadable.

"I didn't mean that. I'm so sorry. I don't know what I was thinking," she said.

"You do know. Don't doubt yourself." He disappeared into his bedroom.

"Jake, I'm sorry." She followed him and then bumped into him as he reappeared holding a boxing bag.

"Are you going to box?" she asked. Had she made him that angry? That upset?

"No, you are." He smiled. "Pressure" by Billy Joel stared to play on his stereo system. "And if that doesn't work, we'll try karaoke. Singing de-stresses, according to my mom's advice for babysitting." He started to sing "Pressure." "I used to play this before exams to psych me up."

Using a stool, he hung the boxing bag from a corner hook in the ceiling.

"I never noticed that hook," she said.

"Probably just as well." "Another One Bites the Dust" began playing. "C'mon—pretend it's Colette or Malaburn." He opened a drawer near the hook and took out some gloves. "Don't let them knock you down." He pulled the gloves on her hands and tightened them around her wrists. She watched as he carefully fastened them.

She firmly kissed Jake on the lips. "You're the best."

"No distractions. I want to see you hit that hard. But watch out for it swinging back."

"Sounds like working with Colette." She took a punch. The bag swung back. She ducked just in time. She paused in her punching. "I shouldn't have taken my frustration out on you. I'm sorry. I want to come, and I'm frustrated that I can't."

"We'll play in the snow another time," he promised.

Chapter Forty-Nine

*A*udrey pulled up her scarf against the biting air as she left the black sedan that had brought her home from work, waving at the driver as she pushed open Jake's building door. She couldn't wait to relax with Jake.

"I'm home," she said, entering Jake's apartment. Biscuit barked. Warm and cozy, the apartment smelled like chocolate.

"About time too," Jake said, appearing in the hallway. He was dressed in flannel pajama bottoms and a gray fitted long underwear shirt. *My favorite shirt on a man.* He kissed her firmly on the lips.

"Just two more weeks and then vacation." She nuzzled into him. "You're so deliciously warm."

"You need some heating up. Can I help you with unwrapping?" He smiled crookedly, his dimple appearing.

"Yes, please."

His hands slid up from her waist to her coat's big pink button, just above her chest. He was taking his time unbuttoning her. She caught her breath, leaning against the wall for support. He held her gaze, his hands slowly working his way down the front of her coat, leaving heat in their wake. He smelled of chocolate. His hands moved to her waist to pull her towards him and they kissed again. She ran her hand through his wavy brown hair and melted into his embrace, letting the feelings take over and silence her thinking. He unbuttoned her last button, and she slid out of her coat.

"Mmm, you taste like chocolate," she said.

"It's a hot chocolate night. Actually, I was in the middle of making some more. I'll put the milk back on. Do you want marshmallows in yours?"

"Yum."

"Coming up." He disappeared into the kitchen, and she followed.

"How was the skiing?"

"Great. Fresh powder this morning, so we got in some amazing runs." He poured two cups of hot chocolate.

"What's your style of skiing—is it a few runs, full ski lodge lunch and then ski some more in the afternoon with a hot chocolate break, hot tub with drinks at 4 p.m.? Or is it wake up at dawn, be on the slopes when the lift opens, and here's your soup canteen, you can eat lunch in the lift?"

He laughed. "Can it be in-between? What's yours?"

"Oh, I'm definitely trending more towards the former than the latter."

"Are you sure?" he asked. "I've never met anybody who brought lunch in a thermos and drank it on the lift. Sure that's not you?"

"It's so definitely not me. Not skiing, anyway." She sipped her hot chocolate.

"How's the trial prep coming along?" he asked.

She carried her hot chocolate into the living room where she could see that he had been reading, if the bookmarked book on the table was any indication, and doing laundry. A pile of white folded laundry sat next to his bags from his ski weekend.

"I think it's all under control, but I'm nervous about my cross."

He placed some napkins on the coffee table and sat on the couch next to her, hot chocolate in hand.

He asked, "Have you practiced it? My dad used to practice with junior associates—and sometimes with my mom."

"We've been so busy; I wasn't sure I should ask a junior associate to practice with me."

"Of course, you should. Your cross-examination is key to winning the case."

"Thanks. That should help me sleep better at night."

"I've got another solution to help you sleep better at night." He rubbed her shoulders. "Yes, your muscles are tight." He maneuvered onto his knees so he was in a better position to massage her shoulders. "Here, you can practice with me. I only know what I've read in the news about your case, but I can be the slimy investor plaintiff." He leered at her in a mocking fashion and sat back across from her on the couch. "So, pretty lady, what do you want to know about me? I'm a simple man, you know, and your company recommended this fund. I put all my life savings into it. And then it dropped. Just dropped. How am I going to retire now?" Jake ended with a wail.

That wasn't exactly the allegation, but more practice would be helpful. Two could play at this game.

"You seem like a smart man—you know that stocks are not a guaranteed investment and that they can fluctuate in value?" she asked.

"Yes, but my financial advisor from *your* company recommended Popflicks, and I relied on his advice. I didn't expect it to drop."

"And you didn't put all your life savings into it, did you?"

"Well, maybe not all," he said.

"You seem like a man who does his research before he buys something."

"Yes, normally, but I don't know anything about stocks." He shrugged his shoulders.

"Nothing?"

"Nothing."

"Please show the witness Exhibit A." She grabbed a napkin and presented it to him. "Isn't this your research folder?"

"It does look like something I often write my research on," he said with a straight face.

"And that is your handwriting?"

"Shucks, yes."

"With all your notes on various stocks?" she asked.

"That looks like my handwriting, but maybe it's my wife's. After a while, when you're married, your handwriting looks the same."

"Your wife wrote this note about investing in internet stocks, citing this *Business Week* article?"

"My wife is a brilliant woman." He winked at her. "But I think I wrote that particular note."

"Is this your handwriting and your note?" she asked. His foot was tickling her leg. *Playing dirty. So distracting. More distracting than I would've thought possible.* She looked away from his face and at the painting on the wall to collect her thoughts.

"Yes."

"There are pages of notes, aren't there?" She took more napkins from the coffee table and showed them to him. He examined the napkins seriously.

"Yes." He shuffled the napkins, took one out, and peered at it closely. "But those are my notes from listening to the investment advisor. I just wrote down what he said."

"Really? It doesn't look like that. It looks like these are your own research. See this notation here."

"Yes, I did research that."

"And did you invest in all the stocks the investment advisor recommended?" she asked.

"I think I did."

"It looks like he recommended some energy stocks, and you didn't invest in those."

"I didn't?"

"No, you didn't," she said.

"Oh yes, I thought that energy was not going to do well. And I was right."

"So, you made your own decisions?"

"Yes, sometimes."

"And you decided to invest in Popflicks, right?" she asked.

He hesitated.

She said sternly, "Remember, you're under oath."

"Yes," he said.

"No further questions."

"Great job." He pulled her onto his lap and she leaned against him.

"That was a good twist with your saying his notes were just his investor's recommendations. I wasn't expecting that," she said.

"Keeping you on your feet. Could he say that?"

"I don't think so. It's pretty clear that his notes are his own research. I don't get the impression he used his investment advisor much. But I should have been more ruthless. I had you in several lies. I need to milk that and stretch it out so the jury doesn't miss that you are lying. I should ask Mohan to practice with me. Thanks." She kissed him. "Are you sure you're not a lawyer?"

"Positive. Just seem to like to hang out with them." He nuzzled her neck. It tickled and she shivered. "Mmm, I missed you. I enjoyed skiing with the guys, but I hope next time you can come."

She lifted her face up to his and looked into his eyes. Jake ran his hand through her hair. She could feel herself relax. She caressed his cheek, feeling the little bristles of his five o'clock shadow.

"I can't wait until we can go away after your trial."

"I can't wait either. And Costa Rica will be warmer."

"All right. Leave it to me. I'm planning lots of fun activities." He kissed her. She wrapped her arms around him and focused on giving all her concentration to this moment, with Jake.

Chapter Fifty

Winnie and Audrey met Colette outside the restaurant. Colette was wearing dark sunglasses, making it hard to read her. She stood off to the side, greeting them with a terse "Hello."

Audrey worried that this pitch meeting was not going to go well, even though it had been surprisingly easy to persuade Colette to join them for lunch with the two executives from Global Capital, a well-known hedge fund. She and Winnie had pitched it as a client development opportunity as well as a mentoring lunch. If anything, Colette seemed shocked to be included. As she should be, noted Audrey to Winnie; it was generous of them to invite her.

Still, the three women had worked well together preparing for the lunch. They'd even had fun. Colette had made them watch a TED talk on body language, and they'd practiced doing the pitch in various power poses. Audrey had been surprised at how much the "leaning back, arms out, feet on the table" reminded her of Tim (even though he didn't actually put his feet on her desk).

As Colette took off her sunglasses, Winnie put her arms out wide and struck a cowboy stance, saying, "Power poses everybody." Audrey and Colette made their own stands, taking up as much space as possible on the sidewalk, and all three laughed.

The restaurant was crowded; it was restaurant week, when the prix fixe menu was discounted. Her father had loved restaurant week. He'd carefully decide which two restaurants he and her mom would visit. She should reignite that tradition when her mom returned. Her mom might be more receptive than she'd been to her trying to revive game night.

The maître d' led them to the table occupied by the Global Capital executives. After the preliminary introductions, Audrey launched into the reason for their invitation.

"As I wrote in my email, both Colette and I are up for partner, and we heard through Winnie's boyfriend that you strongly advise women to work together. We don't want to be pitted against each other."

"We're impressed that your boyfriend attended our panel. Few men braved that room," one of the women joked.

"He's learning," Winnie said. "Your presentation really made an impression on him."

The two women shared their stories about how they'd worked together to be promoted and how having an ally had made the whole process much more fun.

"But didn't you worry that only one of you might make it, and that it would ruin the friendship?" Colette asked, her head tilted as if carefully considering their remarks. Audrey glanced at Winnie—they should've organized this lunch ages ago.

"We did, but we still figured it was worth it."

The five women chatted comfortably as they ate their lunches. The two executives asked some legal questions, which the three lawyers answered easily.

Colette shot Audrey a look, indicating that Audrey should start the pitch for business. Audrey was starting with a soft appeal, with Colette making the closing argument. Audrey could feel her shoulders hunch over, almost as if she was a supplicant. Colette raised her eyebrows at Audrey, pulling her shoulders back. Audrey straightened.

Audrey said, "We're also hoping we can bring in a case to show that we're a team, and expand the parameters so that they realize there's enough business to support both of us as partners."

"This is why women find it hard to be the rainmakers. We feel awkward asking for business," Winnie said.

"We're not asking as women, but because we think we make a great team and will provide you top-quality legal representation. That case we just discussed is only one of the federal securities litigations that Audrey and Winnie have won in the past five years," Colette said. She pushed their bios across the table.

"Last year, Colette won an accounting fraud case, and she worked on many financial cases during her two-year clerkship with a Southern District judge," Audrey said. "We've also all done hostile takeover cases. Feel free to ask us any questions that you may have."

The two women from Global Capital smiled. "We do have one matter we'd like to get your counsel on. We'll ask our in-house counsel to coordinate with you."

Audrey, Winnie and Colette all broke out into huge grins.

"Pitching gets easier the more you do it," the senior investment banker said. "I always remember what my mentor said to me: if you don't ask, you've already got the no. You might as well ask and try to get the yes."

"That's always been my philosophy," Colette said.

"It's just that you have to be prepared for that overt rejection," Winnie said.

"Rejection is fine, as long as it's for legitimate reasons. It's one of the best ways to learn what is working and what isn't working. And you get better each time, as long as you improve based on those rejections," the senior banker said.

"So how can we improve the pitch we just did?" Audrey asked.

"Just rely on your expertise as lawyers. You don't need to appeal to us as women, although we appreciate that. But your track records are impressive, and we wouldn't hire you unless they were. We need to defend our decision to our management as well."

"Thank you. Thank you for taking the time to meet with us and for your mentoring," Audrey said. She was impressed that they had given so much of themselves to the three of them. She hoped she was that kind of role model for other women.

Chapter Fifty-One

udrey microwaved some turkey meatballs for her Thanksgiving Day dinner and re-read Winnie's email from Tuesday:

To: Audrey Willems; Colette Caron
From: Winnie Chu
Date: November 23
Re: Global Capital business development

Just ran into Michael. He told the business development committee about our bringing in Global Capital as a client and they're thrilled—and very impressed. They apparently tried to get Global Capital as a client before—with no luck. Have a great Thanksgiving holiday!

That was good news. Separately, Winnie had invited her to join her and her family in Queens for Thanksgiving, if she wanted to take a break from prepping for her trial. Audrey had declined that invite, just as she had said no to Jake's invite to meet his family and have Thanksgiving with them. She needed to continue preparing for her trial starting on Monday. Jake had understood why she had said no. He'd offered to bring her back a doggy bag of turkey and other fixings. She'd requested apple pie. He said he'd text her a picture of all the desserts and she could choose what she wanted. She was expecting him to say something about his Dad missing Thanksgiving last year, but he'd just looked sad. He said he was looking forward to her meeting his family when her trial was over.

She'd also been nervous about meeting his parents, even though she liked his sister. He was really close with his mom. He'd said his mom hadn't liked Veronika and he regretted ignoring that red flag. And his mom had borne the brunt of a relationship with a workaholic lawyer.

Her doorbell rang. She answered the intercom, and it was a food delivery guy. She wasn't expecting any food.

The man said, "Your mom ordered you a Thanksgiving dinner."

Audrey went downstairs to accept the bag. Back upstairs, she opened the package to find all her favorite Thanksgiving foods. She pushed aside her papers on the table and called her mom.

Her mom picked up on the first ring. "Happy Thanksgiving!"

"Thanks, Mom. This is so sweet of you."

"I felt bad that you weren't having a Thanksgiving dinner."

"Jake is going to bring me a doggy bag," Audrey said.

"Oh, that's nice of him. And I'm impressed that he's so supportive when you're so busy working. At least there's only a few more weeks until the decision."

Her stomach churned. Now that it was so close, it was almost worse. The possibility that she wouldn't make it could become a reality in a few more weeks. And she'd seen firsthand how that had hurt Kevin. And she was afraid. She'd also be devastated. Like Kevin. She felt even worse that her sympathy for his behavior had evaporated. It was seven years of work up for judgment. Her mom was still chatting. Audrey focused on what her mom was saying to drown out her fear. Her mom was offering to fly back to be with her on the night of the decision.

"No, Mom, that's okay. Jake will be here, and I'll see you soon enough in Paris."

They talked a few minutes longer, and then Audrey said, "I'd better go. I have to work."

Chapter Fifty-Two

The imposing cherry wood bench of the judge dominated the courtroom. Audrey organized her documents on the defense team's table. She placed her legal pad to the right of her cross-examination notes and checked once more that her exhibits were in the proper order. Opposing counsel, seated at the table next to theirs, was doing the same. Anderson, the partner on the case, was conferring with Betty behind her. She looked up at the clock that was on the side wall and took a deep breath to calm her nerves. A few minutes remained before their case was called.

The judge's seat was still empty. The American flag hung off to the side of the bench behind the desk of the stenographer. On the other side was the witness box, also in a deep cherry wood. On either side of the bench were two wooden doors, one leading to the clerk's chambers. To her right was the jury box. Hushed conversations filled the room. Anderson and Betty opened the wooden spindled gate in the wooden balustrade—also known as the bar—that separated the front of the court from spectators. They joined her at the table, and Betty gave her a reassuring nod. The large ornate wooden door behind the judge's bench opened, and the judge entered with a swish of his black robes.

The clerk called the court into the session: "Hear ye, hear ye, the District Court for the Southern District is in session—the Honorable Judge Kim presiding. All having business before this honorable court draw near, give attention, and you shall be heard. You may be seated."

Adrenaline coursed through Audrey's body. She was up. Betty had requested that Audrey do the cross-examination of the plaintiff—not Anderson, as would normally happen.

The plaintiff, Fred Smith, sat in the witness stand next to the judge. He was a heavy-set man wearing horn-rimmed glasses and a sharp suit. Arms crossed, his pose reminded Audrey of a bull. She'd met him before, at his deposition. He hadn't been friendly.

His lawyer skillfully led him through his direct testimony: he had invested in Popflicks, but he hadn't known that its CEO had a Facebook account, and he didn't follow him on Facebook. He wasn't even on Facebook. The CEO should make his disclosures via the security filings and not in social media forums. He'd been financially hurt because he hadn't seen the CEO's post on Facebook, and so he hadn't sold his stock when others had.

It was Audrey's turn to cross-examine Mr. Smith. She pushed back her chair; its scraping against the wood floors reverberated in the silent courtroom. Holding her legal pad, she walked to the front of the witness box. Her voice faltered as she asked her first question on cross, and Mr. Smith smirked. Mr. Smith answered her question, but in a tone that made it seem as if he had ended his sentence with the phrase 'little girl.'

"You think of yourself as an experienced investor, don't you?" she asked.

"Well, depends on how you define experience," he said. He'd been coached well by his attorney: don't admit to being experienced or you'll be held to a higher standard. But she planned to prove that he was experienced, so maybe his attorney should have told him to admit it. His answer gave her the perfect opening for her line of questioning.

"Well, you seem like you're your own man. You do a bit of your own research before you invest in a stock, right?" she asked.

"Yes," he said cautiously, settling back in his chair.

"Please show Mr. Smith Exhibit A," she said. A thick folder was passed to Mr. Smith. "This is your research file on JP Morgan, right?"

"Yes," he said.

"And you made the decision to invest in that stock recently?"

"Yes, but this is JP Morgan. It has nothing to do with Popflicks," he said, again in a condescending tone.

"Let's look at Exhibit C—that's from your research folder, isn't it?" There was a shuffling of papers behind her as plaintiff's counsel flipped through paper.

"Yes," he said.

"The first document in the folder seems to be a printout from JP Morgan's website with job listings, correct?"

"Yes."

"Was it your own idea to check the JP Morgan job listings website?"

"Yes."

"Because you wanted to see what type of skills JP Morgan was looking to hire?"

"Yes."

"Because that told you something about JP Morgan's future strategy?"

"Yes. I told you that in my deposition."

"The job listing seeks quantitative analysts to create trading models to assist with proprietary trading on the stock exchange. They're looking for candidates with PhDs in math or finance, right?"

"That's what it says." He leaned back and crossed his legs. "You can read it as well as I."

"Is that your handwriting next to it?"

"Yes."

"What does it say?"

"JPM hiring quants."

"What are quants?"

"That's short for quantitative analysts."

"So that's Wall Street terminology?"

"Well, yes," he said slowly.

She needed to get him boasting of his knowledge. "Have you worked on Wall Street?"

"No."

"But you're familiar with Wall Street terminology?" She looked up at him, hoping he'd see her as looking up at him.

"Yes." He nodded. "I'm pretty Wall Street savvy."

"What are quants? What do they do?"

"They're graduates with math PhDs who create trading models to assist with proprietary trading for the firm on the stock exchange."

"That sounds complicated. What does proprietary trading mean?"

"That's trading on behalf of the firm." He seemed proud to be able to explain it.

"And you circled that and you wrote—that is your handwriting?" she asked to confirm.

"Yes, that's mine," he said.

"And you wrote that note there: 'JPM + high-volume trading = upside.'"

"Yes."

"I understand from that note that you deduced that JP Morgan was about to enter into that high-volume trading market and that seemed like a good opportunity to invest—that's what your note is saying, right?"

"Yes," he said. He puffed up like a peacock.

"And the JP Morgan job listing website—that's not an SEC filing, right?"

"No," he scoffed. "Of course not."

"So, would you say you're an experienced investor?"

"Yes."

Great, she'd gotten him to admit that he was a knowledgeable investor who did his own research and who did not rely solely on SEC filings. She turned and walked back to the defense table and picked up the next exhibit. Her heels clicked loudly on the wooden floor. "Let's turn to the next folder, Exhibit D—that's your research on United, right?"

"Yes," he said.

"And here you kept some articles about their bids for certain routes, right?" She handed the papers to the clerk who marked them in the transcript and then handed them to the witness.

"Yes," he said.

"These articles are printed out within minutes of this announcement about the routes, isn't that right?"

"Yes."

"How is that? Do you have your stocks programmed into your news feed so you get updates automatically?" She gentled her voice so that she sounded mildly curious.

"Yes," he answered. *Yes, he'd admitted it.* She had to remain impassive so he couldn't tell how significant his response was. Now to confirm he received an automatic news update on Popflicks.

"Were you traveling to Istanbul in May?" Audrey switched topics to keep him off balance and distract him from the prior admission.

"No, you already know from my deposition I wasn't."

"It looks like you researched these routes on Travelocity and looked at how many seats were taken—is that why you printed out this article on the consumer demand for flights to Istanbul?"

"Yes."

"You do quite a bit of research when you invest in stocks, yes?"

"Yes."

"And you don't just rely on the SEC disclosures, do you?" She was getting into the rhythm of the cross-examination now. The courtroom had narrowed to just her and her witness. She moved closer to his witness box.

"No."

"In fact, you also get immediate news updates on all your stocks, including Popflicks?" Her glance held his.

"Yes."

"And you received a news update on Popflicks that day, right?"

"Yes, I mean . . ." He looked to his attorney seated at the table.

His attorney stood up. "Objection—leading."

"Overruled," the judge said.

Audrey repeated her question.

"Yes." His face crumpled.

"So, you received the news articles reporting about the CEO's Facebook post?"

"Yes."

"And that was before market close?"

"Yes."

"No further questions, your honor." She'd always wanted to say that. He had learned the news before market close so he could've sold the stock—but he didn't. The responsibility for his loss was his. She turned and walked swiftly to the counsel table and sat down. Anderson grabbed her hand tightly under the table and shook it victoriously, while keeping his face looking non-plussed above.

Rapid whispering occurred at plaintiff's table. The judge adjourned the courtroom for lunch. As the gavel hit, conversations erupted. Anderson clapped her on the back and said, "Well done." Sometimes, Howard, Parker & Smith partners could be so understated.

Betty came over and exclaimed, "That was brilliant. You just won the case for us!"

Counsel for the plaintiff huddled with his client and then approached them. "Perhaps we could have a settlement discussion?"

"I don't think that's in the cards now," Anderson said, "but let's hear your offer."

Betty, Anderson, Audrey, Winnie and Mohan left the courtroom with plaintiff's counsel and stood off to the side in the marble hallway while plaintiff's counsel outlined their settlement offer. Anderson said they'd discuss it over lunch and get back to them.

Anderson said, "I've reserved a private room for lunch at the Odeon restaurant a few blocks away. How about everyone meet back here in about ten minutes? Audrey, can you take Betty and everyone else over and I'll catch up? I told another client I'd call them back at the break."

As Audrey turned to make a discreet break for the bathroom before leading everyone to the restaurant, Mohan came running up to her. "I can't believe you got him to admit that he got an update on the stock that day. I thought that only happened in movies. Unbelievable!"

Audrey flushed with excitement. "I couldn't believe it either, but I had him. I've never seen any investor with such extensive research files. I spent days studying those. And then when I looked at the date and time of his research printouts, it just came to me that he must have programmed news updates."

"Absolutely brilliant," Betty repeated. "If it were up to me, you just secured your place as a partner."

Jake met her at his door with tulips.

"For you!" He handed her the tulips and enveloped her in a huge hug.

"It was brilliant! It was such a rush! I couldn't believe it when he just admitted it—I mean, I was sure of my case, but I wasn't sure I'd get him to admit it. It turns out that you can get admissions in real life."

"Somehow I don't think it happens that often." He kissed her on the cheek. "Come, I've made dinner."

She walked into the living/dining room. "Wow." The lights had been dimmed and soft music was playing. He had set the table with candles and an empty vase with water for the flowers in the center. "A girl could get used to this."

"I hope so," Jake said. "I've missed seeing you these past few weeks, other than passing in the night obviously."

"Yes." She looked into his eyes and reached out to hold his hand. "I've missed being with you too."

"But you're glowing now. Sit down and I'll bring dinner."

"I'd rather follow you about." She leaned into his back as he stirred the pot. "Yes, I'm still so happy about winning, although I'm sure I'll crash soon. It was just so thrilling, and it was so much more satisfying because the plaintiff was such an ass initially. One time, I made a woman cry during a deposition when I made her confess her mistake, and I felt terrible, because I could see that it had been a mistake, but nonetheless, it had to be admitted for the sake of my client."

"I had no idea I was dating someone so ruthless," Jake said in mock horror.

"I'm not ruthless."

"I'm just kidding. You're not remotely ruthless by nature; you've just been trained to go for the jugular at key times. It's probably a good survival mechanism for someone like you."

"Probably. I'm always amazed at how some partners don't seem affected at all by the tension of the fight. Sometimes I just get such a tremendous stress headache," Audrey said. "But, this time, I felt like a boxer with an entourage. Mohan was pumping me up and making me box in the anteroom before we went into the courtroom."

"Sounds like a massage is in order after a hearty dinner."

"I want a bit more than a massage," she said.

He smiled. "Do you think you have enough energy? After taking down that guy on the stand today?"

"I've so much energy to burn off, baby. You're not going to know what hit you."

"Hmm, now I can understand why my mom always says that my dad's legal career is not that bad."

"Did they disappear to the bedroom after a big victory?"

Jake shuddered. "I can't think about that. That's not conducive to . . . I should never have raised that."

She shimmied to the music around Jake, her eyes holding his. He reached out to hold her hand, and she moved just out of reach, dancing.

"Should I put this on a low simmer?" he asked, gesturing to the pot.

She laughed. "I think so. It's getting pretty hot." Jake danced over to her and they kissed. He turned off the pot, and she pulled him into the bedroom.

Chapter Fifty-Three

*A*udrey bounced into the office the next day. She probably should have taken the day off, but they weren't leaving until tomorrow, and she wanted to tie up the last loose ends on this case so absolutely nothing was hanging over her while they were on their trip. She planned to do as little work as possible while on vacation. Gertrude handed her a message from Philip, a senior partner she had worked with several years ago on a big case.

"He'd like to see you in his office as soon as you can—after you've settled in," Gertrude said. "Congratulations! I heard all about the huge win!"

That was nice of Philip to want to congratulate her in person. He showed a bit of a mentoring interest periodically. She dropped her bag by her desk, changed into heels, and walked down the hall towards his office.

His assistant was on the phone, but waved that Audrey should proceed on in.

"Congratulations on your win! It's quite the talk of the firm," Philip said.

"Thank you."

"And you'll be thrilled to hear as well that your former British client requested you. They absolutely must have you on this new litigation. I've already flagged this for the other partners here with regard to your partnership bid, not that you need more commendations, of course, but every bit helps."

"That is flattering. I enjoyed working with them and with you on that last case."

"Yes, you'll need to leave for London tomorrow; they're lining up witness interviews and pulling the documents, but they want to get your thoughts on overall strategy first. Here's the complaint."

A buzzing filled her ears. *Had he said London tomorrow?*

"I'm sorry, did you say London tomorrow?"

"Yes."

"I can't, I'm on vacation. I'm flying to Costa Rica with my boyfriend . . ."

He cut her off. "You'll need to re-schedule."

"Are you sure it can't wait until next week?"

"Audrey, are you serious? The client requested you. They've just been hit with a lawsuit. You can't tell them to wait a week while you fly down to Costa Rica to be with your boyfriend! Just go to Costa Rica next week—or during Christmas. We'll pick up any cancellation fees. You're up for partnership now, and as far as I can tell, you've got it in the bag, but don't get cocky and assume that. Not being there for this client would be one sure way to jeopardize your chances."

Her eyes widened. He was staring at her. She knew what she had to say. She just had to say it. *Out loud.* "You can count on me. I'll make the necessary arrangements to go to London tomorrow."

Chapter Fifty-Four

o, No, No. What am I going to do?
She had to go to London—they had made that clear.
Why? Just when it finally looks like I might have it all—partnership and this amazing guy—it's all going to fall apart. How can I tell him? More importantly, how is he going to react? He hadn't wanted to date a lawyer because lawyers always had to work and prioritized work above everything. Maybe she could promise Christmas and another weekend—like jazz fest in New Orleans—that was several months away. Promise would not be a good word to use since she couldn't, apparently—she had promised this week that she would be free. And she'd thought she would be—she should have been. The case was done. This was like some sort of final partnership test—willing to put career above all else.

The phone rang. It was Jake. Oh no. Maybe she shouldn't pick up.

She answered the phone and said softly: "Jake." Tears welled up in her eyes.

"Audrey! Are you packed? I just got off the phone with one of my friends down there, and he'll pick us up and take us to this treetop restaurant. How's that for a romantic start to our getaway?"

"Jake," her voice was like a croak, she felt like her throat had been stuffed with cotton, "I can't go."

"What!?"

"I have to fly to London for another case tomorrow night," she whispered. There was dead quiet on the phone.

"Are you joking? Because I'm not finding this funny."

"No, I wish, the senior partner called me into his office and said that I needed to go to London to figure out the strategy and do some witness interviews. The client requested me. It's a client I worked for about two years ago. They just got hit with a lawsuit."

"Really? You're like an indentured servant, and you can't say you already have plans? Or just push it back?"

"I said I'm going on vacation and I scheduled a trip to Costa Rica with my boyfriend and I couldn't do it, but the partner said that they couldn't push it back, and that I was expected to do this and I should be happy that the client requested me. And that sometimes plans have to be broken—especially in the year that you're up for partner."

"And that's what you want? I've been through this drill before, as you know."

"I don't want this," she said. "But I can't just give it up—I've worked so hard." Her voice broke.

There was a brief silence.

"Fuck, I'm not doing this. I just can't do this. I can't believe I fell for a fucking corporate lawyer."

"Jake . . ."

"I'm sorry, Audrey." Jake hung up.

She listened to the final dial tone. She couldn't breathe. She had to get out. She couldn't cry at the office. She'd just managed to hold it together in that partner's office.

She hurried out into the hallway to the fire exit staircase. She couldn't take the elevator. Her legs felt like Jell-o and her chest was about to burst. She kept taking big gulps of air as she bolted down the stairs. *I can't take this anymore. It's too much to ask.* She pulled open the metal exit door and burst out into the crowded street. She ran down the block, tears streaming down her face. She made it to the Hudson River esplanade. She gripped the cold metal balustrade, heaving. Wiping away her salty tears, she watched the tug push the bigger boat up the river, against the current.

Malaburn was right. She didn't have what it took to be a partner.

Chapter Fifty-Five

The London sky was pale blue, almost white, as evening approached. Audrey wandered through London's streets back to her hotel, needing some fresh air and space to think. She'd made it through two days now, including the client dinner last night, and she'd carried it off—not brilliantly, by any means, but sufficiently. She remembered reading an article that if you pretend to be happy, that alone could affect your mood and make you happier. She hadn't pretended to be happy, but she'd pretended to be a lawyer—by not allowing herself to think of Jake or that they'd broken up, so maybe that had enabled her to function. So, she did have what it took to be a partner. No wonder so many thought of lawyers as heartless. She'd been able to compartmentalize too when her father had died, carrying on with school, crying at night. Malaburn's criticism that she was too emotional was wrong. Sometimes she worried she wasn't emotional enough.

Still, as she passed through Piccadilly Circus, she couldn't help but stare at the statue of Eros. His arrow had pierced her hard, and her whole body ached as if trying to recover from the injury.

The first day here, when she'd woken up and realized once again that it was true—that Jake had broken up with her—she couldn't move. Her whole body had felt like lead. It had hurt to get out of bed. She'd had to force herself to take a shower and eat something of her room-service breakfast. Eating breakfast had been like chewing sawdust. Camouflaged in her crisp black skirt suit, she'd told herself not to think about it for now—to push it to the side of her thoughts and not let it emerge. But she hadn't succeeded. There had been that moment when her London colleague, the guy who was also up for partner, had said dismissively that the paralegal couldn't make it in because his girlfriend had broken up with him, and she'd frozen, her mind veering off to her own break-up. He'd had to prompt her and ask her what she thought of that last point legally. Even then, she had stared at him blankly.

Her relationship was over. Just like that.

She respected that paralegal—who apparently was a guy who'd been able to stand up for himself and take time for his emotions. Then again, he might really be an emotional wreck. Maybe the fact that she had been able to compartmentalize it, if even just a bit, was a sign that it wasn't meant to be.

She walked by the ticket booths at Piccadilly Circus. Normally, she loved London, and if this had been a usual trip, she would've bought a last-minute ticket to a play and spent her off night at a theatre. Instead, she planned to go to her hotel room, get room service, and cry. Maybe she should also take a hot bath. She felt so drained, her body as sore as if she'd run a marathon.

Eve had suggested he might come around, that he'd realize it was silly to give up what they had just because she'd had to miss one romantic getaway for work. But it wouldn't just be this one time. And both she and Jake knew that. They had barely seen each other this past month as she'd prepared for the trial, working nonstop at the office, sometimes only going home to sleep between midnight and 6 a.m. She remembered a year ago, one of her favorite senior partners shaking his head when their arbitration hearing was scheduled for the week before Christmas, which meant living in a hotel in Louisiana for the month of December. He'd said, "My wife is going to kill me for missing all the holiday parties. She hates going alone." And he was sixty-two. It didn't end. She felt terrible to have canceled on Jake. She'd done exactly what he'd feared would happen.

But it wasn't a real choice. You didn't walk away from making partner at Howard, Parker & Smith for a guy you'd just started dating. They could date for a year and then find out they were irreconcilably incompatible, for reasons other than the current fundamental difference of attitude towards work and life—something probably more mundane, like leaving the toilet seat up—and then it would end, and she'd have given up a partnership for that. No guy would do that—except maybe the broken-hearted paralegal.

She'd called Hunter to get his take on the situation, and he'd said that this was her partnership bid. If it were him, he'd just reschedule and go on a vacation trip when he returned from London. But Hunter's wife didn't work—and Jake couldn't just take off on a whim. Hunter said Jake should understand the demands of careers nowadays, unless he had some crap job, in which case, she should be aiming higher. But Jake understood only too well the demands of her career.

Max had immediately suggested that she fly from London to Costa Rica if she was able to leave London early and surprise him there. That would have been a bold move. And she would have been willing to do that, had he gone to Costa Rica. Instead, they had canceled everything, and her firm had reimbursed the amount of the plane tickets and any cancellation fees.

She had not learned this from a phone call with Jake, whose voice would have told her if there was still hope.

He'd sent an email with the details.

Chapter Fifty-Six

ow she was sick. She shouldn't have been surprised. This was par for the course. She'd try to suppress her emotions and carry on, and her body would finally say: enough of this, and she'd get the flu or bronchitis or some other illness that confined her to bed. She supposed that her body, no longer buoyed by her relationship with Jake, had worn down with work stress and the Jake break-up, and it had just flattened her. Well, that blocked the question of any bold move of trying to reconcile with Jake—at least for the moment.

She'd flown in last night from London and gone straight to bed.

In London, she'd developed a preliminary strategy that the client approved. The judge granted their motion for an extension so they'd have more time to respond to the complaint. The case had now been staffed up heavily. So, there was nothing immediately pressing on the London case for her to do. She emailed the client and the partner and told them that she was going to the doctor.

She then changed her out-of-office message to note that she was sick and she would not be checking email today.

At the doctor's office, she texted Eve that she was back but sick with bronchitis. Eve said she'd make her chicken soup. She texted Max that she and Jake had broken up. Max sent her a text telling her to just talk to Jake. She said, no, on my way back from the doctor—bronchitis. Max sent many sad faces.

> Max: *PS. We will come up with another bold plan when you're better.*

Great, Max would probably have her sky-diving into his yard.

> Max: *Do u still have rock star costume?*

She laughed, which turned into a hacking cough.

> Audrey: *Max, you were rock star. I was groupie.*

> Max: *You're always a rock star to me!*

> Audrey: *Except that I can't sing.*

> Max: *You can lip-sync—can't you? We'll talk soon! Will work on this. Chin up!* ☺☺

She was sure it was just her feverish mind playing tricks on her, but those smiling faces looked like little devils grinning. She needed to get better soon so she had some strength to stop Max's latest machinations.

Around 8 p.m., she woke up again. Eve had texted and said she would bring over the soup whenever Audrey felt like it. She texted Eve that she was going to take a shower, but she would love some soup.

After the shower, seeing her phone blinking red, she picked it up. She shouldn't check it. She had given herself the day off. Still, she did.

To: Audrey Willems
From: Lawrence Malaburn
Date: December
Subject: Associate Mentoring Committee

Audrey, I would like to meet with you today about the associate mentoring committee.

Lawrence M. Malaburn

Well, that wasn't urgent. He must have seen her out-of-office message. Except there were two more messages from Malaburn.

To: Audrey Willems
From: Lawrence Malaburn
Date: December
Subject: Associate Mentoring Committee

Audrey, please respond immediately. I need to talk to you today about the associate mentoring committee. I left you a voicemail on your work number.

Lawrence M. Malaburn

Because that would be the best way to reach a sick person who isn't checking their email—by calling that person in their office.

To: Audrey Willems
From: Lawrence Malaburn
Date: December
Subject: Associate Mentoring Committee

Audrey, I left you a voicemail on your work phone and wrote you three emails. As you know, it is firm policy to respond within 24 hours to emails.

Lawrence M. Malaburn

From clients. Didn't he see her out-of-office message? Well, the twenty-four hours hadn't passed yet.

Eve knocked on the door.

"You aren't working, are you? You look like shit."

"That's how I feel too. Hopefully sleeping and the steroids will help." She took the quart of soup from Eve and heated it up. "Malaburn is mad at me because I didn't respond to his three emails today, even though my out-of-office message states that I am sick and I won't be checking email." Audrey set the soup on the table and slumped into the chair.

"Are you sure you want to continue working in this shark tank? It's like you're down bleeding and they're circling." Eve sat across from her.

Audrey spooned up the soup. "This is soo good. Thank you. I don't know. I'm too tired and sick to think about it now. I'm going to respond to him—within the 24 hours—that I've just gotten back from my doctor and I'm sick with bronchitis and that I would be delighted to discuss when I am better and I'm back in the office. Back off. But without adding the back off."

"Way to act like a partner."

"More like: way to piss off a partner—a week before the decision."

"That too."

Audrey just shook her head. "I'm worn out. I'll cc Tim and ask him to follow up with Malaburn."

"Do it now so you don't continue to think about it."

"You know me too well." Audrey typed a response and put the phone down. It immediately beeped. Both women stared at the phone.

"He probably wrote 'feel better.'"

"You think?" Audrey asked skeptically, picking it up. Her eyes widened and she coughed.

"No?"

"No, he's asking a whole bunch of questions, most of which I'd need to think about. Maybe it's for Tim." She scrolled up to the email addresses. "Except he only sent it to me." She sighed. She added Tim to the email and asked him to respond.

Eve raised her eyebrows. "It doesn't seem like Malaburn wants Tim to respond."

"No. But I need to put myself first. I need to get physically better. And I need some space and time to think about Jake—without passive-aggressive weirdness from Malaburn." She picked up her work phone, opened her balcony sliding door, and dropped the work phone off her balcony. "No work distractions."

Eve looked shocked. "Never thought I'd see the day."

Audrey walked back in and closed the door behind her. "I've just won a court case for Popflicks, settled another case favorably for one of our top bank clients, brought in a new hedge fund client, and canceled my vacation to fly to London for another client at their request. If they don't make me partner because I don't answer emails when I'm sick, then so be it. I'll find a place that will."

Eve clapped. "You go girl."

Her shoulders slumped. "But where am I going?"

Eve hugged Audrey, but with a bit of space, head tilted away, so she didn't get sick too.

"Still no word from Jake?"

"No. And now I'm too sick to call him anyway. And I haven't decided that I should be the one calling him." Audrey sat back down. "I don't know how to persuade him to come back. I'm still a lawyer, trying to make partner, at the beck and call of clients, and I respect his decision that he doesn't want to be a part of that."

"That's okay. Let him have some time away to think about it. He'll be back. You're pretty special—even with your flushed face and hacking cough."

"I'm being careful to wash my hands so I don't get you sick." Audrey took another spoonful of soup.

"Don't worry. You can get some really weird diseases working in kitchens. You don't even want to know." Eve shuddered. "But if Jake doesn't come to his senses, I'm sure Max will come up with some scheme."

"He definitely will. He asked me if I have a rock star costume, so I'm thinking he wants me to pretend to be a member of an all-girl band that Jake will discover."

"Not bad. Except you can't sing."

"Details." Audrey finished up the soup and took the bowl to her sink.

"I'll leave you. Get some more rest. I left another pint of soup in your fridge."

"You're the best."

Still achy and feverish, Audrey called in sick on Tuesday too. She talked to Max but when she sent him a picture of what she looked like, he agreed any seduction had to be put on hold—although he texted that it would be a true love test. She spent the day sleeping in bed—and missing Jake.

Just before dusk, she opened her door to the backyard—not to see if Jake was there, of course, but for some fresh air. Who was she kidding? She did wonder if he was home, even though she didn't want to see him when she looked like this. The light was dimming in the backyard. She admired the preening cardinal sitting in the tree, bright red against the dark branches, but she had a niggling suspicion that something was different about her yard. She looked around again, but her head was too heavy to keep upright. She closed the door and sank back into bed.

When she finally left her apartment to pick up some food supplies, she glimpsed the back of Jake through the window of a bar around the corner. He had said the bar was a real neighborhood find, with such a great atmosphere and playlist. Even though she had lived in the neighborhood for years, she'd never been there. Jake, his back towards her, was talking to a dark-haired guy holding a beer. He had on that worn, soft blue shirt that she loved on him. She felt a pang in her chest. Her breath caught. She walked on quickly so he didn't turn around and see her. *At least he hadn't moved.* She couldn't help hoping that, once she was better and they saw each other again, he'd come back.

When she arrived home, she walked into the yard to figure out what had changed. The fence. Yes, the gap—the gap which they'd used to visit each other—in the wooden fence was boarded up. Three new plywood boards had been nailed in and dirt had been put in the hole dug by Biscuit. Her heart dropped. She hoped there might be a chance of reconciliation, but seeing the new plywood firmly nailed into place, she doubted it. The boards did not fit perfectly. You could see that there had been a gap, as if showing a scar of pain, but now it was a fortress, fortified, battle-hardened—ready to fulfill its mission of setting boundaries and keeping the other out.

Chapter Fifty-Seven

Still sick but not feverish, Audrey went back into the office. She would've liked to stay in bed, but she couldn't take another day off. In three days, the partnership decision would be announced. She could barely sleep at night and the office was tense. Conversations ceased as she walked by. Whispering assistants darted glances at her. Winnie was nervous for her.

As she sat and booted on her computer, her phone rang.

"Audrey, this is Eleanor Rothman."

"How was France?" Audrey asked.

"I solved the mystery." Mrs. Rothman's voice over the line radiated satisfaction. "I tracked down Laila and met her in the south of France. It was awkward at first, but then we saw two other women chatting, and I said they looked like us when we were younger. Then it was like old times. Laila said that she'd asked Pierre for a divorce at the beginning of the year. That was a shock, but less so because of those magazine pictures you showed me. Laila suspected that Pierre had filed the lawsuit to alienate her from me and her best friends as revenge, but she's not sure. She doesn't discuss investments with him, so she has no way of knowing. All her energy is being consumed by their still-private divorce battle, so she didn't want to get involved in this too. And she'd been embarrassed to reach out to me because of Pierre's despicable behavior."

"I thought there had to be another reason, but I'm not sure I expected to be right," Audrey said.

Mrs. Rothman laughed. "Trust your instincts. Both John and I felt it couldn't be the stock trade. John feels much better about it all now, except he feels bad that his friendship wasn't worth more. But as I told him, Pierre's right that we would take Laila's side."

"And is your friendship now okay?"

"Yes, we won't let Pierre succeed in tearing us apart," Mrs. Rothman said. "We wanted to thank you again. John wrote a letter expressing his gratitude for your work to Howard, Parker & Smith. He understands that you're up for partner. We just wanted to do our part to help. I'll tell his assistant to send you a copy."

"Thank you so much. I really appreciate it. Also, this call. Thank you for telling me what you found out."

"It was you who found the first clue. And you validated our sense that it couldn't be about the money. You know, cancer has taught me that you can never be sure how much time you have. You helped me set right an important friendship and avoid regrets. Thank you."

After a few more minutes, they hung up. Audrey felt vindicated. She was happy that Laila and Mrs. Rothman had also managed to rekindle their friendship. It gave her hope that she and Jake could reignite their relationship. But she'd wait until after the partnership decision to call him, because if their talk didn't go well, she could take only so much bad news at a time. She turned back to researching a new angle in the British case.

At 5 p.m., just as she was packing up to leave early, Malaburn called. As she saw his name flash up, her head throbbed.

"Audrey, I've got another case I'd like you to work on," Malaburn said, outlining the case.

She couldn't believe he was giving her an assignment right before the partnership decision meeting. Should she take that as a good sign—that he expected her to still be here on Monday morning after the decision? Or maybe she couldn't read anything into it. They could offer a counsel position and not a partnership position and expect her to be here on Monday. Most people seemed to accept that, hoping that they could make partner in another year. She didn't want to be continually trying for partner, though. And she'd be embarrassed that she'd been passed over. But she wasn't going to do another case with Malaburn.

"No," Audrey said.

"Excuse me?"

"I said no. I'm not free to work on another case with you."

"You just finished your trial."

"Yes, but I'm on another case already. And it's very busy and needs my full attention. Plus, I have the Global Capital litigation."

"The partnership decision is tomorrow."

"So it is," Audrey said, her voice clipped. *I could say yes and then say no after the partnership meeting.*

No. As she'd told Eve, she had established her record. If they didn't make her a partner, so be it.

Malaburn said, "I'll talk to the assignment coordinator."

"That's exactly whom you should talk to," she said.

He hung up.

She rubbed her temples to ease the pressure in her head. *That was probably a mistake.* But she didn't regret it. She finished packing and turned off her office lights.

As she was walking out, she bumped into Colette.

"You look like shit," Colette said.

"Yeah, I'm still recovering from bronchitis."

Colette backed up. "I thought you'd be floating. Your trial was the talk of the firm. It's a pity you had to leave that week and not enjoy the buzz."

"I wouldn't have been here anyway. I was supposed to go on vacation that week with my boyfriend."

"That's rough. Maybe at Christmas you can get away?"

"We broke up. Because I had to work and cancel our vacation."

"That's just wrong. You know that. You're lucky to find out now. And better that it was so blatant, rather than some insidious behavior where they act like they support you but then make you feel guilty when you're working. I make it a principle to cancel one date early in the relationship to test that."

"You do?"

"Yes."

I am not surprised. Audrey nodded. "Well, in the past month, I canceled on some dinners and barely saw him because I was working so much. So, he would've passed that test initially. His father is a lawyer who's canceled lots of family vacations, so this triggered that constant disappointment. I should've known not to schedule our vacation right after the trial."

"You're making excuses for him." Colette held open the door. "I used to hate it when my mom made excuses for my dad."

Audrey wasn't sure how to respond. It wasn't fair to compare Jake to a deadbeat cheating dad. She suddenly had a memory of her mom crying after her dad died. "I hated it when my mom cried after my dad died. I feel bad now that she felt she had to hide her crying because it scared me."

Colette looked surprised. *As she should be. I can't believe I just shared that with Colette.*

"I guess what I'm saying is that there's a lot of emotion and past history in relationships, and sometimes that needs to be expressed or at least addressed," Audrey said.

"Like the way you tried to figure out another reason for why Pierre was suing?"

"Yes," Audrey said, glad to get on less emotionally fraught territory.

"Did you ever find out anything?"

"Mrs. Rothman called me today because she tracked down Pierre's wife in France. His wife suspects he filed the lawsuit as revenge for her request for divorce, to alienate her friends. That's all confidential still."

"Wow, I hadn't expected that, as you know," Colette said and she laughed, shrugging. "I really need to tap into my French roots in my next case."

Times like these, she really liked Colette. Audrey smiled. She wasn't sure she and Colette would ever be close friends, but these were baby steps.

Chapter Fifty-Eight

onight was the night. The partners were voting. Her stomach was churning and thoughts kept circling round and round: what if she didn't make it? After losing Jake? After all these years of hard work? She'd gone home because if she didn't make it, she didn't want to do a walk of shame through the hallways of the firm. Tim and Colette were also waiting for the decision at home. Tim said he would text her when he heard, if it was good news.

Eve and Winnie had offered to hang out with her, but she was too nervous to be with people.

What was she going to say if Hunter called to say she hadn't made it? Maybe she should write something so she was prepared. No, she couldn't do that now; she'd just have to wing it and get off the phone as quickly as possible.

She paced around her apartment. The meeting was taking forever.

She walked out into her yard to spy on whether Jake was home, but the lights were dark in his apartment. He was the only person she wanted to be with; he would've made it fun. He probably would've played "Pressure" again and made her punch the punching bag. She slipped back into her apartment and went upstairs. She searched on her iPhone for songs with "partner" in them, but scrolling through her iPhone music made her sad. Her playlists were now filled with memories of Jake and all the songs he'd recommended. She found some songs about teamwork—potentially useful for a team meeting. She couldn't seem to turn her work brain off.

She found "Pressure" and clicked play. The phone rang. She jumped. She fumbled with the phone to switch off the song. Off. Taking a deep breath, she answered the phone.

"Congratulations!" the voices of several partners on speaker-phone chorused. She sank into the couch in relief. She'd made it. It felt like a load of bricks had been removed from her back. She attempted conversation with the partners, barely registering what she said, until they said they'd leave her to celebrate and tell her friends and family. She texted her mom, Winnie, Eve and Max. Her phone rang.

Tim: *I made it. You must have made it too. Yes?*

"Hi Winnie, I made it," she said. She texted yes to Tim.

"Congratulations! I'm so happy for you," Winnie said.

"Me too. I mean, so happy but I'm also wiped out from the stress of waiting."

"I can imagine. I've been stressed, and I'm not even up for it. I had to work late, so I thought I'd put that to good use. I purposefully bumped into Michael after the partnership meeting. He said I had a good shot at partnership in two years because I was recognized as bringing in Global Capital, and that deal had been significant in the discussions. And you know, I did some more surreptitious prompting."

"As you do."

"As I do." Winnie laughed. "And he said that our bringing in the deal had allowed them to promote the three of you. Before that, they were arguing over which two to make. You know that Colette and Tim made it too, right?"

"Tim texted, but I didn't know about Colette," Audrey said.

"Yes, the British guy didn't make it."

"I feel bad for him." But not that bad.

"All right, the car service just arrived at my door," Winnie said. "Congratulations again!"

"Good night," Audrey said. "Thanks so much again for all your help and thank Jae for suggesting Global Capital."

> Tim: *Do you want to celebrate with dinner tomorrow night?*
>
> Audrey: *Yes, that'd be great.*
>
> Eve: *Woohoo! So excited for you. But I'm getting crushed right now. Table of ten all eating dessert. Haven't these people heard of sharing? Just kidding. Love my dessert people.*

The phone rang again. It was her mom.

"I couldn't sleep. I'm so happy you made it. But I also couldn't imagine you not making it. You've worked so hard," her mom said. "How do you feel?"

As she heard her mom's warm voice on the other end, she almost cried. Maybe it was a release from all the tension. "Ecstatic, but also tired. And so, so relieved. I bought a Levain Bakery cookie to eat either to celebrate or as consolation, but I think I'll freeze it and crash after this. I'm glad it's the weekend and I have time to rest and process it all."

"It's good that you don't have to work this weekend. Maybe you should take a spur-of-the-moment trip somewhere to celebrate."

Is this my mom speaking?

"I've been thinking about what you said to me on that one call. About how dating Jake made you happier and made it easier to shrug off Malaburn's barbs. It's so easy in Paris to take these weekend trips to other countries. It's amazing. You just fly two hours and you're somewhere completely different. I guess I'm learning from you and as I live here about how it's important to recharge. And especially for you now, after all this pressure and breaking up with Jake."

"I'll think about it tomorrow, after I've had a good night's sleep. I feel like I haven't slept well in ages. But I do agree with you."

"You know, I worked so hard after your father died. I buried myself in work because that was how I dealt with the pain of his loss. And I was comforted by the words of the French literature that I studied. But there's another lesson in your father's death I should've recognized: you only have one life, and you should live it fully."

"France is affecting you."

"Well, I'm still learning not to let work swallow me up. But one way is to take the time to savor your successes."

Chapter Fifty-Nine

*A*udrey stared unseeing at the congratulatory bouquet of flowers from Max on her coffee table. Betty had just offered her a job as the Popflicks Associate General Counsel, reporting to Betty. She could hire her own team (a lawyer and a paralegal). That was why Sebastian had joined the meeting—to meet her and give his approval as to whether Betty could hire her. They'd been waiting until she made partner.

She'd been so surprised, she hoped she hadn't given a bad impression. She'd told Betty that she would love to work for her, but she had to think about it because she'd just made partner. Betty had been understanding and told her to take some time to think this over.

She sat on the couch, pulling her hair back into a ponytail. She had been aiming to be a partner at the firm for years now. That was the career ladder at Howard, Parker & Smith: you started as an associate and then a select few were tapped to be a partner.

She'd intended to be one of those few, especially after Kevin had said that she couldn't make it. She'd always been at the top of her class. Eventually she'd planned to go in-house but envisioned that as years in the future. *But what do I want?*

This was a really good job offer, but she hadn't even had a chance to be a partner at the firm. She couldn't give that up. She considered calling her mom to talk it over, but she wanted to think it through first. This was her decision, her life. She was afraid that her mom would see it as akin to her giving up tenure. Being a lawyer for a corporation was risky compared to being a partner. A lawyer in a corporation could get laid off in corporate downsizings.

She looked around her living room, bare of any Christmas decorations except for a small Christmas tree. Despite her mom's suggestion, she had decided not to go away for the weekend and instead planned to spend today decorating her apartment for Christmas (that had all fallen to the wayside with the Jake break-up and the final sprint to making partner). But now she walked over to the small desk in the corner of her living room to procure some paper.

She sat down to list the pros and cons of the two career paths. As she bit her nail, thinking about pros/cons, her attention was caught by a to-do list tacked up on her bulletin board. It was eight years old—a to-do list created when she had first started working at the law firm: sign up for MoMA Junior Associates; hold dinner parties once a month; volunteer; keep daily diary; get a kitten? None of those items had been crossed out, which was why it was still there. She usually didn't even notice it. She had created it before she'd broken up with Kevin and before she'd become so obsessed with making partner. She smelled the scent of pine needles and remembered those happy family holidays, the hiking trips with her family, biking with Jake. Maybe she needed to think bigger about this question: about her life and what made her happy. If the work-life balance was as Betty described, choosing this job was a chance to get her life back.

Tim kissed her on the cheek when he met her at the restaurant. The décor was cutting-edge modern, but given the season, they passed a Christmas tree (decorated only in white lights and white angels) and a silver menorah on the way to the bar to wait for their table. Modern polished chrome chandeliers provided a soft, glowing light. As Tim went to the bar to order drinks, she covertly checked out the scene. Well-dressed men and women mingled over crisply starched tablecloths. Diamond rings flashed in the candlelight. She breathed in the soothing clean smell of orchids. Next to her, a group of men were analyzing a stock deal. On her other side, two women were commiserating over the renovation of their summer houses in the Hamptons. One wore a perfume that reminded her of visiting the first floor of Saks Fifth Avenue.

It was the opposite of the places that she and Jake frequented. And it was seductive. This was the life she'd imagined before Jake. A large minimalist modern apartment on Park Avenue or Central Park West, white couches, modern art, she and her husband heading off to work on Wall Street in the morning with their briefcases, kissing goodbye at the door. She'd not thought much further than that in her daydreaming. But now she wanted the more informal, laid-back fun life envisaged by Jake.

She felt someone next to her look at her and look again. She turned around. *Penny. With auburn hair.*

"Audrey," Penny said. Her eyes narrowed. "You broke Jake's heart. He looks like shit. How could you do that?"

"I—I didn't want to break up," Audrey said.

Tim reappeared. "Here's your drink," he said.

Penny stared at Tim, her eyebrows raised.

This looks bad. This looks like a date.

"Penny, this is my work colleague Tim," Audrey said quickly.

"I hope I'm your friend as well," Tim said, smiling at Penny. "Delighted to meet you." He held out his hand.

"Nice to meet you as well," Penny shook it reluctantly, but said in an aside to Audrey, "I'm still not talking to you."

"Why aren't you talking to Audrey?" Tim asked.

"Penny is one of Jake's best friends," Audrey said.

"Then I'm not talking to you," Tim said. He folded his arms and frowned at Penny. "Jake broke up with Audrey. She just made partner. She should be glowing. Instead, she's like a pale shell of her former self."

Penny crossed her arms. "That's what happens if work is your life."

Audrey's shoulders slumped.

The maître d' tapped Tim on the shoulder. "Your table is ready."

"This was just one time, and it was necessary to make partner," Tim said.

"Was it just one time? I'd be willing to bet I've seen Jake more in the past month than Audrey has," Penny said.

"What if you were about to go on vacation and a theatre called you and offered you the role of a lifetime?" Audrey asked.

"Okay.'" Penny nodded, her gaze meeting Audrey's. "I can see why you're a good lawyer."

Chapter Sixty

As Audrey walked into the office on Monday morning, Gertrude met her with a stack of pink telephone slips ("all congratulations," she said) and handed her another bouquet of flowers. Her office looked like a flower shop.

She was really going to do it. She was going to accept the Popflicks offer and resign from Howard, Parker & Smith. After seven years of striving so hard for this? To give it up? She took a deep breath. Maybe she should spend another night thinking about it. *No.* She'd learned a lesson: pick her partner and her employer carefully. If she'd been on trial the week the British had called, the firm would've never pulled her off her trial to fly to London. They would've substituted another associate. But the firm didn't consider her vacation time to be as important as a client's needs. She wanted a workplace that respected life outside work. That belief underlaid the informal, inspiring atmosphere of Popflicks. And she wanted a boss like Betty, who believed in her and challenged her—for example, insisting that she do the cross-examination. She'd be part of senior management at Popflicks as opposed to a junior partner here. On the negative side, she might be the uncool workaholic.

She called Betty to accept. Betty sounded thrilled and recommended taking at least a month off before she started at Popflicks, stating there was nothing like that free time between jobs once you had a new job lined up. Betty suggested Audrey start in eight weeks, since she probably had to give two weeks' notice and the office was closed anyway for the week between Christmas and New Year's.

Then Audrey called Winnie and asked her if she wanted to join her at Popflicks. She told Winnie that Betty had mentioned previously that a lawyer in the department had transitioned to the business side of things so that was an option, if Winnie decided she didn't want to stay in law. Winnie was shocked, but also excited—for both of them. She said yes.

Audrey walked into the senior managing partner's office. She was nervous. Her feet didn't make a sound on the rich red carpet. A black leather couch sat by one wall. Square mahogany chairs faced the partner's desk. Hard wooden seats, with no cushion; they were not comfortable to sit in, but she couldn't quite believe he'd chosen them for that purpose. She'd never been to his office on the spur of the moment before. He looked a bit surprised. Guarded. She supposed senior partners knew that unprompted visits could mean bad news.

"Do you have a moment?" she asked.

"Of course. Do you have questions about the financial aspects of being a partner?"

"No." She rushed out the words: "I'm resigning. It was a very difficult decision. I was offered a position as associate general counsel of Popflicks on Saturday and I've accepted."

His face didn't betray any emotion. "Are you sure? You've worked very hard to make partner, and we view you as a tremendous asset to the firm—both for your legal acumen and your ability to work well with others. We don't want to lose you." He leaned into his argument, as if relishing a good fight. "Is it the compensation? We're in lockstep here which makes it difficult for us to maneuver, but certainly we can consider it."

"The compensation is good, especially with the stock options, but it's more the lifestyle." She'd been surprised to find out she'd be making more money at Popflicks.

He looked slightly relieved that it was not just better compensation. "I'm not sure that the general counsel work/life balance is that much better than a law firm." He paused. "Remember that in a law firm, you do have colleagues who can help you out."

That wasn't what just happened with my planned vacation. But she didn't want to raise that and look like she quit for that reason. She wanted to leave on good terms.

He said, "Also, you're still the outside counsel. You can say no. You can set parameters. If you're the inside counsel, you don't have that choice. You've got one client and you need to support that client."

But I do get to call outside counsel for help, and then I'm the client. Maybe he could see that that line of argument was not winning. He stood.

"We were on that one case together. And I remember our discussing: how did this happen? How could it have happened? And I was relieved I was being called in to fix it, and not the one who was responsible for it. But if you're the inside counsel—" He sat in the chair next to her and leaned in. "You're on the hook. You've got the potential liability. There's a reason why you may be paid more. As the outside counsel, I've sometimes wondered how my client did something so foolish. When you're the inside counsel, you're on the front line. You're the one responsible." There was a reason he was the senior managing partner of the firm. She worried about liability. But she'd only have liability if she was responsible or involved. And she wasn't going to make a decision that conflicted with the law. She was confident about that.

He said, "It doesn't usually start as a direct conflict. Or so I've learned while defending white-collar professionals. Few have bad intentions. It starts as: we need to get business done. What's the risk tolerance? Isn't this a judgment call? What's the risk of liability? And the risk tolerance moves down the sliding scale."

Audrey thought about how to respond. Outside, it was snowing. The weather channel had been predicting a blizzard with possibly five feet of snow.

"Yes," she said. "I do understand that—especially based on the white-collar cases I've done. I'm well aware of that risk, so that will help. I'm truly excited for this new opportunity. It was a hard choice because I worked so hard to become partner here and I'll miss all my colleagues, but I don't think I can pass this up."

He nodded. "I wish you all the best then. It's been a true pleasure working with you, and we will really miss you. You are a role model to many of the associates and partners here, and I was expecting you to have quite a positive impact on this firm."

Touched by his gracious good wishes, she shook his hand and said thank you.

She stopped by Whitaker's office to tell him she was leaving. He looked sad. "I'm sorry to hear that. You're one of the good ones. I've been telling them for years that you can't hire thoroughbreds and then treat them like workhorses." He smiled suddenly. "We can have a joint departure party."

"I'd like that," Audrey said.

As she walked out of his office, she checked her gut to confirm that she still felt it was the right decision. She did. She had loved working here, loved the challenges and the camaraderie, but if she could have that type of legal work at Popflicks, in a warm and nurturing environment, with a life outside of the office? She was going to grab that opportunity with both hands.

Chapter Sixty-One

The snow was falling thicker now, blanketing New York City in white fluff. Outside in the garden, white snow covered the tops of the branches of the elm tree, contrasting with the underside of its dark boughs, as if outlining each limb and shoot. Even through the cloudy sky, the warm lights beckoned from the windows of neighboring houses, Christmas tree lights sparkling through the swirling snowflakes.

Audrey stood in her purple and blue cotton pajamas, gazing out her sliding glass door at the snowfall in her backyard. At least two feet had piled up against the sliding door. Watching the flurries, she felt that excited little-kid-on-a-snow-day exhilaration.

She'd allowed herself to sleep in; management had sent out an email last night saying the offices would be closed for the expected blizzard, after the mayor announced no school today and the closure of the subway. She didn't have much work anyway; all her cases had been reassigned, and she was just cleaning out her office and transferring any case files and relevant knowledge to her colleagues. Colette was picking up the bulk of her work. Colette seemed shocked—and sad—that she was leaving. She'd suggested they meet for lunch every few months.

She felt at a loss because normally she'd have work to do, but now she didn't. She couldn't visit friends, except Eve and Pete, because the subways were closed. Eve had just accepted a position as the executive pastry chef at a new restaurant that Chef Burns was opening up in Williamsburg. Eve was excited and abuzz figuring out her first menu. Audrey was thrilled for Eve. Maybe she should see if they wanted to meander later in Central Park and work up an appetite to sample more of Eve's desserts.

She couldn't help but think of Jake. Today would have been a perfect day to spend with him. She would get dressed and go to his house. She expected that the lifestyle demands of her new job would be more similar to those of his career. With the next month off, she had time to spend with him, although she was thinking of traveling for a bit—she wanted to visit Australia. But still, she'd be around when she wasn't traveling. It would be different this time. She hadn't changed jobs to get him back; but their relationship and break-up had made her realize that the law-firm lifestyle wasn't what she wanted. She sat down on the bed and bit her lip: did she dare? Butterflies fluttered in the pit of her stomach. What if her workload hadn't been the reason he'd broken up with her? What if it was an excuse? Also, he'd been wrong—he needed to be the one to recognize that.

She didn't have to decide yet. The first thing was to shower and get dressed. She couldn't do anything in her pajamas. As she pulled her clothes out of the drawer, she found a fishing lure she'd bought Jake after that terrible blind date discussing fly fishing. She had thought it would be a funny present. It was a bright blue feathery lure. She found string and tied it to the lure. She put on her coat and boots and then opened up the sliding door of her balcony, with difficulty because of the heavy snowfall. Her boots crunching in the snow, she stepped out and tied one end of the string to her balcony railing and then lowered the lure into his yard, so that it was hanging in front of his glass door, bright blue against the snowy white background. It looked like a bird flying there. It should catch his attention. She felt more hopeful now that she'd done something. Baited her hook.

She went back inside, took off her coat and boots, and left them to dry near the heater. She put on a black turtleneck and black pants—her New York armor. Then she ate breakfast, but she didn't have much appetite. Too nervous at the thought of going over.

She'd put on some make-up first. She looked in the bathroom mirror as she applied mascara. She couldn't believe she was wishing a water bug would appear, giving her an excuse to go to Jake's.

A loud banging on her sliding glass bedroom door sounded. She stuck her head out of the bathroom door and saw a large snow-covered figure at the door. She gasped, startled, until she also saw a snow-covered dog—Biscuit.

She ran to the door. She wasn't sure she'd be able to open it, given the snow, but she managed to—to be greeted by cold rush of air. A large snowman with his dog entered her bedroom.

"Are you okay? What's wrong?" she asked.

"No, I'm not okay. I was wrong. I'm so sorry. I'm sorry I was some caveman boyfriend who asked you to choose between your career and me. My mom said maybe you shouldn't even take me back, but I hope you do. I miss you."

His face was so dear to her. She couldn't help reaching out to touch his face and brush off some of the snow. He caught her hand and held it against his cool cheek.

"I miss you too," she said.

"So much," he added. "I've been looking for an excuse to come over, so with the snow, I thought I should do the neighborly thing and, you know, check on you."

"Your boy scout training?"

"You could say that." He seemed to want to say more, but hesitated. "Plus, I saw a bright blue lure hanging from your balcony. That gave me hope."

"How'd you get here if you boarded up the fence?" She felt like she was dreaming. Biscuit was jumping up on her and trying to lick her. The smell of wet furry dog seemed quite real. And her heart was racing again—a sure sign she was in the proximity of Jake. Plus, he was dripping on her floor, and the small puddle on the welcome mat seemed quite tangible.

He took a step closer. "I just un-boarded it." He took a deep breath. "But I didn't think I'd be this snow-covered when I was pleading my case." He unzipped his jacket. "I should've supported your career instead of behaving like an asshole and breaking up with you when you couldn't go to Costa Rica. I'm really sorry. Can you forgive me?" He looked at her, seeming nervous.

"Yes." She didn't pause to think. She didn't need to. She drank in his face as a warmth at odds with the cold air from outside filled her. "Yes! I hate that I had to cancel—especially when you didn't want to date a lawyer for precisely that reason. I'm so sorry."

"You don't have to apologize. We can always go some other time, whenever you're free. And you can cancel it, but I won't throw our relationship away again. And I'm hoping you want to go sledding today. I bought two sleds while walking Biscuit. You do have snow pants, don't you?"

"I do . . ."

"It's a snow day! And I want to spend it with you." He slid off his backpack. More snow fell into the puddle pooling on the floor. He kept talking. "But let me take off my snow pants before I get any more of your house wet." He took off his snow pants and left them drying by the door. He was dressed in his jeans and a long underwear top that outlined his muscular chest and stomach. "Sorry about Biscuit, but he wanted to see you. He's missed you too. He keeps bringing your slippers to me."

She hugged him. "You've kept my slippers?"

"I couldn't throw them out." He raised an eyebrow. "Not when Biscuit was so attached to them."

"Biscuit has good taste."

"He does. I should trust his vetting more than my own."

She petted Biscuit. "I'll change into my snow pants." She looked into her closet. They were deep inside her closet, but luckily still there. She was so happy Jake was back.

He said, "There are a bunch of good hills I want to try."

"Are you sure they're for the thirty-and-over crowd?"

"They're for the kids at heart, no ageism allowed."

Her snow pants still fit—always a good sign when she hadn't worn them for a year at least. But then she had lost weight after the break-up with Jake. They wouldn't have been her first choice, though, for an outfit to wear when getting back with him. She adjusted the suspenders and zipped up the front.

He was next to her. Their gazes met and that electric charge reignited between them.

"Jake," she asked, "are you sure? Because I'm still a lawyer, and I will have to work sometimes, and there will be cancellations.

Are you sure you want that?" She looked up at him, as she leaned against the closet door.

"I just want to be with you. I'll take what time you have. I'm sorry that I broke us up. I regretted that, but I didn't know how to repair it. I knew I needed to deal with my feelings about my dad. I talked to my dad about it, and that made me feel better. I talked with my mom about how life with my dad was always worth it, even when he had to work. I just had to ask you to take me back and try to convince you that I've learned my lesson and won't do that again. And I understand—I mean, what if one of my major marketing projects had gone belly-up and I had to try to fix it immediately? It's the type of careers that we have, and I wouldn't want it another way, because we're both passionate about our work." He reached out to hold her hand.

"Oh, Jake."

"I miss the way you make me laugh. I miss the way you surprise me—in silly ways or brilliant ways. I love the way your face lights up when you laugh. I love you, Audrey." His voice took on a new urgency. "Are you willing to try again?"

"Yes. I love you so much."

He enveloped her in a great big hug, and they just clung to each other for a moment. Then he kissed her, softly at first, making her feel like she was something precious that he didn't want to break, and then more urgently. They fell back on the bed.

"I think we've been here before," she joked. "Are you sure you want to go sledding? There are other fun things to do when you're snowed in."

He stroked her hair, and as he slid her snow pant suspender off her shoulder, she shivered.

But then he said, "We'll definitely get to that. Sledding first." He stood and pulled back on his snow pants. They walked up the stairs to the front door.

Jake asked, "Do you need to check in with work?"

"No."

"It's not every day a blizzard hits New York City."

"No, it's not every day you get your heart back." She pulled on her winter jacket. "We've got some catching up to do. But we have plenty of time for it—I have the next eight weeks off."

"What?"

"I'm changing jobs."

"But I saw the announcement that you made partner."

"Yes, but then I was offered a job as Associate General Counsel at Popflicks, and I can build my own team—well, my own team of two reports. Most importantly, it should be a better lifestyle. So, I took it."

"Are you sure? You've worked so hard for partner. Even though I was opposed to the hours and the demands, I want you to be happy." He turned and held both her hands. "Truly. I've had some good talks with my mom and the rest of my family about this, although they were completely on your side."

She laced her fingers through his. "You weren't being unreasonable. They didn't see me when I looked like shit, as you so eloquently put it. You made me question my choices, and that's a good thing. And you made me think about what I really want. It gave me the courage to accept this job offer." She smiled.

He opened the front door and then asked, "And Tim? Did you and he try to make a go of it?"

"No. There was a problem I hadn't foreseen."

"Which was?"

"He's not you."

Jake kissed her again hard on the lips. They held hands and raced down the building stairs.

As Jake opened the foyer door, Audrey was surprised to see an Amazon package on the table in the foyer. She started to tell him that she'd hated seeing the ubiquitous Amazon packages after they'd broken up because they reminded her of him when she saw her name handwritten on the box. She looked at him quizzically.

She pulled the tape off the package and opened it. A pink and white book was nestled inside. She looked at the title—*Second Chances*—and then read the packing slip:

Dear Audrey,

The last two weeks have been HELL without you. I made a HUGE mistake. I'm sorry I wasn't there when you needed me. Can you forgive me? Can I have a second chance?
And here's a Mark Twain quote for us: "When you fish for love, bait with your heart, not your brain." But I'm hooked, heart and brain.

Jake

He burst into an explanation: "I wasn't sure if you'd take me back. After I had breakfast with my mom, I ran over to Barnes & Noble to buy it. I decided I'd better put Plan B into action in the meantime, in case you didn't take me back on my first approach."

"What was Plan B?"

"Plan B was courting you with reminders of our relationship. I found this Amazon box and put it in there. I put it in your open foyer right before I came over through the fence. With Biscuit as back-up."

"Yes, yes," she said. They kissed again.

They stepped out the door into the white powder drift building up on the street. The snow was just below her knees. He retrieved the two sleds from his building's foyer.

As he walked back, holding the two sleds, she said, "No hot chocolate or soup thermos? It looks like your boy scout training is falling short here."

He smiled mischievously. "As a boy scout, we've been taught skin-to-skin contact is the best way to keep warm in cold weather. I'm definitely prepared to heat you up."

Audrey laughed. "I'll hold you to that."

They walked to Central Park, holding hands, making their own path in the untouched snow.

Dear Reader,

Thank you so much for reading PARTNER PURSUIT. I hope it left you with a warm, fuzzy feeling.

If you would like updates on new releases and what's going on in my life, please subscribe to my mailing list at https://kathystrobos.com/sign-up/

If you enjoyed reading PARTNER PURSUIT, please leave a review. I would appreciate it so much. I can learn what you liked and you can help other readers discover books they might love. Book reviews are also critical to authors because they increase visibility on Amazon. Amazon wants to recommend books that other readers liked. So, help out an author and another reader today. (It doesn't even have to be me.) A review doesn't have to be long; it can be a sentence or two.

Best,
Kathy

About the Author

Kathy Strobos is a writer living in New York City with her husband and two children, amid a growing collection of books, toys and dollhouses. She grew up in New York City and graduated from Stuyvesant High School and Harvard-Radcliffe University *magna cum laude*. She previously worked as a lawyer. She left law to pursue her dream of writing fiction full-time and getting in shape. She is still working on getting in shape.

Acknowledgements

It's been my dream for so long to hold my first book in my hands. I want to thank my family for encouraging and supporting my dream of becoming a full-time author, specifically my husband Claus and my two children. A special thanks also to my mom, my brother, my sister-in-law and my nieces.

I've wanted to be writer since I was in elementary school. My dad read a story I wrote in high school and took me to a Cynthia Heimel play to encourage me to write.

My critique partners, Giulia Skye and Vicky Tiseros, have been invaluable. I'm always amazed at how they pinpoint ways to improve my novels. I also really value our friendship, and I feel privileged to be on this writer journey with them. Thank you especially to Giulia who encouraged me to publish independently and answers all my publishing questions. I'm so glad I met you on the train to the RNA Conference in Leeds!

A special thanks to Linnea Sinclair and Gay Walley who taught me so much about writing and improved my writing craft exponentially. They are both gifted teachers—although now when I am editing, I hear their voices in my head: "Are the stakes high enough? Is she between a rock and a hard place? What does she feel?"

When I first thought I'd like to try to write a novel for real, I took the Penguin Writer's Academy "Constructing a Novel" course, and I want to thank my teacher Bea Davenport, who said that the dialogue between Audrey and Eve was "sparky." That made my month. She, along with my fellow students, first gave me hope that I could actually write commercial fiction—and not just legal briefs and compliance policies.

I also want to thank the Romantic Novelists' Association and the published authors who volunteer their time to read manuscripts by unpublished writers like me in the New Writer's Scheme and give such constructive feedback.

One of the best parts about this new career is meeting other writers. Thank you to Delphine (my partner in the querying trenches) and Evie Alexander for all the pep talks. I also love the camaraderie and supportive vibe of Anita Faulkner's Chicklit & Prosecco Facebook group and the RNA's RomCom Group. I'm always inspired by the critique group Word-Slingers-Plotters-and-Pantsers, who helped me with my blurb and my first chapters and is a great group for bouncing ideas around. My #TBR pile is enormous, but I love reading all your books and celebrating your publishing successes!

A huge thanks to Heidi and Allison for helping me with the career details for music marketing executives and chefs, respectively. Any inaccuracies are mine.

And thanks to all my friends who read excerpts, brainstormed titles, commiserated about writing, suggested plot points etc.: Michelle, Tammy, Becky, Sharon, Matthew, Charlita, Seetha, Ketsia, Koethi, Seendy, Crystal, Mary, Caroline, Jennifer, Jenny, Annette, Suzanne, Kim, Saika, Anne, Mark, Minke, Richard, Elliot, Nisha, Ruth, Mr. Tony, Jen, Nupur, Lin, Jessica, and all my other friends who cheered me on.

Thank you to my book cover designer, Cover Ever After. I love my covers!

I also want to thank my editors Kathryn Craft, Rachel Lynn Solomon, Julie Mianecki and Emily Poole, all of whom improved this manuscript and taught me more about writing craft.

Thank you also to my blog and newsletter subscribers and to my ARC reader team. I'm so happy to be on a team with you.

Finally, but not least, thank you to you, my reader. Thank you for buying and reading my book. I hope you enjoyed spending time with my characters as much as I enjoyed writing about them and escaping to their world.

Kathy Strobos

For Rory's story, read on for an excerpt from *Is This For Real?* by Kathy Strobos, an opposites attract, friends-to-lovers, slow burn, fake dating romantic comedy (publishing soon).

Chapter One

On any top-ten list of best Sunday plans, today's brunch with my former crush and his new girlfriend would rank number eleven . . . hundred. Times five. But I couldn't say no. We're still friends.

And I'm over him.

Just keep telling yourself that.

Still, there is no chance I will ever say "I love you" to Jamie again.

The subway is oddly crowded for this time of day. I squeeze on, snagging the prime real estate spot leaning against the metal doors, right up against the "Do Not Lean on Door" warning, and hold on to a small sliver of a handrail. As the train approaches Times Square-42nd Street, the conductor announces that this local train is now going express, and groans erupt. Works for me. At 42nd Street, half the train empties out, but it quickly fills back up, as if we've all just exchanged dance partners.

Three stops later, the train car shudders to a stop, spitting me out along with a stream of passengers jostling each other for a place in the ant line marching up the stairs. The last brush-by without even a "'Scuze me" skews my hat, my favorite 1920s-style cloche.

So much for all the time I spent positioning it just right, so I'd look more poised—less cute little buddy—when Jamie sees me again. He's back to New York for a brief visit. I haven't seen him in over a year since he's been living in Singapore. Now if only I can live up to the Hat's "superpower sophistication." I adjust it and push through the turnstile.

Even before I reach the top of the steps to the street, the smell of honey-roasted nuts from the Nuts4Nuts vendor cart at the top is making me hungry.

At least my close friend Rory agreed to join me at this brunch with Jamie and his new girlfriend, so I'm not the rejected third wheel sitting across from the happy couple.

Chambers Street is crowded with vendor tables but not many people yet. The phone store and clothing store with back-to-school sale signs soldier on, not yet joining the other boarded-up stores on this block. And then Michael's craft store. The lure is strong. Not that I need any more crafting supplies, but it seems a waste to be in the neighborhood and not check out its sale selection. But I resist. I want to be first to the brunch battlefield, able to plan my strategy, as advised in *The Art of War*. Not that I've read it, just *The Art of War for Writers*.

My email pings. I'm taking a hodge-podge of online writing courses while I write my second novel, as I query my first novel *Caper Crush*, and it's a comment from my teacher on my latest online assignment: "You're still holding back, playing it safe. You need to scrape your emotions raw in your writing."

I don't think so. I felt naked enough writing that scene. And I'm not sure how much of me I want to expose for public consumption.

Up ahead, Rory is leaning against a streetlight, reading a book. One lock of his brown wavy hair has fallen onto his face, and he pushes it away to join the rest of his unruly mop of hair. He could be modeling menswear, except that the cover of the book he's holding is bright pink and yellow. A romcom book I recommended. He wanted to read other books in my genre so he could compare my draft manuscript to the competition, so I gave him a list of my favorites. He looks up, and our glances catch.

"Like your hat, Penelope. Suits you." Rory kisses me on the cheek.

We push open the door to The Barn. Bells jingle and the buttery smell of pancakes welcomes us. The white-washed wood gives the restaurant an old farmhouse vibe. Vintage signs with pictures of black and white cows and bushels of peaches decorate the walls. We stand in line in the small foyer, waiting to be seated.

I've been seeing more of Rory lately. We're friends from college. I briefly had a crush on him then, but he started dating someone else. When he has a girlfriend, we see each other about once every other month. But he broke up with his last girlfriend about two months ago and now he calls me to get together for brunch nearly every Sunday. My best friend and roommate Zelda, who also knows Rory from college, was like: "Well, he obviously enjoys hanging out with you, but you're solidly in the friend lane with this Sunday brunch thing." Trust Zelda for the straight talk. It's not that I thought I was changing lanes and moving to the speeding girlfriend lane. I'm good driving at a controlled sixty-miles-an-hour, and not hazardously heading-for-a-heartbreak on some highway of love.

"How do you like the book?" I ask.

"It's good. Deeper than I expected. Funny. Affirms all my love-lasts-forever bull. Isn't that what you called it?" His tone is mild, but an undercurrent of frustration pulses there.

"I was drunk when I said that." I'm surprised he remembers. It was at a dinner party several years ago. About six of us were drunkenly arguing over the merits of prenups. I don't even remember how the topic came up, except that we have two friends who are on polar opposites of the issue. As were Rory and I. I was for prenups, he was against. I argued prenups define expectations so there's less chance of angry fights when it ends.

"In vino veritas," Rory says.

"I'd say more like, when drunk, debate points are exaggerated. I shouldn't have called it bull."

"I don't think that works as well. In vino debatus pointus exaggeratos."

I laugh. "Anyway, your belief gives me hope." I hope that Rory finds his true love and that she doesn't break his heart.

He gives me a quizzical look. "So, what's with this fake boyfriend trope? This is the second one with it."

"I like that trope." I tilt my head.

"Do you?"

Something in the way he asks makes me look at him more closely. "Yes. I'm writing a fake dating plot in my new book, *Fake Dating Folly*."

"Why do you like it?"

"I like the getting to know each other slowly." I shrug. "I don't know. So, what happened on Thursday? Did your pitch win?" Rory works in advertising.

"Yes, but. . ."

"They want you to change it? You don't look that happy."

"No. They like the pitch," Rory says. He flushes. "But his wife groped my butt during our celebratory drinks."

"She didn't," I say, shocked.

"She did. I got this weird vibe from her, but I thought no—she's got to be about fifty and my client is right there talking about color schemes—and then, she copped a feel of my butt."

"While he was there?"

"Yeah, like what the . . . I was afraid I'd lose the pitch right there." Rory shakes his head in disbelief. "I jumped, which threw her too. But still, it's freaking awkward."

"That's crazy," I say. Rory still looks upset. "Did she pinch anybody else's butt?"

"I didn't take a poll." He laughs, but then looks serious again. "And we've got another client function this Thursday."

I point at the book. "I know what you need. You need a fake girlfriend to protect you at client functions, like a buffer."

He stills, staring at me. "That's not a bad idea."

"I was joking." But I feel a little thrill of satisfaction that he likes my idea. He takes off his blue jacket, and he's wearing a worn t-shirt that does little to hide his washboard stomach.

"Aren't there any women currently in the running to be a real girlfriend?" I ask.

"No."

"How is that possible?" This brunch line is not moving. The smell of bacon frying is making me even hungrier.

He just gives me his look of annoyance, which is one eyebrow cocked and a slight shake of his head. "It's not like you date a lot. Did I miss the memo where you're dating someone?"

"There wouldn't be a memo."

"Your sister would definitely issue a memo."

I laugh. "A legal memo. To whom it may concern. But seriously, Rory, you're not usually at a lack for dance partners."

"I am now. Marie was always asking me, 'So where do you see this going?' Which really kills any . . . uh . . . magic. And Callie . . ." He presses his lips together.

Another couple enters the foyer behind us. Rory and I move closer together to make space for them.

The man kisses the woman on the forehead and looks deep into her eyes. What if Jamie looks like that at his new girlfriend? I feel nauseous. *No, that would be good.* It would be good if his new girlfriend was his soulmate—better than watching him with a parade of different women I didn't merit joining. He wasn't even willing to try dating me. I probably should have asked him out on a date instead—something less dramatic than saying, "I love you." But since we've known each other since childhood, a "date" didn't seem necessary. Not when I've been in love with him since high school. And somehow, I always thought, at some point, he'd love me back.

"Although I recognize that you don't believe in magic," Rory says.

"I never said that," I say.

"You don't have to. It's the way you never discuss it."

I look up at Rory. "That magical connection can be dangerous."

"Is that bad?" He gives me a lopsided grin.

"Dangerously devastating if he doesn't 'feel the same way.'" *Or you lose that person.* "Or if it leads to too high expectations."

"So, you're just looking for humdrum as opposed to magical connection? That explains . . . Never mind."

I don't deign to respond.

He flips through the book and reads out a line. "No, 'every part of her burned with fire' for you?"

"I'm not particularly looking." I cross my arms.

"But you're writing a romantic comedy."

"But it's focused more on the comedy than the romance—more focused on the caper than the crush." Some people are leaving. One bumps me and I put out my hand to avoid falling into Rory, grabbing his bicep. Rory holds my hand as if we're about to do the jitterbug.

"Hence the title, *Caper Crush*," he says.

"If only the title alone could sell it." I release him.

"You just need one agent and one publisher to love it. And it's funny, especially the scenes with the motley team trying to steal back her painting." He chuckles.

In *Caper Crush*, my artist protagonist has five weeks to find her stolen painting or lose her chance to participate in a career-defining art exhibit. And if she doesn't learn to trust her sleuthing partner, she's going to lose a lot more.

The hostess greets us by name and starts to seat us at our usual table for two, but we tell her we need a table for four. As we settle into the blue booth, I can't decide if I should take off my hat or leave it on. Jamie is supposed to see me in the hat. All I want is one twinge of regret—one second glance, one "maybe I made a mistake." At least while he has a girlfriend. But eating with my hat on seems awkward. Like I've got an appendage coming out of my head. The hat partially obstructs my side view. I don't envy horses with blinders.

The waitress is new. She reminds me of a collie. She's tall, with a narrow face, and friendly. She asks if we want to order now. As Rory explains that we are waiting for friends, I smile at her. Waitressing is tough. I tried it, as the typical side job for a writer, but I'd jot down impressions of my customers while waiting for them to make up their mind, and I'd inevitably miss part of their order. And my boss was not sympathetic to my using his order pads for my notes.

Now, I'm supporting myself by making miniatures to sell on Etsy, staging doll soap operas for my blog and Instagram to increase my sales, and dog-sitting temporary canine roomies who pay my rent.

"So, what about you? Would you act as my fake girlfriend at some client gigs coming up?" he asks.

I stare at him. He lightly presses my open mouth closed. His eyebrow quirks upwards.

"You could consider it research for your next book," he adds.

"Why me?"

"Because you're my best female friend and you won't believe it's for real."

Yes, I definitely won't believe it's for real. I flag down the waitress and ask for a cup of tea. More caffeine is needed.

"Neither will anyone else," I say.

"What? Why not?" He seems genuinely confused. *Cute.*

"Rory, you usually date six-foot-tall gorgeous women. I am *so* not your type."

"I don't have a type."

I snort. "Oh really? Let's look at the evidence." I scroll through the photos on my phone. I'm sure I have pictures of Rory with his last few girlfriends at various events. All of whom will be gorgeous and tall. Rory and Marie, five-foot-eleven-inches and blonde. She was so sweet and together. Here's a picture of Ayanna, his college girlfriend, from Rory's Halloween party last year. She's five-foot-eight, stunning, funny, smart, always up for midnight snacks after dancing. She was my favorite, but now she's engaged. We still chat sometimes on Instagram.

"Okay, okay." He holds up his hands in mock surrender. "No pictures of Callie, huh? Didn't you like Callie?"

"I didn't like Callie."

"Hmm." He looks down at the table.

"Are you sure you don't have commitment issues? These women seemed pretty magical to me." Sometimes I can't decide if Rory has commitment issues or he's such a romantic, that if the relationship is not absolutely perfect, he moves on.

He winces. "I don't think so. But it's important that the relationship feels right." He runs his hand through his hair, which makes his brown wavy hair look even more tousled. "I feel like I'm parroting my dad." His dad is a psychologist who does couples counseling. He faces me. "So, you're saying no one will believe I'm dating you because you're five-foot-five?" He pulls one of my curls and it snaps back. He loves to do this.

I roll my eyes at him. "Whatever. I'll pretend to be your girlfriend if it will help. It will be great research for my next book."

He smiles, and that dimple in his right cheek appears. "Great, then we're on for Thursday. We're having an event with the client that night." A roguish glint comes into his eyes.

I look over at the hostess stand, where Jamie now stands with his new girlfriend. He's wearing this blue shirt that's my favorite on him. I can't see his girlfriend Marla's face, but Jamie is helping her take off her coat to give it to the hostess. An empty pit forms in my stomach. He wasn't even willing to meet me alone. And I had to be the one to suggest we meet. And then I got the lunch slot.

I ask, "Should we start now and see if we can fool Jamie? That will certainly persuade Jamie I'm over him."

"It may even make him jealous."

I laugh. "I don't think so. And anyway, I'm over him." If I repeat it enough, it will come true.

Rory nods, but it's that "you're a poor deluded soul" nod. "He may see you in a new light. As opposed to a completely self-sufficient sister type."

My tea finally arrives. I add sugar and take a sip. "You're right. Why am I writing romantic comedies? I should be writing cozy mysteries with self-sufficient spinsters investigating crimes."

"I didn't say spinster. I'm just saying that Jamie's protective instincts might be raised if he thinks you're dating a big bad wolf like me."

"You're so not a big bad wolf." And I knew that from first-hand experience. I would've spent college as "the girl whose parents died in a plane crash in Peru on their wedding anniversary," which was pretty much how I was known for a while there until Rory took me under his wing. Instead, I spent college as part of Rory's crowd, trading quips around a round table in our college dining hall.

"Okay," Rory says. "So, starting now, we're pretending to date?"

Jamie leans down to kiss his girlfriend as the hostess turns to lead them here.

Jamie will definitely think that I'm over him.

"Yes," I say. *Can't hurt.*

Made in the USA
Middletown, DE
29 September 2021